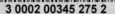

The Secret War

M. F. W. CURRAN

The Secret War

MACMILLAN NEW WRITING

First published 2006 by Macmillan New Writing,
an imprint of Macmillan Publishers Ltd
Brunel Road, Basingstoke RG21 6XS
Associated companies throughout the world
www.macmillannewwriting.com

ISBN-13: 978–0230–00746–8 hardback
ISBN-10: 0230–00746–5 hardback
ISBN-13: 978–0230–00751–2 paperback
ISBN-10: 0230 00751–1 paperback

10   9   8   7   6   5   4   3   2   1
14   13   12   11   10   09   08   07   06

A CIP catalogue record for this book is available from
the British Library.

Typeset by Heronwood Press
Printed and bound in China

For my dad, Kevin Joseph Curran

CHAPTER ONE

Promotion and Resignation

△ I △ Waterloo, June 21st, 1815

Individual names mattered not here. The dead lay in their thousands, and a mere individual was nothing more than a statistic, another casualty to add to the long list that could never be finished. Each bloodied face was nameless, each fallen soldier just one amongst many.

And those bloodied and nameless faces seemed to stretch forever. From Merbraine to Plancenoit there was a vast carpet across the land – a carpet of corpses dressed in blues, reds, greens and greys. Some had helmets, some had caps, some wore distinctive plumes like the feathers of peacocks, all lying in stinking decomposing piles of flesh and cloth, buzzing with flies and crows during the day, and vermin or worse at night.

In some cases it was hard to distinguish friend from foe. Within the mud and blood many were disfigured, some submerged in pools of water. Faces were shattered, cleaved and ruined, and only uniform or rank provided an indication of each man's identity.

Lieutenant William Saxon rode close to the lieutenant colonel, the senior officer astride his grey horse with his eyes fixed on the middle distance where fog hung dismally over Plancenoit. By La Haye Saint the faint smell of blood still lingered even after two days of rain had washed much of it away. It had taken many hours to remove the dead, and here and there French bodies still littered the ground.

Further on, just down a muddy track that curved to the right, was a line of smashed ordnance, their wheels broken and shivered, like ribs breaking through the mist. Bodies spread out from each damaged cannon; some were artillerymen, others were ordinary soldiers from either side, blown apart by the cannonfire before the artillery in turn had been spiked and demolished.

As they passed the frozen corpses, one such cannon just beyond the others caught William's eye. Again it was a wreck – one wheel had snapped in two while the other was reduced to a couple of shattered spokes – but here there was something far more macabre. A British soldier sat on the barrel of the cannon, but his head was cranked back, his face white as bone and mottled. Many spikes – both bayonets and lances – skewered his body and his attackers were not far away. In the main they still clutched their weapons, hunched over muskets or lances, but just as dead as the British soldier, having been killed in the act.

The Allied soldier's arms were held outright, either through rigor mortis or from the many weapons that had turned him into a human pin-cushion. With the sun rising through the patches of mist and fog, the light caught the scene from behind and it appeared to William as though the dead Frenchmen were kneeling at the feet of the British soldier, who sat crucified, his face held high and calling to the heavens. The whole scene seemed biblical in that moment and it appeared absurd to William that in this place of dead flesh some holy symbol could dare to appear without any warning.

Then the clouds strangled the light and the grotesque truth returned: the bodies sitting in the dirt and death of battle, small black swarms buzzing around the corpses in a frenzy to lay their eggs. This was the stark truth. There was no honour left after battle, only death. There were no heroes, only wasted lives. At least the living could remember them. The dead would remember nothing.

William looked away with a mixture of disgust and anger. His short military career had consisted of charging fearlessly into battle, relishing the chance to go up against the best the French had to offer. He never questioned why, nor did he dwell on the more terrible costs of battle – the aftermath, the casualties. But this time it was different. Instead of retiring to camp with the other officers and the remnants of the brigade, he'd accepted the dubious honour of trying to find Captain Mayfair's body. But having seen how the great captain had died (decapitated by a cannonball) the only lead he could go on was regalia and rank. Despite the Herculean task, William eventually recovered the body, though the head was lost forever.

It was on leaving the field that second time that William quietly thanked God he didn't have to look for his best friend, Kieran, amongst the thousands of corpses, knowing that it was only by His grace they had both survived when so many of the regiment had perished.

Lieutenant Colonel Fuller motioned to move on and they did so silently.

Most of the regiments had moved back to camp or to Brussels. Some had followed Blücher's lead and were pursuing Napoleon. Already news had arrived of the Prussians' engagement with Grouchy's depleted army. But at Waterloo, all that remained of the army were the supervising officers and the orderlies with the grim business of burying those who would never leave.

As William and Fuller came by another heap of dead soldiers, a small number of attendants were trying to dig out the fallen bodies of British infantry who had been overlooked the first time. They saluted both William and the lieutenant colonel, and William couldn't help but stare as they pulled the body of a young man who couldn't have been much older than himself from the twisted mess of mud and French corpses.

As they pulled, a French officer rolled away, the top of his head missing, probably from a sabre strike. In his hands he clutched a small wooden cross on a chain, his face a knot of fear and shock.

For years William had been indoctrinated to believe that the French were a faceless enemy, the demon hordes of the 'Monster' himself. If a man wanted to ally himself with Napoleon then he rescinded his right to be human.

Looking at that 'demon' now, with his hand clutched tightly around the cross, William felt himself convulse at the lies he'd swallowed about the enemy. He had felt sick with elation and relief after the battle had ended, but now he felt sicker staring at the officer who could have been a brother had fate differed. This was no monster, but a man. A man who probably had a family; a man who probably had a brother. He may have even been brave right up to the end, but now he was dead, like the others.

Fuller reached over and patted William gently on the shoulder. William closed his eyes and swallowed dryly as they cantered down the path that led to Hougoumont. Although his horse was new (a fresh and rested beast from the stables in Brussels) William followed at a slower pace, still feeling the bruises of battle. He also felt tired to the point of sickness, having not slept properly for almost three days.

'Never a pretty sight, is it, Saxon?' Fuller said as they came by another ditch of dead soldiers and horses.

William shook his head, trying to find the spit in his mouth to answer. 'No sir,' he finally replied, and kept his eyes trained not on the ground but the fog in the distance.

'How many do you think we lost? They're still finding pockets of our boys even now. It'll take days for the whole field to become free of the dead, what with Wellington wanting to find Napoleon.' Fuller paused and rubbed his face gently. He too seemed exhausted. The 1st Dragoon Cavalry had fought fiercely and at great cost.

'How is your friend, Lieutenant Kieran Harte, by the way?' Fuller asked.

William pulled the reins of the horse gently and it bowed its head, its breath engulfing both of them in the cold of the morning. 'Recovering, sir,' William replied, and patted the beast's neck.

Fuller nodded, distracted for a moment. 'I heard he suffered a couple of broken ribs.'

William nodded. 'Just the one rib, sir, and a wound to his side.'

'Bayonet, I suppose.'

'Yes sir. They pulled his horse down with him,' William

added, remembering how he saw his friend fall into a pack of French infantry, his red jacket being swarmed over by the smoke and fighting soldiers.

'But he was lucky you were there, wasn't he? Lucky that the Dragoons managed to pull him out,' Fuller remarked and smiled proudly.

William nodded. 'Yes, he was very lucky, sir. Unlike Captain Mayfair.'

Fuller's expression changed and he seemed pained for a moment. 'Yes, unlike Captain Mayfair ...'

They began to trot again, past a clear patch of ground that had been cleared of both Allied and French casualties. As they made their way to Hougoumont, Fuller paused and asked, 'You were there when Mayfair fell?'

William stopped his horse and nodded gravely. He'd been close enough for the mud and blood to drench his jacket and breeches until he was the same ruddy colour as the ground. And he'd been close enough to smell the death that surrounded him as other men fell under the guns, men he had trained with and known for years. Men he had called friends.

The only friend who managed to escape the slaughter was the one he cared most for: Kieran.

'Yes, I saw him die. Cannonball, sir,' William replied distantly.

'Cannonball,' Fuller murmured. 'Damn shame. Mayfair always wanted to die at the hands of the enemy, not by a cowardly cannonball so far away. Damn bad luck, eh?'

'Yes, sir.'

'But your friend, Lieutenant Harte, was a little luckier.'

'He'll mend, sir.'

Fuller nodded. 'I'm sure he will, just like Uxbridge will go on to fight another day, I'm sure.'

'How is Uxbridge, sir?' William asked. He wasn't too bothered about the earl's health but as the lieutenant colonel was expressing sentiments about his best friend he thought it only polite to ask.

'He'll mend. He's lost his leg, mind. But he'll mend, I'm sure. He's being looked after well.' Fuller turned to him and raised his eyebrows. 'Though I doubt he'll recover enough to lead again. The Earl blames himself for what happened to the cavalry. So many men were killed, and such a hopeless attack on the French cannon seemed like a folly. But between you and me, Saxon, I think we saved the battle. I think we smashed old Boney's plans, what?'

'Yes, sir,' William nodded and watched as the fog lifted again.

'Your Mr Harte ... is he being well looked after?' Fuller ventured.

William smiled. 'You could say that, sir. He's resting in Gembloux.'

Fuller stopped his horse and turned to William. 'Gembloux? What in God's name is he doing in Gembloux? The artillery reserve is in Gembloux, not the 1st Dragoons! He should be in Brussels!'

'He knows someone in Gembloux, sir. A local widow called Katherine. He was given leave to rest there, sir. A privilege you might say.'

'A privilege? Well he's earned it. They all have ...' Fuller trailed off and looked across Waterloo. 'A local widow, eh? Twice lucky, eh, Lieutenant?'

'Yes sir,' William replied.

'And talking of luck, I have some to bestow on you, Lieutenant Saxon.'

'Sir?'

Fuller reached over and patted him gently on the arm. 'We should talk back at the camp, you and I,' he said, and pulled his horse around. William followed at a trot, the smell of death and rot fading as they rode.

△ II △

Beyond La Haye Saint, across the once-green fields of Waterloo, the French bodies still lay in the mud of recent rain. The orderlies and bearers had not reached this far – there were very few

Coalition dead here. In this stretch of land, facing towards the smoking pyres and smouldering ruins of the farmhouse, only dead French infantry littered the ground, those massacred by cannon-fire or the assaulting Prussian cavalry. Among them lay the bodies of officers, of riders and their horses, and even a number of artillerymen who had died fleeing the vengeful Germans. They lay in mounds, or strewn about, and streams of blood congealed around each pile of corpses.

As the dawn lifted with the fog, small shadows began to slink away from the gloom. Here the witches had scavenged for many days, under threat of death by the marshalled officers whose duty it was to ensure the dead kept their dignity as well their valuables. It was a thankless task, yet it was done with honour, regardless of the nationality of the dead.

As the sun broke through a bank of dark cloud, another pair of officers rode up the hill, firing into the air to scare the looters, booting one crone off the corpse of a Coalition soldier as they tried to rout the scavengers. They scattered before them, sure that the threat of a kicking, or perhaps worse, did not warrant the pillaging of more flags and jackets (of which they had looted many over the last few hours). There was hidden treasure still to be discovered, and as the officers rode some of the scavengers from the field, those that remained rooted deep under dead flesh to find the trinkets that would make them a pretty penny.

But not all the treasures were hidden. Some *wanted* to be found ...

An old woman, rubbing her groin and singing a rambling tune, stood over one Frenchman who was lying half submerged in a puddle. His arm was missing and the left side of his face was a rotting mass of bone and mashed flesh. Despite the corpse's condition, she wandered over, having been drawn to it from afar by a call of sorts – a whisper that had reached her ears from almost one hundred yards away. It had been a wordless whisper, the promises blending into each other to form a nonsense, yet to her it was a covenant of discovery, of something important.

She found the trinket peeking from the soldier's jacket,

between two dull buttons, and instantly her hands went to it, bending over in the mud to try and pry the thing loose. Even with the marshalling officers so near, the woman tugged at the jacket using a rusty bayonet to cut away the buttons that held it together. Working feverishly, she cut and pulled until the buttons snapped loose and the trinket slipped from the jacket and into her hands. It was a bronze pyramid no bigger than her palm, and when she raised it to the dim light of day, she could feel it tremble against her hand, thrumming like a trapped wasp in a jar.

She looked about and smiled, saliva dribbling down her chin with excitement. The pyramid glistened as though wet, but the metal was cold and dry, the engravings of some archaic language clearly defined. The woman had no idea what they meant, and cared little. The pyramid was made of a shining bronze and looked expensive. She could sell it in the nearby town and it would feed her for longer than any of the other pickings she had scavenged over the last two days.

Laughing greedily, she wiped her chin and bent to kiss her treasure ...

But as her lips met the object, something rent open her mind, like an eye into her soul. It opened with a sharp flash of pain, and for the briefest of moments she saw a world on fire, of burning rocks and lakes of flame, hissing and moaning with the deaths of millions. At the centre was a mountain of flesh and bone, and on each level of the mountain were hundreds of thousands of grey people – screaming, screaming as though they had been screaming for all of their tormented lives. And there was more – a voice, a nonsense like the whisper, but becoming clearer all the time. At the moment she thought she would understand it, a face appeared at the door, deathly grey with eyes of fire, which seemed twisted into a horrific expression of torment and pleasure that said simply: 'BE GONE!'

The old woman cried out and stumbled back, her left leg sinking into the bloody mud near the corpse of the French soldier. She looked down at her palm and the pyramid had gone. During the vision she had dropped it – she had dropped her treasure! She clutched her groin and uttered a high-pitched moan as she sank to her knees in the filth to find it.

By the time she found the pyramid, she had forgotten the vision completely. She had also forgotten why she had been drawn to the corpse in the first place, and had almost forgotten how she had found the pyramid peeking between the folds of the soldier's jacket. By the time she had put the trinket into the deep pockets of her tattered shawl and made her way from the advancing officers and their pistols, she had forgotten the entire incident, knowing only that she had something special on her person and that the long journey back to Gembloux would be more than worth it.

△ III △

Most of the roads from Waterloo were busy these days, and the road to Gembloux, where the reserve artillery struggled to pull their cannon up the muddy track, was no exception. The road was in a terrible state and they soon found themselves bogged down in puddles and ditches that threatened to overturn the ordnance. William couldn't remember a wetter June, and he wished he was back home in England, in the summer sun of Lowchester. Yet he couldn't complain; he still had his health and so did Kieran. And he had some good news to tell his friend, although he wasn't sure how Kieran was going to take it.

They had been good friends since childhood, after a young Kieran had turned up at the family home, orphaned by a horrific tragedy. The Saxon family had taken him in, treating him as their other son. And William treated Kieran as his brother. As they grew up together, the two became inseparable.

Thirteen years later, having fought two campaigns in the 1st Dragoon Guards, both had risen to the rank of lieutenant. They were equal in everything, except in love. Kieran always had the lion's share, and was seen as more dashing than William. But there was only the slightest hint of rivalry between them, and never enough to divide them. They would gladly die for each other; their friendship was that strong.

But things change, including friendships, and so it was on the day William rode to Gembloux that his and Kieran's paths would begin the inevitable split.

It had been over a week since William had last visited Gembloux. A week of grooming as the lieutenant colonel told him his plans and those of the Earl of Uxbridge. In that week Blücher had fought Grouchy and Napoleon had finally been routed. Several of the other French generals and captains had escaped, some into the East, some to the south of Europe, but they would be hunted down in time. What mattered most was the news of Napoleon's abdication. It was news that spread like the Fever.

Almost everywhere, it seemed, they were celebrating the victory. In Gembloux, the townspeople continued about their business, indifferent to the soldiers' presence. Most were at the market; now and again a farmer herded his cattle across the street. Others simply stared into space, the signs of occupation obvious in certain corners of the town. The French had not harmed them that much during their brief stay, but there were some stories of townspeople being subjected to cruelty as Grouchy's soldiers waited on Napoleon's orders. There were stories of murder and attempted rape; there was a story of a boy being run down by a French rider after he looted the enemy stores. Sad tales to add to the others.

William trotted over to the nest of cottages and shops to the east of the town centre, and dismounted. A young Belgian boy who spoke potted English said he'd stable the horse for a fee. William admired his enterprise and paid him over the asking price, watching as his horse calmly left with the boy who struggled to keep up with the animal.

The inn at Gembloux was modest, yet it seemed to stand out against the other shops and cottages. It was owned by Katherine's father and had been part of the family business for some time.

Looking up at the first floor, William saw there were red

tulips in a window. These were the tulips Kieran had brought Katherine from Holland. The same tulips he'd given her on the eve of Waterloo, not expecting to see her again. They seemed old now, drooping and rusty, and William doubted they had much time left. No doubt Kieran would ride to Holland to get her more, but for the moment all the Irishman could do was rest and make sure his wound didn't open again.

Pulling off his cap, William pushed the door open and walked into the inn. It was quiet but smoky, and a small fire crackled in the hearth. A couple of farmers were talking in the corner and some were glancing at the four British soldiers playing cards in the centre of the room.

When William entered, the soldiers rose and stood to attention. William smiled and nodded back at them, telling them to return to their game. He passed by and went to the bar where an elderly gent with a straggly grey moustache was cleaning the pots. William took off his coat and coughed gently to catch the landlord's attention.

'Sir? I'm here to see Kieran,' William said.

The landlord grunted and pointed upstairs. The man shared Katherine's appearance in the eyes only. He had none of her charm or warmth. William would have scarcely believed the two were related.

'Thank you,' William said, and moved past the bar and began the climb. At the landing, William knocked on the door and waited. The smell of something rich and aromatic drifted by and William's stomach growled.

The door to the first floor opened and a young woman was there to greet him. She was around William's age with long dark hair and a slender face, with smile lines that made her seem more carefree than perhaps she was. Katherine looked more radiant each day, glowing brighter as Kieran grew stronger. On each meeting it seemed it was only a slight change, but she was beautiful, and William thought back on what Fuller had said about his friend being 'twice lucky'.

'I'm not disturbing anything, am I?' William asked.

Katherine looked at him blankly. She could hardly understand a word of English let alone speak it, but she smiled sweetly and opened the door wider to let him in.

The landing smelt of lavender; not overly strong, but enough to mingle with the scent of cooking. It was a blessed relief from the smell of mud and corpses he'd endured over the last few days.

Katherine showed him to Kieran's room and disappeared quietly back to the kitchen, as waves of food-smells made William salivate.

By the look of it, Katherine was a good cook as well. 'Lucky, lucky, lucky ...' William murmured and pushed the bedroom door open.

Kieran was flat on his back and looking distantly out of the window where the tulips stood. He barely noticed William entering the room, and he guessed the Irishman was deep in thought or maybe just resting. On a nearby bedside table sat a drink and the book William had brought him on a previous visit – a copy of Milton's *Paradise Lost*.

'No welcome?' William said. Kieran blinked and stared from across the room. 'Not even a "hello" for the man who saved you?' William half joked.

Kieran's expression changed suddenly to a grin, slightly weakened, but it was better than the grim expression William had seen a week before as they had bandaged up his friend's side.

'Well, I'd walk over there and give you a big hug, my friend, but I believe I would unknit my side again. And that's if I could manage to crawl out of bed to do so,' he laughed and coughed gently.

'How's the rib?'

Kieran squinted. 'Oh that! Fine, fine. Couldn't be ... *better*,' he said, coughing up the last word. 'I must have a word with your horse. I wish he hadn't thrown me so far!'

'Well, I would let you speak to him if he weren't on the battlefield being eaten by crows,' William replied grimly, remembering their mad dash from the enemy lines as all hell broke loose around them.

Kieran made to rise from the bed but William held up a hand. 'It's alright. I'll sit,' he said, and took the stool from the nearby table, perching upon it.

'So, Katherine's looking after you well, I hope?' William asked.

Kieran nodded. 'Yes. She's a marvel, Will, a bloody marvel. I don't know how she puts up with me.'

'Maybe she's in love,' William suggested.

Kieran almost blushed and smiled. 'Maybe she is.'

William tapped the foot of the bed with his boot. 'Are you in love with her?'

Kieran looked at his friend and noticed the disquiet in the question. 'What if I was?'

'Nothing. It's ... It's good that you are. Not many people find love,' William struggled.

'But?'

'But nothing,' William replied, and sheepishly tapped the bed with his boot again.

Kieran pursed his lips and pushed himself up with some effort. 'If you're thinking about your Elizabeth, Will, I assure you nothing happened between us. Falling in love with Katherine will break no honour.'

William looked up. 'Then you *are* in love with her?'

Kieran shrugged and now it was his turn to look distant. 'Perhaps.'

William got up from the stool and went to the window. Down below, a number of townsfolk were helping a local farmer move his cart out of a mud-trap that had formed in the centre of the town. Some of the folk, maybe local farmers themselves, were covered in mud, yet their will was not broken and their enthusiasm held fast as they teamed together to pull and push the cart free.

'I never thought anything was happening between you and my sister, Kieran,' he admitted, still watching the struggle below, 'I know it was more Lizzy than you. No, that's not the problem at all.'

'Then what is it?'

William looked back. 'I just find it peculiar,' he started.

'That I've found love?' Kieran pushed, unsure what this was leading to.

'For all the years I've known you, you never once thought about settling down. Women have thrown themselves at your feet, and for all those you've bedded, never has "love" been spoken by you,' William said, trying desperately to hide his jealousy. Kieran had slept with women that William had looked on as goddesses, and yet his Irish friend cast them aside on a whim.

'Maybe I haven't spoken of love before, but times change. People change. And I have changed. This will not be the only change in the near future, Will. In Katherine I see someone I want to be with for the rest of my life. Is that so hard to understand?' Kieran asked, feeling a little aggrieved.

William screwed up his face. 'How will you live? Here in Gembloux? You don't speak a word of her language and she doesn't speak English. How will you communicate?'

Kieran pondered this and a wry smile came to his lips. 'With our bodies!'

William couldn't help but laugh. 'Oh really! How will you achieve that, what with your body all banged up? With one busted rib and a wounded torso, how would you do that, Mr Romeo, if you please?'

'Ah, my friend. There are more ways of satisfying the flesh than simple copulation!' Kieran replied, and looked pleased with himself.

William laughed again, but felt quite envious. 'Well, if you're truly in love, you'll work something out, I'm sure,' he conceded and sat back down next to the bed.

'So tell me, Will, what happens in our world this day?' Kieran asked, trying to change the subject.

William tried to get comfortable and the stool creaked slightly under his weight, more used to the light frame of Katherine rather than a rider of the 1st Dragoon Cavalry.

'You've heard about Napoleon's abdication?

Kieran nodded. 'It's all they talk about in the streets. You wouldn't believe it to see them, but they're all glad the war is over. Especially Katherine.'

'Because it means you don't have to go running off to fight some damned idealistic battle?' William ventured.

'Something like that.'

William smiled and fell silent.

'Is that it? No more news? Just a titbit that I heard from my sickbed?' Kieran laughed, trying to hide his disappointment. 'What about Uxbridge? What about the rest of the regiment?'

'Uxbridge will survive. Fuller told me he's in good hands. As for the regiment …' William hunched his shoulders and wanted to say something about his captaincy.

'We're getting shipped back to England, aren't we?' Kieran guessed.

William nodded silently, noticing the despondency in Kieran's voice. 'In a few days, the regiment leaves for Rotterdam and from there it's a frigate to Portsmouth. We'll be in Lowchester in a matter of weeks,' he finished, scarcely remembering what home had been like during the brief interlude between the end of the last war and the return of Napoleon. It seemed like years had passed since then.

'They've made me a captain,' William said matter-of-factly, and showed his insignia of rank.

Kieran pinched his brow and leant forward to see if his friend was joking.

'Aye, so they have,' he murmured, and William feared there was resentment there.

Kieran broke into a bright grin and leant back on the bed. 'Congratulations, you deserve it.'

'You don't mind?' William asked, not completely sure if Kieran was being magnanimous.

'Not at all, you always were the better leader. And besides, you pulled us together after Mayfair fell. Any news on Mayfair? You never told me if he survived.'

William shook his head grimly. 'No, he didn't survive, believe me.'

'You've got a lot to live up to, you know? Filling Mayfair's boots like that,' Kieran said sadly.

'Well, that may be, but I'll still have the support of a good friend,' William replied hopefully.

Kieran nodded and looked away. 'Well, that's a thing, isn't it?'

'What do you mean?'

'Well, you see, Will, I'm not sure I'm going to be in the Dragoons for much longer.'

William blinked hurriedly. 'You're being reassigned? To whom? Why? I can try and pull some strings so that ...'

'I'm leaving the Army, Will,' Kieran interrupted and then fell quiet.

William shook his head in disbelief. 'This is because of Katherine, isn't it?'

'Not just that,' Kieran replied. 'I've had enough of killing. A whole gut-full. I've lost too much to war. Katherine has seen her fair share of death as well. I'm not about to make her a widow twice.'

'But, Kieran, there is no one left to fight. The French have been defeated.'

Kieran pushed himself up, his expression doubtful. 'What about the Americans? Or how about the Prussians? And if not them, then maybe it will be Russia next? We live in volatile times; war is a mere whisper away, a footstep from a political disaster. And as we are soldiers, we go where we're told.'

William was crestfallen. 'We knew that when we joined. We knew the risks then as we do now.'

'Yes. But now I have much more to risk. Now I have Katherine,' Kieran replied.

'And you think I don't have anything to lose?'

Kieran turned on his side, the pain visible in his expression. 'Of course you do. But you choose the risk again by accepting the commission. I can't. I won't. All I want is here, with Katherine.'

'You're right, you have changed,' William growled, getting up off the stool. 'I don't know if I'm angry because I feel I'm losing a friend or because I feel you're throwing away your life.'

'Neither, Will.'

'Then what will you do if you're not a soldier? You don't speak the language here. You have no trade apart from soldiering.'

'Maybe I'll become a farmer,' Kieran suggested.

'To toil in the mud and excrement out there, you mean? Does that appeal to you? Are you ready to toil with the other farmers for mere pennies and misery? I know you, Kieran, remember? I've been your friend – your brother – for years, and I know you'll never be happy until you're charging off on some heroic adventure where the odds are stacked against you,' William ranted. 'Christ, you must have been the only one who wasn't pissing their breeches when we saw the French divisions marching down the hills towards us! And you're saying you'll give all that up for Katherine – to be a farmer!'

Kieran sighed. 'I'll do whatever it takes.'

'Fine,' William grumbled, and gathered his sword by the door.

'We've been friends for the length of our lives,' Kieran coughed. '*Please* tell me what you are thinking.'

'I'm hoping right now that you're feverish and that you've had a knock to the head as well as the ribs, as you're not talking like the Kieran I used to know.'

Kieran looked downcast, his weariness showing more as his face grew ashen. He coughed again and reached out towards William who paused and looked down at the hand, taking it gently in his. Kieran's skin felt cold and clammy and for the first time William noticed how weak the Irishman actually was.

'I'm still the old Kieran, Will, it's just that now I want different things from life.'

William nodded and gave his hand a gentle squeeze. 'I'll come by tomorrow, if that's alright by you. If you want to leave the Army I'll make it immediate.'

'Privileges of rank, eh?'

'Something like that. Tomorrow then?'

Kieran nodded and withdrew his hand. 'Tomorrow,' he replied, and watched as William left the room.

At the landing William heard Katherine in the next room,

cooking in the private kitchen whilst humming a gentle tune. It was quiet apart from that. William had a feeling that something had passed. Maybe it was an end of an era, or a friendship. William didn't know, but he felt he had to leave Gembloux before his emotions boiled over.

He descended the steps quickly and returned to the bar at the inn. Still the four soldiers were playing, but their card game was involving and competitive enough for the men not to notice William as he reappeared at the bottom of the steps. William scowled but let it pass and pulled up the collar of his coat as he left the inn and the increasing feeling of isolation.

Outside, he noticed the air growing colder. Like the weather, everything was changing, and he was finding it hard to keep up. Pulling his coat around him, William swallowed his worries and marched off to find the Belgian boy who had taken his horse.

△ IV △

Kieran watched as Katherine removed the empty bowl of soup. She could tell he was watching her and knew well enough what he wanted next. She went over to the bed and his hand went to her backside. She shook her head sternly and said one of the only words she knew in English: 'No.'

Kieran smiled and withdrew his hand. 'No? I'm stronger now. I'm sure I could take it.'

'No,' Katherine said again and giggled.

The sound of her laughing brought warmth to his thoughts and Kieran leant back again on the bed. Katherine was beautiful and it didn't make any difference whether she completely understood what he said. He could tell what she was thinking, and she could tell his thoughts well enough.

As she passed by him with his empty cup, Kieran put out his hand. She leant down and kissed it and then put a hand in her blouse. Kieran beamed as she passed him a piece of cloth. Kieran examined it – a piece of cloth with the letter 'K' embroided upon it. It was a creamy colour and the letter was a bright blue.

'You washed it!' Kieran held the piece to his chest, a dazzling smile on his lips. This had been his first keepsake, one that she'd given him on the eve of battle, and he'd feared it had been ruined.

Katherine leant close and kissed him on the lips, returning to the bedroom after taking the dishes into the kitchen. She went to the window and closed the curtains, pausing only to remove the tulips that had faded over the last daylight hours.

Kieran watched her smell them once with her eyes closed and she sighed, removing them from the vase. Kieran knew she was going to throw them out.

'I'll have to go to Holland again, won't I? I can't imagine this room without flowers!' he grinned. Katherine smiled shyly and looked at the tulips. She pulled out one that had withered the least and gave it to Kieran before returning silently to the kitchen.

Kieran played gently with the flower and smelt it. It was practically scentless and he guessed it had been dead for some time. Looking at how fragile it seemed, he took the cloth Katherine had returned to him and placed the tulip between the folds. He then reached over and opened *Paradise Lost* at the centre of the book, inserting the piece of cloth inside.

Kieran turned to the first page. He'd only read half of the book but had read that many times. There were parts that he couldn't get past, sections that seemed too hard to read (though he never admitted it). Instead he made the excuse that it was the first part of that epic poem that was worth reading – that spoke to him. It was a reminder of William, and now his words came back like ghosts.

What would he do if he left the Army? Katherine could indeed come to England, but how would she fit in? She didn't know any English and he didn't like the idea of Katherine being viewed as an immigrant. America was another choice, but this would mean moving far away from the people they knew and cared for. That still left Kieran with another problem.

William was right: soldiering was all Kieran knew. He was well educated, but he knew that he wouldn't stand doing a menial office job or something involving diplomacy. He didn't fair well with figures, and had no patience to teach. His love was for the outdoors and adventure. Could he really be content with a simple life in a place like Gembloux? Would he miss the excitement of battle?

He leant back and held the book against his chest, his eyes searching the cracked ceiling for an answer, or a clue at the very least. Katherine appeared again with an apple that she quartered and shared with him. His teeth bit through the skin of one quarter, into the sweet flesh, and he smiled as the taste dribbled over his lips and down his throat. Katherine dabbed at the corner of his mouth where some of the juice had escaped. He stared into her dark eyes and ran his hand gently along hers.

'I love you so much,' he heard himself saying, knowing that he truly meant it. It felt right, and so did leaving the Army – and for Kieran, that was good enough.

Katherine looked at him for a moment and smiled again. 'Love Kie-ran,' she tried, attempting to pronounce his name.

'Yes,' he said vigorously and put his finger on her breast. 'I love you.'

'*D'amour*,' she replied. 'Love.'

'*Vriendin?*' Kieran said, reciting one of the very few words he'd learned since staying with Katherine, hoping he'd expressed it correctly.

She rolled gently onto her side and lay next to him, placing her arms around him as though ready for sleep. She nuzzled him for a few moments and kissed his lips.

Before Kieran could reply with his own petting, her hand ran under the blanket towards his groin. 'I'm not sure if I'm strong enough for that,' he admitted gently.

He wanted it so much but he was still weak. Katherine understood the tone in his voice and the sound of caution, so her hand retreated slightly. Kieran laughed, his hand gently holding hers by his hip. He grinned and kissed her gently. 'But I didn't say you shouldn't at least *try*,' he whispered and guided her hand down.

△ V △

Across the sky the dark crept in. It was not the normal settling of night, but as though a bank of black fog was overpowering the light, shrinking daylight into darkness. It came on a tide and the people of Gembloux knew well enough to retreat inside their homes as the night came without the stars or the moonlight.

Inside one hovel a woman squatted in the corner. The place hummed with flies during humid days and smelt of excrement when the owner couldn't be bothered to shit outside. Sometimes she would piss close to the door and her urine would trickle out under it − steaming during winter months, riper during the summer − soaking into the mottled floorboards that rotted in sections along the front room.

The woman stood up and wiped her backside with her gown. She stepped out of the room and closed the door behind her, taking to a broken chair that sat by a pair of boarded windows. She looked through the gaps to the outside world and noticed that night had arrived. The few candles that were lit in the room crackled and spat with animal fat, giving off an onerous smell that quelled the stench of her own excrement as it dried on her gown.

The woman leant over and rifled through the pickings of the previous days. There weren't many more 'expensives' left on the battlefield. Most of the dead had been picked clean by other scavengers. As she brought up a snuff-tin, bloodied but with a family crest adorning it, she narrowed her eyes and opened the little box. To her disgust there was nothing inside except brown sludge that smelt of blood. She sneered and tossed it into the pile of discarded weapons that was littered with the shreds of French flags, Prussian caps and British buckles. These would fetch a few pennies from the local dealer, a distrustful man who bought cheap and sold high, across Europe. He had floated about Gembloux and the other towns as soon as the first of the battles occurred. The man, who went by the name of Vernaldes, had appeared at her cottage twice, demanding to see what pickings she'd found.

21

The woman now pushed these pickings away and reached into her gown for her pride and joy, the bronze pyramid she had found a week ago. She had cleaned it some more, hoping to sell it on. But there was reluctance there, a fearful feeling that she would lose much more if she sold it. She grew possessive and talked to it, thinking that it heard her and would some day reply. She didn't know why, but it felt as though it pulsed with life. A life that was now hers. Vernaldes could have any of the shit she had gathered from the battlefield, but if he tried to take the pyramid from her, she would scratch his eyes out.

◬ VI ◬

The Reserve Artillery had made it back to camp, having almost lost their ordnance in the mud just outside Gembloux. Before night arrived, William had collected his horse and began trotting back when he passed the train of artillerymen and cannon. The lead officer, a lieutenant, saluted him and William returned the gesture. 'I see you managed to move the cannon out of the bog, Lieutenant,' he grinned playfully.

The lieutenant was splattered in mud but had retained his sense of humour. 'Aye, you could say that, sir. It was a damned close thing, I can tell you. A damn sight closer than the race we ran with those Frenchies! I wished now that I had not requested a twelve-pounder. An eight-pounder is an easy pull!'

William laughed. 'Ah well, a little spit and polish will bring it out I'm sure.'

'Aye, Captain, it will. Sorry to say I don't think the same could be said for me and the lads,' he said gesturing to the bedraggled train of mud-soaked soldiers.

'Well, if the other captains say anything about the Artillery not mucking in, I for one will put in a word for you,' William promised. He looked ahead to the twilight on the horizon and sighed as he thought about the long ride back to the provisional barracks in Brussels.

'Thank you, Captain,' the lieutenant replied, and noticed that William was preparing to leave. 'Are you riding back this night?'

'Yes, unfortunately. Just a social call, I'm afraid.'

'Oh? You know someone in the town?'

'A friend of mine is being treated by one of the townspeople,' William replied, and was about to bid the lieutenant a goodnight when the officer trudged over to the horse and patted it gently, careful not to leave a muddy handprint on the charger's fine coat.

'It'll be another cold night in this grey place, sir. Are you sure I couldn't tempt you with a cup of rum and a few stories at the local inn? The Reserve Artillery might not be as heroic as the King's Cavalry, but we have stories to tell that I'm sure would amuse an officer of your humour, sir.'

William pondered the offer, looking out towards the distance where the night had fallen and the shadows had drenched the land. He wasn't expected back at the regiment for a while and he was sure the lieutenant colonel had no more errands for him.

'Thank you for the offer, Lieutenant. I accept,' William said, shaking the officer's hand.

'We'll need to change first though. You could come back to Camp with us or meet up at the inn, if you'd prefer?' the lieutenant suggested.

William thought about being in the inn again and felt uncomfortable at the idea of waiting for them there; Katherine might start to resent his presence. He turned his horse around and dismounted.

'Lead on, I'll come with you to camp,' he replied, and followed the train on foot.

The Reserve Artillery had set up their tents on the outskirts of the town. A local farmer had allowed them to settle in one of his fields. The smell of cattle-dung was quite strong; some of the soldiers had gotten used to it, being farmers themselves, but others had resorted to using snuff to block the smell from their nostrils. As William and the train traipsed into the camp, he could hear faint sneezing away to his left as they passed a campfire situated near a dung-heap. It was all very common, very 'down-to-earth', but William had never been a snob about who he was friendly with, be it the Cavalry, the officers, or the common soldiery.

As they got to the centre of the camp, one of the soldiers took William's horse away to be stabled while the lieutenant led William off to a ring of campfires. The artillerymen saluted William in kind and William told them all not to be so formal. After all, he was from the Cavalry and not their commanding officer.

'No standing on parade, please Lieutenant. My name is William,' he said as he settled down by the fire.

'Dickinson, sir, Brier Dickinson,' the lieutenant replied.

'Your accent, West Country isn't it?'

The lieutenant nodded. 'Cornwall, sir.'

'Looking forward to returning home, Brier?'

'Aye, sir. Aye, I am,' Brier replied distantly and noticed that the others sitting by the fire looked hopeful about going back. 'If you'll excuse me sir, I'll just change.'

William watched the lieutenant leave and turned his attention back to the men around the fire.

'What about you, sir?' one of the soldiers asked. 'Are you looking forward to returning home?'

William nodded strongly. 'Very much so. Back home to Lowchester, to see my mother and father, my sister ... sunny days in England ... I miss them all.'

'Don't we all sir, don't we all.'

A sergeant reached over and handed William a metal cup, pouring some rum into it. Swilling it around, William looked up at the expectant faces of the soldiers who were waiting for him to take a sip. William smiled bravely and knocked it back. He paused to let the burning liquid go down, and then heaved with a short coughing fit.

'By gods, that was strong!' he wheezed.

'Bravo, Captain, bravo! Not many officers, let alone soldiers, can knock back Old Pike's rum.' Brier laughed as he reappeared with a clean jacket.

'Old Pike's?' William coughed.

'Aye, sir, God rest his soul. Old Pike brought some of that

from home. His family used to make it. The corporal gave me a bottle just before Quatre Bras, sir,' Brier said, and looked fondly at the bottle. He buttoned up his jacket and signalled to two other soldiers who appeared from the nearby tents.

'Really,' William replied, and wiped his mouth. 'So where's Old Pike now then?'

'Dead, sir,' one of the soldiers said sadly. 'Lancer got him, sir.'

William fell quiet. He noticed how despondent the soldiers had suddenly become. How many friends had they lost in the battle? Maybe not as many as William – the Reserve Artillery had not been virtually destroyed, as the Dragoons had – but he was sure that 'Old Pike' was not their only colleague who had died that day.

Brier poured William another cup as he stood up by the fire, feeling the rum pulse through his body, making him light-headed. He felt the sudden need to toast the men gathered around him, if not everyone who had fought in the battle. 'If I may, gentlemen, before we go I'd like to raise a cup of rum. Not just to you, or myself, but also to those like Old Pike and the friends I lost at Waterloo. We miss them all dearly and will remember them in our hearts,' he said, and raised his cup. For a moment there was only silence, the soldiers shocked that an officer (and an officer of the Cavalry at that) would raise a toast with the common folk of the Reserve Artillery. But Brier raised a cup and shouted, 'Hear! hear!'

Downing the rum, William coughed again and the camp started laughing, the mood growing brighter once more.

Bidding the rest of the soldiers goodnight, William left with Brier and two privates, to walk back down the road into Gembloux. 'You have an iron stomach, sir, to down two cupfuls of that stuff,' Brier remarked and smiled.

'Looks are deceiving, Lieutenant. I may have a well-educated voice, but I'm a man of the Army – officers and rank-and-file alike,' William replied, feeling a little queasy as the rum sloshed around his innards.

'Something that commends you, sir. Not many officers

would sit and drink with lower ranks. It is a sign of a good officer, an officer that the men love and trust. Your company are lucky to have a captain of your calibre, sir.'

'Several days ago I was the same rank as you, Lieutenant. I was given a field commission following the death of my captain.'

Brier nodded thoughtfully. 'How old are you, sir, if you don't mind me asking?'

William looked unsure and smiled wryly. 'I'm in my twenties, Lieutenant.'

'A young officer with an old head, sir. You have the best of both worlds if you don't mind me saying so,' Brier remarked.

'Not at all. Thank you for the compliment.'

It didn't take too long to return to the inn. William looked up at the window where the tulips had been. A lamp burned inside and the room glowed gently. Kieran and Katherine were probably inside 'communicating' with each other. He felt a sting of jealousy and tried to bat it away as though it was just an irritating fly.

The inn was quite busy with soldiers and farmers. The two sets seemed to ignore each other yet there was a mutual respect. The farmers respected the officers for driving Grouchy and the French from the town, and the officers respected the farmers for their hospitality. William passed a collection of corporals and sergeants. They saluted him and Brier as they took a table by the fire.

Lieutenant Dickinson went to the bar and returned with four draughts of ale. A barmaid followed him shortly and William flinched as he saw Katherine appear at their table. She looked at him and smiled, and William smiled back awkwardly. 'We'll keep this simple,' the lieutenant said, and winked at William. 'I'm afraid she knows very little English apart from what food and drinks we want.'

William nodded, trying to conceal his own knowing smile. 'You come here regularly?' he said.

'Now and again,' Brier replied, turning to Katherine. 'We'd like *four soups* and *bread*, please.'

Katherine nodded and looked at William again, smiling warmly. William returned the smile, this time a little more easily.

'Thankfully she knows what "soup" and "bread" mean,' Brier laughed.

Katherine returned with food and a jug of wine, and the soldiers tucked in hungrily. William was hesitant at first, but after a few mouthfuls he followed suit as he ate the satisfying meat broth. He was right again; the widow was an excellent cook.

William finished his food and talked some more with the artilleryman. With Katherine out of sight, his thoughts returned to the battle at Waterloo. The lieutenant and one of the privates spoke of the attacking French Cavalry trying to break Wellington's squares. It was a story William had heard before but this time the details were pretty graphic and none were spared the details of Old Pike's death, lanced through the groin against his cannon as he tried to fend off the charging French.

William was put in mind of Mayfair's bloody demise, and as the artillerymen finished their accounts they pressed the captain for his own stories.

'I'm sure our tales must pale into insignificance beside your own recollections, sir,' Brier said, and poured William another cup of wine.

'Well, we were in the thick of it,' William began. 'We were charging the remnants of Charlet's troops at the time. We attacked them at the rear and managed to ride some down, and then we went for the guns. We managed to get so far and then they unleashed the lancers on us.' He leant back and looked at the faces glowing in the firelight, all eyes on the captain. 'There was no way we could have seen it coming. You know as well as I do that with all that smoke and with explosions around you, it's difficult to see and hear what is going on, let alone when you're at full gallop trying to hack your way through the enemy. We never even heard the recall.'

'What happened, sir?' asked the youngest of the two privates, who was sitting keenly to his right.

William took a deep breath. 'A cannon blast killed the

Captain. He was one of the first to fall. And then one entire flank of the chargers stammered as they were cut in two by cannon shot and the soldiers marshalled in the square. We rallied around and tried to encircle them, hoping that another square wasn't behind that one.'

'Ah, the squares, sir ... they make mincemeat of cavalry,' said the other private – an older man in his late forties.

William nodded sombrely. 'Yes, they definitely do. But we were doubly unlucky, we hadn't reckoned on the lancers. As we wheeled around, a quarter of our line just disappeared into the panicked lines of the French. They must have killed many then, but by sheer numbers the riders were bogged down and over-run. Another section of the chargers were being taken down at the rear by the guns in the square. And then the middle sections were hemmed between the infantry and the Lancers.'

The elder soldier leant forward and lit a pipe. 'What section were you in, sir?' he asked, puffing away.

'Mid-rank,' William recalled grimly. 'We tried hacking our way out of it but we were getting closer and closer to the square. Eventually, the horses dragged themselves onto the bayonets of the French by sheer weight and pressure. It worked to our advantage in the end with those beasts falling on the ranks of the French, but it wasn't pretty. I suppose with all that fighting with the infantry, we got caught short. Before we knew it, we were overrun and had to make a dash for our own lines.'

William cleared his throat with a short cough. 'I lost many friends in that attack, and my best friend only survived after I dragged him from the floor during a melee when the square finally broke. I and a dozen others from the Scot's Greys rode back towards our own lines. And then we were caught in the crossfire between our own artillery and the French. I never saw those men again. My own horse was hit by a cannon blast and killed. I had to carry my friend through the smoke and back to our lines on foot, hoping to God the retreating French didn't catch us.'

'That would be your colleague who is resting here in this town, sir?' Brier ventured.

'That's right – Lieutenant Kieran Harte,' William replied.

'A good friend, sir?'

'We've been friends since we were children. We're practically brothers.'

'I wouldn't want my brother to be here in this God-awful place, sir!' said the youngest soldier.

'My brother *is* here, sir,' said the elder private. 'Part of Picton's regiment, sir.'

'Have you heard from him, soldier?'

The soldier shrugged and sipped his wine. 'Not really, sir. But I know he's fine. He's always been able to look after himself.'

'And this Lieutenant Harte, sir, is *he* alright?' Brier asked as he poured himself another cup.

William smiled. 'Yes, he's fine. I'm not sure his senses are though. Our barmaid has bewitched him.'

Brier raised his eyebrows. 'He's here?'

William nodded. 'Just upstairs. The barmaid is looking after him.'

'Your friend is a lucky man.'

William laughed. 'Indeed.'

'I'd go as far as saying I'm quite jealous of your friend, but then I've been starved of womanly company since we came to Belgium. Most of the women here look like the back-ends of horses, if you pardon me saying so, sir,' Brier remarked and both privates laughed out loud. 'Apart from the young widow, of course,' he added quickly.

William nodded and thought about Katherine. It occurred to him that his anger and frustration at Kieran was only jealousy. Strangely, that made it easier to swallow. He'd felt jealous a few times around Kieran and his way with women, and he almost always shrugged that feeling off quickly.

'You seem a little distracted, sir,' Brier murmured to William as the other men broke off to a separate conversation.

'Yes, I suppose I am. My friend is thinking of leaving the Army to spend his life with this woman,' William sighed.

'I see. Well, if you don't mind me saying so, I think your

friend could do much worse than marrying her. She is a warm woman – a kind woman – and will look after him. She also stands to inherit the inn. I know it might be below your breeding sir, but a tavern can be a lucrative business,' Brier remarked.

'But that doesn't mean he needs to leave the Army,' William said.

'Well, sir, the young widow might see this differently. The French widowed her after they came by recruiting everyone around here that was fit to walk. Her husband was carted off to fight for Napoleon and spent his last days dying somewhere in Russia. I'm sure she's vowed never to marry another soldier in this world, sir. Soldiering is a precarious way of life, even without a war to fight.'

William nodded thoughtfully. Maybe the lieutenant was right about letting Kieran decide, but it still felt like he was losing a friend. He drained the last of his wine and stretched, feeling the warmth of the fire brighten the edges of his gloom.

'If you want to turn in, sir, there's room in one of the tents at the camp – if you're not staying here at the inn. I'm sorry we don't have any better lodgings, but we don't get many captains around here,' Brier said.

William looked up the flight of steps with a feeling of envy, and nodded. 'Floor-space in a tent would suit me fine, thank you, Lieutenant.'

CHAPTER TWO

What Happened at Gembloux

△ I △

The evening concealed most things and this suited Vernaldes' purpose. The shadows were dense enough to hide the Spaniard's horse down an alley. From there he watched as the British soldiers entered the inn at Gembloux. He was keen to keep his business as anonymous as possible, not wishing to fall foul of the law yet again, be it British or French.

As the evening wore on, the flow of traffic in and out of the inn was diminishing. Vernaldes moved out from the gloom along the main street.

He waited for a moment by the wall of a butcher's shop until he was sure no more soldiers would appear. While the majority of the British Army didn't know him, the local authorities were certainly familiar with his name and his trade. The Spaniard was a merchant in pillage – a man who paid blood-money for weapons and regalia stolen from the battlefields. Some called him a scavenger, who preyed on the weak or dying. Some called him worse than that, and there were times when he'd fled under the threat of incarceration or death. They were the risks, but with such a lucrative business to support his lifestyle of perverse pleasures, he could live with those risks even if it meant dealing with people who were often more dangerous than vipers.

After a few moments, Vernaldes slipped away casually from the butcher's shop. He carried a long thick stick in one hand (to be used as a club if necessary), while in the other he carried a deep sack that looked weathered and stained with blood. The sack would carry all the helmets, pistols, ammunition and flags that he had silver to pay for, no matter what their condition. If the witch had more than he was prepared to pay for, he would come back with a cart and simply take whatever he wanted, one way or another.

The Spaniard had learned from experience that no one missed a dead witch.

This was Vernaldes' third call to Gembloux in as many days. Over the last week, he'd visited the neighbouring villages and towns, calling upon the vermin who had scavenged the recent battlefields at Quatre Bras and Waterloo until there was nothing fit to pillage except the stinking corpses of the dead. It had been a fruitful process, yet now there were more muskets and sabres than the Spaniard could shift. No doubt his brothers in Spain could use them, but he was fast running out of room in his rented cottage outside Nivelles. Eventually he had decided to only buy fine quality loot, and he knew that his next supplier valued this also. She was close to madness, but she could smell something valuable from fifty yards.

Presently Vernaldes arrived at a row of poorly built cottages and a shack that was subsiding as its foundations rotted away. He rapped on the door and waited. The hovel appeared to be derelict and it smelt rotten, but from experience he knew the smell outside would be more pleasant than the smell within. He was glad to be wearing gloves; the thought of his fingers touching any part of this filthy place made him feel unclean.

After a while, he knocked again, and heard a voice from inside. It spoke potted French but was clear enough for Vernaldes to understand. He caught on well and was able to learn new languages at the drop of a hat. To date he could speak English and French fluently and had an understanding of German and Italian. He could get by on the little Greek and Turkish he knew, though he was finding the East Asian languages difficult.

The voice came again. 'Who's there?'

'Vernaldes,' the Spaniard murmured. There was a scuffling and the door was unbolted. The smell hit him and he recoiled, disgusted. The Spaniard coughed and tried to smile at the woman in front of him. 'I trust you have something for me?' he said, gently.

The witch narrowed her eyes. 'Only if you have something for me, dear.'

Vernaldes let the sack drop and pulled out a small purse with his free hand. The witch's dull eyes sparkled into life. 'Let me see what you have there,' she hissed.

The Spaniard withdrew the money and held the wooden stick threateningly. 'Let me see what you have first. Then we'll trade,' he replied calmly.

The old woman scowled and clutched her groin. She murmured something that Vernaldes couldn't quite hear as she turned away to shuffle back inside the house. The Spaniard followed and tried to control his stomach as the smell of shit and piss intensified.

'Christ, woman! Don't you have a latrine?' he moaned and put a hand to his nose. The witch ignored him and sat down by the window, her face half-lit by the candles on the table. She put out a hand and gestured to the mound of buckles, jackets, swords and other souvenirs she'd collected.

Vernaldes glanced at her and bent down to sift through the pile with the point of his stick. It was mostly junk: pieces of cloth that had once been jackets, a belt buckle that shone dimly, a snuff-box with only sludge inside, and a few pictures pulled from corpses. There was nothing of value there; it crossed his mind that he'd been wrong about her.

'Well? What do you want, then? All of it?' the witch asked and grinned to reveal two rows of broken and brown teeth.

'None of it,' Vernaldes said, and straightened up.

The woman leant forward and hissed, 'None! None!' She lunged at the purse but the Spaniard raised his stick again and she shrank back. 'None of it, you say? How so?' she whimpered.

'It's all rubbish. I can sell this shit to no one, crone,' Vernaldes replied, and lowered his stick again.

'But this is good trinkets! Shiny trinkets! They make a pretty penny!' she said, and leant forward to rummage in the pile herself.

'It will make me *nothing*. I will not pay you a penny for this!' the Spaniard replied, and stepped away from her. The crone cried and waved her hands in the air as though she was trying to cast a spell on him. He seized her hands and she cried louder, struggling in his grasp. As she struggled, her gown fell open revealing her shrivelled breast, and the pyramid. It fell from her and landed on the pile.

Vernaldes saw it instantly. 'What's this?' he said, and plucked it off the pile with his gloved hands.

The woman lunged at him again and screamed. 'Leave it be! It's mine! Mine!'

The Spaniard flexed his hand and powered it away in an arc. His stick met the side of her skull, and with a loud crack it sent her reeling back against the chair, blood streaming from the wound on her head.

Ignoring her groans, the Spaniard looked closer at the pyramid and smiled. Although it was made of bronze and not gold, it looked unique and he knew he could sell it for a good price. 'Holding out on me, were you?' he said, smiling.

The crone groaned again, looking up through the blood seeping into her eye. 'It's mine!' she hissed, 'Bastard!'

Vernaldes smiled. 'No witch, it's *mine*.'

The Spaniard raised the stick and lashed down on the woman, the blow splitting open her nose. But the witch leapt up from the floor. Despite her frail appearance, she was strong. She knocked the wooden stick from the Spaniard's hand and then raked his face with her fingernails. Three scratches appeared on his cheek and blood spilled out as he stumbled away from the deranged woman. He dropped the pyramid back on the pile and the witch dived for it. As she did, Vernaldes kicked her in the side and she rolled across the floor with a hateful screech.

Vernaldes went for his stick but the witch pushed it away and attacked him again, trying to strangle him and scratch out his eyes. As they thrashed against the floor, desperately trying to kill each other, the Spaniard's hand flailed against the pile of worthless trinkets until he found one of the rusting bayonets. He took hold and thrust it into the witch's back. Crying out and stumbling away, Vernaldes grabbed her and thrust again and again, until warm blood was running out of her wounds and along his gloves where he held the dull blade.

The witch gave a gentle wheeze and the Spaniard let her fall to the ground like a puppet with its strings severed.

'Dead now?' he whispered and looked down at his handiwork for a moment. He grimaced and pushed the corpse away with the toe of his boot. Dropping the bayonet, he reached down and took the pyramid from the top of the pile, regarding it closely.

It was bronze, he was sure of it, but it wasn't the metal that took his interest, but the strange carvings upon it. Maybe it was a map of some place he had never heard of. A map of symbols and words of people long since dead. The sides of the pyramid shone and Vernaldes suddenly realized he was being hypnotised by it. Shaking his head, he retreated to the table by the window and sat down in the witch's chair.

His cheek was stinging badly and he could feel blood seeping from where the crone had attacked him. He rested the pyramid on the table and took off his gloves to put his rough fingers on his torn cheek. He winced and cursed, spitting at the dead woman. He hadn't expected her to be so strong, so violent. She had been like a rabid dog, and part of him felt infected by her filthy hands.

'Bitch,' the Spaniard murmured and rummaged in his pocket for something to dab his cheek with. As he searched, a small drop of blood fell from his chin. Below was the pyramid still shining, and the drop of blood hit the side of it. As it hit, there was tinkle of metal, almost tuneful, and the Spaniard stopped his searching to look down at the bronze trinket.

The blood was not running off the side of the pyramid, but seemed to fill the strange symbols and pin-pricks along one side, oozing into nooks and crannies with the same tinkling sound, like a small bell. Then came a low thrumming noise, like a bee was trapped inside the object and Vernaldes looked closer, noticing that the symbols were glowing dimly.

And then it was quiet again.

The Spaniard laughed weakly, and frowned. Had he imagined it?

Another drop of blood fell from his chin and again it hit the side of the pyramid. Again it began to ring like a bell, and again the symbols absorbed the blood. Again it hummed, this time louder, as the symbols glowed and the side of the pyramid began to shimmer.

Vernaldes swallowed fearfully. This was indeed something special, but deep in his guts he felt it was dangerous. He leant back and felt a third drop of blood fall from his chin. But this time, instead of letting it fall on the pyramid, his hand caught it quickly just before it could touch the bronze symbols.

Vernaldes held his breath with relief and looked down at the small crimson splatter on his palm. Never again would he let his blood touch that strange hypnotic trinket. Never again would he let that thing glow and hum like a hornet.

Never again would he—

Suddenly the humming intensified. The pyramid shimmered and then seemed to lose cohesion as though its very being was breaking into waves. It glowed fiercely, eclipsing the table.

'Oh my ...' Vernaldes murmured before the roar of a thousand voices assaulted his ears.

'*Be our vessel,*' they said, over and over, lapping against each other with differing tones of demand and threat.

Vernaldes was frozen inside that sound, just as his hand was now at the mercy of a thousand strands of light that broke from the side of the pyramid and wrapped around his fingers, his palm and up to his wrists. In an instant, his skin split asunder and blood gushed out. But the light absorbed every drop and glowing tendrils swarmed up his arm like a nest of fiery snakes, burning his sleeve to ash as they went.

Vernaldes could not find his voice as excruciating pain and

terror overwhelmed him, nor could he move as the light burned over his shoulders and across his neck. His body went into spasm and his muscles seemed to expand under the burning mass of flesh. Limbs tore and burned, hair sizzled, and Vernaldes only managed to scream once before the burning tendrils of light snaked about his mouth and dived down his throat.

△ II △

The inn at Gembloux was beginning to empty and soon only a couple of locals and the British soldiers remained. William was too busy listening to the artillerymen to notice. The drink was lying heavily in his stomach and the chatter was straying from the jokes of the common soldiery to more serious matters. As so often happened following a large battle, soldiers talked about the fallen more and more as they downed more and more ale. Wallowing in this loss was a side of war that William hated.

'He was a good man, Captain, even though he was a drunk,' Lieutenant Brier Dickinson slurred.

William nodded and murmured. 'We lost many men, Lieutenant.' He felt agitated and fiddled with the buttons on his tunic absently. The man Brier had been speaking of was yet another face William would never see, another name he would not remember. Just another to add to the long list who would never return home to England.

'Sir?' asked the junior member of the party. 'Do you think the Frenchies are saying the same thing?'

William frowned. 'What do you mean, soldier?'

'Do you think, sir, that they talk about their fallen friends as well?' the private asked.

'Who cares?' Brier grunted.

'Aye, lad,' said the elder soldier and looked at the young man scornfully. 'Stop talking nonsense.'

William ignored them. 'Of course they talk about friends that have died, just as we do.'

'But they're monsters, aren't they, sir?' the young soldier asked.

William shrugged and drained the last of his ale. 'Perhaps. But not as monstrous as their masters and officers.'

'Have you ever met a French officer, sir?' Brier asked.

'Only in battle,' William replied.

'I understand that many officers have an opposite number they regard as their nemesis, sir,' the elder soldier said, his eyes on his pipe as he emptied it onto the table.

William nodded. 'That is true.'

'Do you have one, sir? A nemesis, I mean?' the young soldier asked.

William pursed his lips. 'Not a nemesis as such,' he admitted finally. 'More of a soldier I would have gladly killed in battle.'

'Who was he sir?' Brier asked.

'His name was Captain Jacques Cuassard. Or as some called him, the "Butcher of Berlin",' William replied. 'He was a captain in Napoleon's cavalry.'

'How did he come by such a name?' Brier asked.

'By murdering almost a hundred Prussian people just outside Berlin, Lieutenant,' William said. 'And in cold blood, for no reason other than to make an example of them.'

'A bastard,' the elder soldier murmured as he filled his pipe again.

'Yes,' William replied. 'An *evil* bastard. They said he fell against the squares near Wellington. Shot to pieces by our muskets.'

'A fitting end to a scoundrel, if I may say so, sir.' Brier laughed coldly and finished his ale.

'Indeed, Lieutenant,' William replied quietly, thinking about how close he had been to suffering the same fate against the French infantry.

'Would you like more ale, sir?' the young soldier asked.

But before William could reply that he would rather not, the door to the inn burst open and the customers around the bar suddenly stopped talking. Like an infection, the silence grew until everyone was quiet. By the bar, a hysterical young man was shouting at the landlord in French.

'Maybe he doesn't like the beer,' Brier murmured, causing the elder soldier to smirk. His smile changed as he noticed the blanched expression on the young man's face and his terror as someone took hold of him.

'Something has happened,' William murmured.

'Looks that way, sir,' the elder soldier replied. 'But it's none of our business if it's something to do with the town.'

William stared at the soldier and frowned. 'We're guests here, soldier, do not forget that. We are gentlemen. If we can help, then we must.'

'Yes, sir,' the private said reluctantly and puffed on his pipe.

The hysterical man pushed himself from the collection of farmers, shouting, '*C'est hors là-bas – la bête!*' William felt the hairs rise on the back of his neck. He wasn't sure what the man was saying but realized that something was very wrong. Even Brier looked uncomfortable now. And when they heard a loud guttural howl from somewhere in the town, like a wounded beast was loose in the streets, the soldiers grew pale.

Another howl came and it echoed for a few moments and then faded again.

'What in God's name was that?' Brier whispered, rising slowly from his seat.

'A wolf?' suggested the elder soldier. William wasn't convinced.

'Whatever it is, I don't plan to meet it,' said the youngest soldier.

Brier looked to William and appeared uncertain. 'Nothing holy could have made that sound, Captain,' he said, and then motioned as the townspeople began leaving the inn. 'See? I think they're doing the right thing. We should go.'

William rose from the table and put a hand to his sword. 'As long as we're here accepting their hospitality we'll assist them Lieutenant, understood?'

Lieutenant Brier Dickinson frowned but knew William was right. He nodded slightly and looked to his friends who were just as worried. William watched a few locals raising their voices towards the landlord. 'Do any of you know what they're talking about?' he asked.

Brier and the elder soldier shrugged, but the youngest private furrowed his brow in concentration. 'I know a little Flemish, sir,' he admitted and turned to the muttering locals as they made their way out. The landlord began stashing the evening's takings into a bag and looked nervously to the door as a steady movement of people passed through it. The young soldier turned back, somewhat paler than before.

'Well lad?' William pushed.

'I'm not sure, sir, but they said, "a monster has broken loose", or something quite like it.'

'A monster?' Brier shuddered. 'That doesn't sound so good.'

'We referred to Napoleon as "a monster" and he's only a man, Lieutenant,' William replied curtly. 'It sounds as though a wild animal has broken into the town, and that's all.'

'I hope you're right, sir,' the young private said weakly.

William watched as the inn emptied and noticed that a few other British soldiers remained, a sergeant and two corporals. All three looked to William for their lead and it made him nervous. It was the first time William had faced potential combat as a captain, even if it was just a bit of local trouble.

'Sergeant, I want you to return to camp and muster a party of men. Say around a dozen. Fully kitted with muskets or rifles. I want you to meet us in the street outside,' William said.

'And do what sir?' asked the sergeant.

'We'll track down whatever made that sound. I'm sure between us we'll find it, whatever it is.'

'It sounds like the Devil, sir,' one of the corporals said fearfully.

'It will be nothing more than a dog, maybe a rabid dog. But it will be flesh and blood, Corporal. I want you to forget your superstitions, gentlemen. There is nothing to fear in the dark except making mistakes. Do I make myself plain?'

The soldiers nodded, slightly buoyed up by William's courage. William would make sure they were certain of themselves as they broke into the night, even if, deep down, he wasn't so certain himself.

Katherine's eyes were wide and full of fear as she looked to the window. Her arms had hold of Kieran so tightly that he felt the muscles around his chest grow numb. Eventually he succeeded in unlocking her arms and crawled from under the sheets, managing to perch on the edge of the bed as he heard another distant howl. His blood ran cold with each inhuman cry of torment. And there was no sense in asking Katherine what it could have been. She wouldn't understand him. Kieran looked to the nearby chair and the jacket that hung over it, his sword glinting in the candlelight.

'I must go out there,' he whispered to her.

She didn't understand the words but understood his intent as he tried to get up from the bed. He groaned slightly as he pushed himself upright. At first he was wobbly on his feet, but Katherine was there to stop him from falling. As his fingers reached for his jacket and breeches, she took his hands.

'*No*,' she said, and shook her head. She pointed outside and said something in Flemish before saying 'No' again.

'I have to, Kate, I have to,' he repeated as he tried to pull on his breeches and shirt. 'Someone might be in trouble. Someone could be hurt.'

He pulled on his belt with the sabre dangling to the side, and grabbed his jacket for the first time since he'd worn it in battle. He didn't know what was out there, but one thing was for sure: it was easier to face trouble standing up, with a sword in one's hand, than lying down naked with nothing to defend oneself with.

Katherine held his hand tightly and pleaded with him again. '*Non!*'

'I won't be gone long, my love. I'll be back soon, I promise,' he said, cupping her cheek with his hand. She stood her ground, naked to the waist, her breasts pert and erect in the cold. Her hair fell over her shoulders in dark curls and it reminded him of how warm she had felt, how moist she had been beneath her dress as he searched with his fingers for that secret place. Making love to her had been like nothing else. It felt good to be inside her and she wanted him there every time. But he was still a soldier, and he still had a duty to protect those people who could not protect themselves.

Kieran hastened and tied his belt quickly. There was another cry, and it was the sound of death. Whatever had caused it was near. Very near.

△ IV △

William finally went to the window facing the street. Beyond the warped glass were flickers of lamplight and the outlines of lit windows from across the street; here and there dashed shadows, some with flaming brands in their hands, some with oil lamps. All the signs were frantic and the sounds of panic did nothing to ease William's nerves.

'Do we stay in here?' Brier asked William, appearing at his shoulder to peer past him into the night. William didn't reply. If they stayed inside they would probably be safe, but whatever was out there would tear through the entire town. There was no militia in Gembloux, only farmers who were probably more concerned about the welfare of their herd than that of their neighbours.

There was another long and terrible roar, closer than the last. It was filled with pain like the previous one, and edged with furious anger. It finished with a more human scream and William flinched at the sound of glass shattering and wood shivering.

Across the street a light went out, followed by another, and then another. Transfixed, William watched as a fourth light winked out with a gargled screech – the sound of death. William stepped away, sick with dread.

'What do we do, sir?' one of the corporals asked. William looked to Brier, who couldn't keep eye-contact with him. He had seen that expression before, and knew that fear and uncertainty had almost taken over the lieutenant. After Waterloo, none of the officers seemed to have the appetite for another battle, and William admitted that right now a confrontation was the last thing he wanted.

He drew his sword and looked to the collection of soldiers. 'We'll marshal the town together and evacuate those we can. When the sergeant returns with the squad, we'll systematically hunt the animal down each street until we catch it.' The soldiers nodded in agreement. If it meant they didn't have to face whatever it was alone, then it got their approval.

Brier went to the window as another crash of glass erupted close by. Someone stumbled from a neighbouring building into the darkness, groping the air before falling into the street to lie still in the mud. Around them, other villagers ran blindly, not knowing how to escape. 'I hope they return sooner rather than later,' the officer murmured.

The door at the top of the stairs opened and William looked up to the sound of feet coming unsteadily down. His eyes widened as Kieran appeared, Katherine close behind. 'Kieran? You should be in bed,' he chided.

'What are you doing here?' Kieran replied. 'You should be in Brussels by now.'

'Never mind why I'm here, you're in no fit state to—'

There was a deafening roar and everyone turned as the sound grew suddenly louder from beyond the window. A great shadow fell over it and then the panes shattered. Brier stumbled back, seemingly engulfed in a torrent of darkness and shattered glass. The other officers froze, unable to do a thing except watch as the torrent unwrapped itself, producing a pair of smoking black arms the size of tree-trunks that folded around Lieutenant Dickinson's head. The lieutenant looked up into the face that appeared from the darkness, and blanched.

There was another roar from the creature and everyone in the room felt it rumble through the floor. They would have grimaced at the sulphuric smell on the air but all were transfixed in terror as the creature wrestled quickly with Brier. With a wet ripping sound, a gigantic black hand appeared around the top of the lieutenant's head and twisted it clean off his neck. Blood spurted into the air, spraying the ceiling and one of the unfortunate corporals who had frozen nearby.

With a thud, the lieutenant's decapitated body fell to the floor and the creature stepped over it, arms drooping, knuckles rubbing against the boards like a gorilla. It stretched its back, letting out a piercing call as it turned its attention to the inn's other occupants.

William raised his sword and stepped back to the door, his instincts telling him to run out as fast as he could. The creature was now fully upright, its crown scraping the ceiling. It was entirely blackened – seemingly burnt to charcoal – its skin still smoking. Thick ebony ribs enveloped every part of its body like it was wearing its bones on the outside, and each limb was swollen and stretched, a twisted knot of bone and flesh. Its mouth opened and row upon row of teeth glistened, saliva and blood dripping down in strings.

During those moments of shock, one of the corporals closest to the creature raised his sword despite the immense terror in his eyes. His breeches were wet at the groin where he'd pissed himself during Lieutenant Dickinson's demise, yet still his basic training had taken over. The creature twisted sharply and its ape-like arms latched onto the officer's chest. Blood sprang from the man's mouth, and the claws retracted pulling the front of his chest away. The officer stood for a moment until his lungs, liver and intestines spilled out onto the floor, and then he too fell down on his face.

It was all too much for the other soldiers. William watched them dive under tables, hiding like frightened children as the monster stepped forward, its bloodied claws dragging against the floor. It turned its flat, blackened head towards William, and with eyes of fire it stared at him, its jaw unhooking once more to reveal a nest of jagged teeth.

William gritted his own teeth but raised his sword, expecting his turn to be next, but the creature moved its attention to the man behind the bar – Katherine's father – who was busy loading an antique pistol that barely looked as though it would fire.

The creature arched its back and cleared the room in one bound. With a trailing hand, it lashed out and caught William in the jaw. He fell to the floor, sliding towards the fire, while his sword skittered across the stone tiles.

The creature landed on the counter and the wooden top splintered under the pressure. As the bar groaned and broke, the creature rose up and held its claws above its head, its burning eyes staring down at the quivering barman.

'*Père!*' Katherine yelled and dived past Kieran, almost knocking him down in her haste.

Katherine's father dropped the pistol and his legs buckled in terror as the creature swooped down, its claws thrusting into the man's belly and back. Kieran tried to stop Katherine as she screamed and sobbed to be let go. All the while, her father was screaming himself, and gurgling blood over his lips as the beast quickly dismembered him. His arms thrashed about, catching bottles of spirits and wine, tugging them off the shelves to shatter on the floor around him, before his eyes dimmed and his thrashings ceased.

'*Père! Père!*' Katherine cried out and finally wriggled free of Kieran's hold. He lost his footing and his sword came free, clattering down the stairs after his lover.

William pushed himself up from the floor, still dazed and sore where he'd been struck. He put a hand to his jaw, and got to his feet. The creature had slid from the broken counter and was now standing on the floor again. It was at least two feet taller than any man, and although it had two arms, two legs and a head, it bore no humanity at all. The smoking pits that were its eyes swung hungrily about the room, looking for another victim, and its long scissor-like talons clicked and flexed, the flesh and blood of Katherine's father still dripping from them.

Clambering over to the fireplace to retrieve his sword, William glanced down at the fire itself. He looked back at the bar and the shattered bottles on the shelves, realizing there was only one thing he could do.

Kieran had found his legs again and reached for Katherine,

but her sobs had died and in their place was a terrible anger. She looked down at her feet and found Kieran's sword.

'Katherine, no!' he cried out, but it wasn't enough.

Katherine screamed and swung at the creature, hitting its side with the scabbard. The creature, not even fazed, exhaled a cloud of sulphuric smoke and lashed out with a claw. It took Katherine in the breast and ripped her open from heart to navel.

'No!' Kieran cried hopelessly as Katherine stumbled back, dropping his sword as blood flooded down the front of her dress. He limped over to her and caught her before she fell.

'No!' he sobbed and pulled away from creature as William appeared with a flaming log in his hands.

'Go back to Hell, or wherever you came from!' William hissed, his face black with soot and wet with sweat.

The monster regarded William cautiously and opened its mouth wide. It barked loudly, like some deranged dog, and snarled as it raised its claws.

William could hear the sounds of the dying around him, the sounds of sadness, of loss, and it was all he could do to control his anger.

'I warned you,' he hissed and tossed the flaming log towards the creature. But he was not aiming for the monster itself, but the bar and the shattered bottles behind it. The log hit the floor and the bar went up with a 'whump'sound, sending a fireball towards the ceiling.

The monster screeched and stepped back as the flames approached it. Without pausing, it turned and charged straight out of the door, taking part of the wall with it.

William stood and watched breathlessly as the beast disappeared into the night, realizing he'd come close to being murdered by that thing.

Kieran's sobbing soon brought his attention back to the devastated inn. William ordered everyone out as the room caught fire. There was nothing in the room that wasn't flammable and it burned rapidly, running across the ceiling and the walls in waves.

'Out!' he cried. 'Get out! All of you!' He pulled a shocked corporal from behind a table and threw him through the hole in the wall where the door had been. The soldier grabbed Lieutenant Brier's sword, pausing a moment to stare at his commanding officer's headless body, before leaving with the younger private, who was almost sobbing. With the two soldiers running out quickly, William went to Kieran who was still at the stairs with Katherine lying in his lap.

'Kieran!' he shouted.

Kieran looked up with tears running down his cheeks. 'I don't think ...' he cried, 'I think she's ...'

'Kieran, we have to go!' William pleaded and picked up Katherine's body as he supported his friend who got gingerly to his feet. They left the inn just as the ceiling collapsed and another fireball tore away the stairs.

The soldiers stood outside in complete bewilderment, and it wasn't until he lowered Kieran to the floor with Katherine still in his arms that William realized how cold it was. It was also beginning to rain, which was a blessing, for it would stop the fire from spreading to the rest of the town.

Wiping the sweat from his smoke-stained cheeks, he glanced about to take account of who was left alive. There were no locals, save for those running blindly about them, and the soldiers in front of him were in bad shape.

'What do we do, sir?' the young artilleryman asked.

William shook his head. He didn't know. What could they do?

One of the walls of the inn collapsed and flames clattered through the upstairs window where Kieran had spent his days after Waterloo. They had made love in that room, such sweet love that it numbed him to think they would never do so again.

Kieran looked down at the white face of his lover, her skin cold, her lips blue, and her dead eyes staring up to the night sky. She was gone. Gone forever. Gone in a moment, and there was no way to bring her back.

'Sir?' said the young soldier again. 'What now? What do we do?'

William ignored him and bent down to Kieran.

'She's dead, Will,' the Irishman said quietly, as though Katherine might be listening.

'I'm sorry, Kieran,' William murmured. 'I'm so sorry.' He put a comforting hand on his shoulder, but knew there could be no comfort. There was no comfort for any of them that night.

△ V △

The sergeant eventually returned with eight men armed with muskets, just as the inn collapsed in on itself. The officer stood with his mouth hanging open as flames tore the building apart.

'Good Lord, sir,' he murmured at William's side, 'what happened?'

William put his sword back in its scabbard and grimaced. 'Plenty of people have been killed tonight, Sergeant. Too many,' he growled. 'I will not let another person die.'

The sergeant glanced at the three surviving soldiers who were soaked through with rain but had at least recovered some composure.

'I need you to take three men and search the eastern quarter of the town, Sergeant,' William began. 'The other five will search the western quarter.'

The soldiers glanced nervously at each other. Clearly none of them knew who or what they were up against.

'I will take these three men,' William said, and gestured to the three survivors, 'and will search the north quarter.'

The survivors nodded reluctantly.

'What are we looking for, sir?' asked the sergeant.

'The Devil,' William replied.

The sergeant laughed and looked to the corporal for a reason for the joke, but the officer was still as pale as the moon and shaking all over.

'Are you serious, sir?' The sergeant frowned.

William nodded.

'Huh ...' the sergeant stammered. 'How will we *recognize* him, sir?'

'If you find him, you will know it,' William replied. 'Do not engage him. Understood?'

The sergeant nodded.

'Fire a warning shot. Then we will come and assist,' William said.

'I'm sure we could take on one man, sir,' the sergeant suggested.

'This "one man" just killed four people in a matter of moments, Sergeant,' William warned him. 'Do not make the mistake of thinking that whatever we face will be human. This is the Devil himself, understand?'

'Sir. The Devil himself. I understand,' the sergeant said humbly.

'Very well, then go,' William ordered, and the soldiers split into their groups as they disappeared into the rain and darkness.

The three remaining soldiers stood by quietly. Only one of them still had a weapon.

'What are your names, soldiers?' William asked.

'Cartwright,' answered the elder soldier.

'Richards,' said the youngest.

'Allan, sir,' said the corporal, but so quietly that William could hardly hear him.

'Alright. Cartwright, stay here. You two, find a weapon. An axe, sword, hammer, anything you can lay your hands on, and get back here in a few minutes,' William said.

The two soldiers trudged away to find something to defend themselves with and William turned to Kieran who had laid Katherine's body in the porch of a nearby house.

'You need to get some shelter,' William murmured and put his hand on Kieran's sword. 'And we'll need this, I'm afraid.'

Kieran's hand held William's. 'I'm coming with you.'

'Not tonight, Kieran,' William said, but Kieran's hand held his fast.

'This is not your choice, Will,' Kieran replied coldly.

'You are under my protection. I can't let you ...' William started.

'It murdered Katherine, Will,' the Irishman seethed. 'Do you think, for one moment, that I will let you hunt this bastard down without me? Do you honestly think I can rest knowing her killer is out there?'

William stared at his friend. His face was awash with rain and tears, and blood had soaked into his shirt.

'You are still wounded,' William tried to explain, but it was no good.

'I can fight,' Kieran replied, and pulled William's hand from the hilt of his sword. 'I'll need this, thank you.'

William bit his bottom lip and moved his hand away. 'Very well,' he said reluctantly. 'We'll find this monster *together* then, even if it damns us all.'

CHAPTER THREE

Hunting the Darkness

△ I △

As news of the horrors spread, the town of Gembloux panicked and its people quickly fled the chaos for the relative safety of the nearby fields. Some dashed past William and the others, saying nothing, keeping their heads down lest they get dragged into whatever fight lay ahead. Others spoke of seeing a bear run amok through street after street, terrifying all who had seen it. On one occasion the two men met a traumatised farmer who spoke of a massacre along a row of nearby cottages. William had no choice but to investigate.

They discovered the first signs of the slaughter 200 yards up the street to the north of the inferno that was the inn. William did his best to hold onto the contents of his stomach as he turned from the remains of a family that was scattered across the front room of one cottage and its doorstep.

'Oh dear Jesus,' Cartwright murmured and made the sign of the cross.

Kieran stood by dispassionately while the surviving corporal vomited over the floor.

'Move on,' William ordered, and the small band of soldiers moved away through the rain, which was now coming down hard.

'How long ago do you think they were attacked?' Kieran said, his voice betraying a fragile sense of calm.

William glanced back at him. 'I don't know.'

'Before or after the attack on the inn?' Kieran said.

'Like I said, I don't know,' William insisted, a little agitated. He wasn't sure what to do. Whatever attacked them at the inn was stronger than any man. It had killed two soldiers effortlessly. With the driving rain and black of night, William wasn't sure they could find the monster at all, let alone bring it down.

As they trudged further away from the centre of town, they discovered more carnage. Corporal Allan found a farmer and his wife, their bodies pulled apart and lying in a burgeoning puddle of blood, while Kieran found a young boy without a head. William looked down and recognised the tunic and trousers of the boy who had stabled his horse. His lip trembled and he closed his mouth tight as fury and sadness threatened to take over.

'It's a trail,' Kieran murmured.

'Yes,' William replied, looking away. 'But where is it leading?'

'Sir!' cried Richards.

William turned and found the artilleryman standing by a row of poorly constructed cottages. He waved from the door of one cottage, a shack that was leaning slightly. As William walked over, he noticed the doorway was completely torn open. The soldier pointed to the door with one hand, while the other was held over his nose and mouth. William grimaced expecting more slaughter. He paused by Richards, who was squinting from the smell, and then stepped inside.

The odour of faeces hit him instantly, but it was not as strong as the overwhelming stench of sulphur that hung in the cloudy air. The room was hazy with smoke, and in the dim light he could see that most of it was blackened with soot as though a small fire had broken out there.

William walked across the room and found a table that was half burnt. Sitting by it was a chair that had been reduced to charcoal, still smoking as little embers glowed from the back and legs. William stepped around it, waving his hand in front of him to part the smoke. As the smoke cleared for a moment, he saw a pile of uniforms, both French and British, on a collection of weapons and regalia. Lying beside it was the body of a woman.

William walked over and knelt down.

'Is she dead?' a voice said by William's shoulder. He turned to find Richards just behind him.

'Yes,' William replied, and screwed up his face as the smell of faeces worsened. It was definitely coming from the old woman, yet apart from the bloodstains around her on the floor, there weren't any other marks.

'Did the monster do this, sir?' the young soldier asked.

William stared at the woman for a moment. 'I don't know, Private. I don't know.' As William straightened up he noticed the rusty bayonet nearby, fresh blood still glistening on its blade. Something felt wrong. This murder didn't appear to have been committed by the creature from the inn.

William shook his head, bewildered by what he had discovered.

'Must have been a fire here, sir,' Richards remarked.

'It looks that way,' William replied as he poked around the pile of uniforms.

Richards touched the table with his boot and the burnt legs shattered, causing the table to crash to the floor in an eruption of ash.

It gave William a fright.

'Good God, Private!' he scolded.

The young soldier bowed apologetically. 'I'll just wait outside, sir,' he said meekly and marched back to the door.

William blew out long and hard. He looked up at the ceiling again and noticed how the burn marks appeared only in a tight circle.

'Sir? I think the lieutenant wants you,' Richards called.

William nodded and began to walk over.

But just as he turned, he saw something glinting from the pile of ash by the wall. He paused, narrowed his eyes and walked over to it. With his boot, he parted the ash and found a metal object half buried by the destruction.

'Sir?' Richards said.

'Just a moment, Private,' William replied as he bent down. He brushed the rest of the ash away, revealing a pyramid that seemed to be made from bronze.

William smiled curiously and went to touch it. But as his fingers closed around it, he felt a strange humming like a vibration in the air. His hand recoiled and he felt suddenly fearful. What it was, William had no idea, but there was something unnatural about it.

William stood up and rubbed his hands nervously.

'Sir? The lieutenant?' the young soldier said again.

'I said *one minute*, Private,' William chided. He looked about the room, flapping a hand to clear the smoke. Coughing again, he walked over to the pile of uniforms and plucked a grenadier's jacket from the stack. He then returned to the pyramid and laid the jacket over it.

The young soldier hopped from one leg to the other. 'Sir, I think that was a musket-shot,' he said nervously.

William stood up again with the jacket wrapped around the pyramid. He went quickly over to the artilleryman and put the bundle in his arms.

'Sir?' Richards questioned.

'I want you to take this back to the encampment outside of town,' William ordered.

Richards frowned. 'I thought we were going after the monster ...'

'*We* are. You're not. This needs to be kept safe until I return,' William said.

The soldier nodded, somewhat relieved that he didn't have to face the creature again.

'Don't show this to anyone,' William warned. 'And don't become curious and look inside this jacket yourself. Understood?'

'Yes, sir,' Richards replied.

'Then go, and quickly,' William said as he heard a second musket-shot echo in the night.

'Where did you send Private Richards?' Kieran asked, as they sneaked down a blind alley towards the eastern side of the town.

'Back to his camp,' William whispered out of earshot of the corporal and Private Cartwright.

'Why? I thought you said we needed every man available,' Kieran hissed back.

'We do. But I sent him back with something I found in that house,' William replied.

Kieran opened his mouth to ask more, but William put a finger to his lips. 'I'll talk more about it later,' he whispered, as screams and shouts came from the next street.

As the sound of fighting grew louder, Kieran began to walk quicker. In his anger he had shaken off the pain in his side, and he was matching William stride for stride. He pulled his sword from its black leather scabbard and overtook William in his eagerness.

William reached out and pulled him back.

'Slow down, Kieran!' he said.

Kieran shrugged off his hand. 'It's mine, Will. Whatever happens, I'm going to kill it,' he growled.

'I understand how badly you want this, but I'm responsible for everyone here. Don't do anything foolish. Just stay close by,' William pleaded.

Kieran slowed down and breathed out heavily. He clutched his side and grimaced as William caught up.

'Your wound ...' he began.

'... Is healed,' Kieran finished. 'I'm fine.'

William wanted to send his friend back to the artillery encampment too, but a third musket-shot echoed, followed by a dreadful scream that could only be the death-cry of one of the soldiers he'd sent east.

'Oh Christ!' he cursed, and led them down another alley to a deserted street. The street was a dead end and at the bottom was a courtyard by an old mill.

'Can you see anything?' William whispered against the sound of rain.

Kieran took a step forward. He shook his head. There was little light here save for a couple of lamps in nearby windows and the distant glow of the burning inn eclipsed by the silhouette of the mill.

William unsheathed his sword and cleared his throat.

'Sergeant?' he said, barely able to raise his voice for fear of alerting the monster.

Seeing several mounds lying in the mud of the courtyard, Kieran took another step forward.

'Sergeant?' William called again, this time louder.

Kieran squinted through the water dripping from his brow. He could just make out the jackets of the soldiers who lay before him.

'Damn,' he murmured and raised his sword.

William signalled the corporal and Cartwright to follow as he crept closer into the courtyard. William noticed the three bodies.

'Are they the men you sent?' Kieran asked.

William nodded.

'They look dead,' the corporal moaned.

'The monster has been here,' Kieran said, not taking his eyes from the shadows around them.

'Maybe it's still here, sir,' Cartwright suggested.

'If it is, then it's made a mistake,' Kieran said coldly. 'There's nowhere to run.'

William glanced at his friend, who was smiling viciously. The Irishman looked back at William and said, 'It's trapped.'

'Agreed,' William replied. His mouth was dry and he licked at the rain that ran down his face. 'Stay here,' he croaked, and stepped carefully forward towards the bodies. With each step, his eyes went from left to right, searching for a sign of their assailant. They found nothing but thick shadows lying in corners, by barrels and under the balcony of the mill.

Only the bodies betrayed the creature's presence.

William stopped to wipe the rain from his hair and face. He

looked down at the torn heaps of flesh that had once been the King's soldiers. He didn't know their names, nor did he recognize their faces, now pale beneath the blood and dirt smeared over them.

'I told them not to engage it, damn it!' he muttered to himself. He was angry. Angry that the soldiers had disobeyed his orders, and angry that he'd sent men out to die for nothing.

'How many bodies?' Kieran called.

William shouted back, 'Three!'

'Weren't there four soldiers?' Kieran said.

His friend was right. What happened to the fourth soldier?

William looked hard again and noticed some movement by a barrel near the mill. He crossed over and found the sergeant propped up against the barrel with his arm missing and bleeding heavily.

'It jumped us, sir ... there was nothing I could do ... before we knew it ... Knowles was dead ... and then it caught Feeney,' gasped the officer, slurring as though drunk.

'Can you walk?' William asked, but realized the man was bleeding to death.

The sergeant grabbed William's shoulder with his remaining hand. 'It's. Still. *Here*,' he said slowly, each word obviously more painful than the next.

William realized his error and caught his breath.

'Where?' he whispered desperately, but the sergeant sighed and blood seeped from his mouth as he slipped back against the barrel. William looked down and found a ragged rip across the bottom of his shirt. In his lap was a pool of blood, and William knew the sergeant was dead.

'Oh Lord,' he said quietly. Still crouched by the barrel, William looked frantically around, his eyes darting to where Kieran and the two soldiers were standing in the centre of the courtyard. There was no sign of the monster, but the late sergeant had seemed certain it was still there. And it made sense. It was a trap, a dead end. This wasn't the creature's error as they had thought. It was theirs.

Pushing away the body, William gripped his sword and breathed in, as he stood up from the barrel.

'Kieran!' he yelled. 'Get out of here! The monster's waiting for us in the darkness!'

At once there was a roar, and from the shadows under the balcony, several barrels crashed to the floor, one spilling its grain into the mud. Behind it lumbered the beast, its ebony hide glistening like leather as it charged at William. William scampered away when the first of the claws swooped towards him, scooping up a barrel to send it spinning across the courtyard with a violent crash.

William almost slipped in the mud, but he continued running towards a wagon parked near a hatch to the left of the balcony. The creature was at his heels, and as it came closer to him, William gritted his teeth and let his left leg buckle. He pushed the right leg straight out in front of him and slid under another swooping claw. Through puddles and mud, he continued to slide, until he was under the wagon itself.

Drenched through, he rolled over, mud filling his mouth. He crawled to the other side of the wagon as the creature bore down on him emitting howls that vibrated the air.

Kieran shouted for his friend, but could see nothing now except the blur of the creature's outline in the rain.

'We'll have to surround it,' Cartwright suggested. 'Try and attack it from all sides at once. It's too strong for one of us, but together we could bring this brute down, sir.'

Kieran turned to them and nodded in agreement. 'Alright. I'll climb up there and try and leap on it,' he shouted, pointing towards the balcony above the creature as it lunged again at William, tearing off one of the wagon's wheels.

'Sir, that's a long leap!' the corporal said shakily.

'I'll use that bastard to break my fall! Just get round the other sides, and grab a musket if you can!'

The two soldiers glanced at each other with dread. 'Good luck,' Cartwright said to the corporal, who looked ready to wet himself.

△ III △

The monster's claws crashed into the bed of the wagon, tearing the wooden boards and showering William with splinters. As one talon lunged down, William struck it hard with his sword. The blow clattered like metal on metal, and the impact rang up his arm. Gasping, he fell back in the mud, just as the other paw crashed through the driver's seat above him. He rolled out of the path of the claws until his back was against the right front wheel.

Every inch of the beast seemed armoured. But every suit of armour had a chink in it, however small. William prayed that it didn't take them long to find it.

Meanwhile, Kieran was pulling himself up the side of the balcony. He climbed on top of the barrels to get a little leverage; the rest of the way was a tricky climb at best, especially with a wound and in wet conditions. If he slipped, at the very least he would be injured and unable to fight. And that would leave William at the mercy of the creature, hidden only be the dwindling remains of the wagon that was being pulled apart piece by piece.

The rain was now lashing down and the air around them was thick with water, making the courtyard boggy and visibility poor. Cartwright had managed to cross the courtyard quickly, stealing the musket from a dead soldier as he did so.

To the other side was Corporal Allan, who was frozen behind a stack of crates. A dozen yards in front of him was a musket, half submerged under the corpse of a soldier; but it was out in the open, and he couldn't bring himself to go and get it. Nor could he see any of his comrades. The rain had hidden the old soldier, and the lieutenant was somewhere over the balcony and out of sight. All he could see was a dim outline of the monster and the sound of howling and crashing wood.

'Must be brave. I must be brave,' he said to himself, holding his breath and using all his strength to push himself out from the crates and across the courtyard towards the fresh corpse. He pushed it aside and began digging for the musket that lay submerged in a bloody pool.

'Must be brave!' he said to himself again as he pulled the musket up. He then searched the body for shot, but couldn't find any.

'No, no, no …' Corporal Allan panicked as he searched desperately for ammunition.

Kieran could see the corporal struggling, and he could see that William had managed to dash behind a row of barrels and sacks of grain just as the monster turned over the remnants of the wagon with its huge arms. It howled and roared with anger as it found William had gone, and Kieran saw its eyes burning feverishly, funnels of smoke coming from each socket.

With William gone, the monster turned its attention to the others, but Cartwright was now in the shadows and Kieran was out of view. Only the corporal was in sight.

'Oh God,' Kieran murmured, realizing the man's error. But it was too late.

The monster growled and stampeded across the courtyard to where the hapless corporal knelt, still desperately searching for powder and shot.

'Run, you fool!' Kieran urged, but the soldier was rigid with fear as he saw the beast emerge from the rain, water showering over its glistening body. The creature hung open its long jaws and dived on him, taking in his head up to the neck. It bit down and Kieran closed his eyes, hearing only the faint struggle in the courtyard and the heavy splashing of rain around him.

△ IV △

Cartwright loaded the musket. He had seen the creature charge into the courtyard, and although he hadn't seen the corporal die, he knew there were only three of them left to face the monster. Raising the musket, he prayed to the Lord that the powder was dry and his aim true.

William was taking a breather, bent almost double as he heaved in and out. He was partly sheltered by the barrels, but he was soaked through and mud clung to his clothes in thick clods. He wiped his sword on his jacket and noticed the groove in the blade where he'd struck the creature.

Every suit of armour has a chink, he reminded himself, and peeked around the barrels to find that the monster was marching back to where the wagon had been. As it came closer, William noticed pieces of the corporal's head slipping out of the monster's mouth. But he was too scared now to feel revulsion, and all he could think of was how to bring the beast down.

Above them, Kieran peered over the balcony and moved quietly across the floorboards. He pulled out his sword and felt its weight in his hands. He wanted so much to push it through the creature's face – for Katherine, and all of the poor bastards murdered that night.

Below him, the monster had calmed and was calculating William's whereabouts. It tramped forward, puddles of mud erupting with each step, and then it moved into the shadows under the balcony.

Kieran's breathing grew quiet and he took another tentative step forward, and then another, but froze as the second step made the floorboard creak loudly.

Beneath him, from the darkness, two flaming eyes glowed fiercely upwards. Kieran stepped back just as a giant paw exploded through the balcony a few feet away. The floorboards erupted into the air, showering Kieran with fragments of sodden wood. He raised his hand to shield his eyes, and the other paw reached forward, pulling the rest of the balcony down. The boards split in the middle and collapsed, tugging Kieran off balance. With his free hand, he caught the edge of the structure and swung himself around so he dangled over the courtyard, while the boards he'd been standing on crashed to the dark mud below.

William shouted and stepped from behind the barrels and saw his friend swinging helplessly from the remnants of the balcony with his free hand, with the other tightly wrapped around his sword.

The creature began groping around the supports, knocking

one aside so that Kieran swung out further. Its other hand moved around to the side and leant forward, trying to grab Kieran as he dangled.

William felt helpless and looked for Cartwright, but the downpour obscured his view. Groaning with frustration, William charged out at the monster. As he stumbled past the body of the sergeant he noticed the officer's broken sword lying nearby. Gritting his teeth, he plucked it from the mud, thrust his own sword into the ground for safekeeping, and used both hands – and all his might – to hurl the smashed blade at the creature. The broken sword left William's hand suddenly, and he panicked, thinking his aim was off.

The blade glinted once and was gone.

The creature bellowed loudly and fell quiet. William thought he might have just clipped the creature, but at least he had its attention. He pulled his sword from the mud and stood back, ready for their confrontation. What he didn't expect to see were the two glowing eyes, more feverish than ever, charging at full speed towards him with the sound of thunder.

As the beast came out of the shadows like a black tidal wave, William saw the hilt of the sword stuck in its abdomen. He felt a moment of elation before the monster swung its claws towards him. William reacted quickly and swung the sabre against them. The impact almost shattered the sword and powered William off his feet. He flew a few yards away and rolled in a puddle, blinded by the mud.

Crawling to his knees, William looked up to see the beast descend on him. In the confusion he thought it might be the end, but there was a loud bang and the creature yelled once more. It held its arm and howled into the air, staggering back in pain and anger. As William dragged himself upright he saw Cartwright advancing, his smoking musket held before him. With the bayonet fixed, he stood over William and shielded him from another attack.

'Sir! Get up, sir!' the old soldier pleaded. 'Before it attacks again!'

William pushed himself up, sliding in the mud. His weapon

was gone, and he was shaking all over. He didn't think he had the strength to defend himself again, but Cartwright handed him Lieutenant Brier's sword, still in its leather scabbard.

'Take it, sir!' Cartwright shouted. 'The lieutenant would have wanted you to have it.'

William tried to reply, but the monster had recovered from the attack and lunged at Cartwright. With a Herculean effort, the old soldier thrust forward, but the bayonet snapped in two against the bone plating of the monster's chest. Its arms enveloped the soldier's torso and, with a gargled cry, tore him open.

William could only stagger away, half blinded, and hopeless.

△ V △

Still hanging from the balcony, Kieran swung and clung onto a support. The wound in his side was throbbing but he managed to shimmy down the post. Letting the sword drop in the mud, he landed gingerly by its side. His heroics hadn't gone the way he'd planned, and now another soldier was dead. William was leaning against one of the barrels as the monster stood before him, ready to attack again. It howled and clicked as the ridge of backbone rippled under its black hide. Its entire skeleton seemed to flex and it bowed, letting the rain pour over its skin.

Kieran was struck by the enormity of the beast. This was beyond Katherine's murder; it was an abomination that could murder the world itself if it escaped. The Irishman could not let that happen, at any cost. Lifting his sabre, Kieran clenched his teeth and stepped forward as William rubbed his stinging eyes.

He could see the creature was pulling at the hilt of the sword in its guts, and in spite of its size, it was making a meal of it, the giant claws unable to find purchase on the handle.

'Feel it!' William shouted. 'Feel the pain, you bastard!'

Squinting still, he readied Lieutenant Brier's sword, the blade feeling heavy in his hands. Every limb felt either on fire or like

63

lead and it was all he could do to stop himself from sinking into the mud to his knees.

With a howl the beast finally pulled free the shattered sword and black fluid jetted from the wound. At first it looked like coffee, but then it shimmered with a gentle blue glow and began to solidify. William wasn't sure whether it was the pain in his head, the mud in his eyes or the dark of night that made him believe, for a moment, that the blood was returning to the wound.

He staggered back and felt his feet slip in the mud. The puddles were deep enough to cover his boots, and the mud squelched underfoot and displaced each step he took. If the creature attacked again, he could parry, but with no purchase he would be on his back among the carnage around him.

William shook away the dirt and water from his face and pulled back his fringe. His eyes were still sore, but he could see the creature limbering up for the final attack, its arms flexed wide to embrace William, its claws clicking in expectation. As its flaming eyes regarded him with malevolent intent, its mouth opened, revealing once more the shards of razor teeth that glistened with blood and strings of grey saliva. The smell of sulphur was almost overpowering and William felt drowsy, wobbling on his feet. He raised his sword weakly, mustering as much strength as he could as he faced the final attack.

But he hadn't counted on Kieran.

The last time William had seen him he was still swinging from the balcony. Suddenly the Irishman came rushing forward, screaming, taking a perfectly-aimed swing at the beast's right arm. The sabre came down between two sections of bone armour, and sliced through the limb just above the elbow, with the sound of metal breaking through wood. The limb fell nearby, twitching weakly in the mud under a jet of black blood. Kieran fell to his knees but managed to pull himself and the sabre out of the mud as the creature found its hacked arm and began roaring terribly. The beast's flaming eyes erupted further, spitting out embers and ash, and its mouth opened wide as it voiced its pain to the clouds high above.

William found his balance and raised his blade, only to find the sense of achievement blighted as the severed arm began writhing furiously. With a crackle of blue light, black tendons of blood writhed out from the limb, reaching out to the stump of the arm as it began to re-knit itself to the stump. Where the tendons suckled they merged with the old flesh, fusing with lightning and steam as the rain splashed down.

To William's horror, the arm was almost attached back to the limb it had been hacked from.

It seemed the creature was invincible.

Groaning with disbelief, and with the realisation that their enemy could not be beaten, William pulled all his strength and courage from his guts, and launched himself defiantly forward for one last strike. One last strike, before he could do no more, before the creature calmly tore him limb from limb.

Still occupied by its wounded limb, the creature looked up complacently at William as he launched himself at it. It dodged the first blow, but William turned again, the momentum of the first swing pulling him around for another. This time he tipped forward and lurched towards the beast. The trailing blade went by in a tighter arc, and sank into the creature's side, snapping in two from the impact.

William rolled slightly and lost his grip on the broken sword, the tip now lost somewhere in the mass of black bone and flesh. From the wound, the familiar tendons of black tar writhed out. More light seemed to seep from within, like a fire trapped within a grate.

William put his hands to his eyes and crawled away from the creature, as it shrieked and waved its paws in the air. Its wounded arm, not yet healed, crackled again with blue light, and here and there the black tendrils writhed. With its one undamaged arm, the creature tried desperately to dig the tip of the sword from its flesh.

Grappling and digging, the beast had forgotten about Kieran. The Irishman clutched his old wound, but was back on his feet with his sword, and now he lurched towards the creature, swinging the sabre into its back. It found a gap in the bones, and Kieran pushed further, driving the blade down. The creature groaned and appeared to buckle. William saw a flash of blue from behind it and then saw Kieran pull out his sword again. He thrust down a second time, and the flash of blue became a torrent, geysering from the back of the creature like a Roman candle. Kieran stumbled back and wiped the rain from his eyes as the creature squirmed and fell to its knees, emitting deep cries that would have been pitiful if the monster hadn't slaughtered so many that night.

Kieran, undeterred by the pyrotechnics, swung the sabre and lopped off the creature's head. In the briefest of moments the flaming eyes were spinning away into the darkness, followed by a trail of smoke, to land somewhere in the rain. This was followed by a silent explosion of light that twisted and arched into the night sky, away from the decapitated monster. From its neck spewed light and ash, a rain that blinded both men as they sank to the ground under the onslaught, covering their eyes. The creature's hide split and burned furiously, a ravenous ball of blue flamed licking the body clean until there was nothing but red raw skin steaming underneath.

Finally the light seemed to depart, carried away into the night and the downpour. The heavy sound of rain drummed in William's ears as he lowered his hand and saw a smaller figure solidifying on the ground. He crawled on his knees and stopped short of the naked corpse – still raw, but awash with blood from the many wounds on its body. Here and there it was matted with hair; a steady stream of smoke came from its groin, where pubic hair burned. The rest of the body was as human as the bodies lying about him, and William shook violently. He leant back and choked. He could see it properly now, the clouds of vapour having blown themselves away, and he could see the corpse for what it was. It had been a man, once – a man who had now lost his head. His right arm had split down the middle and there were wounds to his side and abdomen. He was scarcely a third of the size of the beast they had been fighting.

William held himself against the cold, the idea that none of this was real stammering over his pale lips. He went to gather some kind of response from Kieran, but the Irishman had passed out.

William was alone. Alone in the pissing June rain in the dark of night. Alone and surrounded by the corpses of fellow officers. Alone with his unconscious friend who had lost his lover that very night. And alone with a naked, decapitated man who had single-handedly tried to murder the town of Gembloux. All William could do now was wait for help.

CHAPTER FOUR

Homeward

△ I △

The passing of time had been awkward since Gembloux. There had been few good times since that night, and those often went by too quickly, while the bad times (of which there were many) lingered too long.

William spent most of the month away from Kieran, in contemplation, or writing reports. The privilege of rank had buried him in paperwork – and he was thankful. After all, what else could he be doing? Brooding over a terrible event that would not leave him?

William's report of that night was sketchy at best, but then most of the witnesses were dead. It detailed only the murders of over a dozen townspeople and soldiers by a maniac who had run amok in Gembloux. William's description of the man was vague, but that could only be for the best. Of those who had truly seen the murderer, only he, Kieran and Private Richards had survived. Richards had agreed to say nothing about the affair, and handed William the grenadier's jacket without a word, not even enquiring about what lay wrapped up inside.

'It's none of my business, sir,' the young soldier had said. 'All I want to do is forget about what happened.'

William, too, wanted to forget, but could not. And nor could Kieran. He was a mere shadow of the man that had loved Katherine. He was gaunt, ate little, and often stared in silence.

But that suited William, for he too had little to say. When Kieran did speak, it was of that night, and William was reluctant to say anything on the subject.

Finally, when Kieran asked about the report he had made on the killings, William told him in confidence that he'd lied about it all. Never once had he mentioned the monster. Never once had he mentioned either the shack or the pyramid he had found there.

Kieran said nothing to him after that, for a long time. After a week or so, William ceased to visit him in the company barracks. They had nothing to say to each other, and William began facing the truth that what had happened had killed the conversation between them. It seemed that only a miracle could reawaken their friendship.

William had procured a wooden box during a ride into Brussels with the Dragoons. It was a sturdy box with a lock, and he had put the pyramid inside it, locking it immediately. The key – large, thick and made of iron – stayed with him at all times. He never let it out of his sight.

He'd had the opportunity to get rid of the thing inside, but he was strangely reluctant to do so. He could not rationalize his connection with the pyramid, that object of which he felt so afraid; he could not understand why he didn't get shot of it once and for all. It had exerted a hold on him ever since he'd spied it in the pile of ash in that dank shack at Gembloux.

That had been three weeks ago, and not once had he felt the urge to open the box again.

When the time came to leave mainland Europe and return home across the Channel, William had given up trying to understand why he had kept the pyramid at all. He decided that he would get rid of it when he returned home to Lowchester and the rest of the Saxon family, and that would be the end of it.

As for Kieran ...

Who knew what would happen to Kieran? William certainly didn't. They had grown up together, joined the Army together, and now he was only a stranger. But William couldn't let him go without trying to talk to him. He owed their friendship that at least, and decided he would approach him on the crossing home.

△ II △

After writing a letter to his mother and father, William stretched and took a walk up to the top deck of the frigate *Sussex*, which was bearing them to Portsmouth. They had already spent a few hours at sea and William had been told they would make England before dark, having embarked late at Rotterdam just as the news arrived that the barges would also be late and the horses wouldn't get to Portsmouth until the following day.

For William it was only a minor problem – just something to take his mind off his main concern, Kieran. It amazed and shocked him how much courage he needed to approach his old friend, but they hadn't spoken to each other in weeks, and he feared recrimination. William knew he hadn't been there for him while he grieved, but then he was finding everything difficult himself, and would have been no support.

Selfish? Perhaps, but then he had feared going crazy. Had he really seen a monster that night? Hadn't the rain obscured his view? Or was he merely doing his best to convince himself that he was mistaken?

Outside, the sea air was cold, but the day was bright. William pulled his jacket around him and stepped over to the side of the frigate near the mizzenmast. Kieran was there, one foot on the rigging, staring across the waves. At first he appeared as a man who was content to be at sea, as natural as any other seaman on board – yet on closer inspection William could see that the Irishman bore the brooding expression he had worn over the last few weeks.

William approached and rubbed his hands together, hoping at least to catch Kieran's attention. His friend appeared to ignore him and stared blankly towards the faint line of land far behind them.

'France,' William said. 'I'm glad to see it so far away.'

Kieran said nothing for a moment and then sighed. 'Talking to me, are you?'

William flinched. 'Yes. I know it has been a while.'

'Not so long,' Kieran said. 'But long enough.'

'I apologize,' William said. 'But I have been busy.'

'Writing your reports,' Kieran said candidly.

'Among other things,' William replied, and then put a hand on his friend's arm. 'I realize that I have not been there when you've needed me.'

Kieran laughed under his breath. 'I don't need you, Captain. And I don't need your sympathy.'

William lifted his hand. 'I see. Do I sense a note of recrimination, Lieutenant?'

Kieran turned to him and put his hand in his pocket. He pulled it out to reveal a handkerchief.

'Do you know what this is?' he said.

William looked at the grey piece of cloth and shook his head. 'Should I?'

'Katherine gave me this,' Kieran said, trying his best to swallow his sadness. He unfolded it and between the folds was a pressed tulip. 'This is the only thing I have of hers now. That and my memories. Times ... Times that I will never, ever, have again.'

William looked up from the handkerchief and saw the tears spilling down his friend's cheeks.

'Have you ever felt that way about anyone? Have you, Will?' Kieran asked.

William looked away. 'You ask whether I have ever been in love,' he said. 'No. I haven't.'

'No,' Kieran repeated. 'Then do not attempt to come to me cap-in-hand, Captain. I will never take that kindly. Especially from someone I considered a brother who has shut me out of his life since Katherine died.'

Breathing in hard, the Irishman placed the handkerchief back inside his pocket and looked out to sea.

William felt terrible. It was the worse chiding he'd had, even from his mother and father. From Kieran it hurt badly. And why shouldn't it? He was right, wasn't he?

'I'm sorry, Kieran,' he began, 'I truly am. You are right. I have acted badly since it happened. I didn't – *don't* – want to admit to that night. I don't want to know that monsters live in the night, and I don't want to feel afraid any more. I'm a soldier, and I could face death at any time, yet ... I am terrified of discovering the reasons behind those murders.'

'And you think I'm not?' Kieran said, not looking at him. 'Do you think that I too do not wake in fever almost every night with the image of that creature in my dreams?'

'I'm sure you do ... but I would like it to go away.'

'So would I,' Kieran said, and turned to him again. 'But Katherine is dead. Those soldiers are dead. And you are hiding something. You know more about what happened than you admit to.'

William shook his head. 'You're wrong, I know as much as you.' He paused as several sailors walked past. Bowing his head close to Kieran's, he added, 'But I suspect so much.'

Kieran looked at him. 'What do you suspect?'

'What happened to the old woman. Those burns in that shack. That bronze object I took. Are they all part of the same conundrum? I don't know. But it scares me when I think about it, like I could unlock the same horrors that came to us if I dug deeper into this mystery.'

Kieran looked William square in the eyes. 'Then let me,' he said.

William shook his head. 'And lose the one friend I have?' he said, and smiled hopelessly. 'I almost did, that night. I don't want to face that again.'

Kieran's expression remained as stone. 'If you value our friendship, you'll tell me everything you know or suspect, Will.'

William nodded. 'I do, and I will. But I value our friendship enough not to let you go on this path of discovery alone. No matter where it takes us.'

He squeezed Kieran's arm and left him at the rail of the frigate.

△ III △

The *Sussex* pulled into Portsmouth harbour before evening, the sounds of sailors dashing above deck growing urgent as they hauled the rigging. With the commotion around him and England in sight, William couldn't help but wonder at what his father would make of the letter he'd written. It had detailed almost everything that had happened since Waterloo, but like the report he had given Lieutenant Colonel Fuller, it omitted the truths about the monster.

Buttoning his jacket, William looked into the small square mirror hanging in the cabin. He looked older somehow, and weren't they grey hairs at the side of his head?

Amongst the officers' bunks, he noticed the other lieutenants and captains readying themselves as best they could. Some still bore their wounds from Waterloo, the slings and splints evident against their tidy uniforms. Buttons were polished and buckles sparkled. William helped a lieutenant as he struggled with his buttons, the man having lost most of the fingers on his right hand.

After helping another soldier pull on his boots, William climbed to the top deck and stood with the midshipman, a young boy who could only have been about twelve years old. Around him, the officers of the Dragoons stood and stared with sparkling eyes as they gazed upon Portsmouth, the port growing in detail as the *Sussex* cut through the waves towards the piers and quays. Ahead of the port itself, rooftops appeared out of the haze, flags waving from towers in celebration, the skies above swarming with seagulls.

William noticed that a couple of brigade officers were weeping, others congratulating each other on making it home. One had his cap out and was waving it to the port as though someone might be able to see him. He shouted 'Bravo!' over and over, bringing chuckles from the sailors as they went about their business. Having probably seen it all before, not one of them spared a moment to watch as the port came closer.

Over four months had passed since William had last seen England. Four months of field rations, of bad coffee, of bad sleep, of blood and dirt. Four months that had seemed like four years. Looking on England again, William's heart ached to be back at Lowchester.

The sailors began shimmying up the masts and he watched as boys less than half his age climbed like monkeys up the poles and rigging. He heard the sailors cry out overhead, like the gulls, and the world around him was awash with sounds, his heart beating faster as the port came closer. The midshipman smiled at William, feeling humble next to a veteran of Waterloo.

'It is a splendid sight, isn't it, Captain?' the boy said.

William nodded. 'Yes, it definitely is. Especially after so many months.'

'I have the joy of seeing it most weeks, sailing in and out with cargo, men, supplies and dignitaries,' the boy added.

'I'm envious, lad,' William said, and grinned. 'I've been away too long.'

'Do you have a family to return to, sir?' he asked.

William nodded. 'Yes. Mother and Father, my sister Lizzy ...' he trailed off. He thought about Kieran again. 'And I have brother I need to talk to on my return. I must reconcile with him.'

'I wish you luck, sir,' the boy said, breaking off as their attention was taken by the regimental officers who were pointing to the left of the port.

'Is that Nelson's ship?' William heard a soldier ask. The others joined in with quick comments and speculation.

William turned to the midshipman, who appeared saddened.

'The officers are right, that's the *Victory*,' he said, and nodded gently towards the ship, a black and gold giant against the pier, the sails furled, a single British insignia flying from astern.

'My father was at Trafalgar,' he said. 'Killed by a sharpshooter, sir.'

William looked at the boy's glum expression but couldn't bring himself to sympathise. He'd expressed condolences so many times over the last few weeks that the word 'sorry' had lost its meaning.

William heard the *Sussex*'s captain barking orders as the rest of the crew raced along decks and the frigate moved gracefully towards the quay. The midshipman bid him good day, and left to finish his duties.

Standing alone again, William looked along the side of the ship and again found Kieran at the rail, his eyes staring into empty space. While the other men were celebrating, the Irishman's face was blank, cold, and without any cheer. William strolled down the deck and stopped at his side. Not really knowing what to say, William uttered one word only: 'Home'. He hoped it was a word that meant as much to Kieran as it did to him and that, once at home, Kieran would recover, and their friendship could be mended. That was William's hope, and for a moment there was a promise it might happen. He noticed Kieran smile slightly and the brooding face that had been there since Gembloux vanished for a moment.

The smell of sea air now mingled with the potent odour of fish as the ship pulled in against the quay. It was busy; a hive of merchants, sailors and soldiers mingling with the city folk. Some took time out to salute the soldiers on the deck of the frigate. Amongst the crates appeared marines dressed smartly as they marshalled provisions to be loaded onto the *Sussex* as she came to a stop against the quay.

William gave Kieran a gentle prod and they strode over to the other officers. William began giving orders to unload the ship of the wounded and the regimental supplies. As the officers went about their business, the midshipman came over and shook William's hand.

'Well, sir. Enjoy your stay, you've earned it after the battle,' the boy said humbly.

'As we all have. Could you thank the captain on my behalf for such a smooth crossing?' William asked.

'Consider it done, sir,' the boy said, shaking William's hand again. For such a young lad, he had a firm grip. William marvelled at the boy's resilience.

Had he seen any action on the seas? Perhaps not. But while

the war on land was all but over, there were still pirates sailing the oceans. He stared after the boy as he marched away, and wondered if he would ever see adulthood.

The gangplank was lowered and almost instantly barrels and trunks were unloaded. William rested his hands on the rail and watched as the sailors worked tirelessly to unload the frigate as the carts arrived at the quay.

'No sign of Lieutenant Bexley, sir,' one of the officers remarked as William looked across the harbour for the regimental attaché.

'He'll be here soon enough, lieutenant,' William replied, turning to the officer, who had one arm in a sling. His tunic was a little twisted and two buttons were undone. William buttoned them for him.

'Thank you, sir,' the lieutenant smiled.

'There ... wounded yet dignified,' William joked as he straightened the man's collar.

'Wounded, sir, but I'll mend,' insisted the lieutenant.

Kieran appeared soon after supervising the unloading of the company records and colours. 'All done?' William asked.

'Roberts is getting the men ready,' Kieran said abruptly. 'And Bexley?'

'The lieutenant should be here soon,' William replied. 'Make sure everyone is ready. I don't want to stay in Portsmouth longer than I have to.'

'Yes, sir,' Kieran said formally and returned to the company.

William continued to watch the disembarking troops as the crowds on the quay began to part and a train of wagons and horses rumbled down with Bexley at the head, his face red with exertion. William smiled to himself and waved his hat at the lieutenant, who waved back haphazardly as he pulled his horse to a stop just by the stack of crates, barrels and trunks. The riders on the wagons began to load them as William strolled down the gangplank.

'Lieutenant Bexley!' William beamed.

The lieutenant smiled back, still out of breath, and dismounted. He limped over and held out a hand, suddenly retracting it again when he saw William's badge of rank.

'*Captain* Saxon, is it?' Bexley said, quite surprised.

'Yes, Edward, Captain it is,' he said, and shook Bexley's hand, 'but enough of the formalities, we've know each other too long for that.'

Bexley nodded. 'It is a strange thing to go away for a few months as a lieutenant, and then come back as a captain.'

'Yes, strange it is. And tragic. Captain Mayfair will be sorely missed,' William replied gravely.

'And so will the others. But enough of such grim tidings. This is a time of celebration, Will,' he said clasping William's hands. 'Where is Kieran?'

'On deck, helping with the wounded.'

'He's not a captain, too, is he?' Bexley asked, appearing a little envious of William's promotion.

'No, he's not,' William laughed. 'But he's fragile, so treat him gently.'

'Wounded? But he'll mend, yes? Not like me, sorry to say,' Bexley said looking down at his twisted leg, broken in a fall almost a year ago.

'You can still ride, though,' William remarked, looking at Bexley's grey mare.

'Aye, but not for long at a gallop. Takes all my strength just to hold on,' Bexley said as the first of the wounded came down the gangplank, Lieutenant Roberts leading the way.

'Get them on the wagons, Lieutenant,' William ordered.

'Settling into your role already, Will?' Bexley laughed. 'Well I'd better do some "supervising" of my own before you start ordering me around!'

Kieran helped a one-legged soldier down the plank, half supporting and half carrying the man down to the quay. 'There's about thirty more to come. Gerald's helping them,' Kieran said.

'How's your rib holding out?' William asked quietly.

'It hurts. But I'll live,' Kieran replied, and stretched. He took in a deep breath and looked above, the sky teaming with gulls. Beyond them, the grey clouds were clearing for evening, the sky a crystal blue.

'It should be a good day tomorrow,' the Irishman said distantly.

'Yes, it should. Are you glad to be home?' William asked and stamped on the stone floor.

For a moment, Kieran didn't seem to listen, but then he nodded quietly. 'Yes, I suppose I am.'

'Good, because we'll be in Lowchester in about two weeks and I intend to be in good cheer when I see Fairway Hall again. And I doubt Bexley will give any let-up when we get back to camp.'

'I'll do my best,' Kieran said soberly, and tried a smile that faltered.

William watched Kieran leave for the wagons and the other wounded, fearing that he'd pushed his luck too far by trying to get the Irishman to cheer up.

After helping another lieutenant onto the last wagon, Kieran climbed gingerly onto the back of the rear wagon with the other officers. His rib was hurting again but there was a dull ache inside that he knew was from no physical pain. It was a feeling of loss, and there was no telling when that feeling would heal, if ever.

With a gentle buckling noise, the wagons began to turn around. Kieran held onto the side and looked out to the *Sussex* and then beyond the frigate to the other ships across the port, their masts needling the blue sky. In the distance, other vessels were sailing into port or away, ships like the *Sussex*, or large battleships like the *Victory*. Some were fishing-vessels or merchant ships, splendid in their appearance but dwarfed by their large military cousins.

Kieran sat back against the wagon and felt himself drift as he watched the quay move by at a trot, the fishermen and merchants disappearing with each bounce of the wheels against the cobbles. But then, within the mass of sellers and bystanders, Kieran saw one person who stared after the train of wagons. One person who caught his attention.

Kieran leant further out of the wagon, hanging on to the rear as the vehicle bucked up and down, his eyes on the figure that stood motionless in the bustle of the crowd. It was a middle-sized man, elderly, wrapped in a greatcoat of grey, with white hair tied back in a ponytail. But it was his eyes that caught Kieran's attention – crystal blue eyes, like the sky, watching not just the wagon train itself, but looking directly at Kieran himself.

As the wagons bore them further away, Kieran vied for a better view. Another jolt threatened to unseat him and the Irishman settled himself back to avoid being thrown out of the wagon altogether. With a mixture of curiosity and trepidation, Kieran watched as the old man was swallowed by the bustle of the quay.

△ IV △

The sun had almost finished its downward crawl to the horizon as Captain Dale of the *Sussex* tapped the rail impatiently and paced the deck, appearing to have much on his mind. It had been a few hours since they had landed, and night had come quickly. Most of the supplies had been loaded down to the Frigate's hull, yet the first lieutenant was missing. The *Sussex* would sail in the morning and it would not do to leave without her first lieutenant.

Dale pursed his lips and tapped the rail again. The lieutenant had been sent on an errand across the port to the military store of the Royal Naval detachment on Drake's Quay – a small naval store that provided the *Sussex* with, amongst other things, quality rum – something the captain ensured the crew had their fair share of. After all the actions they had been through and the loyalty of the sailors, Dale thought they deserved it. But the lieutenant, who had never been tardy before, was missing and the night was drawing in like a blanket of darkness. Twilight had fallen and the dim light was fading fast as the lamps of Portsmouth began to shine, the occasional fire crackling in the shadows across the quays.

Dale looked at his pocket-watch and felt his stomach rumble. He'd missed the evening meal, though he'd make sure the ship's cook managed to rustle up something simple when he retired from his vigil.

'Mr Craig!' Dale barked and the midshipman appeared from the lower deck.

'Sir?' the boy said, his eyes shining in the gloom.

The captain frowned and paced the deck again. 'Mr Craig, is it my imagination or is the lieutenant a little late?'

The midshipman pondered and nodded firmly. 'Yes, sir, he should have been here hours ago.'

'Indeed he should!' Dale remarked and snapped shut his watch. 'Indeed he should, but he isn't, is he, Mr Craig? Do you know if the lieutenant had any prior thoughts of going astray?'

'The lieutenant, sir? No, sir, he had no thoughts of going anywhere but the stores, sir.'

'Curious,' Dale replied, unconvinced. He stared out again, the shadows filling the streets as the lamps burned brighter. 'Well he shouldn't have gotten far, lad. If you can, I'd like you to locate the lieutenant and return his arse back to the *Sussex* before I bloody starve!' The midshipman nodded quickly and trotted over to the gangplank. 'And don't go running off as well, understand, Mr Craig?' Dale said playfully but sternly, his bemusement showing as he tapped the rail with his cane.

'No, sir, definitely not, sir,' the boy said quickly and trotted down the gangplank. Dale watched the midshipman disappearing down the quay, his dark figure appearing between the lanterns swinging by the water's edge.

'Sir, begging your pardon, but is it wise to let a young lad out into the night?' the boatswain asked.

Dale glanced at the rough-looking sailor. 'I think Mr Craig has more courage than most boys his age, sailor. Do you think he might get drunk somewhere, or end up in a whorehouse?'

The boatswain smiled. 'No, sir. I see your point.'

'Keep an eye out for them. Tell me as soon as they return,' Dale ordered.

'Aye, sir, I will,' the boatswain replied, and Captain Dale felt a cold shiver creep over him as he retired inside.

△   △   △

Mr Craig marched down the quay until the shop-fronts appeared, dark and empty, with lamps shining from the rooms above. A sailor stumbled by, legs uncoordinated and eyes glazed, with a woman on his arm, daubed in makeup. Mr Craig had seen her before – a whore who plied her trade outside The Otters Arms near the quay where the *Victory* was moored. Jack, the boatswain, had taken him there for an 'education', but he had politely declined going any further.

Mr Craig jogged up a side-street, one of the few shortcuts to Drake's Quay. He had made the journey with the first lieutenant many times. Hearing music from an adjacent street, he noticed a new tavern by the fishing stores behind the second row of houses. The music was fine and Irish, a fiddle and a pennywhistle bringing cheering from within. He wrapped his arms about himself and felt suddenly vulnerable. He was only young, after all, and had grown up in safe surroundings in Southampton. The heart of Portsmouth was a dark heart indeed, and there were plenty of 'bad people' (as Jack the boatswain had put it) who would try to take advantage of him.

'Have courage,' he murmured to himself, 'I must find the first lieutenant.'

The dark was creeping down the alleys as twilight turned to night. In the nest of buildings huddled around the fish market there was not a soul except for a merchant counting his coins with a disgruntled looking fisherman standing by. They began to argue until the merchant noticed the midshipman, and their discussion fell to a whisper.

Mr Craig looked away and hurried on, leaving the fish market for Slough Lane, which stood at the foot of a hundred yards of drinking houses (hailed amongst certain sailors as the 'Full Yards'). A sailor taking on all eight taverns wouldn't return to the ship in any state fit for working, and a visit to the 'Full Yards' was a whipping offence on some frigates.

Mr Craig had never been to a proper sailor's tavern, and those on the 'Full Yards' were notorious. Curiosity got the better of him and he paused by a tavern, watching the shadows at the windows and hearing the cheer within. There was sudden laughter and then a clatter of breaking glass, and Mr Craig stepped back.

But the clatter of glass had not come from the tavern. It had come from one of the dark alleys.

Mr Craig shivered and grew scared. Someone was following him, he was sure of it. Frowning, he backed away and continued on, knowing the Naval Stores were only a few minutes away. His pace quickened and he felt fear creeping up the back of his neck as he moved away from the relative glow of the 'Full Yards' to another empty street lit only by the occasional lamp hanging in a window.

The voices came again, and Mr Craig turned around sharply. 'Hello? I say, hello?' he called out. But there was no answer, not even the sound of chattering. 'Who's there?' he shouted.

A window opened above him and a woman with a sour face leant out. 'Oi! What's all this bloody shoutin'?' she yelled.

With a certain relief, the midshipman looked up and waved. 'Sorry, madam. I didn't wish to disturb you. I thought I heard something.'

'You'll wake the dead, you will! Bloody kids!' the woman shouted and slammed the window. The midshipman sighed; all he wanted was to be taken in by the woman, a little motherly support. He clenched his fists with worry and looked into the shadows again. But there was nothing.

'You're spooking yourself, that's all,' he muttered. 'There's no one there, man.' He shoved his hands in his pockets and walked slowly away.

The next street had more warehouses than homes or shops, and Mr Craig was relieved to see that he was near Drake's Quay. It was only just around the next corner and down an alley. He'd locate the first lieutenant, who was obviously stuck talking to the sergeant at the naval stores (who had so many stories about fighting privateers that sometimes it took hours to escape him).

And then the sound came again, and it was closer still.

Mr Craig froze. This time there were voices, not that clear, but definitely not in a tongue he recognised. The boy stopped and looked around. The darkness in the street was almost total save for the stars and moon that cast a pale and sickly glow. Mr Craig began to panic.

'Who is that? Hello? Who's there? Jack? Is that you?' he said quietly, praying to God this was just another prank by the frigate's boatswain. But there was no answer.

The boy began stepping away gently, his eyes glancing quickly about the dark as he backed off. The chattering returned. It was low and in the shadows, voiced deeply.

And it was even closer now.

'Look, I don't want any trouble, right?' Mr Craig said firmly, but it came out slightly broken and high-pitched.

There was a sudden silence and then a voice hissed out: '*A se pe 'el!*'

Mr Craig didn't know exactly what it meant, but he could hear the intent.

'Oh God help me!' he cried and turned tail. He found his running-feet quite quickly as the voices moved out of the shadows, pulling the darkness with them as they advanced. The midshipman needed no more encouragement to leave. He was at the end of the street in moments, and around the corner, hoping to God that he would make the naval store and the first lieutenant.

Getting to the corner by a tall warehouse, he stopped and his heart sank as, from the alley towards Drake's Quay, two figures appeared cloaked in black, their eyes flashing towards him.

'No!' he gasped and turned away again, fleeing down an adjacent alley, away from the quay.

As he raced down the narrow section, his heart pounding in rhythm with his feet, he tried desperately to remember an alternative way to the quay. At the end of the alley, with the darkness behind him, Mr Craig found a ring of homes. He wasn't sure whether the occupants would help, but at least it was safer indoors bargaining with a landlord, than out on the road.

Gulping down his fear with strangled breaths, the midshipman stepped out of the alley and looked about in case anyone was

83

nearby. He was lucky, the street was deserted. Mr Craig walked silently down it, hugging the shadows to evade anyone who might be following. As he neared the end, he noticed another warehouse with a glowing lamp in the window. A shadow moved across it, probably a merchant, and the boy paused to consider whether the merchant was a better option.

Suddenly, behind him the darkness broke out into the street and appeared as two figures, then three, followed by a fourth. He could make it to the end of the street before they caught him, but what then? The warehouse with the lamp in the window seemed more and more inviting.

The boy flexed his sweating hands and backed off as the four figures began walking towards him. The warehouse, or the end of the street? It was a decision he had to make before they moved much closer.

Mr Craig looked back and his heart sank as two more dark figures appeared, their eyes sparkling in the gloom, staring right at him. They had cut off his way to the end of the street.

'Bloody hell!' he yelped, his mind made up, and ran across the street towards the warehouse, his hands outstretched towards the wrought iron handle at the entrance.

Behind him, the figures were coming closer, not just chattering in low voices, but talking loudly in their foreign tongue. One of them stopped talking and cried out as Mr Craig found the handle and began to pull, the door groaning on its hinges. If he'd only been a little stronger the door would have opened more quickly. He heaved with all his might, until there was a gap big enough to slip through. He prayed the merchant he had seen in the window would be more forgiving than the woman he'd woken before.

The darkness stretched high above into the recesses of the warehouse. There was no sign of anyone. Mr Craig pulled the door quickly behind him but his pursuers were already there. They grunted as he pulled, and he saw a set of fingers between the gap, holding the side and pulling it back open. Straining, the midshipman used his weight and hung onto the handle with all his strength as he tried to close the door, hoping that when he managed it there would be a lock to ensure they couldn't get in.

For a moment he thought the pursuers had given up. Then, without warning, a pair of hands appeared at his shoulders and pulled him away from the door. His grip was lost and he seemed to tumble backwards until another set of hands saved him from falling.

From the doorway the six figures appeared, filling the exit completely. 'No! You must help me!' he shouted to the person behind him. He struggled in their gentle grasp, wanting to run again. But there was a loud thump and pain spread up his back and through his stomach as something hard connected with his kidneys. His legs, already shuddering through fear, weakened again and the boy fell to his knees, holding his hand to his back. The heat of the pain spread up his body and it felt as though his insides had split.

Another hand smacked him against the cheek and he crashed to the floor, sprawling in the darkness. Hands held his hair and pulled him to his knees again, taking clumps of hair from his scalp. The midshipman moaned, unable to see anything in the gloom as tears rolled down his cheeks. 'Let me go! Please!' he choked, half sobbing.

Another blow came from a boot to his stomach and the wind was taken from him. The hand pulled at his hair. Gasping, the boy reared up, as the figures gathered around him. 'I'm an officer! I'm a naval officer!' he gasped. 'Please!' There was no reply to this – nothing at all from his attackers, who simply muttered amongst themselves. 'Let me go!' he sobbed again, feeling the pain reporting across his body.

The muttering suddenly died away and the boy could hear a gentle laughter from ahead, deep in the darkness of the warehouse. He noticed his attackers moving away, apart from the two that held him fast on his knees. Squinting in the gloom, the young midshipman found the gentle glow of the lamp somewhere in the expanse of the building, illuminating parts of the warehouse with a gentle light. Now there was another figure, edged in the faint glow, standing apart from the others. It was this figure that began to laugh.

Nearby, he could hear the clink of chains as they swung above.

'I expected a man,' a voice remarked, sharp and hollow. It was spoken from a distance, but by the time the echo reached Mr Craig's ears it felt as though it was by his shoulder. 'But I've never seen a man weep like this. You're no man, my poor fool. You're just boy. Or a blubbering girl!'

'Go to Hell!' the boy screamed angrily, and sobbed again.

The figure laughed louder now, seeming to linger in the faint light, and then was gone suddenly, like smoke in the wind. Mr Craig thought it was a trick of the light, or that he was hallucinating. His shoulders slumped. His hands were clamped behind his back by grips of steel. He began to pray under his breath that the first lieutenant would find him, or maybe that the captain had sent out a brigade to look for them both.

'To Hell?' the voice mused, closer now, the accent as foreign as those around him. 'How little you know of Hell, boy!'

Mr Craig raised his head and he trembled as he found the figure was now merely feet from him. 'Good, now look at me,' the man said, and a cold hand stroked the boy's bloodied cheek. A wince of pain shot through his jaw and he moaned, watching as the man brought his hand to his own mouth. In the gloom he heard a sucking noise, like the slurping of a dog from a water-bowl. 'Very good. Innocent and pure,' the man said again, his breathing harsh and suffocated. 'I like men with spirit ... like your friend.'

Mr Craig struggled again, but the holds on his arms were solid.

'Now we play a game and one that you must master if you're to leave this dank place alive. Understand me, boy?' The midshipman nodded slowly, unable to do anything else. He was faintly aware of the damp patch spreading around his groin. He tried his best to hold on but with the terror that welled up inside, it had become a losing battle. Urine trickled down his leg, and he sobbed again.

'In this game, I ask a question and you give me the answer. A truthful answer, though, or you fail. And if you fail, you will die,' the man hissed. The midshipman nodded again, but he was feeling faint. The smell of his own blood, and the pain rocking around his skull, was making him feel delirious. He could see faint beams of silver light in the darkness, and the world seemed distant. He was going to pass out.

'Not yet, my friend,' the voice hissed and suddenly there was a cold wet pain as something crashed over him. Instantly Mr Craig was brought back to life and pain howled about him. He moaned and felt ice cold water dripping from his face and clothes.

'Awake now? Good! To the questions,' the man rasped. 'I will ask them once, and once only, so concentrate. What do you know about the guests on your ship? The officers that sailed with you, what can you tell me?'

'Officers?' Mr Craig murmured, honestly remembering little in his fragile state.

'The soldiers you transported from Rotterdam. What of them?' the man asked.

'Cavalry ... riders ... the wounded,' the boy struggled.

The figure bent down to him. 'Go on,' he said gently.

'There were some officers. Down below ... on the lower deck,' he gasped and sagged further as his strength fled him.

'Officers? Good. Now, I want to know about two of these officers particularly. Two young men, a captain and a lieutenant. You must have seen them. How many captains can one boat have? And the lieutenant was his friend. Tell me about them!' the man hissed.

The boy shook his head, his brain making nonsense of the request. 'I don't know them ... I don't know ...' he sobbed.

'*Mendax!*' the man screamed in fury, and struck the boy about the face. His cheek tore open and he cried out, sobbing until his chest ached. 'If you lie to me again, I promise that it will be the last lie your tongue makes,' the voice said, and came closer to the lamp so the midshipman could see his outline. Taller than any other man he knew of, he stood by the lamp, his face shielded by a hood of black silk. 'These are not empty threats, my boy.'

The lamp suddenly veered away and the darkness returned. But as Mr Craig watched from the floor, the light reappeared, growing fainter as it seemed to journey upwards, pulled towards the sound of swinging chains. The boy watched as the lamp began to illuminate a long stretch of chain, then a human leg, followed by an arm. A torso soon followed, red as though dipped in blood. As the light travelled further, it caught a neck that had been ripped open, still seeping, and then came the face: the head of the hanging corpse.

The boy cried out. 'Lieutenant!' he shouted. 'No! Not the first lieutenant!'

'That's right, boy. It seems the first lieutenant of your little boat was also unwilling to help me. I hope it won't be the same with you,' the voice hissed, and again the lamp seemed to melt away within the crowd of figures.

'So again the game commences, and again I'll ask the questions. These men brought an object with them that is very precious to me. Let me describe it to you ... It is small, can fit in the palm of your hand, is shaped like a pyramid and made of bronze ... Have you seen it?'

The lamp reappeared from the crowd and the midshipman squinted at the glare of the single flame.

'... And if you require any motivation to answer me, let it be this: your death will be very, very painful. You will know the meaning of Hell ...'

Suddenly, out of the throng of shadows, the man pulled back his veil to reveal a white face of murderous intent. The man's eyes were the deepest yellow and his mouth was outset, a wide jaw with an array of sharpened teeth like broken glass. The two incisors seemed to grow in the dark as the man began to smile, broadening from cheek to cheek. The smell of blood and piss was quickly overwhelming, and young Mr Craig, midshipman of the *Sussex*, could not stop himself from urinating down his leg again.

'Oh God help me!' he squealed, as the lamp flickered out.

CHAPTER FIVE

The Return to Lowchester

△ I △

William and Kieran arrived several days earlier than planned at the crest of Cosworth Hill, near the village of Dunabbey. William let out a whoop of joy as he spied the Westway Tower of Fairway Hall. It was a warm, summer afternoon and the green and yellow fields burned brightly in the sunshine.

William held his cap aloft and grinned at Kieran who could not help but smile, if only a little.

'We're home, Kieran!' He laughed and reached out to his friend.

'Home,' Kieran replied, and shook his hand firmly. 'It feels like a long time.'

'Yes, my friend, it does,' William said, bleary-eyed. 'Oh Lord, it's great to be back.'

Kieran nodded silently and followed William as he trotted down the bridle path and through the woods that screened the estate from the nearby fields. They emerged from the shade and cantered down a lane flanked by small trees. Ahead of them, a pheasant strolled across their path, disappearing amongst the ferns. The sun shone down, bathing them in a fierce heat. Even the intense summers of Spain had not made them accustomed to such weather and sweat poured down their brows and stuck their shirts to their backs.

The workers that Richard Saxon – Lord of Fairway Hall –

had hired in Dunabbey were planting fresh rows of flowers under the watchful eyes of the grounds-man, Robert. He had seen the two riders from a distance and was now making his way slowly to the edge of the bridleway.

'Mr Saxon! Mr Harte! Thank the Lord you've both returned!' Robert beamed, his grey eyes sparkling within his wrinkled face. The grounds-man had served almost three generations of Saxons at Fairway.

'Thank you, Robert. Are you well?' William asked.

'All the better for seeing you, sir!'

'We're going to give Father a surprise. He's not expecting us?' William said, and winked.

'That's right sir, he isn't. He wanted these flowers planted before your arrival!' Robert said, and scratched his head, slightly dismayed. 'You were meant to arrive here in four days' time.'

'Ah well. I'm sure our surprise will be more than welcome,' William said, stroking the horse's neck as it tapped the floor impatiently with its hoof, kicking up a gentle cloud of dust around them.

'I'm sure it will, sir,' Robert said with a wave, as they steered the horses back down the path.

Trotting down towards the Hall, William felt an overwhelming sense of warmth and love for the building as it grew in detail. The main hall rose out of the shadows, its formidable and ornate wings spreading out from behind the row of Irish yews that hedged the building from the grounds. William soon forgot the sun cooking the uniform on his back and instead feasted his eyes on the walls of Fairway, watching as servants brushed the dust from the steps of the main hall, probably in preparation for their expected arrival in four days' time. A smile came to his lips as they passed under the main gate and William signalled Kieran to stop and dismount. Patting the flank of his weary horse, William looked about the courtyard just in case any of the family were around. But only Skinner, the stable boy, had seen them.

'Masters! Oh glory, you're home!' he said, taking the reins from their hands.

'How are you, lad? You're looking fine!' William said, giving the boy a bear-hug. 'You've grown, too. What have they been feeding you?'

Blushing, Skinner wrestled him off and laughed. 'It's wonderful to see you again, sir. And you, Master Harte.'

'It feels good to be home,' Kieran said magnanimously.

'Where is my father, Skinny?' William asked, using the stable-boy's nickname.

'Out back, sir, with your sister,' Skinner replied, leading the horses away.

'And what about Lady Saxon?' William called after him.

'I'm here, William,' said a voice from afar.

William and Kieran turned and found Lady Jane Saxon standing on the marble steps, one of the servants at her side. She was dressed in a red silk shawl over a silver gown. In her hand she held a green fan given to her by William's grandfather following a visit to Asia. She hardly used the fan except to point at something for the servants to do, but this time she used it to beckon her two boys forward. Lady Jane smiled, but her eyes were full of tears. She climbed halfway down the steps and stopped as Kieran and William looked up from the bottom. 'You weren't meant to be here for four days, my sons,' she said, trying to maintain an air of dignity.

'We were given time off for decent behaviour.' Grinning, William bounded up the steps. He took her hand and kissed it, and then threw his arms around her, causing Lady Jane to cry with happiness.

'William, please, not here!' she sobbed. She turned and dismissed the servants quickly, fearing her composure would crumble. As they filed back into the house, Kieran stepped up and kissed Lady Jane's hand.

'Oh Kieran! Thank God you're in good health. Is the wound healed?' she asked and touched his cheek.

Kieran glanced at William a little surprised, but nodded slowly. 'Yes, ma'am, it is healed.'

She hugged him gently and looped one arm through his and

the other through William's, leading them to the courtyard and then down the path by the western wing, towards the rear gardens.

'Your father did not know you were coming today,' she said, her cheeks drying in the heat of the day. 'He'll have a pleasant surprise when I bring you to him.'

'He is well, then?' William asked.

'He was worried sick about you, until he got your letter. We both were. And Lizzy ...' She tutted and rolled her eyes.

'How is Elizabeth?' Kieran asked gently.

'She is fine. Pining, I expect, but fine,' Lady Jane said, and winked at Kieran.

Kieran blushed and looked away. It seemed as though Elizabeth's feelings for him hadn't changed, even if they were no longer reciprocated. Kieran knew that their meeting would not be easy. His apprehension wasn't helped by his ignorance of William's letter. It seemed natural that William would write to the family, but why hadn't he told him of it before? If William had mentioned his wound, then what else had he said?

As they appeared around the corner of the western wing they found the rear garden in a dazzling array of colours, with the flowers in bloom and the smell of roses and apples scenting the air.

'Robert has done incredible work on the garden, Mother,' William observed, clearly impressed.

'The days have been kind to us. The nights have been short and we've had plenty of visitors. Many days have been spent in the gardens, especially after the news of your victory,' Lady Jane said, and gave them both a gentle squeeze.

'Yes, I can imagine. I just wish we had been here to celebrate,' William sighed.

'We'll celebrate over again, my darling son! You and Kieran will be the honoured guests at a party to praise what you have done. Does that sound to your liking?' she asked.

William looked at Kieran and laughed. 'Well, Kieran, it sounds good to me!' The Irishman nodded and returned his smile with a weak one of his own. His mind was not on festivities but on his imminent encounter with Elizabeth. He knew that her feelings for him were strong. Even though he was treated as family, she had loved him from a young age. It was a love that approached adoration, and at one time Kieran had been tempted by her virginal beauty.

But plenty had happened since then; events that could change a man forever. No matter how hard he tried to bury his feelings, he knew they would not so easily be forgotten. After all, Elizabeth was still just a girl; Katherine had been a woman. The gulf between the two was immeasurable.

As they passed the green arch to the garden, Kieran concentrated on being polite. The last thing he wished to do was give in to frustration and appear scornful. The gardens were alive with insects, and sparrows were singing in the trees. But it was the sound of laughter that caught their attention as they approached the summer patio. Near the tennis court, on one of a row of white chairs, was Richard Saxon, Lord of Fairway Hall, his face red with chuckling as he watched his daughter being spun around by three of the household's children. Elizabeth, her jet black hair curled around her shoulders, laughed giddily as she was turned and turned and turned, her eyes blindfolded. 'No more!' she squealed, but the children kept turning her.

'Enough! Let her seek us out!' Lord Richard roared and clapped. He got up from his chair and took a few steps forward as Elizabeth swayed from side to side, her arms outstretched. She stumbled slightly on the lawn and stopped to hold her spinning head, still laughing but feeling quite queasy with it. The children ran circles around her as her father stood nearby, holding his hand to his mouth so she couldn't hear him laughing. Lady Jane was giggling too, and William couldn't help but let out a sharp chuckle, which he quickly stifled as his mother led them down to the lawn.

'Where is everyone?' Elizabeth murmured, groping the air as one of the littlest children, the house-master's son, ran under her arms squealing. 'Matthew? Is that you?' she cried out. She reached lower but to no avail as the boy ran over to his elder sister and hid behind her dress.

'Hello? Where are you all?' Elizabeth said, and stumbled again. Lord Richard laughed out loud and instantly Elizabeth began wandering over to him. He stepped to the side and moved towards the patio. As he turned he stopped in his tracks and let out a gasp.

'Father?' Elizabeth said, and groped the air once more, hearing his surprise.

William stood a few yards away and brought a finger to his lips; Richard Saxon almost couldn't contain himself. He ran forward and embraced his son, then turned to Kieran. The Irishman held out his hand, but the old man shook his head and embraced him. 'You're here! I thought you were coming in four days' time!' he whispered and stared wondrously at the two men before him.

'We thought we'd surprise you, sir,' Kieran said.

'That you have, dear boy!' he said again and laughed.

'Father? Where are you?' Elizabeth called out, as the children continued to run around her in circles. 'Who are you talking to?'

William winked at his father, and then he and Kieran stepped lightly onto the lawn and towards the game. 'Who's there?' she called out and reached forward, her arms clattering into William's chest.

'Father?' she said, unsure. 'Or is it someone else?' Her hands reached up over the buttons of William's uniform, towards his neck. Before she could touch his face, William took her arms and turned her around again and again. Richard Saxon laughed out loud, and the children fled as Elizabeth wobbled across the lawn, completely disorientated.

'I feel quite sick now!' she slurred, her face pale, her movements lumbering. She turned and stumbled forward, clattering into another body.

'Please, no more spinning! I feel positively ill for spinning!' she complained, as her hands touched the uniform. To the sound of laughter she touched the cheek. Frowning, she fumbled at her blindfold. 'Let me see who I've caught!'

The blindfold fell away, revealing her gentle face, still very young, yet stunningly beautiful. Her bright eyes met Kieran's and the change in her expression was immediate. One moment it was shock, the next it was sheer joy. But Kieran's expression of stone stopped her smile as her hands went to his arms.

'Hello, Elizabeth,' he said gently.

She looked at him questioningly.

William appeared at her side and gave her a hug. 'Will!' she cried and hugged him firmly. 'I can't believe you're both here!'

'I know, Lizzy, I know. I can't believe we're back at Fairway either,' William said, and kissed her on the cheek.

'And you, Kieran, are you glad to be home?' she asked.

Kieran looked away and then smiled. 'Yes. I'm glad I've returned back to my family,' he said, and hugged Elizabeth. His embrace seemed to break the tension and Lizzy was happy again, hugging him back twice as hard and twice as long as she had William.

'How long are you home for?' Lord Richard asked, leading Lady Jane onto the lawn.

'For a while,' William replied. 'I'll need to return to Deramere Barracks in three weeks, but I'll be around for a while yet. Napoleon has gone, and America is not for the 1st Dragoons, sir.'

'I'm glad,' Elizabeth remarked. She hooked her arm through Kieran's and rested her head against his shoulder. 'Fairway Hall has been too quiet without you two. Especially this summer.'

'I doubt that, Lizzy,' William joked, and nudged her gently.

'It is true, my boys. Fairway has never seen a quieter summer. We've let a few staff go over the last two months,' Lord Richard admitted grimly.

'Is there a problem, Father?' William asked.

'Not at all. Only the trade is drying up because of the priva-teers in the Atlantic. I've been assured the situation is improving, but money has been harder to come by than usual.' Lord Richard brooded and then broke into his belly-laugh once more. 'But enough of this! You two are here, and that's all that matters!'

Elizabeth jumped up and down giddily. 'This evening we will eat and drink and you can tell us of your adventures. Father has been very secretive about the letter you sent him, Will, and I for one am curious to find out about what you did over there.' She winked at Kieran, who couldn't help but flinch when her back was turned.

△ II △

That evening a great banquet was laid on, with more food than William and Kieran had seen in months. They said very little as they tucked into pheasant and guinea-fowl, sipping the finest wines from the cellars, until they could consume no more and William let out a loud belch, much to Elizabeth's delight and Lady Jane's embarrassment.

Richard Saxon rested his knife and fork on the table and leant back, looking satisfied. 'Thank the Lord we didn't have to lose Marianne, Jane! I swear she's the finest cook in the south of England,' he said, and leant across the table to kiss Lady Jane on the cheek.

William was making a hat out of his napkin but stopped suddenly, looking up with concern. 'Is the situation that bad?' he asked.

'No, not at all,' he replied, appearing blasé. He raised a glass of red wine and toasted William and Kieran's health. 'Tomorrow we will thank God for your swift return,' he declared.

Elizabeth, who was sitting next to Kieran, gave his hand a gentle squeeze. The Irishman did his best not to squirm under her affections, and let her warm fingers squeeze his. She replied by running them over the top his hand, a little more affectionately than before. Kieran flinched and coughed, removing his hand quickly from hers. After appearing to clear his throat, he said, 'We've been away so long, sir, that I for one would like to know what has happened in the world since we left.'

'The world? Well, apart from you kicking old Boney's backside back to Paris, a little has changed since you left us. It appears that even nature has turned on its head,' Lord Richard began.

'George Terry spoke to me about the heavy frosts we've been having of late. They've been playing havoc with the crops, and Robert is beside himself. He fears the gardens will be decimated if it happens again. One johnny at court suggested it was something to do with a volcano erupting in the East Indies! Can you imagine that? That something happening so far away could affect us over here? Months ago that would seem so unthinkable, and yet you two are proof that something far away can affect an entire country. I have to say, my sons, that the biggest change in our world has come from what you secured across the sea. I have not yet conveyed to you what this has meant to the Court, even to the common folk on the streets. You are heroes to them.'

'Even in the borough they danced for days and some of the veterans told stories of their own battles,' Elizabeth added.

'And those parts of the world we haven't changed? What of them?' William asked.

'They stay the same. The Americans are still a problem. A constant thorn in our side. Trade is down and the wars with the French have meant our ships have been open to attack by privateers. It has cost us much, in men and money, despite what Parliament tells us,' Lord Richard grunted and downed the rest of his wine. 'But England is as merry as ever. There are more opportunities than before. There are new ideas – steam-driven machines and the like.'

'Your father's friend, Mr Grendell, believes we are experiencing a peak in the "history of humanity",' Lady Jane added, beaming.

'Yes, and I believe him!' Lord Richard said haughtily. 'We fly in balloons and soon we may move across the land unassisted by horses and at great speeds. I cannot believe the human race will ever improve on that. This is a golden age we live in, my sons, golden!'

'And how about you, Lizzy, how is life at Fairway?' William inquired with a sly and confident smile. 'Any suitors?'

Elizabeth blushed and looked away, knowing she was being teased.

'Mr Grendell's son has tried courting her. A fine boy and full

97

of the ideas your father was speaking of,' Lady Jane remarked. 'He will be a great industrialist.'

'Yes, that he will. But he's not pretty, nor has he many graces. He is almost eccentric,' Lord Richard said, and leant over to William to add quietly, 'and at times a little too effeminate!'

William snorted out loud and poured himself and his father another glass of wine. Elizabeth was turning inside out with embarrassment and Kieran wasn't looking too comfortable either.

'Enough of Mr Arthur Grendell. Back to you two and what happened over there. Our world is dull and slow, but peaceful. I know little of adventures apart from paying the yearly tax return and playing "blind man's bluff" on a summer's day. I want to hear about your adventures,' Richard Saxon announced and sat back in his chair, raising his glass.

'There's not much to say, really,' William murmured.

'Oh go on, Will, tell us, *please!*' Elizabeth said. 'Was it exciting? You never told me about what you did in Spain, and I only get the gentle version from Father.'

'We wouldn't want to harm your sensibilities, Elizabeth,' Kieran replied soberly.

'Kieran is right. War is not romantic. It is terrifying and bloody,' William added.

'We are adults around this table, and I think even dear Lizzy is old enough to hear what life is really like as a soldier,' Lord Richard said.

'Fine, then, I will tell you some of it. I will tell you that the battle was all it was reported to have been, and more,' William said.

For over an hour, they sat and listened as William, with asides from Kieran, described the battle. They talked about their pride as they met Wellington, their fear as they lined up on the slopes behind the farmhouse and watched Napoleon's army arrive in great columns of blue. Lady Jane held her husband's hand as they recounted the first exchange of cannon-fire, the thunderous noises that ripped about them, the explosions as infantry and cavalry were blasted apart by speculative shots from the French. And they detailed the charge on the French cannon, the disaster as Ponsoby's regiment was massacred by the French lancers, the Dragoons being all but overridden by the enemy, and then the rallying by Hougoumont.

Elizabeth hugged Kieran as William told them of the moment the Irishman fell into the melee of enemy infantry. Lord Richard's face was grave when his son mentioned the death of Captain Mayfair, his father's old school-friend. And when the final words had been spoken, the French driven from their minds, just as they had been driven from the field of battle, a deathly silence fell on the dining room.

Both Kieran and William felt emotionally exhausted.

It was Lord Richard who spoke first. 'A grave victory,' he remarked and gazed over to Kieran. 'And you my boy, are lucky to have survived.'

'Maybe,' Kieran murmured.

'No "maybe" about it, Kieran. Your father would have haunted me to my grave if you had been lost in battle,' he said. 'I promised him I would look after you, and at times I have wondered if letting you join the Cavalry was a wise decision. But then if I can trust my own flesh and blood, then why shouldn't I trust my adopted son?'

'My thanks, sir,' Kieran said. 'My father would have been proud.'

'I'm sure he is. Every day, my boy, he looks down at you and knows there is a son that he can be proud of,' Lord Richard smiled sadly.

'I'm just glad Will was there to save you,' Elizabeth whispered, and held Kieran close, running her soft fingers over his rough hand.

William smiled and raised a glass to his friend. 'I was only too happy to oblige,' he said. 'After all, I know Kieran would have done the same for me.'

Kieran caught his expression, and knew what he was talking about. Back in the dark courtyard with the rain about them, it was

Kieran who had saved William's life at the feet of the monster.

Richard Saxon put down his glass. 'I never once felt that I should have imposed a career on either of you, until now. Knowing what I know, I would have insisted that you both became merchants!'

'But a soldier's life is more glamorous than a merchant's, Father!' Elizabeth protested.

'How can you say that after all we have told you?' Kieran said angrily, removing his hand from hers. 'Murder, killings, and more murder! And why? What was it for? I've had my fill of death and yet I'm no nearer to understanding the reasons for it.'

Elizabeth backed away to the edge of her chair, her mouth hanging open as tears stung her eyes. Kieran bowed his head shamefully as the others sat in silence, shocked by Kieran's outburst.

William stared down at his empty plate and said nothing, hoping that Kieran would apologize first.

'I'm ... I'm sorry ... please forgive me,' Kieran murmured and turned to Elizabeth, unable to look her in the eyes. 'Especially you, Lizzy.'

Placing his napkin on his plate, he rose from the table and bowed slightly. 'If you would all excuse me, I need some time alone,' he said, and left the dining room.

Lord Richard watched him leave, his brow furrowed with concern, while Lady Jane got up from the table and went to Elizabeth's side. She was trying her best to stifle her tears, but she was clearly upset.

'It is as I feared,' Lord Richard began. 'There is a lot of anger in that young man, William.'

'He was coping with it at Deramere, and I'm sure he was feeling better when we returned here. But now ...' William shook his head hopelessly. 'He's probably just tired. It was a long ride from the barracks. I'll speak to him, Father.'

△ III △

The hall from the dining room was flanked with paintings of Saxons-past, dressed in their regalia. The history of the family was long, but only during the last 200 years had the Saxon's enjoyed success sufficient for them to merit being caught on canvas. As William strolled down the familiar hall, he felt the eyes of the Saxons who had built this empire staring down at him. He felt a burden of responsibility that at times was too heavy to take; but that seemed trivial compared to the burden of the events at Gembloux.

At the end of the hall was a small room, a study without books or tapestries, home to a simple table, a chair and a tall, thin window that looked out on the grounds. Lady Jane referred to it as the 'Monk Room', harking back to the days of Henry VIII. It was a hideaway, built because, like his successor, the first Lord of Fairway Hall had an eye for fun, especially enjoying hide-and-seek.

William paused, knowing that Kieran would be inside. The door was thick and painted white to match the wall. A small handle was attached, but from a distance, and to the casual eye, there was no way of telling the door from the wall. William knocked and waited. Finally it opened slightly and William pushed his way through the gap.

'I thought you'd be here,' William said, and sat down at the table. 'When we were younger and you wanted to be alone, I always found you here.'

Kieran was staring gloomily out of the window.

'If only I was the same boy who used to sneak in here,' the Irishman murmured. 'But I'm not. I've changed. I've changed so much.'

'Quite,' William replied bluntly and fiddled with his cuffs. 'You're a man who has gone to hide. And you used to be shy, but no longer. Now you're quite content to shout at the people who love you the most.'

'Will ...' Kieran complained. 'Please. You know I'm sorry about that.'

'Yes, *I'm* in no doubt you are,' William said.

'I'll apologize to Lizzie again before I retire to bed,' Kieran promised. 'And to Lord and Lady Saxon.'

'You used to call them "Mother" and "Father",' William remarked. 'Why the formalities now?'

Kieran said nothing. He looked back through the window, the twilight settling on the outside world apart from where the new moon lit the grounds with a milky glow.

'Do you consider me your brother? Or am I Captain Saxon?' William continued, trying to make a joke of it; but Kieran's expression was sour.

'Of course not. You're my friend,' Kieran replied with some effort.

'But no longer your brother?' William suggested.

Kieran sighed. 'We're not even related, Will.'

'That doesn't matter, and you know it,' William growled. 'Ever since you first came here as a boy, I've treated you like a brother and you've been treated as a son by my parents. Nothing has changed, Kieran. In their eyes you are still their son.'

Kieran closed his eyes. 'I know. I'm sorry.'

'Stop apologizing, for goodness sake!' William said, clearly frustrated. 'I want the old Kieran back. The one who would not apologize unless he had to. The one who had so much life ...'

'The one who hadn't had his heart broken?' Kieran suggested.

Now William went quiet. He stood up from the chair. 'I want to help you, but you won't let me,' he said.

'The only help I require is your belief in what happened at Gembloux,' Kieran said. 'You promised you would talk about your suspicions at Deramere, but you've been avoiding the subject for too long.'

'Because I know it won't help,' William replied, sounding as though he'd had this conversation many times. But it was useless to argue with Kieran. 'If you insist, then we will talk.'

Kieran lifted up his hands. 'I can think of no better time than now,' he said. 'At least we won't be interrupted.'

William sat down again and pushed the door to with his boot. 'Alright. We will talk.'

Kieran waited while William seemed to gather himself. It looked like an effort, and the Irishman tried to second-guess what his friend had to say.

'Let us start with the pyramid,' he suggested.

William nodded wearily. 'The pyramid it is,' he replied. 'What do you want to know?'

'Everything, of course,' Kieran replied.

'Well, I found it in that shack, as you know,' William said. 'What I didn't tell you is what happened when I went to touch it.'

'Go on,' Kieran pushed.

'The pyramid seemed to ...' he stopped and shook his head. 'It seemed to attract me. It hummed and shook as though thunder was trapped inside it.'

'How often did that happen?' Kieran asked.

'Once in the shack and once when I put the damned thing in its box. I have not even touched it with my bare fingers. I was ... I was afraid of what might happen,' William admitted sheepishly.

'Do you think this object is somehow linked with the murders?' Kieran asked.

William did not reply to this.

'William?'

'There is more, Kieran. Did you notice an unmarked grave on the way to Katherine's?'

Kieran nodded. 'A grave set far away from the rest? Yes, I know the one. It was defiled when I passed by it ... Who was buried there, Will? It was that ... that thing ... wasn't it?'

'Not a thing, Kieran, a man,' William replied.

Kieran shook his head vehemently. 'We didn't fight a man! It was a monster! How can you keep insisting that Katherine's killer was a man? You were there, Will!'

'I know! I saw it! But I found the corpse of the monster. It was a man, I swear. He was disfigured, but a man nonetheless. You were unconscious by then. It was I who had to show the magistrates what was left while you recovered at the artillery encampment.'

'But it makes no sense,' Kieran complained.

'Maybe not back then,' William said. 'But now, I have my suspicions.'

'Who was he?'

'A Spaniard, wanted by the law.'

'For what crime?'

William pinched his brow wearily. 'Murder, rape, robbery. It was easy for the magistrates to blame the murders at Gembloux on this man. Who was I to argue with the facts as they saw them?'

'But he was only a man,' Kieran reminded him. 'How did he become that beast, Will?'

'I can only surmise from what I know,' William admitted.

'Then tell me,' Kieran said, though he wasn't sure he would believe what William had to say.

'A farmer had seen the Spaniard two nights before. He was visiting someone to the north of the town. A witch.'

'A witch,' Kieran repeated, his disbelief evident.

'Apparently so. In Gembloux lived a witch who cursed the locals and stole from their farms, from soldiers, and even raided battlefields. When I searched her home I found the uniforms of dead men, badges, weapons, everything. As well as her corpse.'

'The Spaniard had killed her?' Kieran ventured.

'It looks that way, but for what, I cannot tell. I saw the murder weapon. It was a bayonet, rusty and quite blunt.'

'But if this Spaniard was the man I killed ... then why kill her with a bayonet? Why not kill her the way the others died, with tooth and claw, like the animal it was?'

William shook his head. 'Do you think I know the answer to that?' he said. 'You asked me my suspicions, and I've told you.'

'You've only told me the facts,' Kieran declared, 'not what you believe.'

William folded his arms and sighed. 'You want to know what I believe?'

'Of course,' Kieran said. 'I want to know if you believe in monsters, Will.'

104

'Really?' William asked, not happy at all with the request.

Kieran nodded.

William struggled and stood up from the table. 'What I believe ...' he murmured and swallowed roughly, 'I believe the Spaniard was the monster. But I believe something happened to him in that shack. I think this witch cursed him somehow. I think she might have drugged him, turned him into a wild animal. And I think the pyramid is the reason for it all.'

William finished and seemed to sag, having unburdened himself. He looked up at Kieran who said nothing.

'Well?' he asked him. 'Is that what you wanted to know?'

Kieran nodded. 'Thank you,' he said quietly. 'I wanted to hear that. I thought I was going crazy. You never admitted to what really happened and that worried me. It was as if I imagined it all. Thank you for being honest with me, finally.'

'Don't mention it,' William said. 'What is the use of trying to ignore something like this?'

'There is no use,' Kieran replied. 'You just have to accept it happened.'

'And then move on,' William murmured.

'No,' Kieran countered, 'you then find out why.'

William shook his head. 'Do we have to dig further into this, Kieran?'

'You're the one who kept the pyramid. Why would you do that?'

William threw his hands in the air. 'I don't know! I just don't know! That thing ... That thing is ...'

'Is what?' Kieran shouted back.

'There is something about the pyramid that intrigues me. I admit, I'm drawn to it,' William said.

'We need to discover its purpose, Will,' Kieran urged. 'We need to discover what it is, and why someone would commit murder for it.'

'That won't be easy.'

'Nothing is easy,' Kieran said. 'It's just necessity. Will you help me or not?'

William stared at his friend. He looked so old compared to the man he had gone to Waterloo with. There was no joy in his eyes, nothing but bitterness and sorrow. He knew there was vengeance buried there as well. William had a feeling that, if he agreed, Kieran's vengeance would lead them to the edge of darkness; but then, he was his greatest friend, his brother, his kin. How could he let him face the unknown by himself?

'Do I have much choice?' he said.

Kieran shrugged. 'Give me the key to the box if you don't want to be involved,' he suggested.

William ran his fingers over the key in his pocket. He always kept it with him now. He had to be sure the box was locked at all times. 'I would rather keep hold of the key,' he murmured. 'And I will help you.'

'Why? Because you don't want that precious pyramid out of your sight?'

'No,' William replied. 'Because you are my brother, remember? It does not matter if we're not of the same blood. I cannot let you face this alone.'

Kieran looked relieved and put out his hand. William shook it.

'Thank you, brother,' Kieran said. 'And I too have an idea about that pyramid of yours.'

△ IV △

William woke early on the fifth day after their arrival, his sleep troubled by nightmares that had rarely left him since Gembloux. As he walked past the other bedrooms, he listened keenly to the sound of the household whispering from the lower halls and rooms. Already the senior staff were cleaning and tidying while the kitchen maids began preparing breakfast. It had been this way every morning as far back as he could remember, and it was a routine he would never tire of.

He went to Kieran's room and knocked, thinking the Irishman would be near to waking. There was no answer. He pushed the door open slowly, but found the bed empty and Kieran's nightclothes already cast across the unmade sheets. Scratching his head, William went back to his room and dressed himself in a shirt and breeches that Mother had bought him two days ago.

Pulling on his jacket, he trotted down the stairs of the main hall, bidding the staff good morning as they laboured around him, dusting the floors, and the frames of the great paintings, and polishing the handrails.

Robert came in through the servants' quarters and William managed to collar him. 'Master William, sir! Good morrow to you! It isn't like you to be up and about so early, sir.'

'Well, the sun is shining and it would be such a pity to waste a fine day. My mournful Irish friend – have you seen him?' William asked.

'Aye, sir, I have. Master Kieran went riding with Miss Elizabeth an hour ago. They got up at the crack of dawn, sir.'

William nodded and smiled, faintly amused. 'Really? That's good,' he said, though more to himself than to Robert. Kieran had been a little secretive since they had last spoken but at least he was mending his friendship with Lizzy.

Tapping his boot heel with his riding stick, William heard another sound at the door, and the head housekeeper marched towards him, her expression serious. 'There's a gentleman outside asking for you, Master William,' she said uncomfortably.

'A gentleman?'

'A man from the city, sir. He wants to talk to you and Mr Harte, sir.'

'Of course,' William replied, a little surprised. He followed her to the main entrance, where a man stood dressed in a plane brown jacket and cream breeches. He wore spectacles and looked impatient as he waited on the steps while Skinner attended to his horse.

'Captain William Saxon?' the man said.

'Yes? And you are?' William asked.

'The name is Darkwood, sir. Hilary Darkwood.'

△ V △

Lady Jane used to say the borough of Lowchester was not just the centre of the county, but the centre of the world. She had said it with Elizabeth in mind and her young, impressionable daughter was romantic enough to believe it. That is until William and Kieran left for the Peninsular War, travelling across the true world and far away from Lowchester. After that, Lowchester didn't seem so great – merely a star among thousands of stars – and Elizabeth was filled with the need to travel as they had.

'I once asked Father for all these fields,' she said, as they halted their horses at Mazey Top, overlooking the meadows of Dunabbey. The fields and woods stretched to the horizon. The church steeple of Dunabbey marked the village from afar.

'Did he give them to you?' Kieran asked.

Elizabeth laughed. 'He said, "What would you do with such a gift? Would you turn the land to farmland? Would you ride on it all day and all night? Or build a hall like Fairway?"'

'So what did you say?'

'I said I would give it to the poor,' Elizabeth replied, and smiled. 'So Father gave a third of Fairway back to the village. He didn't own the meadows down here, but then we never needed land.'

'Just the trade,' Kieran said.

Elizabeth turned to him. 'William told me that Father has offered you a role in the family business.' Kieran nodded. 'So you accepted?'

'I've seen enough battles,' he replied, trying to appear confident about his decision. 'Maybe life as a merchant would be more agreeable.'

'You could stay at Fairway,' she added, beaming.

'Maybe.'

'The Hall is always a lonely place when you and Will leave. I get lonely.'

'Well, I don't have any plans to leave at the moment,' Kieran admitted and noted the look of hope in her eyes. She steered her horse by his and reached out to touch his gloved hand.

'I'm glad,' she said, and flicked her hair back. 'Do you see that pool over there? The one with the willow at the edge?'

Kieran nodded.

'I'll race you!' she shouted. Her horse was at a gallop before her laughter reached Kieran's ears.

He spurred his horse after her as they raced down the hill towards the meadows, laughing giddily as he caught up, but she was always several strides ahead.

At the pool, Elizabeth pulled up her horse and cantered to the willow. Dismounting, she tied the reins to the tree and walked over to the pool's edge. Kieran dismounted nearby and led the horse over to the pool to drink.

'Do you remember coming down here when you two were boys?' she asked.

Kieran nodded. 'Your brother threw me in here once. He thought he'd drowned me. I held my breath for so long he jumped in to save me. I remember his face quite clearly.'

'Nothing has changed, do you not see?' she said, and ran her fingers across the surface of the pool. 'He saved you again in the battle.'

Kieran nodded. 'Yes. And I saved him,' he murmured.

Elizabeth frowned. 'What do you mean?'

Kieran walked over and crouched beside her. 'Elizabeth, there is a reason why I have been ... why I have seemed so distracted. It isn't just because of the battle, or from my wounds.'

Elizabeth looked away. 'I know Father and Will have been keeping something from me, maybe even Mother. I thought it best not to pry.'

'I thank you for that,' Kieran said, taking her hand. 'It makes this easier to tell you.'

Getting comfortable at the side of the pool, Kieran took a deep breath and composed himself. 'After the battle, I was taken to a place nearby. A town called Gembloux. Before the battle I had met someone in that town, someone I ...' He paused. 'Someone I loved very dearly.'

'A woman?' Elizabeth said softly, her expression disappointed. Kieran nodded. 'You were in love with her?'

Again Kieran nodded. 'Yes. We were ready to make a life with each other, but something happened soon after the battle. Something terrible.' He closed his eyes as he recounted the events. 'A killer was loose in the town. Many people were killed, soldiers as well as locals. But Will and I tracked the killer down and ... and we avenged the deaths of those people. One of those murdered was the woman I was in love with.'

Elizabeth was still reeling from the news that Kieran had fallen in love, but she managed to feel sad for his loss. 'She was killed?'

Kieran nodded with difficulty. 'It felt as though something had been ripped from my life. The same way I would feel if I lost you, or Will, or Mother or Father,' he croaked. He cleared his throat and looked out across the shining pool.

Elizabeth pondered this for a moment and Kieran noticed that her hand was caressing his. 'I wish you had spoken to me earlier about this. I could have helped,' she insisted.

Kieran smiled and touched her cheek with his glove. 'Lizzy, you have helped me more than you know. I couldn't have come this far without you. To ride here – to sit by the pool – all these things would have meant nothing to me without you being here.'

'You mean that?'

Kieran nodded firmly.

'Then I will let you mourn, and still be there if you need me,' she said, and got up from the pool. 'And when you have mourned enough, and if you love me enough, might I be so bold as to think that I might occupy the place that she once did?'

Kieran felt uncomfortable again, but tried to put a brave face on his feelings. 'I don't know, Lizzy. Right now I'm not sure how I feel about anything. Maybe – sometime in the future – I may look at you with those same feelings, but I cannot tell you when.'

Elizabeth nodded. 'Then I will wait for that time,' she said, untying the horse from the willow.

'Come! We must return home before Mother and Father send out Robert and his dogs to look for us,' she said, and mounted her horse.

Kieran, feeling confused again, took his horse's reins and led it away from the edge of the pool. Climbing into the saddle he looked skyward and noticed the clouds massing high above. They were dark, the colour of slate. Taking up the reins, he kicked his heels in and rode after Elizabeth as the first raindrops began to fall.

△ VI △

By the time Kieran and Elizabeth had reached the bridle path running to the main hall, the heavens had opened and the rain drenched them. Kieran wiped the water from his face and grumbled as his clothes stuck to him in the downpour. Elizabeth had taken to fits of squealing and laughter. Skinner dashed out of the stables to get the horses inside.

Dismounting quickly, Kieran shielded Elizabeth from the rain as they raced up the stone steps to the main doors. Overhead there was a flash, followed closely by a roll of thunder that went from east to west. The head housekeeper was quick to open the doors as they arrived at the last step, and was just as quick to close them again when they made it inside.

'I'm a little wet, I think!' Elizabeth giggled, and then proceeded to wipe the water from Kieran's cheek.

'Raining, is it?' William said from the far end of the hall.

Kieran looked up from Elizabeth. 'A little,' he said, and rubbed his wet jacket. 'Nothing a roaring fire couldn't dry, though.'

'Well that will have to wait,' William said.

Kieran's mood faltered.

'We have a visitor,' he said, and led him to the drawing room.

Kieran glanced back at Elizabeth and smiled apologetically. She gave him a slight wave and then disappeared upstairs to change.

William pushed the drawing room doors open and Kieran found a man standing by the fireplace, staring at the portrait hanging over it. As they entered, he stopped staring and turned to them both, regarding Kieran through his spectacles.

'Mr Harte?' he said, and walked over, his hand outstretched.

'Yes,' Kieran replied. 'And you are?'

'Darkwood, sir,' the man replied.

'Of course,' Kieran said, and shook his hand. 'Hilary Darkwood. I didn't expect you here so soon.'

Darkwood looked down at his wet hand and flicked the water from it. 'Quite, sir, quite. I took the opportunity to ride here sooner rather than later. Following your letter.'

'Darkwood?' William frowned. 'Why is it I know that name?'

'Because you were once taught by a mutual friend,' Darkwood said. 'Surely you remember Dr Ergan?'

William nodded and smiled a little. 'Of course I do. He was the finest teacher Kieran and I had ... I mourned his death greatly.'

Darkwood rubbed his spectacles with a piece of cloth he had in his pocket. 'We all did, sir. And none greater than I. But when death knocks upon one's door, there is very little to keep it away.' Darkwood replaced his spectacles on the bridge of his nose and stared at William.

'Kieran sent you a letter?' William asked.

'Yes,' Darkwood replied, and pulled the letter from another pocket. 'It said you needed to see me rather urgently.'

William laughed. 'I apologize if I seem a little bewildered, Mr Darkwood. Kieran has not kept me abreast of events here at Fairway Hall.' He stared at Kieran with more than a little irritation in his eyes.

Kieran took William aside.

'I sent the letter three days ago, after we spoke,' he murmured.

'What did you tell him?' William demanded under his breath.

'Nothing. Only that we found something in Gembloux,' he said indignantly.

'But this man is a stranger. It does not matter if he knew Dr Ergan. You have brought a stranger into this, and I do not like it.'

'He was the only one we could ask. Dr Ergan said that if we ever needed help with anything academic, then we should either go to him or to his friend and colleague, Mr Darkwood here,' Kieran reminded him. 'Do you know of anyone else we could have brought into this? Well, do you, Will?'

William stepped back reluctantly. 'No. You did what was right, of course. There is no one else.'

'Gentlemen? Is there a problem?' Darkwood asked from behind them.

'Not at all, sir,' Kieran replied, still staring at William.

The man began rubbing his spectacles again. 'Well then, I think it is best if I view this strange object of yours. Agreed? Let me see if I can unlock a few mysteries for you.'

CHAPTER SIX

The Battle at the British Museum

△ I △

Lord Richard Saxon grumbled into his tea as he watched his son packing a small case on his bed. William in turn said nothing, but hurried, throwing a shirt and some breeches and other clothes into the case. It took only a few minutes to pack.

'You've only been here for a few days, and now you're leaving again?' Lord Richard sighed.

'We'll return in two days' time, Father,' William promised.

'Your mother only sees you for a minute and now you're riding off to London ...' Lord Richard continued, conveniently ignoring William's promise. 'All because of this fellow, Blacktree ...'

'*Darkwood*, Father,' William corrected.

'Darkwood, Blacktree, I disliked him anyway,' Lord Richard grumbled. 'Sheepish character. Could not keep eye-contact with me for one minute.'

'I would call that *shyness*, Father,' William remarked. 'Mr Darkwood is just a little *withdrawn*.'

'A hermit, you mean,' his father sighed. 'He sounds even more unlikable.'

'Ergan vouched for him, before we lost the good doctor,' William assured him.

'I did not like that Ergan fellow either,' Lord Richard said, and hunched his shoulders. 'Far too eager to bury himself in stuffy old books.'

'He was a good teacher, though,' William remarked. 'And you were happy enough for Kieran and me to be tutored by him when we were boys.'

'True,' Lord Richard admitted, grudgingly. 'He knew how to control the both of you. Tell you stories about knights and dragons and you would sit forever, listening to all manner of poppycock!'

'Dr Ergan was a splendid teacher, sir. And a good choice as a tutor,' William reiterated. 'When he died suddenly, Kieran and I felt the loss, even though we never told you or Mother. Dr Francis did not replace him for one moment.'

'Dr Francis was your mother's suggestion,' Lord Richard said.

William paused in his packing. 'What did happen to Dr Ergan, Father? You never told us.'

'Because you were both too young,' Lord Richard said. 'He was murdered by some Spanish men in Southampton. They were meant to be merchants, but were in fact thieves and pirates.'

'Then the rumours were correct,' William said unhappily.

'Rumours?'

'Kieran and I learnt what happened during our visits to Dunabbey. The Landlord of The Mulberry Tavern told us as much.'

Lord Richard frowned disapprovingly. 'Be that as it may, Dr Ergan was not necessarily a good judge of character. His murder is a testament to the dangers of trusting the wrong sort of people. As for this Darkwood fellow ...'

'He is a respected historian from the British Museum,' William stated. 'Hence our departure for London this evening.'

'But so quickly?'

William nodded. 'Yes. It cannot wait.'

'What is so important that it cannot wait for a few days?' Lord Richard grumbled.

William glanced at the wooden box to the side of his case. 'I cannot tell you,' he said.

'What?' Lord Richard said angrily. 'My own son keeping secrets from me!'

'Father!' William protested. 'I will tell you when I can. But now it is necessary that we keep certain things from you and Mother.'

'We? Kieran as well?'

'Yes. Kieran knows also,' William admitted and put the box in a bag with a drawstring attached. 'It was Kieran who contacted Darkwood.' He picked up the bag and the case, and walked out of his room with his father close behind.

'Please trust me, sir,' William pleaded.

'Is this about your adventures in that town near Brussels?' Lord Richard guessed, as they got to the top of the stairs.

William paused. 'Yes,' he replied, 'this *is* about Gembloux. But that is all I can tell you at the moment.'

'All I need to know is that both of you are safe,' his father said reluctantly.

William rested the bag and case on the carpet, and hugged his father. 'We are not in danger, sir. I promise.'

Lord Richard nodded silently and left him at the stairs. At the bottom stood Kieran who had packed and was waiting for his friend. Standing by him was Elizabeth.

'Do you have to go?' she asked, as William bounded down the steps.

'It's only for a short while,' Kieran replied, as William handed him the sack with the box tied inside.

'We'll be back before you realize you've missed us,' William said, and kissed his sister on the cheek. She rubbed it away petulantly.

'I miss you right now,' she said grumpily.

William took back the bag and walked to the front doors, leaving Kieran to say goodbye.

'Always running away, Kieran,' Elizabeth said.

'I know,' Kieran replied, and glanced to William who had his back to him. Elizabeth looked beautiful in her summer dress; her figure was slim and girlish, but he had no doubt that under the layers of clothing beat the heart of a woman. Any man who married her would count himself lucky.

Kieran reached over to kiss her gently on the cheek, but she moved her face and her lips met his. For a moment they lingered and the kiss seemed to hang forever, the barest of touches on each other's lips.

Kieran moved away suddenly and blushed. 'I ... I ...' he stammered.

'You must go,' Elizabeth said, and sighed. 'I know.'

Kieran left her at the stairs and walked away, not even pausing to say goodbye. He felt agitated; agitated that they had kissed, agitated that it had felt so good.

William stood aside and let Kieran pass, before waving to Elizabeth. They walked down the grand steps of the hall to where Skinner was waiting with their horses. As they loaded the cases and bags over the saddles of their mounts, William looked at Kieran.

'She loves you,' he said.

'I know,' Kieran replied.

'Are you sure you know?' William remarked. 'If you knew how much then you would make an honest woman of her.'

Kieran paused as he checked the horse's bridal. 'Katherine has been dead for less than two months and you want me to think of another woman?'

William shrugged. 'It was an observation. And Lizzy's my sister.'

Kieran climbed onto his horse. 'Leave your observations here, Will,' he warned before trotting away.

'As you wish,' William replied, climbing onto his horse. He glanced at Fairway Hall for a moment, wondering what London had in store for them, before he galloped after his friend.

△ II △

They arrived in London as night fell. Riding to Bloomsbury had been a trial, but thankfully it was not too far now. They had galloped in silence for the most part, as both men had much on their mind: Kieran his kiss with Elizabeth, William the visit from Darkwood.

Despite Dr Ergan's recommendation, Hilary Darkwood had

arrived at Fairway Hall most unexpectedly. If William had been honest with his father then he would have agreed that he did not trust Darkwood either, and felt uneasy about travelling to London on such a precarious errand. But despite his unease, he had allowed the man to view the pyramid shortly after his introduction. Darkwood had taken little time in getting to the point, something that William was quick to remember as they approached Bloomsbury:

'The pyramid, please?' Darkwood had requested again after William had at first ignored him.

'Of course,' William replied, though it took a prod from Kieran to make him leave the drawing room to collect the box from his bedroom. Making sure that no one, neither family nor servants, could interrupt them, William had returned with the box and pulled the drawing room door closed behind him.

With only the slightest sense of melodrama, William reached into his pocket and brought out the key, pausing a while before he unlocked the box. This hesitation interested Darkwood. He pushed his spectacles further up the bridge of his nose.

'I understand you came by this object in Brussels?' he asked.

William nodded as the box unlocked. 'A town just outside Brussels called Gembloux.'

'Foreign, is it?' Darkwood had asked.

'That is for you to decide,' William had replied, and lifted the lid.

Darkwood leant over and peeked down into the box. He frowned and shook his head.

'I've never seen anything like it,' he remarked.

'I doubt many have,' William replied, and looked up at Kieran, who fidgeted.

'Do you have an idea what this is, Mr Darkwood?' the Irishman asked.

'Made of bronze, I think ... It looks quite valuable ...' Darkwood began.

'I was not expecting a valuation ...' William grunted, but

stopped short as his friend scowled at him.

'May I pick it up?' Darkwood asked.

'Of course,' Kieran replied, but William stopped Darkwood and held his wrist before he could reach in.

'Is something wrong?' Darkwood frowned. 'I won't drop it, you know.'

William swallowed fearfully and looked down at the pyramid still shinning out from the box. 'Yes ... I know you won't,' he spluttered. 'I'm just unsure about what it might do.'

'*Do?*' Darkwood murmured. 'That is curious.'

'Let me show you,' William said. Even though he had felt reluctant, he knew a demonstration was necessary. He breathed out slowly and put his hands in the box. As his fingers neared the sides of the pyramid, there came a humming sound, ever so slight, but still obvious to the historian's ears.

'*Very* curious,' he said, delightedly. He smiled and looked at William and Kieran. 'Could I try?'

William looked uncomfortable but stepped back anyway. 'Be my guest,' he said.

Darkwood pushed his spectacles up the bridge of his nose again, and reached in, inadvertently touching the bronze symbols. There was a louder hum now, and Darkwood flinched once, then twice, before recoiling from the object, holding his hand as though it was on fire.

'Mr Darkwood!' Kieran said, and took his arms. The historian could only look around in bewilderment before glancing at his fingers.

'What is it?' William said.

'I touched it,' Darkwood murmured.

'I told you not to.'

'I'm sorry,' Darkwood said, blinking hurriedly. 'But that was most surprising.'

'What happened?' Kieran pressed.

'I saw something. Like a vision,' he replied. 'I saw ... flames ... a mountain of fire.'

Kieran stared at William. He looked more unhappy than ever.

Darkwood closed the box and regarded it fearfully. 'You must bring this to the museum,' he said.

'The British Museum?' William said, unconvinced. 'What good will that do?'

'There are people there who could help, Captain Saxon. Good people. This is beyond me. But I think you are right to keep it in a box.'

William crossed his arms with a 'told you so' expression.

'When shall we come?' Kieran asked.

Darkwood handed William the box and marched out of the drawing room with his hands in his pockets. 'Today, of course,' he replied.

'Today?' William said. 'Why today?'

'Aren't you as curious as I am about what this is?'

'Of course we are,' Kieran replied for William.

Darkwood threw his hands up and held them there, smiling awkwardly. 'Well, I doubt you would want me to take the box to London myself.'

'Certainly not,' William said.

'Well then ...' Darkwood fiddled in his pocket for his watch. 'This was indeed a fleeting visit, but worthwhile. I should get back to London by late afternoon.'

'You came all this way just to see it?' William said.

'Of course. Men in my profession have travelled hundreds of miles just to see a desiccated body wrapped in a shroud. Travelling twenty miles or so from London is no hardship, Captain.'

'We need time to pack,' Kieran had said. 'But we will visit you.'

Darkwood snapped shut his pocket-watch and beamed. 'I'll be at the museum until the early hours of the morning.'

'That late?' William mused. 'Do you not have a home to go to?'

'A home, yes,' Darkwood replied. 'But my life is in that museum. The mysteries of time do not unlock themselves, Captain.'

'Then we'll call upon you, sir,' Kieran said.

William hadn't known what to say to Kieran. All of a sudden his life was being controlled by his best friend and a strange introverted man called Hilary Darkwood. But then these were strange times.

And the vision Darkwood had seen troubled him. William had seen enough flames of late to know that Darkwood's description of a mountain of fire was not pure coincidence. At least he'd been right to keep the pyramid locked away.

The evening smog had grown worse under the summer heat; thick strands of fog and smoke hung in layers about each street. The gas-lamps were like balls of light hanging in the air. William and Kieran noticed very few people out in the dull evening.

They arrived at some lodgings just before eight, and waited as their belongings were carried to their room. After checking in, they left again on foot and searched out the British Museum, which lay to the north.

As they walked, William finally spoke up. 'I hope this isn't a wasted journey.'

'It won't be.'

'How can you be so sure?'

'I can't. I'm being optimistic.'

'That's in your blood. My father says all Irishman are optimistic,' William remarked.

'If you didn't want to come, you should have stayed at Fairway Hall.'

'And let you get into trouble? What sort of friend would I be?'

Kieran shook his head. 'Are you sure it's not because you couldn't bear to part with that pyramid?'

'Nonsense!' William snapped. 'I'd sooner lose that damned thing than ... than ...'

'Than what?'

William halted. 'Than lose my best friend.'

Kieran nodded and looked down at the bag in William's hands. 'So would I. Which is why we're here. If this pyramid has no connection with the murders, you'll be able to get rid of it once and for all. Maybe Darkwood could take it off your hands.'

William lifted the sack and looked a little more cheerful. 'Yes. Maybe he could.'

Kieran patted his friend's shoulder playfully and they moved on down the dark streets, passing shadows in the gloom, until they entered Bloomsbury and found a large building with wrought iron fencing surrounding it.

William and Kieran approached the gates of the museum and two men in uniform approached them.

'We're here to see Mr Darkwood,' Kieran said.

'An' your business with 'im is?' the guard demanded.

'It is a private matter, sir,' William replied impatiently. The guard glowered at William and glanced down at the sword by his side.

'He is expecting us,' Kieran added. 'Even this late.'

The guards grumbled and stared at William again.

'He mentioned that two soldiers would be looking for 'im,' one of the guards said. 'You don't look like soldiers to me.'

'We're out of uniform,' Kieran said.

William shook his head. 'I'm growing tired of this,' he said, and pulled out his sword. The two guards went to their own weapons but William held up a hand.

'Calm down, gentlemen,' he said. 'Do you recognize this emblem?'

The guards stared at the engraving on the hilt of the sword.

'I am a Captain of the 1st Dragoon Cavalry, gentlemen,' William said, and sheathed his sword again, 'and we are expected.'

The guards glanced at each other and nodded, relieved that they didn't have to fight. Standing aside, the guards produced a crudely drawn map.

'You'll find Mr Darkwood 'ere, at the oratory, in the east wing,' one of them said.

'Thank you,' Kieran replied, and took the map.

'Your captain friend should watch his temper, sir,' the other guard remarked. 'And 'is sword.'

William ignored them and marched up the drive towards the steps of the museum.

'That could have been better,' Kieran murmured to William as they walked away. 'What is the problem Will?'

'Nothing,' William said dismissively. 'But the sooner we go home, the better.'

The museum was quiet, having closed its doors to the public some hours before. They met only one person during the walk through the main lobby and the great hall, a caretaker who was sweeping the stone floor. He gave them further directions to the east wing, and they walked alone in the echoing halls of paintings and stuffed animals, pausing to glance at the bones of some creature that had died far away in the past.

'See, William,' Kieran whispered. 'Monsters existed then as well.'

'And dragons once existed too,' William scoffed. 'These bones are thousands of years old, Kieran. Monsters should not exist in the here and now.'

Realizing he couldn't convince William, Kieran led him away from the display and they walked up a flight of stairs to another corridor.

'Where are we?' William asked.

Kieran glanced down at the map. 'We should be near the oratory by now.'

'We are lost,' William said loudly, not caring who might listen. To all intents, the museum was silent as the Dead. 'I've never been lost in a museum before.'

'We are not lost,' Kieran insisted, but his frown suggested he wasn't so sure. 'It should be up ahead. Past those display stands.'

They walked onwards into a long room with a tall ceiling. It was dimly lit and only an occasional oil lamp shed any light in the great expanse. Either side of them were more cases of glass with stuffed animals inside them. There was a bird with a long neck, a tall bear and several pigs and rodents, all frozen into a pose that looked quite unnatural.

William frowned. He'd seen stuffed animals before, but this

was truly macabre. He had never been to a museum like this, and was glad of it.

'I told you he was strange,' he commented. 'Look at all of this!'

'*Keep your voice down,*' Kieran whispered back. 'This is a museum.'

'Who's going to hear us? There's no one here! And if Darkwood can hear us, then great. He can find us!' William replied loudly, his voice echoing about the hall.

'That is not the point, Will. It is about etiquette. You of all people should ...' Kieran began and then fell quiet at the sound of something toppling. There was a crash and a thud. Both men froze.

'Hello?' Kieran called out. 'Mr Darkwood?'

There was no reply.

William glanced at Kieran. 'Ghosts?' he said.

Kieran frowned, his hand on his sword. 'In a museum like this? Why not?'

William noticed a shadow move from behind the stuffed bear in the corner. And then he noticed more movement up ahead by a peacock in a display case.

His hand gripped his own sword. 'Do ghosts answer back?' William asked.

Kieran flexed his hand on his sword hilt also. 'Not usually. Though, I've never met a ghost, just a monster.'

'Do monsters talk back?' William murmured.

'Experience tells me they don't,' Kieran replied nervously.

'And neither do assassins.'

'Now you're just being paranoid,' Kieran replied as he looked about the hall, the shadows moving around them. 'Maybe they're just curators. Friends of Darkwood's.'

'They could be friends of Darkwood's,' William replied, drawing his sword as a shadow moved swiftly behind the closest display case. 'But I doubt they're the academic type.'

'Maybe they're just being friendly,' Kieran said, and pulled his sword out completely.

'A welcoming party?' William suggested.

'Something like that,' Kieran said, backing against William as several figures appeared to his right.

'Not sure if these boys are going to be very welcoming, Kieran,' William joked nervously, his back meeting the Irishman's.

As they watched, shadows cut off both exits, and from the darkness and behind the displays more figures appeared, almost a dozen cloaked men with gaunt faces. One by one they pulled weapons from their cloaks: knives, swords, axes, even a crossbow.

'I hate it when you're right,' Kieran gasped.

'So do I,' William said weakly as the men closed in on them.

William kept his eyes on the man with the crossbow, the only one of these would-be assassins who had the ability to kill at long distance.

'Come now, boys,' Kieran suggested aloud. 'Surely we can sort out whatever problem you have as peaceful gentlemen.'

'*A se pe 'el,*' one of them hissed back as they closed in.

William laughed. 'That would be a "no", then!' he said, and swung his foot around, kicking the base of the nearest display cabinet, which housed a small stuffed wild boar. It rocked over and almost crushed the man lurking behind it. As it shattered, the strangers attacked.

William broke to the left and brought his sword down on their weapons, as Kieran dived opposite and parried away an assailant with a dagger. The man was swift and quicker than Kieran as he stroked the air with the short blade. Kieran winced as the dagger knicked his hand, but the Irishman had been sword-fighting since he was a child. He feinted to the side, brought up his blade in an arc and ran it across the man's face. He croaked once and fell back, clutching at his gashed features as blood poured from the wound. As he stumbled, Kieran swung the blade again and opened up the man's belly.

William, facing two attackers at once, parried their sabres one after the other. As one tried to strike, William sent another display case crashing down. Both men dodged out of the way, but

William thrust his sword quickly into the nearest man's chest. The tip of the blade disappeared within the black cloak, and the man fell backwards clawing at the air in vain. The second attacker swung wildly at William, who casually cut him in two before turning to three more assailants queuing to fight him.

Kieran meanwhile was wrestling a man with a mace. It had swung too close to his nose, and he managed a well aimed fist that sent his attacker backwards. Kieran then kicked him hard and the assailant fell through a display case containing a long-necked bird. Then came a swishing of air, and Kieran ducked just as a crossbow-bolt struck another display mere inches from where Kieran stood. Before he could find the shooter, two more attackers fell on him with knives. He fell to the floor and wrestled with them, losing his sword. One plunged a knife into his thigh, and Kieran yelled out furiously. He grabbed the nearest man and head-butted him, feeling the man's nose split under the blow. Then he grabbed the second's arm and bit down hard. The attacker moaned and rolled as Kieran flung himself upon him. He took the bloodied blade and thrust it again and again into the man's chest until his thrashings ceased. Getting to his feet, he stumbled over to his sword and then went to the man with the broken nose, who was still kneeling in the broken glass. The attacker looked up, his grey eyes staring angrily behind his smashed face. Kieran regarded him only for a moment before he ran his sword through the man's neck. The man fell to the floor at Kieran's feet. Tying his belt around the cut in his thigh, Kieran spat some bloody phlegm to the floor and turned his attention to William, who was tackling the others.

William was outnumbered and needed help. Kieran gripped his sword and hobbled over. As the Irishman lurched towards the battle, the display cabinets to the left shattered and there was a dark blur as something came at him. It swung and hit him on the side of the head, sending him reeling against a broken cabinet. Pulling himself up, he saw swirling darkness, like a storm of night, whirling to the floor amongst the dead attackers. At once, the darkness fell away in strands of black cloth, and standing there was another man, dressed in leather armour. His face was pale and white like bone, and his long black hair seemed to have a life of its own as it settled eerily about his shoulders. He looked down at Kieran, who grimaced as he looked into two unearthly yellow eyes.

'You have something of mine, Lieutenant,' the man with yellow eyes hissed and pulled out a long black sword carved with ancient symbols. Kieran shuddered as the sword appeared, almost five feet tall. The man brought the black broadsword up to his face and smiled, two sharp teeth appearing from behind its white lips.

'One way or another, you will give it to me,' the man said, and advanced on Kieran.

William parried blow after blow as three of the shadowy attackers drove him into the corner. With each parry he felt weaker. The odds were against them, despite the number they had slain. There was no sign of Kieran, who he'd last seen wrestling with two of their assassins at the other side of the room, and he had no idea if his friend was alive or not. One thing was for sure – their assailants were well trained and fought ferociously. But William was a Captain in the Dragoons, and if he could survive Waterloo and Gembloux, he was damned if he was going to die at the British Museum.

The men pushed him back a few more steps. William felt the display case housing a bear against his back. The men, their faces almost completely covered by satin cloth, continued to lunge with sword and knife. William pushed them away when he could, but with only one free hand it was a difficult task.

'Argh! Enough of this!' he yelled and swung around the bag in the other hand. It completely surprised his attackers and the bag struck the head of one man. The box inside emitted a loud moan which shivered through the air. As the man fell to the floor, his comrades stepped back fearfully, regarding William's new weapon. They stared at the sack and one uttered a shriek.

At once two more attackers appeared, and William's shoulders dropped. 'Oh Lord,' he murmured and decided to turn tail. He dashed down an aisle of cases with the attackers in tow, pausing only to throw some of the displays down in front of them. One shattered and the lead attacker slipped and fell into the case and was skewered by the shards of broken glass. But the remaining assailant didn't even hesitate as he swung his axe at William. William ducked, stumbled, and swung the bag around in reply, just missing the axe-man, who stepped back at the last moment.

Turning again, William ran to the other side of the room and found Kieran being driven back by another assailant, this one different to the others.

'Where is it!' the man with yellow eyes demanded as he struck blow after blow against Kieran's sword. The Irishman felt his arms ringing until numbed by the continuous impacts. His sword was chipped and weakening, and his arms were like lead. He knew very soon he wouldn't be able to stop the black broadsword from cutting him down.

'Tell me!' the man screeched.

'In Hell,' Kieran spat back and the man screamed, before thrusting the blade towards his heart. Kieran fell under the sword as his knees collided with the floor. He then rolled and crawled away as the black sword came down an inch from his ankle, chipping the stone floor with a sharp clang.

He turned on his backside and shuffled away until his hands felt shattered glass on the floor. There was nowhere to turn, and the man with yellow eyes brought his sword down again. Kieran raised his own sword and connected with a loud report. The shock went up Kieran's arm and into his skull, and he fell back. His sword had been shattered in two.

The man with yellow eyes stepped over him and looked down at Kieran's defenceless form, his pallid expression feverish.

'What are you?' Kieran demanded. 'You're no man.'

The creature smiled at Kieran and nodded. 'I am your executioner. Tell me where the Scarimadaen is.'

Kieran heard William fighting nearby. He was holding his own for now, though that wouldn't last for long. 'Never!' Kieran replied finally, swallowing his fear. He closed his eyes as the creature raised its sword. He heard him scream out and then there was another crash of swords very close by.

Kieran opened his eyes, expecting William to be in front of him fighting for his life. He didn't expect to see an old man, half a foot smaller than himself, wrapped in a silver coat, armed with a bright blade and trading blows with the creature.

'Damn you!' the creature said.

'Time you fought with a professional, my cursed friend,' said the old man through deep breaths as he pushed the creature back. Kieran got gingerly to his feet and watched in amazement as the old man began bettering the creature. It was all he could do to take his eyes off the duel, but William's groans caught his attention and he turned behind him to see his friend struggling hand to hand with an club-wielding lunatic with a shaven skull. William was wounded in the arm, yet still he was holding the hand wielding the club that threatened to come down on his skull. His sword had gone, and so had Kieran's, but that mattered not. The Irishman launched himself forward and punched the maniac repeatedly in the kidneys. He groaned and fell sideways, allowing William to push aside the club. He then wrestled it out of the man's arms, and after Kieran kicked him between the legs, the club-man fell to his knees and William recovered his sword, cutting the man's head from his neck.

'Thank you,' William gasped. 'Where's your sword?'

'Broken,' Kieran replied.

William frowned and then heard the fighting in the centre of the room. 'Who in God's name is that?'

'I don't know. Some creature and some old man,' Kieran breathed. 'What is going on, Will?'

William shook his head and grabbed the bag that had been beaten out of his hands by the club-man. They hobbled together to the centre of the room with nothing but one sword and the club Kieran had lifted from William's attacker, expecting a gruelling fight with the remnants of the assassination squad. But the several survivors were standing by and watching as the old man in the silver coat outfought the man with yellow eyes.

The old man seemed to grin as he pushed the creature away, ducking blow after blow of the black broadsword like a man half his age. As the creature lost patience, it growled and thrust wildly towards him. The old man stepped aside and brought his glinting sword down in a blur, severing the creature's hand.

The thing with yellow eyes screamed and held onto the stump, staring down at the hand as it turned to ash on the ground. He hissed at the old man and shoved him aside, before snatching the broadsword from the stone floor. Slipping the weapon inside his cloak, he wrapped it about himself like a shield. With a blast of air, the cloak blurred into a tornado and hurtled up towards the ceiling to one of the narrow windows high above. Kieran and William heard glass shattering and then the whirlwind was gone.

Their eyes fell to the old man, who was standing alone with his sword at his side. The other assassins had also disappeared in the commotion.

'Wha—' William began, and winced as pain shot through his arm. 'What the hell was that?'

'A vampyre,' the old man said, his back to them.

'A what?' Kieran asked weakly, limping over to the old man.

'A lesser daemon of our world,' the old man replied, and sheathed his sword. He turned around and faced them with a look of indifference. 'Some might say you were lucky to escape, my friends. But then you've faced more terrible dangers than this before.'

William held the bag out of view, suspicious of the old man's intentions. 'What do you know of the dangers we've faced?' he demanded.

The old man smiled. 'I know about Gembloux,' he replied, and came forward into the light. He was around five feet tall, and beneath his silver coat he wore a sand-coloured uniform. His hair was long and white, tied into a ponytail, and he sported a small beard.

'Who are you?' Kieran asked.

'My name is Engrin Meerwall,' the old man replied, smiling, 'and I have been looking for you both for three months.'

CHAPTER SEVEN

Engrin Meerwall and the Iberian

△ I △

William stared out of the window of their lodgings onto the smog-blanket of London at night. Although his arm ached, the wound wasn't as deep as he had first feared. Only the skin had been torn; the flesh and bone beneath had hardly been touched. After cleaning it, the old man calling himself Engrin Meerwall dressed the wound and William pulled on a fresh shirt.

'You've done this before,' Kieran remarked as the old man turned to him and began cleaning the shallow knife-cut in his thigh.

The old man nodded. 'Many times, my young friend,' he said, and then attended to the slight cut across Kieran's hand.

Kieran flexed his bandaged hand into a fist. 'It's good. Not too loose, and not too tight. Thank you.'

The old man bowed.

'I still think we should have stayed until the authorities arrived,' William grunted. It was the second time he had mentioned this since they had returned from the museum.

'And what would that have achieved, Captain?' Engrin asked and sat down opposite the fire that Kieran had hastily lit on their return to their lodgings. 'Talking to the authorities would not have saved Mr Darkwood's life, nor the lives of the two guards at the gate,' Engrin explained. 'Both yourself and Master Harte would be under suspicion for their murders by now. As it stands, their suspicions will now fall on the bodies of your would-be assassins, while you are both free men. More importantly, if you *had* stayed, the enemy would have known where you were and they would have returned, and in greater numbers.'

'But I thought we defeated them,' Kieran said.

Engrin shook his head. 'I'm afraid not. They are surprised, maybe slightly shaken. But soon they will return to find you.'

'Why did they kill Darkwood?' William asked. They had found him slumped over his desk with his throat cut.

'Because he was connected to you two,' the old man replied. 'They were after the object you have in that bag over there.'

William cast his eyes down at the bag lying near the fireplace, the flames crackling and spitting nearby. It was all he could do to keep himself from throwing the bag onto the fire. 'I wish I had never taken it,' he murmured, his eyes still on the bag. 'One good man has died because I took it. I wonder how many more will die.'

Kieran collapsed wearily into his chair. 'It wasn't your fault, Will. I was the one who brought Hilary Darkwood into this.'

'Then we are both to blame,' William conceded. He kicked the edge of the elaborate rug and looked up at the old man with an expression of determination. 'You promised an explanation, Mr Meerwall.'

'That I did,' he said, and pulled off his silver coat. He hung it over the arm of the chair and rubbed his hands together. 'Do you have anything to drink, gentlemen? I must admit to being quite parched.'

William sighed but crossed the room to get a bottle of wine. He poured the old man a glass.

'Thank you,' Engrin Meerwall said, and took a couple of gulps. 'Thirsty work, fighting, isn't it?'

'These men ... our attackers ...' Kieran began.

'They are known as the kafalas,' Engrin said.

'*Kafalas?*' William said.

'Servants of Count Ordrane of Draak.'

'What would a count want from us?' Kieran asked.

'He is not just a count. The title means nothing. He wishes

to have dominion over all mankind,' Engrin said grimly. 'He is this world's most dangerous enemy, and what he wants, gentlemen, is the very thing in that bag.'

'The pyramid,' William said. 'I thought as much.'

Kieran stared silently into the flames. Both men fell quiet, knowing they had landed themselves in trouble.

'Unfortunately, you have both been plunged into a conflict that you will not easily be able to clamber out of,' Engrin said, and sipped more of the wine. 'You are marked men, gentlemen. They will hunt you down wherever you are.'

'Because of the pyramid?' William said.

'Among other things,' Engrin replied.

'But how did they know we were here in London?' Kieran asked.

'They followed you, as I did, from Gembloux. At Portsmouth they murdered two crew members of the *Sussex*, a boy and a first lieutenant,' Engrin said. 'I suspect they told the vampyre that you were from the 1st Dragoons, and where you were stationed.'

'But that would lead them to Deramere,' William said, piecing everything together.

'Yes,' Engrin replied. 'That is exactly where they went, Captain.'

It began to dawn on Kieran that something had happened there. He glanced at William who appeared ashen. 'What has happened, Mr Meerwall?'

'A soldier under William's command was killed in suspicious circumstances five days ago. The regiment sent riders to Fairway Hall to contact you but you never received the letter they were carrying. I found the two riders dead yesterday morning. The letter had gone.'

'Do you know the contents of this letter?' Kieran asked.

'I know only that the lieutenant's name was Bexley, and that you were to return to the barracks immediately.'

William stumbled against the wall and bent double as he was struck with an overwhelming sense of loss. 'Bexley,' he sighed painfully.

'Oh God, Will. Bexley,' Kieran moaned. 'What is happening?'

'Bexley would have known nothing about the pyramid!' William exclaimed. 'Why kill him?'

'Because they wanted to know who you were and where you were,' Engrin replied.

Kieran flinched. 'If he'd told them, that would have led them to Fairway Hall.'

William's eyes grew wide. 'No,' he said. 'Not there!'

Engrin held up his hands. 'They must have discovered you were leaving for London, gentlemen. They wouldn't have been able to attack the Hall and then you in London so quickly.'

'That is not good enough, old man,' William growled, and walked over to his belongings, checking his sword. 'We must leave immediately.'

Engrin pushed himself up. 'And travel by night? Not wise.'

'The night will conceal us from the enemy,' William replied, and motioned to Kieran to get up.

'The enemy loves the night, Captain Saxon. It will conceal nothing,' the old man said coldly.

William stopped and turned to him.

'You still do not realize who you face,' Engrin said. 'This is a vampyre, a creature of the night. We know very little about them, except that they never attack in daylight, only at night.'

'They look like monsters,' Kieran remarked.

'That isn't far from the truth, Lieutenant. They are lesser daemons; they straddle the thin line between mortality and immortality.'

'They cannot be killed?' William said.

'It is possible to kill them,' Engrin admitted. 'Just as a daemon can die through decapitation, so too can a vampyre. And that is the one and only way to stop them.'

'Is it the same thing we fought in Gembloux,' William asked. He had stopped packing; a draught of wine was quite tempting.

'No,' Engrin replied. 'You destroyed a daemon. A creature brought into our world through the object in that bag.'

Kieran tapped the bag with his foot. 'This?' he said. 'This conjured the creature?'

Engrin walked over and picked up the bag. Untying the string, he looked inside, shivering just slightly.

'An innocuous-looking thing, isn't it? But highly dangerous,' Engrin remarked.

'But we killed it. We killed the daemon, so why is it so dangerous still?' William asked.

'Because in this war nothing really dies, Captain. You destroyed the *host* of the daemon, but the spirit itself returned to the pyramid.' Engrin drained the last of the wine from the glass.

Kieran looked down at the bag and his face contorted into anger. 'Then we must destroy it! By flames it must be removed forever,' he said, snatching at the bag.

Engrin held it fast and stared into Kieran's eyes. 'It will not burn, Lieutenant. Be sure of it. Mere flames are not enough to destroy this object. There is only one way it can be destroyed safely.'

'How?' Kieran asked.

'It must be taken to Rome and disposed of there,' Engrin replied.

'Rome?' William said, bewildered. 'Why Rome?'

'Because there, in the Vatican, we have the means of purging this object for eternity. Those tools lie in Rome. And that is where you both must go.'

'To Rome?' William laughed angrily. 'You are toying with us, surely?'

'I do not jest, Captain,' the old man said.

'You realize that is impossible,' Kieran said. 'We are soldiers. We cannot just leave.'

'Rome holds the answers you seek,' Engrin said. 'You are not safe here, gentlemen. Here, in England, I cannot protect you. You must leave with me.'

'Out of the question, sir,' William scoffed. 'We are not leaving England. We would be court-marshalled for desertion!'

'I understand,' Engrin agreed and went over to his coat. He rummaged deep in the pockets and pulled out a letter. Opening it carefully, he held it up for both of them to see.

'What is that?' Kieran asked.

'A letter to Lieutenant Colonel Fuller from the Archbishop of Canterbury, "requesting the services of both Captain William Saxon and Lieutenant Kieran Harte, that they be transferred to the Papal State immediately",' Engrin replied.

William leant closer, narrowing his eyes as he read the letter and looked at the signature. 'It is perfectly *real*, Captain. This was signed by the Pope himself, and Arthur Wealsey.'

'The Duke of Wellington?' William gasped. 'Surely not?'

Engrin nodded. 'We have friends in lofty places, Captain. The Church has more power than you know. The agreement for your release was sought within days of landing at Portsmouth,' he said.

'But why?' Kieran asked. 'Why us? You're here for the pyramid, so why bring us to Rome?'

Engrin smiled. 'Because you are needed, Lieutenant. As I said, you have stumbled into a conflict which you will not easily pull yourselves out of. It did not start tonight, and it did not begin in Portsmouth. The moment you destroyed the daemon at Gembloux was the moment your destinies were set in stone. Like it or not, you are now involved in this secret war.'

'What secret war?' Kieran asked.

'The war that has raged for thousands of years, between Heaven and Hell.' He noticed William rolling his eyes. 'Mock if you will, Captain, but you trust your own eyes, don't you?'

William said nothing.

'Or perhaps you don't? After all, I recall that the report you wrote on the events in Gembloux failed to mention the existence of the daemon? Am I correct?'

William grew angry and his nostrils flared. 'How do you know about that report?' he demanded.

'Friends in lofty places,' Engrin reminded him. 'I have read it. A surprising piece of fiction – though no doubt more credible than what really happened.'

William stormed forward and Kieran stepped into his path to stop him from doing anything unwise. 'Do not dare tell me what

I should or should not have written, sir! I am a soldier, and soldiers do not see monsters! What else was I supposed to write?' he shouted.

'You acted properly, of course,' Engrin replied, folding his arms. 'You do trust your eyes, then?'

William calmed down. 'I trust what I can see, touch, smell and hear,' he growled back.

'So you agree that daemons walk our streets?' Engrin asked.

William wanted to deny it, but couldn't.

'Good,' Engrin said. 'Because that is what this war is about, gentlemen. That is why it is a secret – because people like you, Captain, do not want to believe in it. But you have both seen enough to know it is all true. Which is why you must come to Rome.'

Kieran wandered to the window. 'If we are ordered by the Duke of Wellington himself, then there's nothing to stop us from going,' he murmured.

'Except our family,' William added. 'What about my family, Mr Meerwall? Do you propose I leave them?'

Engrin nodded.

William was about to respond when a sudden knock at the door silenced him.

Kieran and Engrin froze, and William pulled his sword from the black scabbard.

The knocking came again.

'Yes?' William said.

'It's only the landlord, sir,' a voice said from behind the door. 'A rider has arrived. From your father.'

William glanced at Kieran. 'A rider?' he mouthed silently.

'Maybe we should see him?' Kieran whispered.

William frowned. 'Very well, send him in,' he said, his hand gripping the sword tighter.

Kieran walked over and unlocked the door, opening it quickly as William stood ready. The door opened and the landlord, Mr Tate, let out a yelp of surprise as he stared at William's sword. 'Oh sirs! I'm sorry to be disturbing you!' he exclaimed.

Behind him was the stable-boy they knew from home.

'Skinny?' William said, his frown deepening.

The stable-boy smiled awkwardly. He was red-faced and out of breath.

Kieran appeared around the side of the door. 'What are you doing here?' he asked.

'Lord Richard sent me, sir,' Skinner replied. He stared at Engrin with suspicion.

'Come inside, boy,' William said, and turned to the landlord, added, 'I'm sorry for giving you a fright. We weren't expecting visitors.'

'Of course,' Mr Tate said sheepishly. 'Goodnight, gentlemen.' The landlord hurried away and Kieran locked the door again.

'Well, tell us why you're here,' William pressed the boy.

'There's been a tragedy, sir,' Skinner said. 'Robert the grounds-man was found murdered in Dunabbey.'

William put a hand to his mouth.

'Robert?' Kieran said, and took Skinner's arm. 'Are you sure?'

The boy nodded, appearing afraid. 'They found his body an hour after you left. Your father sent me because the other servants were combing the grounds for intruders. Lady Jane and Miss Elizabeth were sent to the Grendell house, sir.'

'They are safe?' Kieran asked.

'Yes, sir. Very safe,' Skinner replied.

'And do they know who killed Robert?' William asked.

Skinner shook his head.

William blew out through his cheeks and paced the room, while Kieran sat down, his mind racing through what could have happened. Both men knew there was only one choice open to them.

'Skinner, ask Mr Tate downstairs to fix you a room under my father's name,' William said. 'You've ridden enough tonight and it's too dark to send you out again.'

Skinner looked relieved and smiled boyishly. 'Thank you, sir.'

'Go,' William said, and Skinner left the room.

Nobody spoke for a long time. Engrin sat fiddling with the

drawstrings on the bag, until Kieran spoke. 'Will, if this is true, we can never see Fairway Hall again.'

'What are you talking about?' William replied distantly.

'They killed Bexley, Will. They killed Darkwood, and now Robert. They'll kill Father, Mother, and Lizzy if we don't stay away from Fairway Hall. Can't you see that?'

'No, I cannot believe that,' William protested miserably. 'Everything I have is there. And now you're saying we cannot return?'

'Your friend is right, Captain. If they have killed someone in the employment of your father, then you cannot return there. Not for the foreseeable future. And certainly not while you have the pyramid in your possession.'

'Take the pyramid, old man, and good riddance!' William barked at him. The old man frowned and walked away, leaving Kieran to calm William down.

'You are not helping, Will,' Kieran remarked and held his arm.

'I cannot believe you trust this man!' William scowled, struggling free. 'What evidence do we have that all this is the truth? How can we trust him?'

'He didn't send Skinner. Your father did. And the man saved our lives,' Kieran reminded him.

'I know. But what he asks in return is too high a price!' William replied.

'We have little choice,' Kieran whispered to him. 'Would you risk everything? The lives of the family?'

'No. Never,' William heaved. 'But all I want is to return home.'

Kieran shook his head sadly. Both of them knew that this was now impossible.

Engrin pulled on his silver coat. 'I'll take my leave, gentlemen. There is a ship at Southampton that is leaving for Naples in two days. The ship is called the *Iberian*. I will meet you there in the evening.'

Kieran nodded. 'We'll be there.'

Engrin shook Kieran's hand. 'Goodbye, Lieutenant,' he said, then addressed William. 'I am truly sorry for what has happened, Captain, but nothing I can say will help you decide on the best course of action. Only this will help,' he said, pointing to his heart.

He turned and went to leave.

'Wait,' William said.

'Yes?'

'Take the pyramid with you,' he said, picking up the bag. He tossed it over to the old man, who caught it with his left hand.

'You trust me with it?' he said, glancing down at the bag.

'No,' William replied, and closed his eyes, 'I just want it out of my sight. It has cost me too much already.'

Engrin drew the strings and nodded. 'Until then, gentlemen.'

Watching him leave, Kieran rubbed his face wearily. 'There is much to reckon with,' he murmured. 'We should sleep on this Will.'

'Not yet,' William replied. 'You go to bed. I have a letter to write. Perhaps the hardest letter I've ever written.'

△ II △

They awoke early the following morning. Neither of them had slept well. William had been up until the small hours, writing to the family. It had been a work from the heart but excruciatingly secretive. He wanted so much to tell them what was happening, if only so that he could ask for his father's guidance. William was a man, but only of twenty-five years and he lacked experience of life, always looking to his father for guidance when decisions needed to be made. But not this time. This time the choice was his and Kieran's.

Though, if he was being frank, there had been no choice at all.

'Give my love to Elizabeth,' he had written at the end of the letter. 'I hope to be in contact again soon. Your loving son,

William.'

William had rested his quill sorrowfully by the parchment and considered again what they were doing. He had no idea when they would return to England, no idea when it would be safe to see the family again, and no idea if and when Elizabeth would be able to hug Kieran again. He picked up the quill once more and added an 's' at the end of 'son'. He then wrote Kieran's name next to his and folded the letter.

As he slept (uncomfortably in the chair by the fire, with the letter on the table nearby) he had broken and disturbing dreams. When he stirred the following morning, he was glad to be awake.

At first light he gave Skinner the letter with some instructions: 'Take the main roads. Steer clear of the short-cuts, even if it takes longer to ride. And on no account must you stop. Even if the horse is tired.'

Skinner looked at his master and appeared worried. 'Sir?' he said.

'Yes,' William replied.

'Where will you be?' he asked.

'I cannot tell you,' William replied, and embraced the stable-boy. Skinner looked uncomfortable with it and more afraid than ever.

'But sir,' Skinner protested.

'No more questions, lad,' Kieran told him as William walked back to their room alone.

'When are you returning to Fairway Hall?' Skinner said.

Kieran frowned. 'I don't know,' he replied sombrely. 'Now go.'

Skinner left them to pack their belongings, and Kieran hoped he would arrive safely in Lowchester.

With all that could be done now completed, they left London and travelled the long road to Southampton. The journey took almost two days, but eventually they arrived at the port and the harbour master directed them to the *Iberian*, a sixth-rated frigate at a weight of 600 tonnes. It was not the largest ship they had sailed on, and could have been likened to a chamber pot.

Still, a ship was a ship, was a ship. It had sails, it had a crew, and judging by the ordnance being loaded on it, it had at least some fire-power.

Waiting on the quay was Engrin Meerwall, smiling from ear to ear at their arrival. 'I'm glad you're here, gentlemen,' he said.

Kieran smiled in return, but William scowled, and under his breath said, 'I'm not.'

Once on board they were introduced to the captain of the ship, a gruff man with experience gleaming in his eyes. Captain Gerard told them proudly that his was the fastest freelance ship in Southampton, and had the finest crew in the Channel. Neither Kieran nor William disputed such a claim, especially after the captain was kind enough to give them quarters next to his own. They were to travel as dignitaries and the news softened William's mood.

'You're a Saxon, eh?' Gerard said as they toured the top deck. 'There's a name synonymous with trade.'

'Yes, Captain,' William replied. 'My great grandfather was a merchant in the Americas.'

'Yes, yes! I've heard of the fellow. But things have changed now, haven't they? America is not the same place of opportunity since those damned rebels have taken it over!' the captain grumbled, pausing to bark orders to the crew as the boat made way from the quay under the late evening sky.

Once underway, the *Iberian* glided gently from the port and out towards the Channel and a starry horizon, a gentle breeze taking her sails as the sound of waters dividing rose up from below. The crew of the frigate were efficient and vocal as they prepared the ship and steered it through the throng of fishing vessels and past two battleships moving in from the Channel. Unlike the *Sussex*, the *Iberian* slipped out from the port in secret, with not a single cheer.

William stood on deck, watching the pinpricks of light from the city move farther away. Kieran walked over. 'Goodbye,' William murmured distantly. 'It doesn't seem so long ago that I was saying hello.'

Kieran gave him a friendly squeeze on his shoulder. 'We'll see it again,' he comforted. 'We've seen England fade into the distance many times before Will.'

'Not this time,' William replied. 'This time I fear I will never see her again.'

Shortly, Southampton was simply a collection of bright dots on the horizon, and Kieran and William waited on deck until twilight turned into night.

Soon they were making their way towards the Portuguese coast and down by the Bay of Biscay. 'We'll be in Naples after we've stopped at Gibraltar,' Gerard said on the quarterdeck. 'This is a trading ship, after all, and we have cargo to deliver. But we'll have sight of the Italian coastline in less than a month from now.'

'We're aware of the *Iberian*'s itinerary,' Engrin said, as Kieran and William waited nearby.

'Good then. Well I hate to be rude, but I have chores to attend to tonight and will not be able to dine with you until tomorrow. Mr Murray is a fine cook, and I'm sure your meal will be the best on these seas!' he said proudly. 'As, I hope, are your quarters.'

'They're excellent, Captain,' William replied, glad to be sailing in comfort for once.

The captain laughed. 'Good, good! All part of the service, eh, Engrin?'

The captain winked at the old man, who led Kieran and William quickly away back to their quarters.

'What was that about?' William asked suspiciously.

'I have known Captain Gerard for a long time,' Engrin said, opening their cabin door. The cabin came with four bunk-beds either side of a long table and chairs. At the end of the room was a narrow window that looked out to sea.

Engrin opened his trunk and pulled a sword from beneath his clothes. 'Here,' he said to Kieran and tossed him the blade in its scabbard.

The Irishman pulled the sword free and smiled. 'Solid craftsmanship,' he remarked.

'I always carry an extra sword in case I lose my preferred

blade,' Engrin said. 'While I'm sure our journey to Rome will be free of trouble, I insist you are armed for your own protection.'

Kieran bowed with thanks and regarded the sword gratefully.

Engrin sat down at the table and pulled out his own sword and a cloth from the trunk. He unsheathed the weapon, laying it gently on the tabletop. The sight of the blade pricked William's curiosity and he emerged from his sulk as his eyes alighted on the unusual workmanship. He stared at the sword, shining in the lamplight like a mirror, and asked, 'Is that steel, or some other metal?'

Engrin lifted the sword up and gently passed it to William.

'It's very light,' William remarked, somewhat surprised as he weighed it in his hands.

'Yes, a light sword but well balanced and extremely sharp and strong. It was a gift to me from someone who knew the art of sword-making. It is steel combined with other metals, very much like the Samurai swords of the East, but fashioned in a more European style.' Engrin took back the weapon.

'You must have special friends to receive such a gift,' William suggested.

Engrin nodded, and cleaned the blade in silence. William returned to his bunk, knowing he would get nothing more out of the old man on this subject. It would be many days before they landed in Naples. There was plenty of time to think. He lay back and stared at the wooden ceiling, thinking about Fairway Hall and the life they had reluctantly left behind.

△ III △

The following days crawled by. Life at sea consisted of routine and yet more routine. During those lingering days of long horizons and quiet nights, Kieran and William often talked of what had passed and more importantly, what might happen to them in the future. It was the kind of talk they had relished as young men before their adventures in Spain, but now the future felt like a millstone around their necks. Never had they been so uncertain about their fates.

Engrin had told them little of what to expect, but insisted they trained while the crew of the *Iberian* toiled. 'Not one minute should be wasted on this journey, gentlemen,' he said, and while at the beginning William baulked at taking orders from the old man, eventually he began to grudgingly like the fellow's company. William was amazed how quickly he discovered hidden depths in his sword-play; Engrin seemed to bring the best out of him. The old man even allowed William to use his unique sword on one occasion, and the results were impressive, much to the dismay of Kieran, who found himself with his back against the deck, his newly-acquired sword lying nearby with a small notch in its blade. His arm was numb for a day and William kept apologizing to him for delivering such a blow, though secretly he delighted in teasing him.

On the third night, as they journeyed down to Gibraltar, William stood alone on the top deck and practised new moves with his sword. Before, his style had been offensive, a rider's style, suited to 'carving men into pieces', as Engrin remarked. But now it was graceful; he was able to feint like a ghost, and his parries always turned into attacks on the second turn. His balance had improved and he moved elegantly, not like the cavalry officer he had been.

That night, moving up and down the quarterdeck, swinging his sword this way and that, he paused as he noticed someone watching him.

'You're learning quickly,' Engrin said.

William's cheeks reddened, having been caught in the act. 'Thank you,' he breathed and sheathed his sword. 'You're a good teacher.'

Engrin smiled and gestured him to come over. Both men stood at the railing and looked into the black sea. It was a calm night and the moon played against the water.

'Do you trust me, Captain?' Engrin asked.

William shrugged. 'More so than I did before,' he admitted.

'Good,' Engrin replied. 'Because you will need to have complete trust in me when we arrive in Rome.'

William rested on the rails thoughtfully. 'What is waiting for us in Rome, Engrin?'

The old man smiled. 'Revelations.'

William shook his head. 'You asked me to trust you, yet you will not trust me with the truth,' he said indignantly.

'I have not lied to you,' Engrin rebuked.

'Nor have you told me everything,' he said. 'The pyramid, for instance. What does it do, precisely?'

Engrin pursed his lips. 'Very well. The pyramid is a door to the spirit of an unholy creature. A cage for a daemon.'

'And opening it releases the creature?' William pondered. 'But when we destroyed one in Gembloux it was only a man.'

'It is not the creature that is let loose, William, but the creature's spirit. Once released it possesses the living.'

William frowned. 'You die?' he asked.

Engrin nodded.

'And what of the soul?'

'Once a daemon takes your soul, no matter how strong you are, it burns to ash beneath the weight of the creature's fiery spirit, until there is nothing left,' Engrin said. 'Death is the only release.'

William put a hand to his chest and felt his heart beating beneath his fingers. 'Could I ... Could Kieran have been taken by the daemon?' he said, horrified by the possibilities.

'You were both careful enough with the pyramid,' Engrin said. 'Kieran told me you only ever touched it whilst wearing gloves. That is a start. Direct touch seems to tease the device, but only one thing can unlock it.'

'And that is?' William pushed.

'Blood,' Engrin said.

William flinched. 'Anyone's blood?'

'Just that of the living,' he replied. 'It takes over a person's blood and then their soul. It is like a disease, but one that comes with fire and burning light. It is swift and agonising. And there is no cure.'

William wrapped his arms around himself. 'I would never have believed you, if it wasn't for what I have seen,' he said. 'Tell me more about the vampyres.'

'Their blood is dried and dead, yet they are kept alive by the energy that burns within the pyramids. The Count is a cursed animal that has lived for thousands of years with a daemon trapped inside him. He is able to create more creatures like himself – more vampyres. But each time he creates another, he weakens the daemon within. The one we fought in London is weak compared to some. He is skilled in the dark arts of warfare, but his power is lesser.'

'But greater than either Kieran or I,' William remarked.

'Only because you were surprised,' Engrin replied. 'Now that you know what your enemy is, you will defeat it.'

The old man patted William on the shoulder and turned to leave. 'And now I think you have learnt enough for one night. You will have bad dreams if I tell you more. Goodnight, Captain,' he said.

'William,' he replied. 'Call me William.'

'William it is.' Engrin smiled and wandered away into the shadows.

△ IV △

They stayed at the port of Gibraltar for twelve days, longer than expected. Captain Gerard apologized and ensured that his guests were compensated with bottles of fine wine.

On the thirteenth day, William woke late and dressed quickly, noticing that Engrin and Kieran had already risen. The day was blindingly bright and the sea was about as calm as the pond under the Willow tree at Lowchester. There was a gentle roll to the ship but one that could hardly be felt as he climbed the steps to the upper deck. Kieran was there, cupping his hand over his brow as he stared out across the sea under the glare of the noonday sun.

'Gerard has promised that we will arrive in Naples sometime tomorrow,' Kieran said, and rested on the rail, squinting.

'He keeps apologizing to me for the delay in Gibraltar,' William mused and wiped his sweating brow with a handkerchief. 'Engrin told him apologies weren't necessary. So he apologized again and sent down another bottle of wine!'

Kieran nodded thoughtfully. 'That is the attitude of one who greatly respects his guests.'

'Talking of respect, I must pay Gerard's cook my respects,' William mused. 'I'm famished!'

'We've eaten already,' Kieran smiled. 'But feel free to find some scraps.'

'Well, thank you,' William sighed. 'Where is the old man, by the way?'

'Up there,' Kieran said, pointing to the crow's nest.

William cupped his hands over his eyes and looked up, squinting again. Standing with one foot on a beam, his hands gripping the rigging, Engrin looked out to sea, searching the horizon. 'He holds no fear, does he?' William mused.

'It appears not,' Kieran replied. 'He thinks highly of you, though.'

'Me?' William said.

'We've talked about you,' Kieran said frankly. 'He told me that you are fine soldier and good with a sword. He is glad he discovered us.'

William nodded. 'So we can fight in this secret war of his?'

Kieran shrugged. 'Maybe.'

'What if I don't want to fight?'.

'Do you think we have a choice?' Kieran said.

'Every man has a choice. It is part of being a man. We are no different.'

'Yet the wrong choice could cause the deaths of the people we love,' Kieran said.

William brooded. 'You think this Count will pursue us back to England if we return?'

'I would, if I was him,' Kieran replied. 'We killed one of his

149

kind, killed his servants, and have something he holds dear.'

'And you think that being away from Fairway Hall will stop the family from being attacked?' William said bitterly.

'There would be no reason to attack them. We're here, Will. At sea, and heading to Rome. Why attack our loved ones in England?' Kieran said.

'To lure us back there. As bait.'

Kieran laughed. 'That would be foolish.'

'Would it?' William said, more afraid than before. 'I had doubts when we left Southampton, and now they grow upon me. I fear for my father, my mother and Lizzy. I should be there to protect them.'

Kieran took William aside. 'And your return could doom them. That's the choice, Will. It is a risk, but at this moment, I think we're making the right decision. If we had stayed, the vampyre would have found us. Fairway Hall would be ruins and everyone that we hold dear would be murdered. The pyramid would be in the enemy's hands, and there would be no vengeance for Bexley, for Katherine, for Father, Mother ... nor Lizzy, for we would be dead as well. Perhaps by leaving for Rome, we have lured our enemies away from England. Perhaps the family is safer now.'

William closed his eyes. 'I know,' he murmured, 'I know. I just pray we've made the right decision. If I lost them ...'

Kieran squeezed his arm. 'You won't. We will see them again when this is over.'

William smiled hopefully. 'Of course. You're right. I'm acting like an old woman.'

'You're acting like a responsible son,' Kieran corrected him.

'Yes,' William laughed, 'I suppose I am.'

'And who would have thought that?' Kieran said.

'Years of war change a man. I thought you'd had enough of it.'

Kieran's brow knotted. 'I had. But now I want vengeance, Will. Now I know why it happened, all I want is to ensure it never happens again.'

'You mean by serving in this secret war?'

Kieran shrugged. 'I haven't made up my mind yet.'

'It sounds like you have,' William said.

'I thought you were hungry,' Kieran reminded, unsubtly changing the subject.

William felt his stomach growl. 'Yes. Well, we'll talk about this after breakfast, or whatever scraps the cook has left me.'

William left Kieran under the mizzenmast, and the Irishman felt it safe to put his hand in his jacket pocket. He pulled out the tulip wrapped in the handkerchief. He didn't open it, but felt it gently in his hand, knowing, deep down, that it was a sign of his own weakness to cradle it so dearly. It was the only thing he had left of hers and it reminded him of his loss, though he knew William's reaction would be to toss it over the side of the ship. He would say that Katherine was gone, that there was nothing he could do to bring her back.

'But there is always vengeance,' Kieran murmured, surprising himself that he'd said it aloud. Looking sheepish, he pushed the cloth back inside his tunic.

A voice sounded above him, and he looked up to Engrin, who was pointing to the horizon behind them. Kieran could make out a shadow, obscured somewhat by the dazzle of the sun on the ocean. He crossed from the rail and walked over to the rear of the ship, staring out again. It was the first ship they'd seen in the dozen days since leaving Spain. Some of the crew stared out thoughtfully, others muttering to each other.

Was it so strange to see a ship in the Mediterranean? He doubted it, but something in Engrin's voice had unnerved him. What had he seen? No doubt he would learn of it at dinner later on.

Feeling his skin burn under the glare of the sun, Kieran buttoned up his jacket and returned to his quarters, leaving the sailors with their concerns.

△ V △

On Engrin's advice, Gerard had given the two men in the crow's nest specific orders to watch the pursuing ship. It had gained almost fifty leagues on them since its appearance around midday. The *Iberian* was running at full speed, with all sails unfurled, and they were likely to arrive at Naples in good time. Already the day was beginning to fade.

The first lieutenant scuttled around the crew nervously as the ship gained on them. On two occasions, William had noticed that the captain's first officer was deeply concerned; he had overheard the words 'unnaturally quick in this weather' a few times. Gerard wasn't too worried, just curious to know who was trying to out-sail him. The ship showed no registered colours, and yet it bore no signs of being a pirate vessel or a privateer. Despite this, he issued orders for the crew to be ready for any 'funny business' from the pursuing vessel. What arms they carried were pulled out and the cannons below deck were cleaned and made ready for action.

In the dining room under the quarterdeck, Captain Gerard had dismissed all concerns by the time the first course arrived at the table. 'With the removal of the French and due in part to the operations of His Royal Navy in the Atlantic, the Mediterranean has been free of piracy or privateer actions for many months,' he said to his guests between sips of wine. 'Frigates and a battleship patrol this region, so I doubt very much they would let in any ... how can I put this? Undesirable seafarers?' He smiled and winked at Engrin.

The captain's guests smiled politely, but nervously. Kieran and William had watched the ship gaining and they could feel the tension amongst the crew, especially from Engrin, who had been quiet for most of the day, spending the afternoon hopping from foot to foot and staring out to sea.

'However, complacency has claimed ships in the past,' Gerard continued. 'And even if it is simply a trading ship, battle-readiness is good practise for the crew. Days at sea with not much to do can drive a man to slovenly behaviour and a few drills will sharpen their wits!'

Engrin gave a short nod, but looked worried nonetheless.

Over the first course, a rich broth of vegetables and salted meat, Gerard spoke about the life of a merchant, burying their concerns about the pursuing ship with anecdotes from his new career. 'I've made a considerable amount of moneys from trade over the last few years. Not bad for someone who was once merely a deck officer,' he said, his eyes glazing over as he reminisced.

'And a lieutenant at Trafalgar,' Engrin added and turned to William and Kieran. 'Though Captain Gerard is sometimes too modest to mention it!'

'Tosh, sir' Gerard grunted. 'I just don't believe that talk of battle goes well with eating. It gives me frightful indigestion!'

'The *Iberian* was a Royal Naval frigate, was she not?' Kieran asked.

'Aye, she was. And one of the first. She was originally called the *Kent* but she was decommissioned shortly after the war. I was promoted to captain, after Captain Tiverton was killed in a skirmish off the coast of Spain. Originally it was planned that we would continue pursuing privateers here or in America. But the *Kent* had been damaged too much during its last action and would not withstand another pounding in battle. To completely rebuild and restrengthen the hull would have been as costly as building a new frigate, so they passed the *Kent*'s name to a third-rated frigate under another captain,' Gerard said, pausing to clear his throat.

'You went on to command a battleship, then?' Kieran asked.

'No sir, I passed up the opportunity, and retired. As a gift from the admiralty for my years of service I was given this frigate and renamed it the *Iberian* after the Peninsular Wars I fought in. It was a simple task then to create a small trading company and build contacts across Europe and North Africa. I am glad to say this has been highly profitable.'

William agreed. 'My great grandfather believed so, sir. He also

153

began his trading company under humble origins.'

Gerard smiled rosily. 'I hope fortune favours my affairs as it did your great grandfather's. To have a trading company such as the Saxons' would indeed be a great achievement.'

William raised his glass in appreciation. Despite Engrin's brooding air and Kieran's nervous appearance, William felt strangely relaxed around Gerard.

The captain rested his spoon in the empty bowl and sighed contentedly. 'What did I tell you, gentlemen? Is that not the best broth you've tasted at sea?' he asked, looking pleased with himself. William and Kieran nodded quickly.

'We have very few comforts here, so we make do,' Gerard said, folding and unfolding his napkin. 'It makes a pleasant change to have such company on the *Iberian*. These dogs around me are good men, but rough as three-day stubble. They are uneducated, rowdy and with not one cultured bone between them. However, they are the finest crew I've sailed with.'

William raised his glass again, feeling a little drunk. 'Here, here, sir!'

'They also recognize danger, even if her captain does not,' Engrin murmured.

Gerard glowered at the old man. 'For goodness' sake, man, that ship is far away ...'

'And closing on us,' Engrin remarked. 'I apologize if I seem nervous, but we are sought-after men.'

Gerard frowned and glanced at his other guests. 'You think a vampyre would attack us here, in open sea?' he said.

William felt a shiver as Gerard said the word 'vampyre'. Before, the only people to mention such a creature were he, Kieran and Engrin. Now there was another believer and one that William thought had more credibility than even Engrin. 'You know about vampyres?' he asked Gerard.

'Know about them?' He smiled, though it was without humour. 'I have faced and killed one.'

Kieran looked up from his bowl.

'You are not the only ones to have seen the dark places of this world,' Gerard said. 'I too have faced vampyres, and once a dae-mon. If it is a vampyre, then we'll be ready for him.'

Captain Gerard wiped his mouth on the corner of his nap-kin. He then rose from his seat, looking perplexed. 'If you'll excuse me, gentlemen, I've lost my appetite.'

Kieran was about to say something but Engrin held him fast. The captain left the room in silence and William shook his head. 'Have we insulted him?'

'No,' Engrin replied. 'He is worried for his crew. A privateer could be bested, but he knows that a vampyre would kill many men. If it is a vampyre our captain could lose his crew, even his ship.'

'He sounds prepared for it,' William remarked.

Engrin shook his head. 'There is a difference between prepa-ration and resignation. Anyway, we should finish our meal. If there is a battle, you'll need a full stomach.'

The three of them ate the next course in silence, thinking about what might happen, while on deck, Captain Gerard stared out to sea through a telescope. The ship was coming closer and closer.

CHAPTER EIGHT

The Blackest of Waves

△ I △

Even the heartiest, warmest meal could not keep away the gnawing chill of uncertainty as the darkening at the sky's apex fell to the horizon, where a thin strip of blue light lay, as if stubbornly refusing to succumb to the approaching night. But this faded quickly until there was only the stars and the crescent moon ducking behind the occasional cloud in the sky. For Kieran it was a sublime sight but one tempered with anxiety.

The ship at their heels was closing quickly.

William stood close by, shoulders hunched, breathing out gentle clouds of air that blossomed and melted almost instantly in the cold. His cheeks were rosy and he stamped his feet to keep warm. It did not seem to help.

'A chilly night, gentlemen,' Gerard grumbled, rubbing at his arms.

'Yes,' William replied, 'it is quite cold.'

'You'd think I would be used to cold nights like these, Captain Saxon, but no ... they still take me by surprise,' Gerard admitted. 'And you, Lieutenant, how do you fare in such weather?'

'I tolerate it, sir,' Kieran replied, but his thoughts were elsewhere.

Engrin came over to them, his arms wrapped around himself. His concern was clear as he glanced back up to the crow's nest.

'They've gained another league on us, Captain Gerard,' he said, frowning.

Gerard waved his hand dismissively. 'I'm sure there's nothing to fear. Sardinia is barely fifty miles from here. In daylight we'd probably be able see the coastline. She's probably running for that little island.' The first officer, who had taken station by the steps to the quarterdeck, nodded in agreement. He was nervous, but took heart from his captain's scepticism.

'Running is right,' Kieran murmured to William. 'How much has she has gained in the last half-hour?'

William looked up at the *Iberian*'s sails. They were hardly moving – the gentle breeze not enough to pull them faster than a crawl – yet the closing ship was sailing as though a strong easterly gale was howling across the sea. William felt unnerved. The whole scene was surreal, with every man at his post, waiting for something to happen.

Waiting for a sign maybe, or perhaps even a miracle.

Gerard paced the quarterdeck and pulled out his telescope, looking long and hard to the rear. Shutting the telescope, he beckoned to his first lieutenant who came up the steps. Whispering something to him, the first lieutenant shouted up to the crow's nest.

'Can you see any sweeps or markings?'

The lookouts signalled 'No'.

'It's almost night, Captain,' Engrin whispered. 'Perfect for attack. Perfect for a vampyre?'

Gerard bowed his head and paced the deck again. The first lieutenant waited with William and Kieran. All three men were worried.

'What should we expect?' Gerard asked, turning to Engrin, with his hands clasped thoughtfully behind his back.

'The ship appears to be larger than the *Iberian*. Probably fully crewed, by kafalas or privateers. Either way, they will be armed,' Engrin said.

'A ship that size could out-gun us,' Captain Gerard considered. 'They could even sink us. This ship wasn't refitted for battle.'

157

'They won't sink us,' Engrin dismissed. 'Be sure of it. They will board us instead.'

'Then it will be close-quarters,' Gerard sighed, 'and bloody.'

'Perhaps your men should arm themselves with swords and anything else to hand,' Engrin suggested.

Gerard nodded and motioned to the first lieutenant. 'Make it so,' he murmured and then paused, taking hold of the officer's arm. He looked at Kieran and chewed the corner of his lip. 'And muster eight men with muskets and swords.'

The first lieutenant nodded and marched away, barking orders to the rest of the crew. Gerard looked at Engrin, who appeared pleased. He then glanced at Kieran. 'How are you at fighting at sea and in close quarters, Lieutenant?' he asked.

Kieran shrugged. 'I can hold my own, sir.'

'Good,' Gerard said, 'I'm putting you in charge of a flying platoon at the centre of the deck.'

Engrin appeared to want an explanation. 'With a flying platoon we can plug the gaps in our defences,' Gerard told him.

'And where would you have me, Captain?' William asked.

Gerard smiled. 'You are a captain, so you can choose your own ground. Though I must admit that if we lose the lower decks, we are as good as sunk.'

William nodded, taking the hint. 'I'll see you below, gentlemen. Good luck.'

'And you, Captain,' Gerard said, shaking his hand.

Kieran faced his friend calmly. 'You don't mind fighting up here by yourself?' William asked.

Kieran laughed. 'Not at all. Engrin will be nearby. How about you? Below deck with the artillery?'

'Some things never change,' William replied. He placed his hand on his friend's shoulder and squeezed it.

'Good luck, Will,' Kieran offered.

'Don't do anything heroic, Kieran,' William replied. 'That's an order.'

Kieran laughed. 'I'll try not to.'

While they were getting into position, the first lieutenant

returned, a little paler. 'They're almost on us, sir. In a few minutes time they will be in range of our guns.'

'And then we will know whether they are friend' – Captain Gerard glanced behind them again towards the shadow on the darkening seas – 'or foe.'

One of the lookouts shouted down. The pursuing ship was gaining speed.

'It's the Devil's work, sir,' the first officer murmured. 'There is barely a breeze.'

Gerard wheeled down to him and opened his mouth to chastise the officer, but Engrin took the captain's arm and nodded. 'He may be right, this is unnatural,' the old man whispered.

'Could they have such powers?' Gerard replied.

'After hundreds of years no one knows for certain the powers of Ordrane's followers, nor of Ordrane himself. There are stories of great storms issuing from the Carpathian Mountains that have swallowed whole armies. Of gales that have torn villages asunder. Of rains and floods that have drowned whole towns. These are just stories, of course,' Engrin admitted, 'but there is a dark miracle occurring here. Be sure your men are not blinded by it.'

Gerard nodded and pulled his sword free. 'The kafalas are flesh and blood, are they not?'

'Yes, Captain,' Engrin replied.

'Then leave these gypsies to me and my men,' he growled and trotted down the steps to the main deck. 'I will leave the phantoms to you!'

While Gerard bellowed to his men, Engrin stood with Kieran. 'I apologize to you both,' he said, 'I did not think they would attack us at sea.'

'No need to apologize,' Kieran replied. 'If it weren't for you, we'd be dead in London rather than in the Mediterranean.'

'Remember, fighting at sea is very different to fighting on land,' Engrin lectured him. 'The space for combat is tight, and there is nowhere to retreat to except the sea, where you would surely drown. When you fight your opponent, cut him down with one strike, or use quick stabbing motions. And whatever you do, do not take your time or you'll have no room to manoeuvre.'

Kieran took in the advice and gripped the handle of his sword tighter.

'You'll do fine,' Engrin promised. 'Good luck, Lieutenant.'

'Watch your back,' Kieran replied as he climbed down the steps to the flying platoon.

Engrin rubbed his hands together and stared back to the sea. The ship was closing in on them and the darkness was almost total. Only the lamps shining upon the deck of the *Iberian* gave any source of light; there were no lights at all on the approaching ship.

Praying quietly, Engrin made a sign of the cross and drew his sword.

◭ II ◭

The men in the crow's nest watched keenly.

'Anything?' the first officer called up to them. One replied with a short wave, telling him 'no'; this only made Gerard pace some more.

In the gun-room below deck, the gunner and boatswain kept calm, exchanging worried glances as the men talked of omens and rumours about the pursuing ship being manned by French ghosts or the Devil himself. 'How could a ship sail so fast?' one had said.

'There isn't a ship in Europe that could sail so quickly under calm weather,' another added.

'I hear there are no crew.'

'I hear there are crew, but they are wraiths ...'

The boatswain did his best to halt such speculation, but he could do only so much. In truth, they were all worried. If the ship turned out to be a merchant, they would all breathe a sigh of relief and maybe speak about what happened at length in a tavern in Naples.

The frigate creaked with its movement against the sea. In the background were the nervous sounds of breathing from the crew, waiting for the order to stand down, or fire.

William appeared below and pulled together a team of six men to wait near the steps to the deck. 'If they break through, we hold them here,' he said. The men accepted his order only because they were frightened. None of them recognised his rank. But that was just fine, as long as they followed his lead.

'Above all else, we cannot let one of them in the gun-room,' William pressed. 'They'll sink the ship. Understood?'

'Aye,' each man replied, though their eyes betrayed how afraid they were.

'And remember, you also fight for the man at your right. Defend him, and you defend yourself,' William said as shouting came from above. 'I'll be standing at your left.'

'And who will defend you, sir?' asked one of the men, a young sailor with barely enough years to cultivate a proper beard.

'Don't worry about me, I'll defend myself,' William replied. 'Are you prepared to defend this ship with utmost bravery?'

The men nodded and breathed in and out quickly, composing themselves.

'Very well,' William said, 'take your positions.'

Across the ship, the anticipation was the same. No one spoke, no one dared to make sudden movements, and most were scared. The closing vessel was now 200 yards away, almost within the weapons' range. Gerard stopped pacing and began tapping rhythmically on the rail with the handle of his sword.

'Lieutenant?' he said, and the first officer came over. 'Have they seen anyone on deck yet?'

The officer looked up and yelled to the crow's nest. They waved back to signal 'no' once again.

'No one?' Gerard said. 'That's hard to believe.'

'At this rate we'll be in range in minutes, sir,' the first officer remarked, his voice betraying unease.

'Very well,' Gerard replied, and looked up to Engrin.

'You know my mind, Captain. I'd fire as soon as they get in range,' the old man called down to him.

Gerard shook his head and stormed impatiently up the steps to the quarterdeck. 'You'd fire on a vessel be she friendly or not? Clearly you do not know my responsibilities, Engrin. I cannot fire unless provoked,'

Engrin turned him. 'This is not the French we're dealing with, nor is it a privateer. Where are the crew? Why would they be hiding? Heed my warnings, Captain, before it's too late!'

Gerard met Engrin's eyes and faltered. He went over to the rail and motioned for one of the other deck officers. 'Are the guns ready just in case?' he asked.

'Aye, sir,' the officer replied.

'Satisfied?' he grunted at Engrin. The old man said nothing, but continued to stare behind them at the ship as it quartered the distance between them in a minute.

Up in the crow's nest, the two sailors stared out and tried to catch a last faltering glimpse of the ship as it dipped finally into darkness, the very shadows overwhelming the detail of the deck.

'At what range can we fire?' Kieran asked one of the men in the holding party.

'We can fire some of the 'eavier guns at 'undred yards, sir. The rest at around fifty yards,' one of the sailors replied. 'That's if we get a chance to.'

Captain Gerard shouted up to the crow's nest for a report. Again, they replied that they could see little. There was still no sign of anyone on deck, yet the ship continued to gain on them.

Engrin walked up to Gerard and they exchanged words again, this time more privately. 'I cannot order them to fire on that ship. There is no sign of belligerence, and as I do not see privateer or French insignia on her, sir, my hands are tied,' Gerard whispered to Engrin.

'I understand. Just be ready to return fire if you need to,' the old man murmured.

On cue, the men in the crow's nest began shouting.

'What is it?' Gerard called to the first officer.

'Movement, sir, they thought they saw movement on deck!'

Gerard went to the rail and barked out orders to the crew. 'To your positions, but stow those muskets! I don't want to see a single musket pointed at that ship. They'll be plenty of time for that if needs be!' The crew scuttled about, some hunkering down behind the rails, others shadowing masts and bulkheads.

Kieran ordered his men to crouch by the main mast, some kneeling by bulkheads, other using barrels as cover.

'Have you ever fought in a battle, sir?' asked one of the flying platoon, an old seadog with a missing eye.

'Once or twice,' Kieran grimaced back.

'At sea?' asked the sailor.

'No,' Kieran admitted.

'Just keep yer 'ead down, sir,' the sailor clucked and grinned.

Kieran nodded, feeling somewhat like a novice.

Gerard began shouting again. 'Get someone over there with a lantern to signal the other ship once it comes about, and find out who the hell they are. They should have seen and heard us by now!' Gerard bellowed.

The closing vessel was almost within the hundred-yard firing distance.

Down below, William approached the gunner. 'Here they come,' William murmured. 'How are your men?'

'They're chewin' the wood from the 'ull, they're that anxious about it, sir,' the gunner replied. 'They'll fight like bastards if they have to.'

'They may have to,' William replied. 'We'll do our best to stop them from getting in here. You just make sure you can put a few holes in that ship.'

'We'll try, Mr Saxon,' the gunner replied. 'If they're trained like the French they will fire at the masts and the rigging. We'll fire on the roll at the guns. The Cap'n is a fine tactician.'

'Let's hope so,' William murmured and crossed the room to the six men at the steps to the upper decks.

△ III △

Above them, a deck officer leant out from the side of the ship as a crewman lowered a lantern from the mainmast yardarm. The deck officer plucked the lantern from above and began swinging it in the direction of the closing ship. He then began shouting out to it, hoping the sea would carry his words.

'Ahoy there! Ahoy!'

Gerard leant out on the rail and glanced at the first officer. Still there was no response from the other ship. 'Distance, Mr Grayson,' Gerard said.

The first officer looked keenly at the distance between the *Iberian* and the other ship. 'Almost ninety yards, sir,' he replied.

'Damn it,' Gerard murmured and looked up at the crow's nest, but again there was nothing to report. 'Try calling them again.'

The deck officer leant out once more and swung the lantern, calling out to the other ship.

Almost casually, a plume of smoke rose from the forecastle of the closing vessel. The air around the deck officer shivered for a split second and then the man disappeared in a spray of crimson. A moment later a loud boom heralded from the other ship as the sound hit them.

Gerard stood in shock, his jaw hanging open. It happened so quickly that most of the crew were in an equal state of bewilderment. The silence that followed seemed to last an eternity, but it was merely seconds until the closing ship fired a broadside that rang like thunder. The space between the vessels was instantly filled with smoke, and then chaos reigned as the side of the frigate was pounded with a roar of gunpowder and shattering wood.

A number of shots fell short, but several found their target. Cannonballs shattered the rails where crewmen were hidden, one taking the head of an unfortunate sailor and the arm of another. A dismembered crewman was riddled with splinters as a yard-wide hole appeared beside him at the rail, the ball proceeding to smash through a bulkhead. Another shot managed to shatter the fore topgallant yardarm, sending it clattering to the deck onto an unlucky sailor who'd run there to avoid the cannonade.

As the world around exploded into splinters, Gerard flinched but held his ground. 'Return fire! Return fire!' he bellowed, mortified by the damage the first broadside had done. The order was carried swiftly along the line and before the closing ship could send another broadside their way, the *Iberian* replied with all portside guns.

For a moment, it sounded as though the very sea had cracked open and was about to suck in all and sundry. The frigate rocked heavily with a thunderous volley that rang in Kieran's ears; he winced as the ten cannonballs tore across the sea between them, adding a bank of thick black smoke that obscured the enemy ship.

No one could confirm any hits, but many could hear them landing in the water. There was a slight cheer as the sound of timbers being smashed echoed from the smoke.

The second enemy broadside followed, closer than before. Kieran instinctively ducked as the one-eyed sailor had suggested, and the heavens seemed to open again with bright orange flashes and rolls of thunder. The rails to the port of the frigate were chewed up into shards of wooden shrapnel. Those who weren't killed outright by shot and cannon were nailed with slivers of wood a foot long that skewered hapless seamen as they ran blindly from the carnage.

Another shot hit the main mast, and a large chunk was blown out near the topsail yard. It groaned and appeared to give for a moment, but the rigging held it in place.

Again the *Iberian* replied, this time more blindly than before. The cannonade ruptured across the smoke, appearing to hit nothing until a series of crashes came from the enemy ship.

Gerard ran out to the rail of the quarterdeck and tried to order the chaos. 'Get them down! Get them under cover!' he yelled wildly at the first officer who had blanched and was almost completely inert. He tried to compose himself and made to move out to the crew when another broadside erupted closer still. He held his ears and cowered as shot and ball flew towards them. Again the rails were battered and more of the main mast took a pounding.

A number of shots found their way across towards the gun-room and the cockpit, and those below deck suddenly had a taste of the carnage that was happening above. A shot managed to strike the guns and a few men were dashed by shrapnel as their cannon was split open and the port was blown asunder. Some screamed, their faces peppered with shards of burning-hot metal and wood.

Gerard hung onto the rail even as the bulkhead a couple of yards away was smashed open, the rigging falling about them. 'Return fire with everything we've got!' he yelled, his voice increasingly hoarse.

Engrin lurched up to him, his head bowed from the shots fly-ing nearby. 'They're going to board us, Gerard!' he shouted.

The captain growled back, 'But they have no crew!'

'Then who's firing that cannon?' Engrin shouted.

Gerard grimaced and looked across the deck to his crew spilled over it, either dead, mortally wounded or in a state of total panic.

'We won't be able to outrun them, Captain!' Engrin prompted.

'Damnation!' Gerard shouted. 'Mr Grayson, prepare to repel borders!' The first officer nodded as the *Iberian* fired another broadside.

'They're tearing the ship apart!' Kieran shouted as another yardarm came crashing down. 'Keep covered!'

As he put his hands over his ears, hunkering behind a hatch that had been almost obliterated, he recognised the body of the one-eyed sailor. He no longer had a head, and it was all Kieran could do to hold on to the contents of his own stomach. The old sailor had been crouching by his side, and wasn't it he who had told Kieran to keep his head down?

His platoon was down to seven men.

Cursing under his breath, Kieran motioned to the others to keep down.

Gerard was also ducking, as musket-balls tore up the quarter-deck. 'Engrin, I have veterans of Trafalgar here, but most of these men have never seen combat. What can we do?'

'Make sure the attackers do not get to the lower decks, Captain!' Engrin replied. 'They're not just after me and the two officers, but also something else.'

Gerard stared at Engrin questioningly. 'What have you brought upon my ship, Engrin?' he demanded, under another volley of musket fire.

Engrin shook his head. 'Neither the time nor the place, Captain,' he shouted back.

Gerard growled and crawled over to the steps. Even with his first officer marshalling the men, they were in disarray. Gerard called him back and Grayson scuttled over, his composure still weak but a little more confident than before. 'Mr Grayson?' he said calmly, and ducked as a chunk of wood clattered by him.

'Sir!'

'Have a deck officer get down there and tell them to con-tinue firing all they have until there's no distance between us and them!' Gerard ordered, leaning over the rail to hear. 'And have Lieutenant Harte ready his party.' The first officer nodded and departed again.

Gerard straightened up once more and clenched his hand around the handle of his sword. 'Judgement Day comes early,' he murmured and looked pensively through the blackened smoke for sight of the enemy vessel.

Quietly, under a lull in the cannonade, Engrin made his way from the quarterdeck to the main deck, his sword dancing in front of him in preparation. Another volley of cannon-fire sounded so close he thought it came from the *Iberian* herself. The yard of the spanker to the rear shivered and the sail tore with a great ripping sound, crashing partly to the deck and partly into the sea. At once the *Iberian* replied, its rate of firing increasing, and there was thunderous roar as the portside guns opened up along the flank of the vessel. In that brief moment, fire appeared in the smoke, illuminating the enemy vessel in full. She careered out of the smoke and Kieran watched in horror as she lurched towards the side of the frigate. Knowing what was about to happen, Kieran hung onto a bulkhead just before the impact. Others weren't so lucky.

Below, William and his men rolled with the ship as it was buffeted. Other sailors lost their footing and fell. Engrin grabbed hold of a fallen yardarm and steadied himself; only the rail stopped Gerard from falling.

As the smoke cleared, Kieran could see the yards of the other ship tangled into the rigging of the frigate. It groaned with all its might, sounding as though it might tear itself apart with the strain. It was chaotic, but at least the smoke was fading fast and the cannonade was silenced.

Then followed intense volleys of musket fire. They raked the *Iberian* – flashes and plumes flowering all along her right side and across her deck, cutting down a number of men as they scrambled to their feet. Some fell to the deck stone dead, others clutched mortal wounds that squirted jets of blood. Kieran ducked once more as shots ricocheted around them.

Raising his head again, he signalled the platoon to load their guns. Captain Gerard bellowed an order to return fire, but apart from the smoke of the muskets there was little to fire at. The very few lanterns that had survived the broadsides were being shot to pieces by musket fire. Still, Kieran turned to his flying platoon and gestured them to sight the enemy ship.

'And ... Fire!' he yelled and their muskets and rifles crackled in the darkness. It was impossible to see if they had hit anyone, but returning fire was better than doing nothing at all.

'Reload!' Kieran shouted and noticed that other sailors were firing back where they could.

Some were still hunkered down, exchanging shots, but others, mostly young sailors, were cowering, and some were dead or dying; blood ran along the boards of the deck in tiny streams.

The first officer was against the main mast, which creaked audibly under the pressure of the enemy yard clamped against it. He looked up with worry and shouted to a nearby midshipman to get an engineer. The man nodded and stood up to leave, and then his head was sheared away in a spray of blood as a musket-ball cracked through his skull. He fell down quickly and rolled out of sight, leaving the first officer to stare incredulously into the space the man had once occupied.

Mr Grayson clenched his teeth to stop the gorge from rising in his throat. It was all too much to take, and his knees weakened suddenly. Kieran dashed from cover to attend to him, believing him to be wounded. 'Are you hit?' he asked. The first officer looked at him blankly, his face as white as a sheet.

Finally he shook his head. 'No, I'm fine,' he said weakly.

'We have to get these men into cover!' Kieran shouted at Mr Grayson, who could only shake his head.

'No!' he shouted back.

'What are you talking about, man?' Kieran exclaimed.

'The Captain,' the first lieutenant replied. 'The Captain says we must be ready to repel borders!'

Kieran agreed. 'Very well. We'll plug the gaps where we can!'

The first officer nodded and wiped his mouth. Glaring at the men around him, he ordered them to shoot at the smoke and to fix bayonets to repel borders. He ordered others to fight at their posts and defend in ranks, then left to return to the quarterdeck.

Captain Gerard was motioning again, the last surviving midshipman scuttling over, unwilling to share his fellow officers' fate. Barely listening to Gerard, the man looked wildly around him as more shots were fired and more men fell to the deck. In a matter of minutes one third of the frigate's crew was either dead or dying.

Gerard yelled again at the midshipman, but the poor man was too scared to follow his orders. He shook his head frantically and dashed for the stairs, running through another volley of shot that cut him apart. Gerard brought a hand to his face and slumped in despair. There was no way to organize his men – they were in chaos. 'Hopeless,' he murmured. He looked up as he heard his voice being called.

Gerard opened his eyes and a faint smile came over him as Mr Grayson, dodging musket-balls, ran down towards the quarterdeck. 'Mr Grayson! Try and get some of those cannons up here! I want to hold the entire deck! And where are the other officers?'

'Mostly dead, sir. One of them is below in the gun-room, the others are gone.'

Gerard nodded gravely. 'It's up to us, Mr Grayson. Try and pin down those skirmishers!'

'Aye, sir!' Grayson said, leaving quickly.

Kieran rounded the main mast and crouched by a barrel of grain that had already been riddled with shot, its contents spilling out across the deck. He signalled for the other men to follow and soon they were all hunkered around him. A sailor was slumped next to the barrel, as though kneeling in meditation, but wearing a wet crimson bib that was starting to congeal where his neck had been gouged by a musket-ball. Kieran grimaced and pushed the dead man over, trying to clear a shot for one of the sailors behind him. One of his team pulled up his musket and fired it to the left of Kieran's shoulder. The crack was loud enough for Kieran to flinch.

'Are we hitting any of them?' one of the sailors shouted.

Kieran shook his head. 'I have no idea. I can't see a thing out there except for the occasional flare. This is crazy, we can't see to aim. Some of your men appear to be retired marines, yet even they are having difficulties. We'd see them clearer if the sun was up or ...'

'Or what?' the sailor asked.

'Or if their ship was on fire! If we could fire their sails we could see them and they wouldn't be able to pursue us!' Kieran said.

'You'd be shot before you got up there, sir! And you'd fire our sails too! Their yards are caught up with ours!' the crewman said, pointing towards the sails of the frigate.

'We must do something. They're cutting us down!' Kieran insisted.

Meanwhile, the first officer was threading his way amongst the positions. Organising a pocket of ex-marines, he moved back from the forecastle to the mainmast. Halfway, he paused by a stack of crates to look up at the sails. There was an unusual sound – screaming from high above – and he quickly remembered the men in the crow's nest.

Suddenly, the platform was covered in a strong black shadow and the sails around it were turning red, something spraying over them. One after the other, two bodies fell from the crow's nest and crashed somewhere on the deck below. Aghast, the first officer looked up frantically and saw the shadow spread further, unfurling its wings. It appeared to blot out the crow's nest completely and then it swooped from the position, soaring down towards the deck. It went for a number of men firing from a hatch, and the first officer ran to warn them. 'Down! Get down!'

Two of the three men crouched as Mr Grayson ordered, but the third man was clearly bewildered by all the shouting. In a matter of moments, the shadow swooped from behind and there was a flash of black metal as the shadow eclipsed the man in an instant and then was away again. Across the deck, the sailor's head bounced and rolled, his decapitated body toppling like a felled tree. The first officer followed the shadow as it disappeared behind one of the sails.

Engrin had seen it too and left his position at the foremast. He came over, dashing past Kieran without a word, his eyes trained on the shadow's last position.

The first officer ushered the two men down the hatch and into further cover, just as the shadow swooped again. It came from the mid-ship, spiralling out of the night, flickering against the moon-white sails. Mr Grayson turned on his heels and raised his sword as it came for him. Black steel flashed keenly in the darkness and Grayson lashed out with his sword. The blades met and the black weapon sliced through Grayson's sabre. The blade continued its course and cleaved the first lieutenant's side from belly to spine, running him open in an instant. Mr Grayson stumbled and looked down, watching his insides fall out onto the deck. Then he fell to his knees, and then to his his face, a river of blood splashing out in front of him.

Engrin had watched this from afar, his eyes staying on the shadow as it disappeared once again into the topsails. The old man ran over and knelt by the first officer, turning him over to find Grayson's dead eyes staring back. Looking away, he rolled him back, just as dozens of kafalas, servants of Count Ordrane of Draak, flooded over the shattered rails of the frigate and onto the deck of the *Iberian* like a black tidal wave.

Kieran saw them too, a horde of men, cloaked in dark colours that camouflaged them within the gloom of night. Moments later the deck was teaming with them; all were armed to the teeth, with daggers, axes or swords. Those sailors who fled in terror were run down mercilessly, while those who faced them weren't much better off. Soon, even the veterans were struggling to hold their ground.

Kieran ordered his men into two ranks. After several of the attackers cut through the sailors at the rail, the men charged towards them. 'Fire!' Kieran yelled, pointing his sword at the oncoming horde. The holding party fired one volley and the kafalas fell.

'Reload!' Kieran shouted, and stepped into the breach as two kafalas sprang forward behind their dead comrades. Remembering Engrin's advice, he wielded his blade in a powerful arc, cutting down the first kafala. He then wrestled the second, and thrust his sword into his guts twice. With both kafalas down, he leapt back to the ranks of the holding party, who brought their muskets to bear again. Another wave of kafalas came for them, and Kieran grimaced, knowing that this was going to be a long and painful battle.

'Fire!' he yelled again and the muskets replied at once, filling the air with smoke and death.

△ IV △

While Kieran was holding the main deck, William and his own men waited at the steps of the gun-room. The sound of fighting above was nerve-shredding and one of the crew looked as though he would wet himself. Of William's men, only one had a musket, the others making do with swords. He just hoped their attackers would be similarly armed — a well placed rank of rifles would knock them dead before they could draw a breath.

William glanced at the men and offered words of encouragement. 'Remember, fight to your right, and don't give them a chance. They will give you none. If they take the gun-room, we're finished.'

'Aye, sir,' they replied nervously.

The sound of something rolling, like a barrel on the deck, thundered above, followed by screams and shouting. And then they appeared, the kafalas, charging down the steps in their dark cloaks.

William glanced at the sailor bearing the musket. 'Third left!' he shouted and the sailor brought up the musket and fired at the third kafala, who was standing above the others, behind them on the steps. The shot to the head was accurate and cut away the man's veil in a spray of blood. The body toppled and landed on his comrades, who fell like dominos, sprawling to the deck where William and his men stood. Instantly William and the next nearest sailor sprang forward, driving their swords into their backs where they lay. They leapt back as more kafalas ran down the steps, some slipping on the blood of the dead.

'For life! For your Captain!' William shouted and rushed forward, the men following closely.

Stumbling over the bodies of the fallen, the kafalas lunged but were surprised by the tactics of the defenders. As one went to strike the sailor opposite, the sailor to his left struck him in the side. In moments, six more dead kafalas were added to the heap.

Breathing hard, William grinned at the crew. 'That's it, boys! We'll show them!'

Covered in blood and sweat, the crew grinned back deliriously as another wave of kafalas charged down the stairs.

Above them, the battle was taking its toll. Gerard had organised the remnants of the crew into a tight fighting group, but they were being overwhelmed by the number of kafalas pouring from the enemy vessel.

Engrin, still chasing the shadow, came by him, cutting down two kafalas in his path. The captain was wounded in the side. Engrin peered down and flinched. 'It's worse than it feels!' Gerard shouted as a round of musket fire spluttered from his tightly-packed crew.

'You should go below!' Engrin said.

'And who would lead my men? My officers are dead.'

Engrin turned and found Kieran and the holding party still fending off the attackers, a large pile of kafala bodies lying about them. His five remaining men were making a good account of themselves.

'No!' Gerard shouted, waving his sword in Kieran's direction. 'I need him there. He's holding them back, but not for long.'

Engrin gritted his teeth. 'I cannot lead them,' he said. 'The vampyre is here, on this ship!'

'I know!' Gerard replied. 'Who do you think gave me this wound?'

Again Engrin glanced down. 'You're lucky he didn't kill you!'

'Not luck, old friend,' Gerard replied. 'One of the crew threw himself in the way. He cut the poor bastard in two, and then managed this ...'

The captain held the gash with his left hand. Engrin knew how painful a wound that deep must be. 'I insist ...' Engrin began.

'Insist away, Engrin!' Gerard spat. 'If we lose this deck then no one will be alive to patch me up!'

Engrin nodded gravely.

'Just get that flying bastard!' Gerard demanded.

Engrin left the captain and made his way to the main mast again, where he sparred with a kafala whose only weapon was a long dagger. Dodging the swipes of the blade like a twenty-year-old, the lithe old man side-stepped and thrust his sword through the man's ribs. Pushing him over, Engrin marched defiantly to the mast, his eyes on the sails, waiting for the vampyre to swoop again.

△ V △

William's squad were holding still, but the fallen kafalas were making the place more cramped. He found himself knocking elbows with the sailor next to him as they traded blows with the advancing enemy. His arm brushed his comrade to the left, and he felt himself being jostled by the struggles around him. It was an accident waiting to happen.

'Push them back!' William cried. 'Make room!' The sailors, at first, didn't appear to listen to him, so he made them follow his example and shoved the attackers away before he despatched them. Eventually, after killing two more and wounding another, William had made himself more room, which the others began occupying. One plucky sailor managed to fire his musket through the melee, taking out another approaching kafala. The body fell down the steps and up-ended another who William cut in half as he fell.

Grinning with blood-lust, almost punch-drunk with the gore flying in front of him, and sick to the depths of his stomach with fear and adrenaline, William kept going through the horror, hacking away at wave after wave of cloaked attackers.

They were holding them back, but for how long?

The pernicious kafalas were trying to rally by the hatch as they were driven back by William and his men. With their dead lying about them, the attackers appeared to falter. Instead of rushing their position they came in ones or twos and were systematically hacked down or shot. The sailor with the musket hunkered down and began picking off kafalas, loading and reloading with the speed of a crack rifleman.

There was a sudden boom from the gun-room and commotion from within. The enemy ship was firing again, this time on their guns.

A kafala rushed at one of the sailors with his axe. The sailor went to lunge forward but paused and looked down as he saw a throwing-dagger buried in his chest. The sailor to his right, still fending off another kafala was struck in the shoulder with the axe, cleaving him through the ribs. At once he fell, and only William's timely intervention halted the axe-man from killing another.

Cutting the kafala down, he ripped the dagger free from the dying sailor and hurled it back, almost blindly at one of the kafalas above, striking him in the side.

'Hold them!' he implored as he pulled the dying sailor from the melee. But as he looked down he noticed a faint dribble of blood seeping from his mouth and that glassy-eyed look.

William cursed under his breath as he realized they were losing. More cannon sounded and the ship was rocked by explosions from the room beyond. Still William fought blindly on, hoping that Kieran was still alive.

Kieran had half his men, yet those remaining continued to fire in two ranks while Kieran plugged the gaps. The number of kafala dead was mounting, but for every one of the enemy that fell, two more seemed to appear.

And Kieran's men were running out of rounds.

Kieran struck down another of their cloaked assailants, and yelled out as one sneaked to his blind-side on the left and cut him across the ribs. In fury, Kieran grabbed the man's head and butted him. Reeling back, he swept up his sword and carved the kafala's face in two.

Another scream, and another of the holding party fell. It was beginning to look hopeless.

'Back!' Kieran shouted to the remaining three men. 'Back to the rear hatch!'

The sailors fired another round and dropped their muskets, pulling out their hand-weapons. As they fell back, the tide of kafalas turned on them, and for a moment it seemed as though they were the only crewmen left alive on deck.

'Fire!' cried a voice and a volley of musket fire cut down half a dozen kafalas, the others faltering. Behind them charged Captain Gerard and the remains of the crew. As they fought through to Kieran and the platoon, Gerard laughed hysterically, blood dripping from his face.

'I'm glad to see you, Captain!' Kieran shouted, the captain's wound obvious.

'You call this a flying platoon, sir?' Gerard joked.

'I'm afraid it looks pretty grim, Captain,' Kieran said, raising his sword. 'But if I'm to die, then let it be at your side!'

'I'll drink to that,' Gerard replied, 'if I ever see a bottle again!'

Both grinned and then plunged with the sailors into the deepest crowd of kafalas.

△ VI △

The melee closed in and William saw the kafalas' confidence was growing. Now it was *they* who were being pushed back, towards the doors. The last two men held them off as best they could with sword and bayonet, but William knew it was only a matter time – maybe minutes – before the kafalas broke through.

William brought his shoulder to bear on the nearest kafala. The attacker fell to the stairs and William stepped back as another kafala filled his place. He barely drew breath before he knocked the next attacker in the face with the hilt of his sword. The man stumbled back and there was a brief respite before yet another kafala appeared, and the routine continued. Several were cleaved while another had slipped down the steps, breaking his neck in the fall. William was faintly aware he'd been standing on one of the dead sailors for the last few minutes as they tried to hold the kafalas back, but space was at a premium and the dead carpeted the foot of the stairs, piling up around them. It was not numbers that held the kafalas now but the narrow passage down the steps and the barrier of corpses. Across the passage they fought three men abreast. Each enemy wave was comprised of fresher kafala fighters who'd endured only minutes of battle, wheras the weary sailors of William's squad were nearing exhaustion.

The guns in the room behind them had fallen silent, and William feared the worst. He glanced at the two desperate men and made a decision. He was not happy about it, but what choice did he have?

'I'm going inside!' he shouted. 'I'm going to form a party to relieve us!'

The nearest crewman glanced at William with worry. 'We won't hold them if you go, sir!'

William saw their desperation and raised his sword at another wave of kafalas descending the steps. He leapt forward and cut the legs of two of them, then plunged the sword into a third who collapsed on him. William pushed the body aside and staggered back.

'I have to go!' he implored.

The two sailors glanced at each other, and knew William was right. They nodded nervously and wearily, but raised their swords as one.

'Just keep them here for a few minutes longer while I get reinforcements. I'll get a cannon up here and we'll blow them to Hell!' The crewmen looked at William and their faces were a little more optimistic.

'I won't be long!' William promised, knowing too well that he'd never see either man alive again.

'We'll hold them, sir!' one man finally replied. 'Just bring that cannon out as soon as you can!'

William lunged forward, taking the nearest kafala in the neck so that he fell back on the others, giving the two sailors a modicum of breathing time – before pulling himself quickly through the gap in the doorway to the gun-room beyond.

△　△　△

Seconds after William pulled himself through the door, a huge hand fastened onto his neck and lifted him off the ground. Choking, he felt the blood balloon in his head. His tongue flapped about and he wheezed as his very breath was stolen from him.

'No, wait! He's one of ours!' a voice cried out nearby. Instantly the grip relaxed and William could breathe again. He felt the floor at his feet and tried to balance, but his legs gave out and he fell, only to be saved by the very hands that had nearly choked the life out of him.

'Very sorry, sir,' a deep booming voice said.

William's vision adjusted from the dull blur, and he looked up into a pair of dark eyes in a big round face strewn with stubble. The man was huge, his arms as thick as his legs, with hands the size of shovels. He steadied William with care and smiled apologetically. 'I fought you woz one of dem,' he said slowly.

Another man appeared at his side and took William's arm. 'Sorry, sir, we had no idea,' the man explained. 'There're no officers left alive down here, sir. The gunner copped it, and the boatswain was blown up.'

'No officers at all?' William managed to wheeze.

'No, sir.'

'What about the guns? Why aren't they firing?' William asked.

'Their ship is far too close, sir. We'd risk damaging ours,' another sailor said from afar.

William staggered across to one of the guns and leant on it for support. 'That hasn't stopped them from firing at us.'

'They're crazy sir, they'd sink us both!' said the sailor.

'Well, we have more important things to deal with,' William said, and turned to the door, pointing at it with his sword. 'They're going to come through here sure enough. I need you to hold the door as long as you can.'

'What about the men on the other side?' one of the gun-crew asked.

William knew that the men he had left would be killed, if they weren't dead already. Ignoring the question, William pointed down at the nearest cannon. 'I need to turn this around to face the doors,' he ordered. 'And I need some shot.'

'We have no shot left, sir!' one of the men exclaimed.

William noticed that the contents of the gun-room had been thrown about. Lying around were planks, tools, spilt grain and cannonballs. There were also smashed barrels, pools of blood, and several bags of nails.

'Nails!' William shouted. 'Use the bags of nails. Ram them down the gun barrel.'

The crew looked at each-other and nodded, quickly hurrying to pull the gun around. There was a crash outside and the crewman who had half-strangled William bounded to the door and braced it with his weight. Two other sailors joined him and used their strength to keep it shut as William's gun-crew worked. They laboured quickly, their faces awash with sweat, and while their movements were steady, sometimes those nervous hands would drop a bag of nails or spill powder.

Throughout those short few minutes, William stood with his sword ready, holding his nerve and sometimes his breath as the three crewmen held the door fast. His heart hammered as the sound of banging began to reverberate against the door and he realized the sailors on the other side had been killed.

'Come on!' William urged as the cannon was turned and the barrel loaded with bags of nails. The door shuddered continuously, driving one of the sailors back a foot. The large crewman gritted his teeth and heaved forward bracing the door further.

The gun-crew loaded the last of the bags and another wad. They pierced the cartridge cloth and primed the touch-hole with powder as William glanced anxiously towards the door. It was suddenly pierced with sword-points and one of the sailors cried out, clutching his palm that had been sliced open. The second sailor bolted from the door fearing he'd be skewered also, but the large crewman remained, as the points of weapons pricked his flesh and gentle streams of blood trickled from his arms and legs.

'Hurry!' William shouted to the gun-crew.

A long blade shivered a section of the door and second point lanced the giant through the knee. He looked down, his expression of pain masked by rigid determination until he was lanced through the thigh. He groaned, yet still he held his place. More blades followed through, spearing him in the gut, the forearm and then his neck. Blood poured out of him but the large sailor held onto the doors until all strength and life left his body. As the kafalas behind pushed the door ajar, the pinned sailor went slack and toppled over onto the deck, the impact shaking the boards where William stood.

'Ready!' one of the gun-crew yelled, just as the kafalas poured into the room. William stood by the cannon and held his breath. The kafalas halted when they saw the cannon and William's embittered and merciless expression.

'Fire!' he growled.

There followed a tremendous explosion, far louder than anything William had experienced during the cannonade before. His head shook as though struck by a strong punch, and he cursed himself for standing so damned close. Reeling back, he looked up through the smoke and heard a series of muffled shrieks.

As the smoke cleared there was a bloody scene – men literally nailed to the bulkheads; men rolling in agony in burgeoning pools of blood that poured like red wine across the deck to where William and the crew stood. More intruders were stumbling blindly about, their limbs intact but blood pouring from wounds that peppered their bodies. The first rank of men, almost a dozen kafalas, had been shredded. The second row had been grievously wounded, some bleeding to death amongst the first rank. The third row – those who were about to charge into the gun-room – now stood shocked to the marrow to see their comrades slaughtered so easily.

William could see it in their eyes, the faltering confidence, the doubt. The fear.

It was all he needed. 'No mercy!' he cried out, and the crew, buoyed by the havoc wrought upon the enemy, joined his cry.

They pulled out swords, clubs, hammers and anything else to hand, and rushed forward.

The wounded kafalas, those bleeding to death, were dispatched instantly. The others – those who had not suffered from the cannon blast – managed to stand their ground for a few moments before they bolted. Soon the steps were conquered. 'Secure the deck!' William shouted, blood and sweat dripping down his face.

△ VII △

Continuing to attack the kafalas, Kieran and Gerard failed to see the blanket of darkness sweeping down on them. Looking up at the last moment, Kieran saw the sheen of a blade coming towards him and ducked just in time. He felt hot liquid splatter his neck, followed by a gurgled cry from behind and turned to find a sailor spitting blood through his shattered and cleaved face. His skull was split in two from the forehead to the lips, blood gushing down the crevasse in between.

As the courage of the other sailors broke, Kieran pushed aside the dead man and yelled, 'Take cover!' to the rest, in case the creature dived again.

Above, leaning from the rigging off a yardarm, the vampyre stared down and gloated as his servants closed in. He recognised the lieutenant by the smell of his sweat and the glint of his eyes. He had been close to killing him before in the museum, and he would not fail this time. But the old bastard who had taken his arm was nearby; the vampyre spat onto the deck, cursing Engrin and vowing to tear his heart out.

But Engrin had seen the vampyre, too. He waited patiently, despite the fighting whirling around him; when a kafala came too close, Engrin showed his intention, cutting the man down with one swing of his sword.

The vampyre watched and smiled. It was time to settle old scores.

Engrin saw the darkness swoop down and he raised his sword. Instead of attacking him outright, the vampyre halted in mid-flight and floated to the deck, his feet treading the air gently. As he landed, he raised his black broadsword.

'You have a new arm,' Engrin remarked casually.

The vampyre nodded, flexing his gloved hand. 'Yes, old man,' he hissed, 'and I'm eager to kill you with it!'

'Really.' Engrin smiled.

The vampyre growled, seemingly put off by Engrin's confidence. 'I won't just kill you outright, I promise!' he hissed. 'No, I'll take your legs so you'll crawl over to me and beg for death. I'll take your arms and roll you over like a tortoise in its shell. Then I will piss on you, and when you've been defiled enough, I will boil you slow in a pot and serve you to the dogs!'

Engrin's eyes narrowed. 'You talk too much,' he remarked.

The vampyre flung back his head and laughed gutturally, his black blade dancing towards Engrin in a whirl of glinting metal. Engrin was almost taken off guard, but his sword connected with the vampyre's and he felt the impact shoot up his arm with a flash of pain. Despite the discomfort, Engrin held his ground and retaliated, driving his sword at the creature. Now the vampyre parried and then moved into the air, pulling himself off the deck as though climbing an invisible rope. Engrin leapt high and swung out, nicking the vampyre's foot with his sword. The creature howled and spiralled towards the mast, catching hold of the rigging as he looked down at the wound. It was hardly deep and already mending, judging by the faint blue mist writhing around it. 'I owe you for that one as well, old man!' he hissed.

Engrin strode over and looked up at the creature. 'You call this a fight? Cowards hide. Can you not fight me without your childish games?'

'And ruin my fun?' the vampyre laughed back. 'I will enjoy gutting you. I'll savour every moment.'

Engrin raised his sword again. Laughing deeply, as if thunder were trapped in its belly, the vampyre flung back his head and let go of the yardarm. It spun through the air like a tornado, lashing towards Engrin with swathes of satin and flashes of black steel. Engrin swung his sword in an arc as the creature approached. Again there was a whirl of metal and Engrin felt his sword connecting. The impact gibbered through his arm, the muscles numbed by the blow. As the creature flew past again, Engrin dropped to one knee and picked up a discarded dagger. He hurled it at the vampyre and the blade disappeared inside the tornado of darkness. Instantly the spell was broken, and the vampyre fell to the deck.

Engrin dashed over, growing more tired with every passing moment. Where the vampyre had fallen he found a black mass crouching on the deck, dead sailors all around. 'You spoiled my parlour trick,' the creature murmured.

Engrin nodded, weighing his sword. 'Yes. And that won't be all I'll spoil, foul creature.'

The vampyre clucked in the back of its throat and it rose up until it towered over Engrin. 'You think a simple dagger can harm me? How naive you are!' it said, and his gloved hand appeared from within the cloak, the thrown dagger glinting between the fingers. The vampyre dropped it nonchalantly to the deck and kicked it aside.

'I know more about your kind than you realise,' Engrin said.

'My *kind?* I am unique!' it hissed back, amused.

'Don't flatter yourself. You're nothing more than the bastard-creation of something unholy,' Engrin stated coolly.

The vampyre nodded. 'That may be. But I'm no lap-dog to the King of Shit-eating, the one who pisses on you and expects devotion! Do you see me demeaning everything I am? I am the truth, and the holiest are the liars, living in a wretched state of absolution! Hah!' the creature laughed and walked forward, Engrin backing off a little. 'Would not the world follow me to the foot of the Carpathians and beg my Lord for immortality if they knew the truth? The truth that death is absolute no matter if you have sinned or not. Would not the world kill itself?'

'There is no immortality for you. Tonight, you will be destroyed as others of your kind have perished,' Engrin announced and swung his sword towards the vampyre. The creature parried easily and Engrin lunged again. Once more the vampyre parried, driving Engrin against a fallen yardarm. Out of breath, the old man straightened himself and held his sword up, in case the creature tried to strike back. Instead the vampyre looked at him and smiled, shaking its head slightly.

'Oh my! It appears we're tiring! Such a shame, this was meant to be entertaining.' The creature levelled its sword at Engrin.

For the first time, Engrin lost his cool. Maybe a few years earlier he would have taken this contest in his stride, but time had caught up with him. His stamina was a pale reflection of what it had once been, but he still had his cunning and determination.

The vampyre twirled the sword in an arc and lanced it towards his Engrin's shoulder. Engrin dodged it, parried the following blow and jumped over a nearby body, landing to deliver his own strike. The vampyre registered surprise but caught the strike easily with the edge of his sword, the black blade inflicting a deep grove on the side of Engrin's weapon. Engrin stepped back and swung again, repeating the arc with a second and a third blow. The vampyre predicted a fourth but Engrin leant to his left and brought the blade up. The creature reacted quickly and parried the blow, but Engrin drove his blade on, pushing the creature back. The vampyre retreated into the air, hissing as it spiralled up into the rafters of masts and yards.

'I thought,' Engrin panted, 'I thought you said you were better than I?'

The vampyre scowled and stood on the yard-arm, his balance perfect. 'I am growing weary of this contest,' it hissed. Wrapping its cloak about itself, the vampyre leapt again. It dived towards Engrin and as the old man raised his sword, the vampyre expanded, its cloak flying open. The edge of the cloak hit the tip of Engrin's weapon with enough force to push it aside. Then the black sword drove straight into the old man's shoulder. Falling back against the mast, Engrin moaned with pain, and dropped his own sword as his hand went to the wound.

The vampyre landed gently a few yards away. He turned and

walked up to Engrin who clutched at his wound, his eyes betraying both pain and defiance.

'And so our meeting ends,' the vampyre said casually, several of his kafalas close behind. 'You will die here, old man. But before you do, where is the Scarimadaen?'

Engrin spat on the floor. 'Where you'll never find it. You'll have to tear this ship apart to get it!'

The vampyre smiled. 'Check below deck,' he hissed to the masked men behind him. They left quickly, dodging the battle at the main mast, where Kieran and Captain Gerard were holding their ground.

'And your friends?' the vampyre asked. 'Where is the other one?'

'Go to Hell,' Engrin growled.

'I'll find him eventually, old man,' the vampyre said, and kicked Engrin's sword aside. 'I have killed so many men like you. Your war is lost. We have won, old man.'

'As long as one of us draws breath, it is you who will lose!' Engrin spat back.

The vampyre stared at the old man and shook his head. 'Defiant to the last. Let us see how defiant you are when I unleash a daemon upon this ship.'

△ VIII △

William looked on as the men tried their best to lift the cannon over the mound of corpses by the steps. It was proving difficult.

'It's no good, sir,' one of the crew said. 'We'll need to clear them out of the way.'

William looked frustrated. 'Then clear them!'

He climbed the steps and got to the hatch. Looking across the deck he saw the tired crew struggling hand-to-hand with the kafalas. It was a gruesome sight, with bodies spilling across the deck in piles, rivers of blood running across the planks. Even in the meagre light of the few lamps swinging over them, William saw enough to know that it had been hell up here.

Desperately, he searched for Kieran, but in the darkness it was difficult to distinguish him from the enemy. For a moment he caught sight of Captain Gerard before several kafalas leapt on him and he disappeared under the onslaught.

And then he caught sight of Engrin, hunched against the main mast. In front of him was the vampyre, his long black hair curling over his shoulders, his bone-white skin glistening in the moonlight. He was smiling at Engrin and gesturing to him with his black sword.

'Engrin!' William yelled, and the vampyre turned to him, grinning terribly.

'No, William!' Engrin shouted back. 'To the quarterdeck! The pyramid!'

William turned and saw that the door to the rooms underneath the quarterdeck was open. He dashed across the deck, leaping the bodies of friend and foe, until he came within a yard of the door.

'William! Watch out!' he heard Engrin yell. He sensed the air moving swiftly behind him and instinctively fell to his knees. He looked up as the vampyre landed in front of him, its black sword close to cleaving his head in half.

'You,' the vampyre hissed, staring at William with its deep yellow eyes.

William got to his feet and raised his sword.

'You will not stop me, Captain,' the vampyre said. 'The pyramid is mine.'

Behind him the kafalas reappeared, one with the drawstring bag in his hands. They flocked around their master, their weapons ready.

'Is that all you want?' William said calmly.

'No. I also want your and your friend's heads,' the vampyre clucked. 'As for this ...' The creature ripped open the bag and lunged inside to pluck out the wooden box. Regarding it curiously, he looked up, a little amused.

'Do you have the key?' the vampyre asked politely.

'No!' William replied.

The vampyre shrugged. 'Never mind,' he said, and dropped the box on the deck. He then swung down with his broadsword, shattering the lid. The pyramid fell out, glistening and glowing in the moonlight. There was a faint hum as it came to rest at the feet of the vampyre.

The creature looked down, almost transfixed by the shining object, before raising his eyes to William. 'You were the ones who destroyed the daemon at Gembloux,' he said. 'Do you care for a re-match, Captain?'

William swallowed nervously as the vampyre's smile spread further. Laughing hollowly, the creature bent down to pick up the object. But at that moment, several things happened at once:

Engrin shouted 'No!' in desperation ...

Kieran pulled Gerard from the crowd of kafalas ...

William made a final charge on the vampyre ...

... Just as the world around them exploded in a ball of bright blue light.

At first William thought the daemon had arrived. The light blinded him, and the force of energy that rippled through the deck, knocked him against the rails. He stumbled and rolled, his sword falling from his hands as he lost orientation. The sound that followed the explosion lifted him off his knees and he rolled again until his back was against the rail.

Blinking, he could make out a ball of light expanding on the deck, with a shadow seemingly trapped inside it. It opened up like a pair of wings before exploding with a dull thud and a rumble.

Out of it came a darkness more intense than that of the vampyre. The creature, whatever it was, was crowned with bright golden hair. The kafalas looked up in terror as the figure brought out a short silver sword that flashed like summer lightning.

Rubbing his blurred eyes, William watched in total bewilderment as the kafalas were slaughtered in seconds. The vampyre backed away from the pyramid and leapt into the air, landing on a yardarm high above.

This wasn't a daemon, it was something else.

William rushed across to Engrin, who was still struggling by the mast. 'What is that?' he shouted.

The old man shook his head. William took his arm and they lurched awkwardly across the deck, pausing only to defend themselves against a kafala who charged wildly towards them. William thrust his sword into the man's belly, barely stopping as he helped Engrin towards the quarterdeck.

'Wait,' Engrin murmured. 'The pyramid.'

William looked down and saw the pyramid lying in a puddle of blood. It was glowing feverishly and little blue strings of light licked around its edge.

'I thought you said it needed blood to open itself,' William said.

'The blood of the *living*,' Engrin reminded him.

William nodded and reached down to pick it up.

'William, your hands!' Engrin warned him. William grabbed a veil from one of the dead kafalas and wrapped it around his own hand. He plucked the dripping pyramid from the bloody pool and held it gingerly, as the blue flecks of light writhed and spat before dying completely. He then carried Engrin inside the room, leaving the battle behind them.

△ IX △

Kieran could see that the raiders had lost their appetite for battle. Gerard, wounded but still fighting, had noticed something else.

'Up there!' he yelled.

Kieran looked up to find two figures duelling across the masts. 'Who is that?' he said.

'The vampyre, and some*one* or some*thing*,' Gerard replied.

Kieran rubbed the sweat and blood from his face. He wiped his hands on his jacket and turned around. The rest of the sailors were battling hard. A group had appeared on deck with a cannon. 'Get it over here!' Kieran yelled at the struggling men. They hastened their efforts and the cannon rolled across the deck towards them. Gerard gestured the direction to fire.

Another pocket of kafalas stepped towards them over the mounds of corpses, but faltered as they spotted the cannon.

'Quickly men!' Gerard urged.

The kafalas stopped and began to step back.

'Load it!'

Some began to retreat hastily. Others hesitated.

'Loaded!' shouted the gunner.

'Fire!' yelled Gerard, and the cannon erupted, firing nails across the deck. The shot shredded the front line of kafalas, who fell to the floor instantly. Others stumbled about clutching at mortal wounds, while the back ranks limped away to the rails of the deck.

'For the *Iberian*!' Gerard yelled, his sword outstretched. 'Charge!'

As the remaining crew charged, Kieran felt himself being buffeted along, and he too launched into the nearest kafala, cleaving him open. He then felled a second, who was already missing an arm. The wounded raiders were being slaughtered, but Kieran had no compassion or guilt: death was too good for these bastards.

As his sword came down again and again, his strength failed him and he fell to his knees. Crawling over to a barrel, he rested, breathing heavily.

It was only when he heard a heavy thud nearby that he looked up. In front of him was the vampyre, but he looked different somehow. His yellow eyes were wide and somewhat terrified, and he was clutching his hip as bright blue smoke sizzled from beneath his hand. The vampyre had not seen Kieran but was looking skyward as something else fell to the deck. It was a man, as tall as the vampyre, with golden hair down to his shoulders. The man crackled with blue light, and in his hands was a shining silver sword of a kind Kieran had not seen before.

The vampyre raised its black sword and struck down. The burning short-sword connected with it and there was a flash of light as it parried the blow. Then followed another strike and another flash.

And then another.

And another.

Kieran held his hands to his eyes as the duel continued in a maelstrom of light and sound. Between the flashes he could see that the vampyre was being forced back again and again. When the creature went to rise from the ground, the golden-haired warrior gripped its coat and pulled it back to earth, punishing him with wound after wound. Slowly the vampyre began to lose energy, appearing to wither. It held its sword to parry a strike but the warrior of light palmed aside the black blade and swung his sword around in a tight arc, slicing through the vampyre's neck. The creature belched a small column of light and dust from its severed neck, before turning instantly to ash and crumbling to the ground.

Kieran stood back, staring at the warrior with golden hair. It turned around and looked down at Kieran with solid black eyes.

'Who ...' Kieran stammered. '*What* are you?'

'*Dar'uka,*' the man replied, his voice like thunder. He raised his head and stared towards the enemy vessel. Sheathing the sword beneath his mighty cloak, the warrior ran across the deck and leapt from the main mast across to the enemy vessel. It was a huge leap, but he made it seem effortless.

Kieran clambered over the bodies and stared across the black waves at the enemy ship, which was lit by intermittent flashes of blue light. Now and again, dark figures fell over the side and into the sea. The sight was eerie: the kafalas died in almost complete silence, apart from the clanging of metal on metal.

Around him, he noticed that the battle on the *Iberian* had ended. The survivors leant on rails and bulkheads, standing in pools of blood and gore, their heads bowed. Kieran did not know how many had died, but he knew they had made a good account of themselves. The number of kafala dead outnumbered the crewmen lost, yet still barely a third of the *Iberian*'s men had survived.

Gerard stumbled over to Kieran. The Irishman looked down and saw that the bloody stain on his shirt had spread. 'You should see the ship's surgeon,' Kieran suggested.

'The ship's surgeon is dead,' Gerard said weakly.

'Then let Engrin see you,' Kieran said, 'I think he's dressed wounds before.'

'Engrin is one of the wounded,' Gerard remarked.

Kieran frowned. 'When?'

'The vampyre ...' Gerard replied. 'He cut him.'

Kieran looked across the deck and found no sign of the old man.

'Your friend ... Saxon ... He's taken him inside,' Gerard said, trying to lean on the rail without tearing his wound further.

'You really should be in your quarters,' Kieran suggested.

'With this ship at our side?' Gerard replied.

Kieran looked across at the enemy vessel noting the damage done to it and the faltering shadows on the deck being destroyed by the blazing warrior.

'They're no longer a threat,' Kieran remarked.

Gerard shook his head and with some effort he pointed to the masts. '*There.* The rigging is tied up with ours. It needs to be cut free before we can make distance between the ships.'

Kieran looked up and noticed, even in the gloom and smoke, the rigging fouling theirs.

'How can we get across?' Kieran asked. He was exhausted and he could barely lift his arms, much less his legs.

Gerard slumped a little. 'Swing across.' He grimaced with pain.

Kieran shook his head. He looked about him at the tired faces staring over at the enemy ship. They were all weary, or wounded, or both.

Kieran sighed, and pulled himself up. He was not going to be able to do this alone, and he considered an alternative. Whoever that warrior was, he had defeated the vampyre and driven the kafalas back from the brink of victory. Kieran wondered if he would bow to a simple request.

'Hey!' he yelled with all his might. 'You there! Can you cut the rigging?'

The other crewmen looked at Kieran with complete bewilderment.

'Please!' he shouted again, his voice hoarse. 'Cut their rigging!'

Gerard looked at the Irishman and then back at the ship. The flashes of blue light continued but were dimmer than before, flickering like distant fireflies over the enemy vessel's deck.

Kieran sagged but pushed himself up on the rail for one last try. 'Warrior of light!' he hailed. 'Can you cut the rigging?'

The flickering continued for a moment and then disappeared. Kieran sighed again and sank to his knees. 'It's no use ...' he gasped. 'Someone needs to go over there ...'

'Wait ...' Gerard said, and pointed to the enemy vessel. With a dull thud and a loud splash, the rigging was cut from the enemy vessel, the trailing edge slipping into the sea.

Gerard began laughing and the crew cheered.

'It appears he heard you, my friend.' The captain grinned and patted Kieran gently on the shoulder.

The Irishman relaxed and closed his eyes, murmuring a quiet prayer.

'Thank you, thank you, thank you,' he added as he looked up into the stars above him. He noticed a figure emerging from the crowd of sailors, picking his way over the bodies of crew and kafala. It was William.

'You're alive,' William said, slightly amused.

'As are you,' Kieran smiled back.

William leant down and picked up his friend, supporting him as they stared over the rail towards the receding enemy ship.

'We won?' William asked.

'It seems that way,' Kieran murmured.

'Did you see him?' William said.

'The warrior of light?' Kieran replied.

William nodded.

Kieran shrugged. 'I think I did. I'm not sure who or what he was, though. But he took care of our vampyre.'

'Not to mention the enemy ship,' Gerard remarked. 'An angel on our shoulders.'

As the distance between the *Iberian* and the enemy ship widened to one hundred yards, there was a large thud, like concussion erupting from its deck, and a blue thunderbolt shot up from the enemy vessel and into the sky.

Kieran watched transfixed as it disappeared into the night, before there was a catastrophic explosion from the enemy ship. It began below their main deck and ripped along the hull of the vessel, blowing out its sides before the quarterdeck was engulfed in a final bang, showering flame, smoke and wood panelling unto the sea.

'Gods,' Gerard murmured.

'What was that?' Kieran gasped.

'Their magazine,' Gerard replied, and looked skyward. 'Our friend fired their magazine.'

'I suppose that finishes the battle, gentlemen,' William murmured as they watched the ship burn and sink under the black waves.

A quiet fell on the deck. The conflict had lasted barely half an hour, yet the price had been terrible. Now was the time to reflect on what had happened, to remember the fallen, and thank God that they themselves were alive.

CHAPTER NINE

Agents in the Shadows of the Church

△ I △

Engrin's instructions to Kieran were flawless, and he followed them without hesitation, meticulously cleaning Gerard's wound. The captain did his best not to cry out and clenched his teeth hard around a cane as Kieran cauterised the wound and William held onto the captain of the ship. With the sweat pouring from his brow, he heaved as Kieran sewed the lips of the wound together and then bandaged it.

Sitting back on the chair in the centre of their quarters, Gerard hung his head and breathed heavily.

'It will do until we get to Naples,' Engrin remarked. The old man was pale and looked older now than before; a fragile old man rather than the lithe fighter who had battled with the vampyre earlier that night.

Gerard inspected his side and nodded to Kieran. 'My thanks,' he breathed as he pulled on his jacket.

'You should rest,' William suggested.

'And who would command my crew, sir?' Gerard croaked. 'All my officers are dead. I will have to promote a few of my men first.'

William glanced at Engrin, who had not the strength to reason with him.

'How many were lost?' Kieran asked.

'Two thirds of the crew,' Gerard replied. 'Another third are bloodied. I don't think one man on this ship survived without at least a nick on the cheek.'

'I'm sorry,' Engrin murmured. 'The Papacy will compensate you for the loss.'

'It's not the loss of money that bothers me Engrin,' Gerard said. 'Was it all worth it?'

Engrin stared at Gerard, his eyes red with pain. 'Yes,' he groaned and then fell quiet.

Gerard nodded, though he was finding it hard to convince himself.

'Enough gloom, gentlemen. Let us be thankful that I have a ship to command at all,' he continued. 'And whoever that angel was, I would like to thank him personally.'

'As would I,' Kieran said, a little distantly.

'But who was he?' William asked. 'Engrin?'

The old man shrugged and looked away.

'That golden haired warrior ... he spoke to me,' Kieran admitted.

William raised his eyebrows. 'And said what?'

Kieran shook his head. 'I'm not sure. It was a word I've never heard before. A foreign word. He wasn't from England.'

'Nor any other land I know of,' Gerard remarked. 'In certain ways he resembled the vampyre.'

William nodded. 'I agree. He seemed ... well ... *dead*.'

'Whoever he was, he defeated the kafalas and the vampyre,' Engrin eventually interrupted. 'But I doubt we will have any-thing more to do with him. The matter is closed.'

There was a noise from the deck above and Gerard groaned. 'What now?' he said as he pushed himself slowly up from the chair.

'You're in no fit state to go anywhere, Captain,' Kieran remarked.

'And you are not captain of this boat, Lieutenant Harte,' Gerard growled back. 'When you become an Admiral, you may tell me my business.'

They watched the limping captain leave their quarters and

William picked up the pyramid. He'd retrieved the box from the deck but the lid was smashed and it would not lock.

'We need to find somewhere else to hide this,' he murmured.

'My trunk,' Engrin suggested. 'It should be safe there.' The old man winced again.

'Engrin, you need to be looked after. Tell me what to do,' Kieran prompted.

Engrin looked up, unsure.

'You instructed me with Gerard's wound, I'm sure you could do the same with yours,' Kieran suggested. 'Unless you have no faith in me.'

Engrin smiled slightly. 'I have faith in you. I have less faith in my own ability to stand pain. I'm too old for this kind of thing.'

The sound of voices rose outside and William fidgeted. 'Do you need my help?' he asked. 'If not I'll find out what is happening out there. It does not sound encouraging.'

'Go,' Engrin replied. 'Kieran will do just fine.'

William patted his friend's shoulder as he walked past, letting him treat Engrin alone. He opened the doors and stepped out into the corridor and then to the world outside. The smell of blood and smoke was as strong as it had been before. Already a small detail had been formed to carry the dead crew below.

Above him, on the quarterdeck, Gerard stood with his new first officer, one of the gunners that had fought alongside William. Both men were peering towards the black horizon.

'What is it?' William asked as he climbed up the stairs.

'A ship,' Gerard groaned.

'Not another!' William moaned as Gerard passed him the telescope. He squinted down it and found the ship speeding along towards them.

'What do you make of her?' Gerard asked.

William shook his head. 'It's too dark with the night upon us like this. It could be friendly.'

'Or it could be another raider,' Gerard suggested and took the telescope back from William.

'And if it is?' William asked.

Gerard laughed bitterly. 'We'll have to hope that angel returns. Look at my men, sir.'

William turned from the sea to the sailors shuffling about on deck. They were deathly quiet apart from the occasional sobs from the wounded. All had one thing in common, and that was the blood on their clothes, be it from a friend or foe. None looked fit for battle.

'We cannot survive another attack,' Gerard said, and looked up to his torn sails. 'Nor can we outrun them.'

'And there's not enough men to fire the cannons,' William added grimly.

As both men waited and minutes passed by quietly, one of the sailors came dashing down the deck.

'Sir!' he panted. 'Sir!'

William readied himself for grim tidings.

The sailor, no more than a boy, had his arm in a sling and two cuts across one cheek. He bent double and breathed hard.

'Spit it out, lad!' Gerard growled.

'The ship, sir ...' the boy gasped, and then smiled. 'She has the King's colours.'

Gerard smiled. 'The Royal Navy?'

'Sir!' the boy replied, just as relieved as the captain.

William leant back on the rail and wiped his forehead with the back of his hand.

'Thank you, lad,' Gerard replied. 'That must be the finest news I've had all day. You may even get a promotion for it.'

'A promotion, sir?' the boy said, and clapped his hands.

'Back to your station, sailor.' Gerard turned to William. He was shaking with relief and blowing out his cheeks.

'A close call,' William remarked.

'Aye,' Gerard said. 'Hopefully they will help us with our repairs. And we'll have an armed escort when we arrive in Naples.'

William nodded and cast his eyes over the deck. 'Perhaps it would be wise to dump the bodies of our erstwhile invaders into the sea, Captain.'

Gerard glanced down at the corpses.

'Privateers can be explained,' William continued. 'But these men ...?'

'I see your point.' Gerard noticed a sailor walking over to the quarterdeck. In his hand was a long black broadsword which he had obviously picked up from the deck. Gerard climbed halfway down the steps and took the sword from him. Weighing the blade in his hands, he was astonished at how light it was.

'Sailor,' Gerard began, 'you are now a temporary deck officer. Get the decks cleared of the enemy. Dump them into the sea before that naval ship reaches us.'

'Aye, sir,' the sailor replied, and hurried away.

William regarded the sword, realizing that it had probably taken Lieutenant Bexley's life. He felt triumphant that revenge had been delivered, yet he felt no relief from the burden of the battle. Bexley had been revenged, but their own lives were still in danger as long as they remained with the pyramid.

Gerard climbed back to the quarterdeck and handed William the black sword. 'This is yours,' he said.

'Mine?' William replied, staring down at the blade now resting on his palms, remembering how animated it had been in the hands of the vampyre. Now the sword was cold and lifeless, though it wore the blood of many men on its edge.

'I can't accept it, Captain,' William murmured. 'You should keep it as a trophy.'

Gerard held up his hands. 'I will not let one piece of that infernal creature stay on my ship, Captain Saxon. And I don't need a memento to remind me of what we fought for. Engrin said it was worth the loss of life, and I believe him. I have learned through bad experience that the old man is often right. You would do well to listen to him in the future.'

'I listen to him now ...' William began.

'But you do not *believe*,' Gerard interrupted, 'and that is the key to fighting this war. Believe what you see, but believe what you are told as well. Whether you like it or not, you are now part of this conflict, Captain Saxon.'

Hearing it from the Captain of the *Iberian* hammered the

news home and William looked afraid. Gerard took hold of his shoulder, his grip strong despite the wound in his side.

'You have doubts, I see,' he said. 'Push them aside and open your mind. It will be the best weapon you have. It will be your wits and instinct that keeps you alive in the times ahead. Use them.'

William nodded. 'I will, and thank you.' He shook the captain's hand and retired below deck, where he found Engrin asleep and Kieran sharpening his sword.

△ II △

The naval vessel, the *Sheffield*, pulled alongside the *Iberian* in the early hours of the morning. With the assistance of the ship's crew, they repaired the *Iberian*'s sails and tended to their wounded. Engrin was relieved to discover that the *Sheffield* had a first-rate surgeon. He patched-up Engrin's shoulder quickly and painlessly. Gerard was examined and Kieran was praised for what the surgeon called 'a bloody good field dressing'.

All signs of the kafalas had been removed and there was little talk about who their attackers had been. 'Privateers,' Gerard had told the captain. 'We managed to repel borders but at a terrible price, as you can see.'

'And the enemy ship?' the captain had asked.

'We sank it,' Gerard had replied. 'A lucky shot to their magazine.'

Gerard discovered that it was the enemy ship burning on the sea that had caused the *Sheffield* to investigate. Gerard thanked his luck. It would have taken several days to get to Naples with a battered mast and torn mainsail, rather than the day-and-a-half it eventually took them under the protection of His Royal Highness' Navy.

The journey was quiet, and William took time to rest, sleeping below or watching the *Sheffield* sail alongside them. Engrin said little, but kept staring at Kieran. An hour from Naples that the Irishman decided to find out why.

'Is something on your mind, Engrin?' he asked as they ate lunch in what remained of the shattered dining-room.

Engrin looked away and ate thoughtfully. William noticed this as well and shook his head, making a face at Kieran.

'Engrin, you've been quiet ever since the battle,' Kieran remarked.

'How is the shoulder?' William ventured.

Engrin put down his fork with a piece of salted pork on the end. He looked at William and then Kieran before flexing his shoulder. 'It will heal,' he replied.

'I'm glad,' William said. 'I was worried for a moment.'

Engrin bowed his head and chuckled quietly. 'I'm sorry,' he said, 'I have been terrible company.'

'You have an excuse, old man,' William joked. 'It's not often a vampyre lances your shoulder and you live to tell the tale.'

Engrin agreed. 'That night was a night of many sights, gentlemen.'

'Especially the warrior of light,' Kieran added.

'Yes. Indeed. The warrior of light,' Engrin repeated and fell quiet again.

'It's him,' Kieran suddenly realized and sat back, putting his hands in his lap. 'You're thinking about our saviour, aren't you? Is that why you've been quiet?'

Engrin seemed to brood.

'You know who he is, don't you?' William pressed.

'He is a beautiful terror,' Engrin murmured. 'And that is all you will learn today. No more questions until Rome.'

'What?' William asked, his fury rising. 'After all we have been through? After trusting you?'

'I have neither the will nor the strength to answer any more questions until Rome,' Engrin replied calmly. 'I hope you will forgive me.'

William opened his mouth but Kieran elbowed him in the

201

ribs. The Irishman could tell how fragile Engrin was. William bit his tongue.

'Fine, but on the condition that all questions are eventually answered,' he conceded.

'Agreed,' Engrin replied. 'Now if you will excuse me, we are nearing Naples and we need to be ready. It will be a long ride to Rome, gentlemen.'

△ III △

The *Iberian* limped into Naples just after midday, beneath grey cloud and drizzle. The merchants of Naples had risen early, pushing out wagons of fruit from the orchards in the surrounding hills, or herding livestock down through the town for their place at the port. The dismal weather did not dampen their enthusiasm as they began trading, a fact not lost on William as he peered over the rail of the frigate.

After donning more robust travelling clothes, Kieran went back to his luggage and quickly rifled through the rest of his clothes to see if everything was there. His eyes alighted on the handkerchief he'd hidden away and his heart leapt for a moment. There was a stain there, of sweat and blood. He unwrapped it quietly, hoping the flower inside wasn't damaged. Finding it intact, he breathed with relief and allowed himself to run his finger over the brittle petals.

'My dear Katherine,' he murmured and felt a tear sting his eye. Brushing it away, he wrapped up the handkerchief and slipped it into the breast pocket of his clean jacket.

On deck, Kieran found Engrin and Gerard exchanging goodbyes. He stood back, too far to hear them but near enough to see how close they were. Engrin, his arm in a sling, shook Gerard's hand and then embraced him. The captain of the *Iberian* looked sore, but he remained cheerful to the end as he approached William and Kieran.

'So, gentlemen, it is goodbye,' he said.

Kieran reached forward and shook his hand firmly. 'My thanks, Captain,' he said. 'We are indebted to you.'

William followed suit and held Gerard's hand tightly. 'When this is over, Captain, I will speak to my father about what happened here. Maybe a venture between Gerard and Saxon could be arranged?'

Gerard beamed. 'I would be delighted, sir!' the captain replied, and clapped his other hand on William's.

'It would be *our* honour,' William added.

Engrin ushered the men away, pausing to glance back at Gerard. He said nothing, but his sorry expression spoke volumes.

As they walked down the gangplank to the quay, Kieran heard Gerard say something to Engrin.

'Look after them, old man. The war is turning, as you warned. We could all use some divine intervention.'

Engrin seemed to nod and smile. Kieran felt suspicious. There were so many secrets and revelations in this new world. What sort of 'divine intervention' was Gerard talking about? It crossed his mind to tell William, but his friend was already having trouble coping with this adventure as it was.

'How long will it take us to get to Rome?' Kieran asked.

'Five days. Maybe longer,' Engrin replied.

'Will there be more vampyres?'

'There could be many things between Naples and Rome,' Engrin said. 'The Apennines hold many dark secrets – many dangers still. But vampyres? I doubt it. Count Ordrane would not have heard of his folly so quickly. He cannot send out another of his servants before we reach Vatican City. We should be quite safe.'

William sighed and scratched one of his cuts that was itching. 'I trust you have arranged horses?'

'The finest horses, William. And the fastest. I must get you to Rome immediately as there is a lot to do and many things to talk about.'

Several minutes had passed on the quayside when a thin man with black hair and a small beard waved to Engrin. He wore a slate-grey uniform and rode a jet-black horse. Behind him were three other horses tied to his. The man waved up to Captain Gerard as he stood on the quarterdeck.

The *Iberian*'s captain waved back. 'Peruzo? Is that you, Peruzo?' he shouted.

The man with the beard nodded. 'I see you have been through a storm, my friend Captain!'

Gerard smiled bitterly. 'Yes, Peruzo. And it was quite a storm.'

Noticing Engrin's frown, the man called Peruzo dismounted his horse and tied it up with the others.

'We were expecting you earlier, but heard there was a delay. Cardinals Issias and Devirus are waiting for your return,' he said, glancing warily at William and Kieran.

Engrin nodded. 'Good. We'll be leaving shortly. But I need you to ride ahead with this and our luggage,' he said, and handed the man a letter. 'It details everything that has happened since I left for Brussels. Give it directly to either Cardinal Devirus or Cardinal Issias. Not to anyone else. Not even to Lieutenant Cazotte. Understood?'

Peruzo nodded.

Engrin gestured to his trunk. 'And don't let this out of your sight,' he added. 'It holds something *very* important.'

Peruzo stared down at the trunk, something dawning on him. He nodded strongly. 'Of course. I have a number of brothers outside of the town waiting for my return. It should be quite safe with us.'

'Do not stop, Peruzo,' Engrin insisted. 'Stop for no one.'

Peruzo nodded and attended to the luggage.

As Engrin led William and Kieran to their horses, William looked unsure.

'Will the pyramid be safe with him?' he asked. 'After all we've been through I'm surprised you would trust it to one man.'

Engrin turned aside and said, 'Peruzo is a fine officer. I would trust him with my life. He is entirely loyal to our cause, Captain Saxon. Under his supervision I have no doubt the pyramid will arrive in Rome.'

William shook his head. 'Your faith in people is commendable, old man. But so far we've been attacked in a museum and at sea. What makes you so sure they will not try to attack us on the way to Rome?'

Engrin slid his foot into the right stirrup and paused. He turned to William and shook his head. 'I cannot be sure, Captain Saxon. But you of all people, as a soldier and a gentleman, know there are risks in every venture. As I said before, Count Ordrane will not learn of the defeat of his ship so quickly. It will take several days for news to reach him. It will take us only five days to arrive at Rome, and by then we will be safe. Time is on our side,' he added and pulled himself up to the saddle, swinging his leg over. 'But we should not waste it arguing.'

William sighed and held up his hands. He gave up the discussion and mounted.

'Welcome to Italy, gentlemen,' Engrin said, and smiled as he led them away, down the quay through the throng of traders. The ride out from Naples took longer than expected, due to the condition of their guide: Engrin looked weak as he rode ahead of them, and Kieran was concerned. With a five day ride ahead of them, it was on his mind to suggest that the old man should rest first. It seemed Engrin possessed an uncanny ability to read the Irishman's thoughts.

'I have ridden in worse conditions than these, Lieutenant Harte,' he said as they trotted through the suburbs. He looked ahead and saw blue sky breaking through the grey. 'The weather will clear the further north we travel.'

'If you insist,' Kieran replied. 'But if at any point you look like tiring, we will stop.'

Engrin looked as though he would protest, but instead he smiled. 'Of course,' he conceded.

By late afternoon, the city was far behind them. Ahead lay a dusty, rugged track into the barren countryside with the Apennines to the east. For the first hour they said little to each other and stared silently out towards their surroundings.

Ahead, the mountains soon appeared as the sun disappeared.

They made camp in the fields that merged with the flanks of chestnut and cypress trees huddling on the fringes of the pass, and it was while they sat around the campfire that William approached the subject of Elizabeth. 'Each day we spend here is a day when Elizabeth will not wait for you,' he said to Kieran out of the blue, his eyes on the flickering flames.

Kieran rolled over to face him, and knitted his eyebrows reproachfully. 'I never asked her to wait for me, Will.'

'But she will, Kieran. And she has done so for many years, with or without your encouragement,' he said regretfully.

Kieran frowned. 'I want to return to Fairway, Will. I miss home as well. I promise you, we *will* see England again.'

'But when?'

'When we've found what we're looking for,' Kieran replied.

William shook his head. 'I found what I was looking for, Kieran – Bexley's murderer – and now he is dead.'

'But it was the warrior of light who killed him, Will. And it doesn't finish there, does it? Do you think this Count would stop looking for us?' William didn't reply. 'They followed us to England, to the *Iberian*, so they'll follow us anywhere. Even back to Fairway.'

'What you imply, then, is that we cannot return home until this Count is defeated?' William suggested.

Kieran smiled bitterly. 'You want me to tell you something you already suspect?'

'I know we cannot return until this war is over.'

'The war will never be over,' Engrin said suddenly, having overheard their conversation. They had assumed he was asleep.

The old man sat up and poked the fire with a stick. He looked more like the Engrin they had met in London. The hours of riding had not tired him but reinvigorated him. Kieran guessed he'd been sleeping in the saddle for the most part of the afternoon.

'What do you mean it will never be over?' William asked.

'This war has lasted thousands of years, maybe even longer. It is the oldest war,' Engrin replied. 'It will not be over in your lifetime.'

'You're telling us we'll never be able to return home?' Kieran said.

'I'm saying that your return home will not be governed by whether the war itself is won or lost, but by the outcome of the battle ahead. Our fight with Count Ordrane is just a sideshow, part of the pantomime of death that has played in front of audiences since the beginning of Time.'

'What does that mean?' William asked and then looked at Kieran. 'What does he mean?'

'Sleep gentlemen, you've earned it,' Engrin said, and turned on his side, leaving William frustrated.

'Does he think I can sleep after what he has just told us?' William groaned.

Kieran shrugged and got comfortable. 'I think I could sleep through a battle.' He closed his eyes, leaving William to stare into the fire alone.

△ IV △

The next day came and went without much discussion, under grey clouds and rain. When dusk came again the clouds cleared and what little light was left turned the countryside gold and green. The old man considered where next to make camp.

Eventually they found a place under a row of orange trees some distance from the road. Engrin thought it best they kept out of sight. From the road they would appear as nothing more than farmers sitting around a fire near the field they'd been working on. It was a pretence that would not last on close inspection, but at least they could see any potential attackers approaching from the slope.

As they gazed into the small fire, Engrin regarded his guests.

'I have been reluctant to tell you certain facts over the last couple of days,' he admitted, 'but there is a reason for my reticence.'

The words came out of nowhere and neither William nor Kieran had expected the admission.

'I cannot tell you everything without a way of qualifying it. You know of daemons because you fought one. You know of vampyres and kafalas because you have fought them also. And you know of the pyramids because you have seen one. The other truths I must tell you are harder to prove. That is why I have not been forthcoming with the answers to your questions. It is vital that you believe what I have to tell you. So far I have given you shards of stories, pieces of the picture which make little sense and only conjure more questions. Questions that lead to yet more questions. That must now stop, until you know everything. I stand by my decision to be vague, until we reach Rome.'

'What is in Rome – if you permit me at least *one* question?' William asked churlishly.

'Answers,' Engrin replied. 'To *all* your questions.'

'Even to the one about returning to England?' Kieran said.

Engrin nodded. 'Even that one. But I warn you both, the answers may not be the ones you wish to hear.'

'That sounds ominous, old man.' William yawned and turned on his side, closing his eyes. 'And just a little cryptic.'

Engrin laughed. 'You should be used to my replies, Captain Saxon.'

'William,' he murmured. 'Call me William.'

Engrin settled back against the trunk of an orange tree and very soon William was asleep. Kieran remained awake, his thoughts too muddied to let him sleep. He stared into the flames, glancing now and again at Engrin who remained quiet for almost an hour.

'Who is he, Engrin? Who is this warrior?' Kieran asked eventually.

Engrin stared back at Kieran, his blue eyes reflecting the fire. They shone now, like they did the first time they had met, and it was clear the old man's strength was returning.

'I know you said you would not answer any more questions, but my instincts tell me this is one answer I will not find in Rome,' Kieran said.

'You are right. But may I ask you a question first?'

Kieran opened his arms. 'By all means.'

'What did the warrior with the golden hair say to you?'

Kieran thought for a moment. 'I can't really remember ...'

'Please try,' Engrin insisted.

'Something like "bark" ... "The Dark" ... "Daruke" ...' Kieran struggled.

'*Dar'uka?*' Engrin suggested.

Kieran's eyes alighted on the middle distance as the word unlocked the memory. In his mind's eye, he suddenly saw how grand the warrior had looked, his golden hair flowing out behind him like he was standing in a gale, though the passing time was almost languid or dreamlike. He was taller than a normal man, like a giant cast in stone. He looked unreal, pale as the moon but darker than the night. Kieran had asked him a question and the warrior had turned to look down at him with those solid black eyes. Then came the word:

'Dar'uka.'

Kieran blinked and gasped, feeling suddenly unburdened. '*Yes* ...' he whispered. 'That is what he said.'

'It is his name,' Engrin said. 'The only translation we have for this word is "plainsman". They are the oldest creatures in our world. Older, we think, than even the vampyres.'

'How do you know all this?' Kieran asked.

'Because it is written in the oldest book of Man,' Engrin replied. 'Written in a language that came before ours by thousands of years.'

Kieran could scarcely imagine that far back in history, but listened closely. 'Are they on our side?' he asked.

'Well, they are not on the *other* side,' Engrin replied, and smiled. 'Though it is sometimes hard to understand exactly whose side they are on.'

Kieran pondered this. 'Will I see him again?'

'He can never be called upon and only attends when he sees fit. It is for that reason the Papacy have never believed them to be true allies, but rogue elements. Are they instruments of God? I do not know. Many brave men who have fought against the minions of the Dark have fallen when they have most needed the aid of these beautiful terrors. The three of us have been fortunate enough to see one, and to receive his help. Let us hope we are not put in a situation where we must pray for his aid again.'

Kieran nodded. 'Amen.'

Engrin clasped his hands together and fell quiet again, but Kieran's curiosity had been pricked.

'What else do you know about them?' he asked.

'Another time,' Engrin replied. 'Sleep now. We must rise early and reach Rome as quickly as possible.'

△ V △

They left the grove early the following morning and headed further into the countryside towards Rome. William said little for most of the journey, aggrieved that he was not permitted to approach the old man about any subject apart from the weather and their surroundings.

On the fifth day the outskirts of Rome appeared from behind a range of chestnut trees. As they trotted through the glorious sunshine, they glimpsed their first sight of the shimmering city. It appeared over the hill with bright domes and towers, buildings stacked on the side of hills, and streams and roads meandering between the villas. The sun caught the golds and silvers of the city and seemed to set them on fire.

William stared and felt his heart quicken as he surveyed the beauty of Rome. He couldn't help but feel its majesty. In the distance stood the walls of the Coliseum, glowing under the rays of sunlight. Then there were the twin towers of the Piazza di Spagna, and beyond the river Tiber the ashen dome of Saint Peter's Basilica. The roofs of the villas seemed ready to melt into shadow, and save for the few citizens going about their daily chores – washing, or carrying food – the city seemed almost asleep.

Engrin trotted his horse over the ridge and down a track,

through the fringes of the inner city, with Kieran and William following closely. It didn't take long to ride through the empty streets of Rome's inner district, beyond the villas and the catacombs. As they rode through the Palatine district towards the more affluent centre, the streets began to grow busy with courtiers and people of money.

After another hour's ride, Engrin halted his horse and both men looked ahead. In front of them, lit magnificently by sunlight, was a boulevard that stretched across to a range of buildings and a domed construction. It was quiet apart from the hooded and robed men drifting silently across its expanse.

'This is where we begin, gentlemen. The Vatican,' Engrin announced and pointed down the boulevard towards the halls and walls of buildings that sat in pastel colours.

'Down there?' Kieran said.

'Down the Via della Conciliazione and beyond, my friends.'

William held the reins of his horse tightly. He was unsure whether to go on or not. Though he knew he could leave whenever he felt like it, Engrin's talk of legends and eternal wars made him think that maybe this was his last chance to turn back. Behind him lay a life in Lowchester, but a life full of fear the Count would attack him and his family when least expected. Beyond him was a path of equal uncertainty, but one which would at least keep his family safe for the foreseeable future.

'Are you ready to see the truth, Will?' Kieran asked him.

William shrugged nervously. 'I'm not sure. Are you?'

Kieran gripped the reins of his horse tightly. 'Well, we've come this far. And we have faced great dangers ...'

William nodded. 'Yes, that is true,' he admitted. 'But it isn't the path behind us that scares me.' Pulling on the reins he rode up to Engrin.

'Ride on, old man,' William said. 'In Naples you told us that there are risks in every venture. Maybe this risk is one worth taking.'

△ △ △

Engrin guided them down the boulevard and to the steps of the basilica – a great domed building coloured in whites and greys. At the stone steps were a handful of men waiting to greet them. They were lined up, facing down the boulevard, and at the front were two men dressed in grey. Standing above them at the top steps were three figures dressed in scarlet robes and red caps.

The first of the scarlet men nodded to Engrin as they halted at the steps. He smiled crookedly; his face was younger than Engrin's by many years, yet he was almost as old as William's father. The second man was older and had a small beard and moustache. He nodded but restrained any expression. The third – a stern and grey-skinned man – did nothing but stare at William and Kieran.

'Your Eminence,' Engrin said as he dismounted.

The first man smiled again and reached over to pat Engrin gently on the arm. 'Please, Engrin, no formalities here. I trust your journey from Naples was comfortable enough after such a horrific time at sea?'

Engrin nodded. 'It was.'

'Are these the two you spoke of?' the second man said coldly, while the third continued to watch Kieran and William, who were fidgeting under his gaze.

'Yes, Eminence. I would like to introduce you to Captain William Saxon, and Lieutenant Kieran Harte,' he said, and gestured to both men. They in turn bowed slightly to the scarlet men.

The first man grinned and clapped his hands, clearly enthused. 'Excellent. I am Cardinal Issias, and this is Cardinal Devirus,' the man said, and gestured to the bearded cardinal who simply inclined his head towards them. He then looked to the third man, his smile faltering a little. 'And this is Cardinal Grisome. He has come directly from Pope Pius.'

Engrin watched Grisome suspiciously, but bowed respectfully. The cardinal did little to return the gesture.

Grisome smiled thinly and spoke in Latin to the other cardinals. William understood a little of what was said, and what he understood he disliked. Grisome was distrustful of him and

Kieran, and was clearly unhappy about them being there. William was tempted to tell the cardinal that the feeling was mutual, but his grasp of Latin was poor and he couldn't remember the words needed to express his anger.

Cardinal Devirus replied curtly and it appeared enough to rebuff Grisome. 'Then I will take my leave,' Grisome said, and glanced at William and Kieran once more. 'You will find Rome a comfortable city, gentlemen, if you leave it in peace.'

The cardinal disappeared back inside the basilica and Engrin shook his head, looking questioningly at Cardinal Issias.

'We will talk later,' Issias promised. 'But first we must invite our guests on a tour.'

William and Kieran dismounted and stretched, thankful to be out of the saddle.

'I hope that you will find your stay in Rome very pleasant and worth the difficult journey,' Cardinal Issias said as he led them up the steps of the basilica. 'Cardinal Grisome is correct in one respect, the people here are very hospitable. This is a beautiful city and still one of the wonders of the world!'

Behind them, moving as quietly as the evening breeze, the two men in grey uniform took the horses and led them away.

Cardinal Issias was friendly enough, and his knowledge of the Vatican was immense. But the history of the Papacy and the many works of art inside the basilica began to bore Kieran. He was only interested in the cardinals' role in the secret war – everything else seemed superficial. Art seemed to lose its beauty, and what was history compared to the legends spoken of by Engrin?

After the tour they walked down the last halls of the basilica in silence. Presently Engrin whispered something to Issias in Latin, and while William caught most of what was said, there were moments in the conversation that were beyond him. The only information that made any sense was something to do with a 'secret army' and 'problems in the Americas'. Finally they spoke of Count Ordrane. Kieran also tried listening but he knew little Latin, and understood less than William.

After strolling through the gardens, accompanied by Cardinal

Issias' remarks on Man's love of plants and flowers, they came to a great hall guarded by two men dressed in yellow and blue, each holding a staff. They bowed slightly to the cardinals and stepped aside. The great oak doors behind them swung open with a rusty groan.

Beyond these doors was a hall with a low-ceiling, lit by oil lamps every dozen yards or so which caused the marble floor to glisten. The sunlight from the courtyard outside glowed feverishly through the tall windows that lined the left wall of the hall, illuminating the ornate decorations on the walls and the ceilings. The hall was impressive – more impressive than anything William had seen at Fairway Hall or any other of the great houses of England.

High above, along the ceiling of the hall, were scenes from the Bible and pictorial representations of saints. There were obscure coats of arms and texts in Latin, and, in the centre of the largest tile, opposite a set of crimson double-doors, a flaming sword with the Devil cowering beneath it.

Cardinal Issias smiled at William and Kieran as he rummaged in his robes for the key to the door. Devirus said nothing, while Engrin stood proudly watching his young friends as they gazed about in wonder. 'Where are we?' Kieran whispered, as Issias unlocked the double doors.

'We're deep inside the San Damosa, my young friends. Near the courtyard by the Secretariat of State. We have rooms here to welcome guests, or for debriefings,' Engrin said as the cardinal pushed the doors open.

'This is the office of the Papal Sword,' Issias announced.

'Papal Sword?' William asked.

'A name, gentlemen, among many other names for what we do here,' Cardinal Devirus said, finally. 'We are a secret secretariat dealing with concerns somewhat more tangible than faith and divination.'

Issias led them into the room beyond, also lit by candles and an oil lamp burning in the corner that gave off the smell of primrose. The room was quite large but held little furniture. On one side of the room was a desk with a crucifix set above it, while two book shelves stood on the other side. In the centre of the room were five chairs and a carpet that seemed centuries old. It looked like a tapestry to William and he stepped on it gently, fearing that his dusty boots would damage it.

Kieran and William were motioned to sit. Engrin took up his own seat opposite them, next to Issias and Devirus.

Issias lifted the hem of his robe and settled, his hands in his lap like an old maid. His face was rigid, yet the crooked smile remained. Devirus, on the other hand, seemed to be permanently scowling.

'So, gentlemen, here we are,' Issias began. 'You must be wondering about many things by now, am I right?'

Kieran nodded eagerly. 'There are a hundred questions we'd like to ask,' he said.

'Of course there are, Lieutenant Harte. You would not have come all this way otherwise,' Issias said, and tapped his fingers together. 'But before we answer your questions, I will tell you a little about what we do here. Then you can rest and we'll start again tomorrow. I believe it will be a bright day like today, am I right, Cardinal Devirus?' Devirus nodded silently. 'Engrin will take you to a place not far from Rome. It is a village hidden away in the hills and quite safe from the outside world. You will rest there and I will speak to you again – in depth – tomorrow afternoon. It is not my intention to bombard you with revelations so soon after your journey.'

'Of course. Thank you,' Kieran said.

'Firstly, you must be wondering who we are. The cardinal and I are more than officers of the Church. We are also commanders in the standard sense. We administer faith and strategy to the ongoing struggle,' Issias said.

'The "struggle" with whom?' William asked.

'The Damned, Captain Saxon, the infernal armies of Hell,' Issias answered. 'Ours is not a simple struggle with faith in God or the Church, but a conflict with those who embrace evil and make it flesh.'

215

'Daemons are loose in the streets, gentlemen,' Devirus announced. 'Not just sinners or those who are capable of sinning, but flesh-and-blood daemons. These are creatures utterly composed of terror and rage. It is our mortality and strength of spirit that matches their power. And we have our army.'

'Army?' William frowned. 'But the Papacy has no army.'

'The Church does not recognize us, Captain Saxon,' Devirus interrupted. 'Or rather, they wish not to know.'

Issias puffed out his chest and locked his fingers. 'The Church does not publicize what we do here. They would rather fight faith or the notion of sin, and at the very extreme, witchcraft. After the inquisitions of the late sixteenth century, they no longer believe in open conflict with the sword, only with prayer. While we also believe in this nobility, we know that prayer alone will not stop the flesh and blood of the infernal.'

'Which is why we have our secret army,' Devirus added.

'But why not use the armies of those countries who are loyal to the Papacy?' Kieran asked.

'There are many facts that we would not want to be made public. Apart from the questions that would be raised by the intervention of heads of state across Europe, there is the issue of what might happen should the world realize the Devil walks amongst us in the flesh and not just in spirit.'

'It would be too much of a shock for the civilised world,' Devirus added. 'Cultures would fall apart. Some would embrace the power of the Devil and we would be over-run by daemons, while the God-fearing would become paranoid and there would be a new era of unjust persecution. The Inquisition, which we have fought long to end, would become a tide of horror, where even the innocent would perish.'

'Chaos, my young friends, would aid the Devil in his work,' Issias said distantly, locking and unlocking his hands.

Issias stifled a yawn. 'We will stop here, my young friends. It is it growing late in the day and you have travelled far. You still have an hour's journey to Villeda to contend with, so we will convene until the morrow.'

'One more thing,' Kieran asked. 'The pyramid ... did it arrive safely?'

Engrin glanced at the cardinals who both nodded. 'It is in our custody and waiting for exorcism.'

'Exorcism?' William asked.

'Destruction,' Engrin quietly explained as he bent forward to them.

Issias rubbed his hands together and straightened his scarlet robes. Engrin and Devirus rose and lead them from the room, with Issias a few steps behind. As they came to the door, both William and Kieran noticed Engrin murmuring something to Devirus, who nodded gravely and replied quietly in Latin.

'Until tomorrow, gentleman,' Issias declared. 'A carriage is waiting by the courtyard to take you to Villeda.'

They expressed their gratitude, but their enthusiasm was much muted as they watched the two cardinals disappear down the ornate hall. Engrin tried to look cheerful but noticed the two officers' dismay.

'I know,' the old man said, and shook his head. 'I realize your meeting was brief, but it seems there are serious issues at work here that I wasn't privy to.'

Engrin led them back down the hall of the Secretariat towards the main doors.

'What issues?' Kieran asked as they made their way to the steps of the basilica and the waiting carriage.

'Cardinal Devirus has informed me of a breach in security within the Secretariat. It is quite serious,' Engrin said in a hushed voice, pausing as they passed the guards in yellow and blue.

'Before I left for Flanders, I was aware that certain operations were failing. Agents have been killed in suspicious circumstances and a few monks of the Papacy have died in ambushes in Spain and the Far East.'

They moved quickly down the courtyard flanked by lamps and arches near the walls of the Vatican, and Engrin continued, this time at a slower pace. 'When I left, Cardinal Devirus and I agreed that somehow information within the order was being transferred to the enemy by recreant tongues.'

'Do they have an inkling who this traitor is?' Kieran asked.

The old man shook his head. 'There are only a few who work within the strategy of the Secretariat. They are a dozen or so bishops and cardinals with a few pilgrims like myself. Cardinal Grisome has been sent to the Secretariat to ensure security becomes an issue. But if there are any further breaches without swift resolution, they may well close down the Secretariat.'

'Will we be safe?' William asked.

'Yes, in Villeda we will be secure,' Engrin said.

'What is Villeda?' Kieran asked.

Engrin beamed. 'Villeda is a shard of Eden. And it is there that you will begin your learning.'

CHAPTER TEN

Maps of Gold

△ I △

Outside Saint Peter's, a congregation of pigeons had flocked around the steps, feeding on the scraps of food left there by a passing bishop. Behind the squabbling birds was a plain carriage with two drivers in grey uniforms.

As Engrin, William and Kieran climbed down the steps, one of the men signalled to Engrin who held up his hand.

'Our ride,' he announced to William and Kieran, climbing into the carriage. 'Your belongings should already be at Villeda, gentlemen.' Engrin used the hilt of his sword to tap the roof, and the carriage began to roll forward steadily.

'Our drivers up there, who are they?' William asked suspiciously.

'They are part of the Order,' Engrin replied.

'Order of whom?' Kieran asked. 'I understood there are many Orders inside the Church.'

'The Order is of Saint Sallian,' Engrin replied, 'a saint few are familiar with outside the Vatican. He became the figurehead of our cause because he is a secret within the Papacy.'

'Under the circumstances, that makes sense,' William remarked. 'A secret saint for a secret army.'

'Indeed, but he also has the notoriety of dying doing battle with a daemon,' Engrin mentioned.

'Now I understand why I've never heard of him before,'

Kieran said. 'His deed has never been recorded, has it?'

'Not in the usual books, my friends. There are a couple of tomes in the archives, but they have never been made public,' Engrin replied

'Are you part of this Order?' William asked.

Engrin crossed his arms and shook his head. 'No. I work for the Secretariat. The Order is an instrument of the Secretariat.'

'To wage their war?' William added.

'Exactly,' Engrin replied. 'What is a commander without his army?'

'And how big is this army?' William asked. 'Something so secret cannot be that huge.'

'There are almost 200 men in the order.'

'Only 200?'

'The monks of Saint Sallian are the finest fighters in Europe, I assure you.'

William seemed unimpressed. Engrin leant forward, his face close to his. 'A monk of the Order trains from fourteen years of age until he is twenty-four,' he whispered. 'That is ten years of training in faith and wisdom, and fighting techniques acquired from as far away as China. It is a fighting style unlike anything you have seen on the continent.'

'And guns?' Kieran asked. 'Do you have firearms?'

'We have Baker rifles, the finest. We also have cannon and several other weapons that are not commonly known about,' Engrin replied. 'A monk learns to use over twenty different weapons and becomes an expert in at least eight of those.'

William's unimpressed expression began to crumble. It did sound remarkable now. He was used to being one the best swordsmen he knew, but if Engrin's boast was good, then he could quickly become outclassed by a simple monk.

As they rattled along the paving stones and cobbles, many villas and a piazza passed by the window. They slowed down to let a group of courtiers saunter in front of them; William watched as they gathered around some women on the street corner. Kieran pushed the cabin window down to let some air into the stuffy interior, and he caught a whiff of jasmine or some other fragrance. Craning his head out of the gap he admired the trees flanking the street and the flowers in many of the villa windows. Rome was a beauty, much more so than smoggy London.

Kieran closed his eyes and drank in the smells. When he eventually settled back, he suddenly felt weary as the days caught up with him. He began dozing and then jerking awake as the carriage turned suddenly up backstreets and past intimate squares marked only by a couple of corner-shops and the occasional frothing fountain.

When at last they hit another straight road and the carriage began rocking rhythmically again, Kieran's eyelids drooped despite his efforts, and he fell into a deep, dreamless sleep.

△ II △

He was jerked awake some time later and his eyes fluttered open to find Engrin talking up to the driver in Latin. William leaned out of the carriage to stare down the road ahead. Groggily, the Irishman straightened up and rubbed his face.

'What's happening?' he asked.

William shrugged. 'Something's up ahead.'

Kieran looked out of the window and found they were in the countryside. He rubbed his eyes and yawned. 'How long have I been asleep?' he asked.

'A good hour or two,' William replied.

'Really?' Kieran murmured and glanced at Engrin who simply smiled.

The Irishman looked out towards the sky and noticed the sun had passed its peak and was beginning its decent. Immediately in front of them was a short range of olive trees that looked out on an orchard that stretched to a small lake in the distance. Farmers were working nearby and some children were helping pick the lemons from the trees, playing under the adults' supervision.

'This is Appiella, a grove owned by a respected man called

Paolo. We are not far from the village of Villeda, now,' Engrin said.

As they rolled slowly by the lemon orchard, the farmers waved at Engrin, recognising the old man by his long silver beard and hair. A number of female lemon-pickers, their long hair tangled up beneath small headscarves, giggled and gestured at Kieran and William as they passed. Kieran noticed that their hands were wet with lemon juice, and there were faint streaks on their dresses. As they rode by, the sweet citrus smell seemed to lift him and Kieran closed his eyes again, feeling the afternoon sun on his face.

William opened a canteen of water and swigged from it. He passed it over to Kieran who took it appreciatively. As the carriage slowed on the outskirts of a village hidden in the cleft of the hills, William gestured out of the window and the Irishman gazed out as they rounded gently up a road through a cluster of hills. The road broke into a slender valley, cupping a poplar plantation on one side and a corn-field on the other, the village of Villeda nestling in the dip. Down the gentle slope to the village, two men stood at the side of the track smoking thin pipes, talking to each other in hushed whispers. Both men leant on farming tools, a scythe and a fork, and both wore short-swords around their waists. As they approached, both men raised their eyes at the carriage, the first one staring intently, while the second broke into a smile and shouted something to Engrin. The old man nodded slowly and waved.

'They're waiting for us,' Engrin told William and Kieran. It was the most cheerful the old man had been since they had met him in London, and it lightened their spirits to see him smile so broadly and appear so relaxed.

'How well do you know this place?' William asked, suspecting Engrin's attachment with Villeda was more than perfunctory.

'Very well,' Engrin sighed, still smiling. 'As I told you, it is our own piece of Eden.'

Kieran grinned at the thought and even William appeared disarmed by the remark. He looked out of the window expectantly, hoping this was one boast that held up.

At the edge of Villeda the welcome was warmer. On seeing

Engrin, a number of elderly villagers waved and called out, their rich accents filling the air with joy and elation. All appeared to celebrate the old man's arrival, and this rubbed off on William and Kieran, who were treated with similar elation as they stared out of the window.

'His fame precedes him,' William whispered sardonically, as Engrin called out to the villagers from the cabin.

'Like a conquering hero,' Kieran whispered back.

As the carriage turned again, trotting down the street at a leisurely pace, the busy village centre grew quiet again and William watched as small cottages moved lazily by, their eaves supporting garlands of ivy and flowers. It was a pretty little place, quaint and quiet, and the heat of the late afternoon sun brought with it the smells of herbs and flowers.

The cottages soon gave way to long fields, and then tall trees which reached over the road, creating a natural arch.

William sat back and looked to Engrin. 'Are we still in Villeda?' he asked.

'We are out on the outskirts. Near the monastery,' the old man replied quietly.

'Of the Order?' Kieran said.

Engrin nodded. 'It is called Saint Laurence and has stood for 600 years. One of the oldest monasteries in Italy, gentlemen, and one of the most respected. This will be your home while you are here.'

Soon the carriage slowed to a halt and William looked out of the window to find they were at a large stone wall with a wrought iron gate across the entrance. On either side of the gate stood three men in grey uniforms, each carrying rifles and wearing swords about their waists.

Engrin opened the carriage door and stepped out, signalling Kieran and William to stay inside. William managed to peek beyond and saw a large building standing a dozen yards beyond the walls. The stone was grey, like thick smoke had stained it, and the gates themselves stood beneath a broad arch alive with ivy that hung about it like green drapes.

After a few minutes, Engrin returned to the carriage and beckoned them out. William and Kieran climbed out and both could feel their leaden limbs ache as though they were dragging chains behind them. The prospect of a bed and some sleep was inviting.

Engrin waved a hand at the guards and they stepped aside, one of them opening the gate as they passed under the arch. 'The monastery of Saint Laurence is also a training-ground for the Order,' Engrin announced proudly, his intonations echoing gently in the long arch which led to the courtyard.

'Those men in the grey uniforms – were they from the Order?' Kieran asked.

Engrin nodded as they walked into the courtyard. 'They are used around the Secretariat for minor functions as well as field operations. Some are just noviciates; some are foot soldiers. It is sometimes difficult to distinguish between the two as there are no observed badges of office or rank among the Order. Captains and lieutenants wear the same uniforms as the foot soldiers.'

William didn't approve of this. 'How is a chain of command respected without obvious rank and file?'

'These are not peasants or criminals or mercenaries, William,' Engrin replied curtly. 'These are disciplined monks of the Order who train for years before they arrive on the battlefield. And when they fight, they do not battle in squares of men, or in rank or file. No, they fight in companies, as skirmishers; each man is easily a match for five average soldiers in armed combat. They follow orders without question and will do so with God in their hearts for they are not afraid of dying for what they believe in.' William fell quiet, reluctantly impressed.

There was a slight fragrance in the air and the courtyard was lined with pots that held some unknown yellow flower. Kieran paused to look at the surroundings and then jogged after Engrin and William, another question forming in his mind. 'Are the 200 men housed here?' Kieran asked as they walked down through the shadows of the basilica's courtyard, the sun peeking above the roof-top to illuminate the fountain in the garden.

'Largely, though some operate abroad. The remaining monks are formed into companies of thirty to forty, each led by an officer – though admittedly we do not have many experienced officers to lead the companies,' Engrin said quietly.

They climbed the steps of the courtyard and followed the old man down the hall and through a single door. Here the gloom made way for a candelabra that lit the space with an orange glow. There was a musty smell in the air. Against the far wall was another door, this one ajar. 'These are your quarters, gentlemen. They are simple, but then you are soldiers and should be used to such conditions,' Engrin said.

Kieran sighed. 'Sleeping with a roof over our heads will be enough.'

William nodded slightly. 'I personally am famished. I hope the food here is not as simple as the quarters.'

'The food *is* simple,' Engrin admitted and then bowed close to William, smiling, 'though it is also *tasty*. It may not be the same standard you'd expect from home. But food is food, and I'm sure it will taste better than field rations.'

William scowled.

'Have no fear, Captain. You will be well fed and watered. Then you must rest. I will send for both of you in the morning, so sleep well,' Engrin said, turning away from them. 'Tomorrow will be a long day.'

△ III △

Kieran and William ate late and alone in one of the mess halls across from the courtyard. The cooks brought them some simple soup and cheese and bread. William stared at the meal with dismay, but softened after trying it, for the food was as tasty and satisfying as Engrin had promised.

Having eaten enough, they retired to their rooms along the deserted corridors. Outside, night had fallen sharply and William felt a sudden chill. They had said little to each other over their meal and were silent during their stroll from the mess hall to their quarters. It was only when they had settled down on their beds that William thought to speak, the silence gnawing at him.

'Are you awake?' William whispered.

'God knows why, but it appears so,' Kieran sighed. 'I should be tired but I can't sleep.'

The bunks were meant for monks and not officers, Kieran found as they lay looking up at the narrow window high above their beds. Save for a simple table, the only furnishings were the two single beds William and Kieran now lay upon. Their belongings were arranged at the foot of each bed.

'I can't sleep either,' William admitted, rolling onto his side. 'And it isn't just the bed that's the problem.'

'How so?' Kieran asked.

'This whole place is uncomfortable. I feel unsafe, especially around the cardinals. I don't trust them.'

'But they're cardinals, Will. I'm sure we can trust them,' Kieran said.

William grunted, and then said after a long pause, 'I don't like the sound of this traitor in the Papacy.'

'I wouldn't worry about it. Why would a traitor come after us? We are nothing in this secret war of theirs,' Kieran grumbled. William heard his friend pull the sheet over himself.

Settling back, William thought about Lowchester and Fairway Hall. He tried to blot out everything he could about the battle on the Iberian and the ride to Rome, thinking about Fairway Hall: about the rides across Lowchester and the smell of roasting pork in the evening; about days spent in the fields, talking to the local farmers and merchants, and the smell of freshly washed sheets, clean and sweet. And the faces of Mother, Father and Lizzy, smiling in the summer haze.

Fairway Hall was far away, William knew.

Kieran half woke to the sound of knocking as though a bird was gently tapping on the door. At first the knocking was light, but it was followed by a series of firm bangs that jolted him fully awake. He leapt up from under the sheets, his hand going instinctively to his sword by the side of the bed.

Looking about, Kieran found that William was already awake and had his hand on a dagger he had hidden under his pillow. The door opened without warning and sunlight burst through, causing them to squint. 'Good morning, gentlemen,' a man said from the doorway. He stepped inside the room, partially blocking the glare so that they could see who had woken them so suddenly. He was about average height and dressed in the grey uniform of the Order. He had a wide grin, but his expression was free of warmth and appeared to be taking great pleasure in waking them suddenly.

'I am Lieutenant Cazotte, and you are our guests,' the man said, and leant casually against the door, arms folded. 'I trust you slept well? The beds can be a little hard, I hear, though you are both tough British soldiers and should have no fear of hard beds, is that not true?'

'We expected Engrin,' William groaned and put down his dagger.

'The old man will meet you at Saint Peter's. I am to take you there. You have ten minutes to dress or I leave without you. But then you are British soldiers and are always on time, is that not true?' Cazotte said, and began laughing.

'How well did you sleep?' Kieran murmured after the lieutenant had left them to get dressed.

'I didn't,' William grumbled, pulling on his boots. He tied on his belt and checked his sword. 'How about you?'

'I slept fine. I was too exhausted to do anything else,' Kieran admitted.

William nodded and felt envious that his friend had slept so well while he had been wrestling with his doubts. The scent of primrose leaked into the room from the hall outside and the two of them breathed in other scents of oils and wild flowers as they left their cell and made their way down the corridor adjacent to the courtyard.

As they walked over to the arch and the main gates, they noticed monks training at the foot of the courtyard. They were stripped to the waist and sweating in the early morning sun as they sparred with staffs. Each staff was as tall as a man and would have weighed as much as a musket, if not more, yet they twirled them in their hands like they were merely twigs.

William and Kieran paused for a moment to watch a pairing stand off from each other, not bowing but looking into each other's eyes with deep concentration. Then they patted their staffs twice with their hands and launched into attack. The monks traded blows and parried each strike, their hands a blur as they danced with the weapons, sweeping them over their heads as they tried to strike each other. One managed to turn his back and swing the staff behind him, missing his opponent by a hairs-breadth. The man ducked and jumped, bringing his staff down on his opponent's arm. With a crack the man fell to the ground. William grimaced, believing the man's arm had broken. But the monk lifted himself gingerly, flexing his shoulder, and although he appeared to be in pain, nothing had been seriously damaged.

Kieran glanced across from the monks and found an old Chinese man sitting cross-legged and watching his students closely. For the briefest of moments, Kieran caught the Chinese man's eyes and the old man nodded towards him; then, as though it had never happened, he was back to his students, clapping his hands twice for another pair of monks to begin sparring.

William nudged Kieran's shoulder and the two men left the courtyard quickly, remembering Cazotte's ultimatum.

The Italian was sitting next to the driver on the carriage as they appeared from the main gates of Saint Laurence. 'I had given up on you. We would have left, had you been any slower,' the lieutenant grunted from above, and turned to the driver. 'I thought the British were always on time. I thought they were tough. They are weak and lazy and never on time. Is that not true?'

The driver said nothing but shrugged, waiting until Kieran and William had climbed inside the cab. Kieran climbed in without a word, and William followed, glancing up at the Italian with a look of contempt. The lieutenant only laughed at William and barked at the driver before he had a chance to close the carriage door. Then they were away, rattling down the road under the branches of the trees at a greater speed than their ride to Saint Laurence.

They slowed a little as they drove through Villeda, but once they had passed the final cottage on the outskirts, the lieutenant urged the horses on, and the carriage raced again, churning up clouds of dust in its wake.

Inside the cab, William held onto the door as the carriage bucked and reared against the pot-holes, Cazotte urging the driver to go faster and faster. He had an idea the lieutenant was enjoying himself at their expense. There was a bump and William hit his head against the roof of the cab, cursing the Italian loudly.

Kieran said nothing and stared out of the window towards the countryside, which he'd seen little of having dozed for much of their journey from Vatican City. He quickly found there was much more to the land than he had first suspected: endless fields of crops, cattle grazing, plantation after plantation of grapes, lemons, apples and oranges. The sun had risen only an hour or so before, and it lay low, casting a bright orange sheen on the world.

Kieran was more astonished when Rome eventually appeared from behind the crest of a hill just over half an hour after they left Villeda. He could see all the way to the basilica in the distance. Now and again, men gathered on corners pointed to the carriage as it bore them away to Vatican City.

They were soon at the steps of the basilica. The carriage drew to a halt and William heard Cazotte climb out. Guessing that the lieutenant wasn't going to open the door for them, he leant out and unlocked it.

'What time is it?' Kieran said to William, who was trying his best to stifle a yawn as he climbed out onto the pavement.

'Time to learn something,' Cazotte replied. 'Today you will come to know the true meaning of the world. I hope you won't be terrified.' The lieutenant broke into harsh laughter again.

He would have continued to chuckle, and maybe taunt them some more, had not Engrin appeared silently from the doors at the top of the steps. Cazotte stopped immediately and stepped back, allowing William and Kieran to climb the steps. He signalled the driver, and the carriage moved off, down to the stables at the rear of the basilica.

'Good morning, William, Kieran. I trust you are rested?' Engrin said, his manner fresh and jovial. Both men nodded, though William tried to stifle another yawn.

'Very good. Come now,' the old man said, choosing to ignore William's tired expression. 'We must find Cardinal Issias.'

△ V △

The halls of the basilica were busy that morning as bishops and cardinals strolled by. Cazotte walked a few yards behind William, Kieran and Engrin, pausing occasionally to bid good day to passing officials. William could feel the lieutenant's gaze on his back and it made him uncomfortable. He didn't trust this Cazotte fellow, yet it appeared that, by default, he was their appointed chaperone at Saint Laurence.

'The Order has been fortunate to find so many men who are pure of faith and strong of arm,' Engrin said as they passed the Hall of Martyrs. 'Lieutenant Cazotte is a particular example of how fortunate we have been. He is a soldier who has loved his faith enough to renounce material conquests and delusions of Earthly power for the championing of Good over Evil. He is clear example to us all.'

William glanced at Cazotte who simply smiled, satisfied with the compliment. 'I am but a humble servant making his way through a time of chaos,' he said, and then murmured to Engrin a few words of Latin regarding 'redemption' and time spent as a 'mercenary'.

William hung back and turned to Cazotte as they came to the corridor near the main courtyard. 'You were a mercenary?' William asked cautiously.

A flicker of surprise registered in Cazotte's eyes. 'You know your Latin. Yes, I was a mercenary. But I renounced it to follow a true path. I know all about power and its hunger. And I know all about those who would follow such a path without considering why. I have learnt this from two masters of greed: the French and the British.'

Cazotte's expression was contemptuous as he stared at William. He flinched under the lieutenant's gaze, but could not bring himself to back off. 'You talk like a man who has had bitter experience,' William remarked.

'I served Napoleon, as I served the Coalition. Bad times. I served the French in Egypt, and I served the Allies in the Peninsular. If there was ever a moment when Man fought for the wrong cause, it was then. I saw men benefit from the deaths of others, and for what? A medal? Some pennies? Maybe a whore's love? And then death comes for them,' Cazotte said solemnly. Regarding him closely, the lieutenant then stopped William as Kieran and Engrin walked on ahead.

'Do not think that this is personal between you and me, Captain,' he whispered, as a group of bishops shuffled past. 'I will never respect you, because I know what an officer in the British Army represents. They are arrogant and pompous, and have little respect for the consequences of their actions – only delusions of honour and pride. They do not respect the will of the people; to many, war is simply a game. This is just a matter of principle, you understand. But if my view is to change, then you will have to work very hard, Captain.'

At the courtyard, by the cyclical basilica of Saint Augusta, two guards dressed in the traditional blue and yellow uniform of the Papacy stood by double doors with their pikes. They stepped aside as Engrin pushed the doors open, and Kieran, William and Cazotte followed him in.

The corridor beyond the double doors was low-ceilinged, almost like a wine cellar, and quite bare. On the other side of the doors were two other guards. These were dressed in the grey uniform of the Order and appeared far more formidable with their swords and rifles. They didn't salute Cazotte or Engrin, but the lieutenant had a few words for them in Italian that seemed to put a smile on their faces.

'These are the catacombs,' Engrin said, his voice echoing down the long tunnel. 'They are similar to the Vatican Grottoes and were designed for a similar purpose. The tombs are for those who have died in the conflict against the damned, the resting places of men who have lost their lives through battles with daemons or vampyres and their servants.'

'Are there many here?' Kieran asked as they came to one tomb with a figure of a knight carved into the stone lid.

Engrin nodded solemnly. 'Yes, there are many, *too* many,' he said running his hand over the image of the knight, with a look of sadness.

Leaving the tomb of the fallen brother, they journeyed deeper underground, down ramps and small flights of steps. They were now many feet below the city. At this depth the only light in the catacombs were the intermittent lamps burning in the alcoves along each stretch of corridor. The burning oils could do nothing but add to the stale tang of the air as they travelled onwards.

'Where are we, Engrin? I feel we have been walking for all ages,' William moaned. They hadn't seen a soul in almost an hour, and the corridors seemed as bare and featureless as the ones before.

'We're in the sub-section below the fifth tabernacle, near the tomb of Saint Sallian,' Engrin replied, and glanced at William over his shoulder. 'We're not far from the Map Room.'

As they came to the end of the corridor, there was another bend that rose up a ramp towards a flight of steps. From there, a narrow tunnel stretched a dozen yards or so towards a darkened alcove. At the alcove was a single door guarded by four monks of the Order. They stood like statues on either side of the entrance.

Kieran noticed how their swords on their belts glinted in the light of the underground lamps. Each monk held a spear that barred the way. But it was their stony expressions that made them appear so formidable, as though they would stand fast in the path of the Devil himself.

Cazotte took his place by Engrin and spoke to the monks in Latin. One by one, they stood back and Engrin moved past them. He pushed the door with both hands and there was a low groan as it swung slowly open. The door must have been at least a foot thick and able to withstand great force. They entered, with the Italian bringing up the rear. The door closed behind them with a thud that shook the stone floor.

The next room appeared to be another tomb of sorts, lit by two corner oil-lamps that gave off a fragrance unfamiliar to William and Kieran. It seemed to lift them and make the stale air more palatable.

Engrin bid them over to the far side of the room, where a red curtain formed an entrance to the inner catacombs. The way was low and Kieran ducked as he passed under, but William banged his head on the ceiling. He cursed quietly and heard Cazotte chuckling in the darkness.

The corridor was narrow and low, and so gloomy that it was hard to find their way. Then all at once there was light, and Engrin emerged from the corridor with a smile, followed closely by Kieran and William. Straightening up, William was surprised by the change of scenery.

The room they had entered was lavish and draped in tapestries which appeared to be many centuries old. Each one seemed to bear different motifs, as though collected from around the world. On closer inspection they all seemed to depict the battle between good and evil. William examined a silver cup in an alcove; engraved on the surface was an angel laying low a beast breathing fire.

William turned his attention to the voices coming from above them and looked up to find light glowing from windows carved in the rock a dozen feet overhead.

'What's up there?' Kieran asked.

'Is that the Map Room?' William suggested.

Engrin nodded and put a finger to his lips, then led them up a flight of stairs to the gallery. As they climbed, there was more light, which seemed to illuminate the air around them. It appeared as though daylight had somehow found its way down into the heart of the catacombs. It was composed of a myriad of different colours, a spectrum which was almost dazzling.

William glanced up and saw Kieran gazing around him as he reached the top, his mouth open in awe. When he too arrived at the gallery, William could understand his friend's astonishment. The gallery itself was circular – with diameter of at least forty feet – and the walls were carved with an elaborate image of a serpent. On the other side of the gallery were a series of arches from which the coloured light appeared to emanate. As they walked slowly about the gallery, there were more treasures to be found – shelves of books and alcoves that burned feverishly with lamps or candles in ornate holders. Some of the candles appeared to have been burning for years, their stands dribbled with long lines of wax.

William was entranced by the treasures around them but Kieran moved towards the arches and peered down to the voices coming from below. He gasped and turned back to Engrin.

'The Map Room?' he ventured and then turned to William with an expression of astonishment. Engrin nodded and ushered William over to where Kieran now stood. He too leant over and looked down to the source of the coloured lights and voices, gasping like his friend.

In the centre of the room below, engraved upon the floor, was a map of the known world, depicted in gold – every continent, every island, every place known to civilised man.

The lights they had seen from the stairs came from the markers on the map. Standing on Italy was a candle with a bright blue flame that fizzled gently. Nearby, merely a foot away in the

North of Italy, stood a yellow flame that flickered to and fro, and to the north was a large red candle casting a pool of crimson light beneath it.

Across the map were other flames – red, blue, yellow and green, a kaleidoscope of colours that painted rainbows on the walls of the gallery.

'I have never seen its like in my life,' William gasped. 'A map of solid gold?'

'A strategist's map,' Engrin said proudly. 'What it is made out of is irrelevant, my young friends. Gold is quite resistant to the markers, as you can see. If silver had been more resistant, or bronze, then the map would have been carved from those metals. Its value lies purely in its function.'

'What do the flames represent?' Kieran asked.

'The influence of the Devil, the might of the Papacy and the regions of unrest.'

'Which are which?' William asked.

'The blue flames for the righteous, the red for the damned, and yellow for the cautious. Sometimes we deploy other flames as we see fit. Green flames are sometimes lit for victory; eternal smoke for defeat,' Engrin replied. 'There is a man in Rome who specialises in these unique markers. He is quite the magician, conjuring blue, red, green and yellow flames from the simplest of candles. It is purely alchemy I have no doubt, but they serve a great purpose.'

'The largest red light to the north of Italy,' Kieran said. 'Does that represent Count Ordrane?'

'Yes. In the Carpathian Mountains. You have keen eyes, Kieran. That marker is bigger than the others and has been burning for centuries now, since the Map Room was built.'

'Centuries,' William murmured. 'So the Count is immortal?'

'Did someone mention Count Ordrane?' a voice said from behind them.

The three men straightened up and found Cardinals Issias and Devirus standing nearby. Issias was beaming, while Devirus scowled.

'Your Eminence, I was describing the function of the Map Room,' Engrin explained.

Issias held up his hand. 'Please, please, don't let me interrupt you, Engrin. I asked you to give our guests a tour, after all.'

Cazotte stepped forward and bowed to the cardinals. 'Your Eminence,' he said, and put his hand in his jacket, producing two letters.

'Ah, news I see,' Issias murmured and Cazotte passed the letters to Devirus. 'What fortune do they bring, Devirus?'

The bearded cardinal looked over the first one and cleared his throat. He began to reply in Latin, but Issias frowned and held up a hand. 'Please, Devirus. We have no secrets from our guests now, do we?'

'If you insist,' Devirus grunted. 'The first letter is from our Man in the North, near the border of the Carpathians. It appears the regent of that province is reluctant to help us ... And the second piece of news is graver still.'

'What has happened?' Issias asked.

'The Scarimadaen from Gembloux is missing,' Devirus replied, glancing at the two guests.

'Scarimadaen?' William said. 'You mean the pyramid?'

'You said it would be safe,' snapped Kieran. 'You said it would be destroyed!'

'I believe this is another act of the traitor in the Secretariat,' Devirus suggested. 'Only the Secretariat knew of the Scarimadaen from Gembloux.'

'How could this have happened?' Kieran demanded. 'Even after your assurances? You said that once in Rome the pyramid would be safe.'

'I know, I believed it to be so ... but ...' Engrin paused, 'I did not believe that the traitor in the Papacy would be so daring.' The old man looked to Devirus.

'Was it not delivered to the Furnaces as instructed?' he asked the cardinal.

'Yes, the Scarimadaen was delivered, but between here and deliverance to the Furnaces, the original was switched for an imitation,' Devirus said, reading the rest of the letter.

'Then that settles it. There is a traitor here,' Issias declared.

Devirus folded away the letter. 'May I suggest that we place restrictions on the centre of strategy here in the catacombs and in the city above?'

Issias shook his head. 'No, that will restrict the work we do, but we should increase security and be more vigilant.'

'We have recorded the destruction of over 200 pyramids,' Engrin whispered to William and Kieran. 'That's 200 fewer daemons.'

'But how many does that leave?' William remarked.

'We understand from writings that there could be over 600 Scarimadaens in all,' Devirus said.

'So that still leaves 400 pyramids,' William stated. 'I believe you are struggling uphill.'

'There is still much to learn,' Engrin announced. 'Please be patient, my young friends.'

'Gentlemen,' Issias said, walking over to them. 'You have seen but a little of our world; now I must ask: how long will you be staying?'

Kieran shrugged and looked to William who appeared a little agitated. 'I'm not sure I understand your question,' he said, though he secretly understood what it implied.

Issias locked his fingers. 'It is a simple question, Captain Saxon. You came here with Engrin to protect the Scarimadaen. Since it has disappeared, you are free to return home.'

William shook his head. 'I was under the impression the Count would attack us if we dared to.'

Issias nodded. 'Perhaps. Though we cannot be certain of it.'

'Cannot be certain?' William repeated, a little angrily. 'But there is a risk?'

'Count Ordrane knows who you are, and what you did in Gembloux. He can include many servants and a vampyre in the list casualties caused by you and Kieran,' Engrin said. 'So there is a risk he will seek revenge on you.'

'And if we stay away, would he dare attack Fairway Hall?' Kieran asked.

'Who can say for certain, but it is very doubtful. Ordrane's interest would lie with you only,' Issias said.

William blew out his cheeks. 'Then that settles it. I will not put the family in danger. We will stay for a while, if you'll allow us.'

Issias smiled. 'Very well. But we will require your services, gentlemen.'

'In what capacity?' William asked.

Issias gazed over the map. 'Not many can claim to have fought a daemon and defeated it. You have also survived an attack by a vampyre, and I understand from Engrin that you proved yourselves on board the *Iberian* during the sea battle.'

William and Kieran nodded cautiously.

'You are both veterans of war, survivors of Waterloo and other campaigns. You are young, brave and strong,' Issias continued. 'Perfect for the Order.'

'We are not monks,' William said.

'You do not need to be,' Issias replied. 'Cazotte is not a monk either. He earned his place through devotion, training and reputation. Peruzo too. We have some officers in the Order who are monks, but most are not. Mercenaries, soldiers and even former criminals have led our men into battle. Monk-hood is not a prerequisite.'

'I accept,' Kieran blustered, grinning.

William frowned at his friend. 'This is not a game,' he hissed at the Irishman.

'And I am not playing one,' Kieran hissed back. 'But while we are under their protection, should we not offer something back?'

William pondered this and reluctantly agreed. 'We will serve the Order, while we are here,' he replied. 'What will become of our rank?'

'It remains,' Issias said. 'You will be a senior officer, and Mr Harte retains his rank as lieutenant.'

'And the British Army? Will they not be looking for us?' William asked.

'They will be contacted and, as far as possible, told of the situation. I am sure we will have their complete cooperation,' Issias said, and mused for a moment. 'And as we are in debt to you for all that you have done thus far, I will send someone to watch over Fairway Hall.'

'Someone?' William said.

'A guardian angel,' Issias smiled. 'I trust there is a nearby town to the hall?'

'Dunabbey,' Kieran replied.

'They will be stationed there,' Issias said, and looked to Devirus. 'Could you arrange this?'

Cardinal Devirus nodded.

'Lieutenant Cazotte will look after you while you are at Saint Laurence. You will train with the monks and Engrin will answer your questions,' Issias added.

'We must leave you now,' Devirus announced. 'Issias and I have to meet with Cardinal Grisome on the recent breach of security.'

Issias sighed and nodded wearily. 'Of course. Until we meet again, my young friends,' he added and walked away to consult with the scowling cardinal.

'You have embarked on a great adventure,' Engrin said as he led them away from the Map Room. 'But it is one fraught with danger and revelation in equal measures. You do realize that, don't you?'

'We've faced both a daemon and a vampyre,' Kieran reminded him. 'And our luck holds out still.'

'If you intend to join the Order you will need more than luck to survive. The Order will not just train you to become a better fighter, it will train you to become a stronger person in spirit. And it will not be easy.'

Kieran appeared resolute. 'I am not afraid of hard work.'

William agreed. 'Nor am I. Who will be training us? You?'

Engrin shook his head. 'No. Cazotte.'

Chapter Eleven

Hard Lessons

△ I △

William was convinced that Cazotte took particular pleasure in waking them early the following morning. The lieutenant clearly had a purposeful vindictive streak. He disliked Kieran, but seemed to take special satisfaction in angering William, who would have surely stabbed him when he came to wake him, had Cazotte not tipped him out of bed first.

'Time to get up,' the Italian growled. 'Training begins in ten minutes. Be in the courtyard.'

William didn't see Cazotte leave but muttered something about him being 'a bastard'. Kieran said nothing and quickly dressed, strapping on his sword as William fumbled about in the gloom.

'Come along, Will,' Kieran motioned, as his friend pulled on his boots.

'I'm coming as quickly as I can ...' he grumbled. He hadn't slept well since they had returned from Rome the evening before. Everything they had learnt that day had filled his mind with doubts. He had woken several times in the night with questions trembling on his lips. If Kieran had suffered similarly, he hid his weariness well.

Having dressed, they stumbled down dark corridors, using an oil lamp to guide their way.

'I can't believe he's woken us so early,' William griped.

'Cheer up, Will. It's not so early, see ...'

William looked out of one passing window and saw pink sunbeams stretching from the hills. They passed dormitories which were empty apart from a few monks brushing the floors.

'I wonder how long they have been awake,' Kieran whispered.

William nodded, realizing they were probably lucky to have slept in so long. Minutes later, they arrived at the courtyard; it too was deserted.

'Where is Cazotte?' William asked. 'He said to meet us here ...'

Stepping out into the yard, they looked around, their eyes adjusting to the gloom.

'We must have been mistaken,' Kieran said.

William was tempted to fly into a tirade about their shoddy treatment, but stopped when he saw several cloaked figures emerge from various exits. They were hooded in dark robes, their arms concealed within. William turned to find that several others had blocked off the door from which they had come.

'Will,' Kieran said, and his hand went to his sword.

'Who are you?' William demanded.

The figures halted, and then in a blur, each figure tossed back their cloaks to reveal clubs in their hands. Without warning they attacked. William pulled his sword free and parried the nearest attacker, his sword ringing against the wood. He swung and ducked and swung again, his blade hitting wood time and time again. Kieran was not faring much better, but had managed to cut down two of the figures before one struck his wrist and he yelled out in pain and dropped his sword.

On seeing his friend disarmed, William lunged to protect him, punching an assailant in the face before parrying a blow intended for Kieran's skull. He then turned and knocked the club out of an attacker's hand before driving his knee into the man's groin. The assailant fell to the floor, and William pounced on him, pulling back his cowl to skewer the man between the eyes. As the hood flew back he saw the face of a young man, fearful as he looked at William's sword.

'Enough!' was shouted from across the courtyard.

The cloaked attackers stopped and then lowered their clubs. One by one they pulled back their hoods. William and Kieran gazed upon them in bewilderment. They were all monks.

The man William had pinned lay back with his hands in the air, completely passive. William shook his head and stood up, letting the man crawl away. As he regarded the others, he was surprised to find those cut down by Kieran's sword pulling themselves to their feet. Now each of the monks revealed in turn the armour under their cloaks, the only injury being to the bloodied nose and lip of the monk William had punched.

From the shadows the voice emerged, clapping limply. 'Not bad,' Cazotte said as he walked towards them.

'What is the meaning of this?' William demanded.

'A test,' the Italian replied. 'I wanted to see how much you already knew.'

'By hurting my friend's hand?' William pointed at Kieran who held his damaged wrist.

Cazotte shrugged. 'That wasn't intended.'

'Intended!' William exclaimed and started towards him.

'Will!' Kieran stopped him. 'I'll be fine. Nothing's broken ... Just bruised.' The Irishman flexed the wrist gingerly.

William crossed his arms angrily like a petulant child. All he wanted was an excuse to smack the Italian around the face.

'I hope we didn't wound anyone,' Kieran said.

Cazotte smiled and glanced around at the monks. 'A few bruises and cut lips, but they've had worse, Lieutenant Harte.'

Kieran half bowed to them and the monks bowed back before melting into the shadows.

'You rushed in to save your friend, Captain Saxon. Under normal circumstances that would be considered a weakness. Here, I would say your compassion for your comrades is an asset,' Cazotte explained.

William appeared humbled and nodded. 'Thank you,' he uttered, with some difficulty.

'You still fight like an old woman with the grace of an elephant. If we had been fighting for real, you would be dead.'

William snarled at him, but Kieran nodded in agreement.

'Can you train us to be better fighters?' the Irishman asked.

'I thought you'd never ask,' Cazotte answered.

△ II △

With the sun fully risen, William and Kieran watched uneasily as three rows of ten men, all stripped bare, had their heads ritually shaved and every area of their body examined by a hunched monk with an eye-glass, in the courtyard. Despite being naked, the monks looked far from uncomfortable standing on parade. He hoped that neither Kieran nor he would have to endure such a ritual.

'What is happening here?' Kieran whispered to Cazotte.

The Italian smirked and for once his mockery was aimed at others. 'They are initiates, and this is the test of purity.'

'Do they have to stand naked?' William complained.

'Why do you ask? Are you afraid that you will have to stand naked with them, British?' Cazotte grinned, apparently reading his mind. 'They are shaven, as initiates of most religious orders are. But they are also checked.'

'For what?' Kieran asked.

'Concealed weapons and marks of the Devil,' Cazotte replied. 'We have enough problems with spies in the Secretariat.'

William looked across the lines of men gazing straight ahead.

'Do not worry, Saxon, you do not need to go through such a test,' Cazotte mocked.

William opened his mouth to reply but bit his tongue.

'I have no problem with being naked nor seeing others so,' Kieran said, turning to Cazotte calmly. 'Though there is a difference between being naked and being humiliated.'

'Humiliated? Hah, this is nothing! It is necessary for the security of the compound. It ensures none of the Count's agents can infiltrate Saint Laurence. After all, would you wish to sleep with a dagger under your pillow every night?' Cazotte said, and raised his eyebrows at William.

Again William held his tongue.

'I see,' Kieran replied. 'If it is deemed necessary, then ...'

'Believe me, it is.' Cazotte glared at Kieran, but the Irishman held the Italian's gaze. 'Enough of being a spectator. Now you must be trained.'

He led William and Kieran away from the courtyard down a cold narrow corridor built from rough stone. It was dark and uninviting, but they followed the Italian closely until they reached a long hall. It was quite immense and flanked by table after table of weapons.

William raised his eyebrows and blew out his cheeks. 'Lord, you are prepared,' he remarked.

Cazotte nodded. 'Every weapon known to man is in this room. Only a brother who has mastered four of these weapons can be deemed ready for combat.'

'Four?' William murmured and approached the first table. There were a number of strange-looking knives. William was impressed with their craftsmanship, but they didn't seem so formidable. He walked to the next table and found some sharp steel stars.

'What are these?' he asked.

Immediately, a monk appeared in front of him, surprising William. He was old and hunched and looked up at William with a strange smile. He said something in Latin and William managed to piece the sentence together.

'You throw them?' he murmured.

'Is this your choice of weapon?' Cazotte asked.

William shook his head. 'I would not know where to begin with them.'

'If you wish to be trained in their use, only Master Yu knows of this discipline. It is part of the Asian art of combat,' Cazotte told him.

William stepped away and glanced around the other tables. His eyes alighted on a line of sabres of different lengths and shapes.

'You are not in the cavalry now, Saxon,' Cazotte grunted.

'Then why have these here at all?' William said, picking up

one of the swords. 'Are you saying the Order has no horses?'

'Of course it does,' Cazotte replied.

'Then this is the first weapon I wish to master,' William said as he stared at the sabre in his hands, an almost perfect weapon and one that would have brought a smile to the finest rider in the Dragoons.

'Pick another weapon as well,' Cazotte ordered.

William looked up from the sabre and saw the cold expression. 'Another?'

'Another,' Cazotte insisted and gestured to the other tables.

William put down the sword and looked around. He saw all manner of hand-weapons: maces, hammers, daggers, spears, staffs; but none appealed. He then came to the firearms and looked down at the rifles. Lifting one, he felt how heavy it was. A formidable weapon. Close-quarter fighting was one thing, but firearms always evened the odds, especially when fighting cavalry.

'The rifle,' Cazotte said, and picked up another from the table. 'You wish to master the Baker rifle?'

William glanced about in case he was missing anything. Then he nodded.

'Very well,' Cazotte said. 'The sabre and the rifle. Conventional, but fair.'

Kieran returned to them with a grin. 'I couldn't decide, so I went for the broadsword.' William looked down at the long weapon he was lifting with great effort.

'You are jesting,' William said.

Kieran shook his head, his expression suddenly serious. Cazotte looked down at the sword, almost as big as Kieran, and laughed again, slapping the Irishman playfully on the back. 'If you can master that, Harte, then you will forever have my respect. But perhaps a smaller broadsword for now.'

Cazotte walked over and found a second sword, a little shorter than the one Kieran cradled, but a vicious-looking weapon nonetheless. Kieran looked at it and frowned. He obviously preferred the bigger weapon, but nodding reluctantly, he returned its larger and heavier cousin to the table.

245

Cazotte regarded their choices and nodded. 'So it begins,' he declared. 'Your training will be hard, sometimes brutal. You may come out of it with a few scars. But you are both soldiers, and should expect no different.'

He leant forward to both men and smiled humourlessly. 'I myself will ensure you are treated as badly as the other monks, and just as hard. There will be no favouritism, and I expect no weakness.'

'You will get none, I promise you,' William guaranteed.

Cazotte cracked his fingers and laughed. 'I'll make you remember that, Saxon. So, to your first test: how to handle a Baker rifle. And I know just the man to teach you.'

△ III △

Cazotte took William alone to a field at the back of the monastery, at the bottom of which were several mannequins made of straw. Tied to each one was a picture of a face painted on canvas, and each one was clothed.

William halted and stared out towards them, frowning.

'Target practise?' he asked.

'Maybe, if you don't shoot yourself in the foot first,' came the reply. The voice was not Cazotte's. Indeed, it sounded English.

William turned and found a round, ageing man with stubble and a wounded eye which had all but disappeared under scartissue. William tried his best not to grimace at the fellow's disfigurement.

'This is Wilcox,' Cazotte said.

'A pleasure meeting you,' William said, his hand outstretched.

Wilcox grunted and brushed past him towards the mannequins.

'A friend of yours?' William said.

'A colleague,' Cazotte replied. 'He will train you in how to fire a rifle, Saxon. I will return in a few hours to mark your progress.'

The Italian clucked in the back of his throat, and swaggered away, leaving William with Wilcox. who just seemed to wander around William, regarding him suspiciously.

''Ave you ever fired a rifle before?' he growled. William met the man's one eye and shook his head.

'Never?' Wilcox pressed.

'Should I have?' William replied.

'You're a soldier,' Wilcox said.

'Yes, sir, that I am. The Cavalry.'

Wilcox glowered at him. 'The *Cavalry*. Posh whores riding on their fancy 'orses with their swords thinking they're 'igh-'n'-mighty ...'

William stepped back, his mouth hanging open at the insult.

'What's the matter, Saxon? Never 'ad anyone talk to you like that?' Wilcox said.

William pressed his lips together. 'No,' he said.

'I expected not,' Wilcox mused. 'I would 'ave been flogged by now, eh? 'Ung maybe? You're not in the British Army now, boy! 'Ere you'll do as I say, when I say it!' As he ranted phlegm and spittle came forth, landing near William's boot.

This fellow was worse than Cazotte, and it stung more because he was English. Perhaps the only other Englishman in all of Villeda.

Wiping his lips, he reached down and grabbed William's rifle, checking it carefully.

'What is this?' he asked William.

'A rifle.'

Wilcox growled and threw the rifle back at him. 'Wrong! It is a Baker rifle. It is forty-six inches long, .625-inch calibre, with a thirty-one inch barrel, bayonet extension and sighted for 300 yards. It weighs over eight pounds.'

William looked down at the weapon, noting the weight. 'The stock is English walnut, isn't it?' he asked.

Wilcox spat at his feet. 'Don't be clever with me, *boy*. I'll do the teaching 'ere!' he growled, pacing about in front. ''Old it as you think you should.'

William lifted the weapon with his left hand under the stock and his right hand supporting the butt, with his forefinger against the trigger.

'Don't point that bloody thing at me!' Wilcox smacked William's hand with the short cane he held in his left.

William snarled and stared back at Wilcox, thinking that it wasn't by accident that Cazotte had chosen this man to train him. Even if he had decided on using the staff, or the spear as his choice of weapon, no doubt this Wilcox would have been his instructor.

'Pull it to your shoulder!' Wilcox yelled, smacking his shoulder with the cane. 'Gods! 'ow the 'ell did you become a soldier? Your father buy you a commission?'

William bit his bottom lip until he felt blood seeping into his mouth. This foul-mouthed individual was trying his patience and the lesson was only minutes old. Wilcox took hold of the rifle, showing William what he had to do.

'See?' he gestured. ''Ands 'ere, rifle-butt against 'ere. You don't do that an' you'll miss the bleedin' target. If you don't lean into it, the kick will break your collarbone!'

He then tossed back the rifle to William who caught it with both hands.

'Now do it again!' he demanded and William lifted the rifle. He mimicked the instructor perfectly, but Wilcox slapped his hand as his finger wavered towards the trigger.

'Never put your finger near there unless you wish to fire it! Damn and blast!' he roared.

William, his hand sore, moved his finger away. It was a good thing the weapon wasn't loaded, for he was tempted to fire at Wilcox.

Wilcox examined the rest of his stance and grudgingly admitted it was fine.

'You know how to fire one of these things?' he asked.

'Squeeze the trigger?' William ventured.

Wilcox snarled and brought his stick down but William caught the blow with the barrel of his rifle which it hit with a clang. The swiftness of his parry surprised Wilcox.

'Don't do that again,' William told him. 'There might be no rank in the Order, but if you hit me again, by God I'll put you on your back.'

Wilcox stared at William who met his gaze firmly.

'You think you're so sure of yourself,' Wilcox remarked. 'I've 'eard all about you from Cazotte. Spoilt rich kid found 'imself in trouble.'

William nodded. 'Maybe. And I'm sure Cazotte also told you that I defeated a daemon and faced a vampyre and survived. Not to mention my experience as a soldier in Spain and Waterloo.'

Wilcox rubbed his chin thoughtfully.

'Did he not mention that?' William said, noticing his faltering expression.

Wilcox cleared his throat and spat to the floor. 'Before you fire that thing, you'll need to load it,' he continued, a little more civilly.

Wilcox taught him for the rest of the morning and into the afternoon. William learned to load and shoot, his first shot close to the target, his second was spot on. Even Wilcox grudgingly admitted that William appeared to be a natural.

Finally Wilcox threw up his hands and declared that training was over for the day. He said nothing as he departed, leaving William alone in the field, with the smell of gunpowder on his fingers and smoke hanging in the air.

He picked up his rifle and examined it. The barrel was still warm. He hoisted the rifle to his shoulder and squinted down its sight. He was still unable to load and fire as quickly as Wilcox, who could squeeze off four rounds per minute compared to his poor two. The man was swift and accurate, despite his bulk and only having one eye, yet William knew he could better him with enough training.

'You're a natural, I hear,' someone said behind him. Cazotte leant against the wall of the monastery, absently fingering the grip of his sword.

249

'It was your idea to put me in the hands of Wilcox, was it not?' William asked.

Cazotte nodded.

'The man is a bully,' William remarked.

'I know,' Cazotte replied. 'That was the point.'

William snarled and squared up to the Italian. 'Why is it you hate me so, Cazotte? Is it because I won't be intimidated?'

Cazotte looked frankly at William and smiled. 'My intention was not to bully you. If you think I have, then I apologize. I thought the British were tougher than that. It seems I was mistaken,' he said, obviously hoping to anger William even more. 'As for Wilcox, he hates the aristocracy for subjugating his people.'

'His people?' William said.

'He is Irish. His people are Irish. They have suffered because of British rule. *Your* rule,' Cazotte said plainly.

'He doesn't sound Irish,' William frowned.

'Nor does your friend, Harte,' Cazotte said. 'Wilcox is not his real name; that was discarded so he could come here as a free man. He is wanted for the killings of several important aristocrats from Ireland.'

William narrowed his eyes and seethed. 'And you made him train me?' he said, disbelievingly. 'Do you know how close we were to fighting each other?'

'Quite close, I would assume,' Cazotte said. 'But again, that was the point. I wanted to test you. I wanted to see if you would back down or come out fighting. As it happened, I was correct.'

'Why? What did you think I would do?'

'You would come out fighting,' Cazotte admitted and folded his arms. 'The monks of the Order are well trained and obey without question. But they need leaders. In time, I think you may become one, as you have a strong spirit. You are also a natural fighter. It has taken you four hours to master a weapon that usually takes men days. I wonder if your skills with the sword will come so easy.'

'Then this is all a test?' William said.

'Partly,' Cazotte replied, and began sauntering away. 'One thing you can be sure of, Saxon. I still dislike you.'

△ IV △

William trudged wearily into their room and slumped down on his bed, feeling secretly proud of his accomplishments that day. He had procured some grease and polish from the weapons store on the way back. Sitting alone, he began cleaning the rifle.

Eventually Kieran hobbled in, his leg strapped. William frowned and pushed the rifle aside, regarding his friend closely. As well as the strapped ankle, he had a cut on one cheek.

'What happened?' William asked.

Kieran hobbled over – a little gingerly, but he still appeared cheerful. 'I sprained my ankle,' he said, and sat down slowly. 'Bloody silly, really. I dodged under one of the swords and bent back too much. I went over.'

'Painful,' William remarked. 'And the cheek?'

'Revenge for splitting the lip of a monk,' he replied, and laughed.

'You split his lip?'

'With the hilt of my sword,' Kieran sighed. 'They tried to teach me to fight like a gentleman, Will, but you know me ...'

'You fight dirty,' William mused, remembering their fencing lessons as young men.

Kieran shrugged. 'I do what I must,' he admitted. 'It may be unorthodox, but I'm still alive. I doubt I would be if I just used fencing techniques. Anyway, Master Yu says I'm making progress. How did your lessons go?'

'I have a bigot for a tutor,' William murmured. 'He hates me and all I represent. Still, I put him in his place, and discovered that I am a natural shot too.'

'Did you tell them you had fired a rifle before?' Kieran said.

William shook his head.

'So you didn't tell them that you used to go hunting?' Kieran laughed.

'I didn't want to get his hopes up.' William grinned and glanced down at the rifle. 'Damn fine weapon. Better than anything Father has.'

As he stroked the greased barrel with a piece of cloth, Cazotte appeared at the door.

'You are both wanted in Rome,' he said, 'and will travel in the morning.'

'Rome?' William asked. 'For what?'

'The message didn't say.' Cazotte glanced at Kieran. 'Your ankle is swollen?'

Kieran nodded and patted it. 'I'll be fine. I heal quickly.'

'Good,' Cazotte said, 'I wouldn't want any injuries to slow your progress. The brothers say you fight like a wolf. You have already earned their respect. That is a good sign.'

Cazotte left then, leaving Kieran particularly cheerful with a grin like a Cheshire Cat's.

'Respect, eh?' William said.

'I guess a few cuts and bruises make you one of the men,' Kieran said, folding his hands behind his head. 'Just like the Army.'

'Mmm,' William pondered, secretly envious that his friend had made a bond with the monks already.

'So, tell me more about your tutor?' Kieran asked.

William almost told him, but then he recalled how Kieran had come to Family Saxon in the first place. Kieran was the son of a Lord in the south of Ireland. While the Hartes did their best to support the surrounding communities, they had their hands tied by British law. One day two brothers were caught stealing food to keep their family from starving. Lord Harte had had no choice but to enforce British law, and they were hung, as any other would be hung.

And then the attacks started, on Harte's staff, and once on Kieran himself when he was just a boy – he was almost run down by a shadowy rider while walking with Lady Harte. This act finally drove Kieran's father to send him to England. At the age of eight, Kieran moved to Fairway Hall, the home of Lord Harte's schoolboy friend. Lord Harte and Lord Saxon had known each other since they were boys and it was hoped that William and Kieran would soon bond.

They might have bonded sooner, had news not arrived at Fairway Hall three weeks later that Lord and Lady Harte had been murdered on their estate by Irish rebels. The news devastated them all, but Kieran could only retreat into himself. It took him over two years to recover.

Kieran was waiting for an answer. Even if there was no evidence that Wilcox was responsible for his parents' deaths, William knew that the knowledge that the man had been one of the rebels involved in killing English aristocrats would be sufficient to rouse hatred in Kieran, and quite possibly a desire for revenge.

William folded his arms and shrugged. 'Like I said, he's bigot,' he replied finally, 'and he seems to dislike me.'

'Why?' Kieran asked.

'Because I'm a captain and his superior,' William said nonchalantly. 'Either that, or he didn't appreciate my threats to punch him out.'

Kieran opened his mouth in shock and then laughed out loud. 'That would do it!' he declared and slapped his thigh. 'And I thought I was the rash one!'

William let him laugh, but made a mental note to keep him away from Wilcox.

△ V △

There was no sign of Cazotte the following morning as they trudged to the gates of Saint Laurence. William strapped on his new sabre, while Kieran elected to keep the sword Engrin had given him in London. The broadsword was mighty, but he had yet to master it and the shorter sabre was familiar.

A carriage waited outside. Two monks sat atop it, one clutching a rifle. William ventured a few words in Latin and the driver replied.

'What is it?' Kieran asked.

'I simply wanted to know where Cazotte is,' William said. 'Apparently he was not invited to the Vatican.'

Kieran made a face and it turned into a grin. 'Is he out of favour, I wonder?'

William shrugged and climbed in. After a day of being cooped up in the monastery with Cazotte and Wilcox ridiculing him, he was glad to be away. Engrin and Cardinal Issias always made them feel welcome, though it was curious that no one seemed to know why there were being summoned.

The carriage moved away slowly down the road from Saint Laurence, in the shade of the trees. William stared out of the window and felt calmed by the gentle rocking. Kieran also looked content, despite his bandaged ankle and the nicks on his cheek.

'When are you taking sabre training?' Kieran asked.

William shook his head. 'Who knows? When I've mastered the rifle?'

'You can shoot well enough, can't you? Unless Robert lied to me that time.'

'When was this?' William asked.

'When you went hunting a few years ago, Robert said you shot a pheasant while lying on your back. He said you slipped and fell, but when the beater startled the pheasants in a thicket you bagged one almost 300 yards away.'

William remembered and smiled. 'Yes, I recall that happening,' he said, though secretly he hadn't been lying down but kneeling, and it was more like 180 yards. Still, Father had been impressed by his accuracy.

'It isn't my accuracy that is letting me down,' he said, 'but how quickly I can—'

There was a sudden bang and the sound of wood tearing near the frame of the door. Bits of wood showered down into the cabin. Kieran looked up, dumbstruck.

'What on earth ...?' William murmured and then came another shot, ringing from the valley outside. It struck one of the driver's above and there was a moan as he slipped to the ground.

William looked out and saw a shape in grey uniform roll into a ditch behind them. Another shot and the horses went wild and

254

began to stampede down the road, the remaining monk up above yelling at them. He was wrestling for control, but the speed and rocking of the carriage told William the horses were unrestrained. He and Kieran hung on to their seats as best they could, Kieran grimacing in pain as his ankle gave way again.

For a moment, the cabin ceased rocking, and then with an immense crash it turned over and the world around them tumbled. William's vision was punctuated with flashes of white pain and then hurtling greens and yellows. The wind was crushed out of him and his vision flashed with a million lights as he was tossed about. Darkness followed and the sound of crunching timber filled their ears.

Then, finally, the cabin rolled to a halt.

William opened his eyes, one filling with blood, and looked about. The carriage was on its side, with the roof of the cabin dented in several places. Kieran was unconscious against the door, a steady trickle of crimson from his temple coming down his check and chin.

'Oh God ... *Kieran*,' William slurred and crawled to his friend. The breath against his hand told William he was at least alive, but he had no idea how well he was. He tried to wake him but he was out cold.

He could hear distant voices.

'Kieran ... I have to move you,' William said, though more to himself than his unconscious friend.

The voices grew as William pulled and pulled. He pushed open the door to their prison and bright sunlight invaded, making the pain in his head even worse. It was all he could do to keep from fainting. As he climbed out, half stumbling into the open air, he gazed about, bewildered by their surroundings. They had landed in a ditch by a field of corn; the horses had disappeared as well as the driver who had fallen from the carriage. The other driver was dead, half crushed under the carriage, only his legs sticking out.

More voices came to his ears, and they sounded aggressive.

'Shooting,' William murmured, remembering what had happened. He looked to Kieran and began pulling him out of the ditch, into the shoulder-high crop. He managed the task as the first voices approached the road behind the rolled carriage. They talked in Latin, and another language, one which William couldn't understand.

He pushed Kieran deeper into the crops and pulled out his sabre, though he knew he would be no match for an outnumbering foe, especially in his dazed condition.

And then he noticed the rifle lying a few yards away from the carriage on his side of the ditch. Gritting his teeth, he dashed for the weapon, then went to the body of the crushed monk and began pulling at his belt where the cartridges were held. Grimacing, he pulled with all his strength. Ignoring the pool of blood he was kneeling in, he tugged until the belt came away.

The voices came closer, one voice in particular, and William feared he would be found. Without hesitation, he half-cocked the lock and grabbed a cartridge, pouring some powder down the barrel. He bit the ball away and spat it in after the powder and rammed it with two swift strokes as footfalls came around the corner of the wrecked carriage. He set the lock to full-cock just as a man in a brown jacket and cap appeared, a sword in one hand and rifle in the other.

Their eyes met. William stared at the man, trying to judge his intentions.

Friend or foe?

The man yelled out and rushed at William with his sword.

Foe.

Smoke filled the air and the man spun backwards in a spray of blood. He fell to his knees, crawled and then fell on his face. It was enough time for his comrades to appear and for William to load again.

Now came three other men, also dressed in rustic clothes and carrying guns and swords. They paused briefly to look at their dead friend before attacking William, who barely managed to cock the lock before firing again, hitting the nearest man in the belly. Luckily the man stumbled back into his friends, buying William precious time as he pulled out the sabre. The other two attacked and William parried against their blows, his movements awkward and slow. Despite the strength pouring out of him, he managed a few tricks, sliced through the stomach of one of them, before the other thrust the tip of his sword into William's arm, opening up the old wound from the British Museum. The pain was excruciating and his fingers let go of his sword as he stumbled against the carriage. He put his heel in the pool of blood and slipped, falling against the cabin with a thud as his head hit a panel. He was aware of another commotion, a horse galloping down the road, before he passed out completely.

CHAPTER TWELVE

A Simple Errand

△ I △

William felt as though he'd been sleeping for weeks. His head was heavy, painfully so, and there was a horrible metallic taste in his mouth. Every muscle seemed to hurt. Opening his eyes, he saw Engrin perched on a stool by his bed.

'Awake, are we?' the old man asked.

'I don't know ...' William slurred.

'You were struck on the skull,' Engrin told him.

William blinked in recognition. 'Struck? When?'

'Yesterday.'

William closed his eyes. 'Yesterday. We were travelling ... to Rome?'

'But you never arrived,' Engrin said.

William frowned painfully. He opened his eyes wide and looked around the room like a frightened child. 'Oh Lord ...' he murmured. 'I remember now. We were attacked ...'

'Yes,' Engrin confirmed gravely.

'And Kieran?' William said, and then stopped, fearing the worst.

'He lives, but he will take a little longer to recover.'

William managed to push himself upright, but winced, and would have fallen had Engrin not held him up.

'You were lanced in the shoulder,' the old man said.

William squinted through the pain and leant over to his side. Gingerly, he pulled away his shirt and found a series of stitches across a small wound.

'It was shallow, thankfully, and is healing quickly,' Engrin remarked as William made himself comfortable. He looked about and found himself in a long whitewashed room with a number of beds in it. In a bed on the far side of the room lay Kieran, resting but quite pale. He strained a little to see him, but the effort sapped more of his dwindling strength and William had to relax again.

'Rest easy,' Engrin said, and pulled the sheet back up to his shoulders. 'You need to preserve your strength. Kieran is in good hands.'

'What happened to us, Engrin?'

'You were attacked outside Villeda,' the old man began. 'You and Kieran were found unconscious next to your carriage. The drivers were both killed.'

'By whom?' William pressed. 'I remember killing two of them ... who were they?'

'You killed three,' Engrin said, 'and at first we thought they were only bandits. Even this close to Rome, the hills are not entirely safe. But later we discovered they were hired men.'

'Hired?'

Engrin shifted on his stool and leant forward. 'One of the bodies had a mark on its arm.'

'What mark?'

'The mark given to all the servants of the Count. The leader of the ambush was one of Ordrane's men – a kafala. He was waiting for you.'

William's skull ached. 'I don't understand,' he moaned. 'How did he know we were going to Rome?'

'Because we did not request your presence,' Engrin said grimly.

'You what?'

'We did not send for you and Kieran. The message was sent by this agent, to lure you into a trap,' Engrin replied.

'You were outwitted by something so simple?' William said.

'I can only apologize, William,' Engrin said sadly. 'We did not know. We did not suspect that they would go to such lengths. The brothers at Saint Laurence assumed the courier from the Vatican was genuine. He wasn't. Nor was the letter. When the kafala's body was taken to the monastery, he was identified as the one who bore the letter.'

'Gods,' William murmured and held his head in his hands.

'I'm sorry,' Engrin apologized again.

'You mentioned a mark,' William said. 'What is this mark, in case I see it again?'

'A series of lines, waves if you like. Each time a kafala carries out a mission successfully he is branded with a wave. Once he has five waves, he is turned,' Engrin replied.

'Into what?'

'A vampyre,' Engrin said. 'It is an honour for them. It is why they serve the Count – the promise of immortality. Our friend had four waves on his arm, so he was regarded highly. That is why the Secretariat is so concerned with this change in events.'

'So the traitor has revealed himself,' William said.

'No, he was not the traitor. This kafala has never been seen in Rome before. The true traitor has been working within the Secretariat for some time now. It is doubtful the traitor is linked to this.'

William thought for a moment. 'Cazotte sent us, Engrin.'

Engrin looked at him and after a few seconds he shook his head. 'The traitor isn't Cazotte.'

'Are you sure?' William said. 'How can you know?'

'Because he saved your lives,' Engrin replied.

William fell silent.

'Cazotte suspected something was wrong. He interrogated the brothers who were handed the message and then looked through the message himself. It was signed by the Secretariat, but forged, and not a good forgery. Cazotte doesn't usually check messages such as this, but thought the vague request was strange, particularly coming from Cardinal Devirus. His suspicions grew and finally he Cazotte galloped after you.'

'Why didn't he stop us from going if he believed something to be wrong?' William asked.

'Because, apart from Cazotte, no one believed anything was wrong; even Cazotte felt foolish for being so suspicious. He killed two of your ambushers and chased off the others. He found you against the carriage and Kieran in the grass. One of those he killed was our kafala.'

'Then I should be grateful,' William admitted reluctantly. 'But it is a pity he didn't keep the kafala alive.'

'Cazotte realises this as well,' Engrin sighed. 'He admits to losing his temper. But then two brothers had been killed and he was enraged.'

William grimaced. 'How much disaster can follow one man, Engrin?' he said weakly. 'Why us?'

'Because of Gembloux. Because of the *Iberian*. And because the Count is afraid of you. We believe he will do anything to have you both killed, and that is why both of you will be sent on an errand as soon as Kieran is well enough.'

William frowned. 'An errand?'

'The safest option is for you to leave here while the Secretariat unmasks the traitor and his plans. When all is secure, you can return to Rome without fear of reprisal.'

'Yet we cannot return to England,' William said. 'He will follow us there, won't he? This is no longer about the pyramid.'

Engrin seemed to agree.

'Can the Count be defeated?' William asked.

The old man shifted uneasily on his stool. 'I won't lie to you. He will survive long after you and I are mere bones underground.'

'So this is how it is? Exiled forever?' William lay back and looked at the ceiling. It was whitewashed but covered with dust and spider-webs. 'We'll stay, then,' he sighed, feeling tired once more. His eyes closed and he slept, Engrin pulling the sheet over him.

△ II △

Outside Engrin's villa in Villeda, a number of children were playing with a sheepdog in the sandy street. They had been playing with the animal for a good hour and the sun was near its peak in the cloudless sky, making the ground around them shimmer in a haze. William didn't know how they managed to keep running about in such heat, and marvelled at their energy.

Finally, after much laughing and screaming, the dog became more and more excitable until it broke into a loving frenzy, pinning one of the children to the floor and licking her face as the others screamed and laughed some more.

William smiled as he watched, feeling a warmth he hadn't felt in a while. Kieran, who looked pale, sat in the chair nearby. He still appeared unwell, but had complained when William told him he was planning to meet with Engrin alone. Reluctantly William agreed to allow his damaged friend to come along.

'Do you believe in prophecies?' Engrin asked.

'Prophecies?' Kieran croaked.

'Visions of the future, or stories of what may be. Do you believe in them?'

William shrugged and Engrin passed him a large soft roll to dip in the garlic and olive oil. It had been their first tasty meal since the attack three days before. They had been instructed to eat a very bland broth and coarse bread to help them mend.

'Visions,' William said. 'There was an old man who lived in Dunabbey who had visions. Do you remember, Kieran? Everyone thought he was a little mad? We later discovered he drank too much.'

Engrin laughed. 'I see. So all prophets are drunks?'

William didn't reply and dipped his bread again.

'There have been many prophets and many prophecies, and not all have been drunks or delirious,' Engrin explained. 'Some have been saints or holy men. There was one man – a Frenchman called Nostradamus – who was wrongly believed to be a prophet when in fact he was merely a translator. It was said he prophesied many things that may have happened already. He foresaw Napoleon's rise to power and has foreseen other events that might happen in the next century. Catastrophic events that could mean the end of the world.'

William looked up from his bread. 'Nostradamus? I think I've heard of him. A Frenchman from the sixteenth century?'

'The same. His writings have been marginalized but we at the Secretariat believe differently,' Engrin said. 'We know the text from which his so-called prophecies originate.'

'You speak of a book?' Kieran whispered.

'I speak of the oldest book of Man, Kieran,' Engrin replied. 'It is written in a language only a handful of men have translated through the ages. One of those was a physician called Michel de Nostradame. He was in fact the greatest translator known to the Vatican, and he had a great and keen intellect. A man of many talents, yet he was compelled by an appetite for power, and abused the knowledge given to him.'

William put down his food and sat back. 'As I recall, his work was open to interpretation. Indeed there are a few who consider him a crank and fraud,' he said.

'That was our fault, I'm afraid,' Engrin admitted. 'Or rather the Papacy's. The knowledge Nostradamus gave to the world was never meant to go further than the walls of Vatican City, and thankfully, most of it didn't. Nostradamus only translated a fraction of the history of Man but he used that information to fuel his prophecies.'

'But how? How can a book influence what happens in the future?' William asked.

'This no ordinary book, but a blueprint of the cycle of man. It talks of three brothers – in essence, three Anti-Christs – who will cause a war on Earth. No one is sure if it means now or later, though it speaks of a soldier who will unite Heaven and Earth against the Devil. Nostradamus thought this meant a soldier would open the land to heresy, but we at the Vatican believe it means that soldier will face the Heretic and the Devil on the field of battle at some point in history. Some even say that time is now,' Engrin added.

William sipped the wine slowly from his cup, realizing what the old man was driving at. 'A soldier? You mean either Kieran or myself?' he said, smirking. 'And I thought it was I who was struck on the head!'

Engrin crossed his arms. 'I understand your scepticism, but

the translation clearly states that a soldier will emerge from the *wars* and lead an army against the Devil.'

'There have been many wars, Engrin. Our war with Napoleon has been only one. How sure are you that the text does not relate to a future war?'

Engrin couldn't reply.

'You can't be sure, can you?' William reasoned. 'Mayhap you are eager for this prophecy to come true because you are losing this war. Mayhap you want either Kieran or I to be your savours, but we are instead only men.'

'Mayhap I am not the only one who suspects that one of you may be the man described in the text,' Engrin replied. 'The Count wishes you dead, because he believes the prophecies as well, even if you do not.'

William considered this for a moment. 'I've had enough lucky scrapes in the past six months to think that someone was watching over me, maybe Fate. And not just me, but Kieran as well. If there is a guardian angel then he must be run ragged trying to save both our necks. Fate is destiny and destiny can be controlled by no man,' William conceded. 'We are at the mercy of this prophecy then, old man. If it comes true ... well, we'll just cope with that when it happens.'

'Well, enough of such talk for now,' Engrin suggested. 'The pre-ordained is hard for the soul.'

'Agreed,' William said, rising from the table. 'If you will both excuse me, the wine has gone quickly to my bladder.'

Engrin laughed gently and watched him leave. He then looked to Kieran who was watching the streets. He had said very little that afternoon and at times looked frail.

'How are you feeling?' he asked.

'I've felt worse,' Kieran replied, trying to appear comfortable.

'I understand the training was going well,' the old man ventured.

Kieran nodded.

'What weapons were you mastering?' Engrin asked.

'The broadsword and the sabre,' Kieran replied.

'The broadsword?'

Kieran nodded.

'A formidable weapon.' Engrin pondered for a moment, his thoughts elsewhere.

'Is there something wrong with my choice?' Kieran asked.

'No. Not at all. Just curious,' Engrin replied. 'Have you ever wielded one before?'

'Never.'

'Was your decision influenced by anything or anyone in particular?' Engrin asked.

Kieran looked uncertain.

'Yes?' Engrin pressed.

'The *Dar'uka*,' Kieran admitted.

'I see,' Engrin smiled.

Kieran turned himself about in the chair, though he struggled to do so. 'Is there anything more you can tell me?'

Engrin shook his head.

Kieran appeared deflated.

'Kieran,' Engrin began. 'Both you and William will be leaving here soon. And perhaps, if you are lucky enough, you will see this *Dar'uka* again. This "plainsman".'

'I hope so,' Kieran replied.

'And if you do, please promise me something,' Engrin asked.

'Anything.'

'Come back and tell an old man the story!' He smiled, his eyes sparkling.

For the first time in days Kieran smiled back. 'I promise.'

William reappeared and sat back down at the table. 'So, what have you been talking about?'

'Oh, very little,' Engrin replied. 'Only your training.'

William groaned. 'Oh. That.'

'From what I hear you have both done extremely well,' Engrin said.

'My instructor hates me.'

'I see,' Engrin replied. 'But his lessons have already paid off. You killed two of the ambushers in the field with a rifle. Had

265

you not been trained, it is doubtful you could have achieved that.'

'I've had my hands on firearms before,' William admitted, 'I just didn't tell Wilcox.'

'Really?' said Engrin.

'I don't want Cazotte or any of his friends believing they can put one over on me,' William explained. 'In everything, I try to have the advantage.'

'Don't get too carried away with hiding your skills, William,' Engrin suggested. 'You are being assessed for your role in this errand.'

'Oh yes, the *errand*. When are you going to tell us what this errand entails?' William asked.

'I won't be,' Engrin replied, 'the cardinals will do that. I am but a messenger.'

'Always ducking questions, and always the cryptic,' William remarked with a shake of his head. He grinned at Kieran and they drank some more, their thoughts on more peaceful times.

△ III △

'The boy is called Carlos, and this is his peer, Marresca,' Cazotte said.

William regarded the young men, stripped to the waist, their expressions calm.

'They're just boys,' William whispered to Cazotte. 'You wish me to spar against them?'

Cazotte nodded. 'Of course I do. If you cannot beat an initiate you are worthless to me.'

William stared at the Italian, waiting for him to say it was a joke, but Cazotte turned to the initiates and clapped his hands. Cazotte then bowed to Master Yu who stared on, po-faced.

William took his position at the top of the courtyard and drew out the sabre, still in its scabbard. He stared back at the boys and Cazotte. William didn't like this one bit. The monks of the

Order were famed for their skills and mastery of sword-fighting, but these boys were only initiates. How much could they know?

Master Yu pointed at the boy called Carlos and the initiate stepped forward, raising his sword in the air along the length of his chest, the blade also in its scabbard. He bowed to William, who bowed back. Then Master Yu clapped his hands and the initiate stepped forward.

William swallowed nervously. He didn't want to be defeated by a mere child (although, to be fair, the boy was only eight years younger than himself) but at the same time he didn't know how far to take the sparring.

The boy attacked and William parried. The initiate was an awkward opponent. His sword skills were minimal and crude (his thrusts had no aim and his parries lacked control) but he was also resolute and enthusiastic. The boy concentrated on every movement from his opponent, and responded confidently. With each subsequent parry, the initiate grew more controlled and was able to predict with greater accuracy the attacks of his opponent.

In short, William's adversary was learning too quickly.

The old Chinese mentor sat by the edge of the courtyard on a little reed mat, watching the duel calmly, betraying little interest towards either William or the initiate. The sparring had lasted almost twenty minutes and the sun above the courtyard was cooking William in his shirt and trousers. Rivers of sweat were pouring down his back and he could feel his shirt clinging to every inch of his skin. He understood now why the initiate was stripped to the waist, wearing only a simple pair of trousers made of the same stone-grey material worn by the monks. His head was also shaven. The boy showed no perspiration at all.

Eager for an end to the contest, William lunged again and the initiate parried. William leant back and swung the sword sideways, catching the initiate off guard. He parried again but was pushed off balance as William advanced. The young man swung back but lost his footing. With a dusty thump, he landed on his backside and the sword fell from his grasp.

William was somewhat relieved, and walked over to help the

young man up. The initiate nodded at William and then bowed to Master Yu, who remained impassive as ever.

'Bravo, Captain Saxon! You spar well.' Cazotte clapped and swaggered over to him to whisper: 'Though if the initiate was any slower a cripple might have beaten him!'

Master Yu scowled at Cazotte but the lieutenant ignored him, placing a hand on his own sword. 'I wonder if you could fight like that against the enemy.'

'You forget, Lieutenant, I have fought a daemon.' William wiped the sweat from his forehead.

'And a vampyre, and in Spain, and at Waterloo,' Cazotte teased. 'How can I forget when that is all you tell me? I haven't forgotten. But you had help then, and maybe this daemon was unlucky. Maybe this daemon was a little slow, yes?' The Italian laughed.

William put his sword out and smiled, despite feeling tired from the heat and the sparring. 'Maybe we should find out if that is so? Do you think you're the measure of me? Eh, Lieutenant?'

Cazotte looked doubtfully at William and for a moment he thought the Italian was going to back down. 'It would be my pleasure to teach you something,' Cazotte said, unbuttoning his grey jacket. He tied back his hair and pulled out his sword, in its scabbard.

'I would not like to cut you, and disfigure that beautiful face,' he mocked.

William snarled and pulled his own scabbard away, letting it clatter to the ground. 'Do you think you frighten me, Cazotte?'

Cazotte rubbed his chin and nodded. 'Very well,' he said, pulling away his scabbard. 'I will only nick you. Do you think you have the dexterity to do the same?'

'Shallow wounds only? Yes, I can do that,' William said, 'but I'm not promising you won't be scarred.'

Cazotte shrugged and walked around William, his sword out in front of him. 'Who would notice one scar amongst many,' he said, pulling off his shirt. His back was ribbed with scars, most probably caused by a whip. His chest was also a nest of scar tissue, from small nicks to long wounds.

William faltered. This is not the British Army now, he thought and unbuttoned his own shirt. He pulled it off and laid it behind him so he too was stripped the waist. It was refreshing to feel the air and sun on his back and arms.

Cazotte smiled, faintly amused by William's unmarked skin. He soon concentrated again and stepped forward with his sword. William knew this fight was going to be tougher than the one with the initiate. He would not be fighting against a novice. Cazotte was a veteran and an unknown quantity. He had been a mercenary in the war and had survived, and William knew there was a distinct possibility the Italian would outfight him.

The boy Carlos and Master Yu sat quietly, the mentor whispering something to the initiate who nodded. For him this would be a learning experience. To William it was going to be a question of pride.

'En garde,' Cazotte said casually. William stood with his sword pointing forwards, and looked the Italian square in the eyes. Cazotte moved in a blur and William felt the tip of the sword miss his cheek by inches. Blinking, he backed off and ducked to his left as another of Cazotte's blows came close. The Italian was quick and William's fears had been demonstrated in the first few moments of the contest. He realized that Cazotte could have the measure of him and deliver a good scar to remind him of it.

The lieutenant turned on his heels and swung low towards William's legs. He dodged, lifted his legs and bashed the hilt of the sword into Cazotte's ribs. The Italian stumbled to the side and cringed as pain blossomed up one side. William caught his breath. Cazotte was fast and controlled but he could not defend as quickly as he could strike.

The Italian rubbed his side as a reddish mark spread over the skin and scars where he'd been struck. He glowered at William and snarled. William readied his sword again. The Italian rushed forward and twirled the sword one way and then the other. Both swings were unpredictable and both almost caught William off-guard. He parried the first and dodged the second, but as he turned, the Italian swung his elbow into William's face. With a smack, William reeled backwards, seeing nothing but white light, feeling pain scream up into his head. He stumbled and felt blood coming over his lips and down his chin. Shaking his head, he put a hand to his nose which was bleeding well. He looked up and found Cazotte grinning at him with satisfaction.

'I hope I haven't permanently marked you, British. I doubt it will stop you from charming the ladies,' he mocked and paced around him, waiting for William to raise his sword.

'*Bastard*,' William hissed and tried to snort out the last of the blood from his throbbing nose. He raised his sword again and the Italian beckoned him on. William lunged, and Cazotte stepped back to swing his own sword towards him. This time William parried it but dodged the other way catching Cazotte by surprise. As the Italian swung his arm around to catch William again, it only found thin air. William lifted himself and thumped the handle of his sword on the back of Cazotte's head. The Italian fell to the ground and slumped forward clutching his skull.

William stood away and wiped the blood from his chin.

'I hoped that hasn't marked *you*, Lieutenant,' William grunted, sniffing as he felt another trickle of blood run over his lip. The Italian crawled over to the side of the courtyard, where he touched the back of his head tenderly, the blood on his fingers testament to the force with which William had delivered the blow.

'Didn't Bexley teach you that trick?' came a voice from courtyard steps.

William looked up and could only smile as he found Kieran standing there dressed in a shirt and trousers. His smile weakened as the pain in his nose made him wince, but he sheathed his sword and strolled over, dabbing the back of his hand to the bloody mess. Kieran looked weak, but at least he was well enough to stand.

'Walking now, are we?' William asked.

'Yes, and it appears not too soon. In my bed for a few days and already you're getting yourself into trouble,' Kieran remarked, glancing at Cazotte who was dabbing the back of his head with a handkerchief.

'Not at all. We were just sparring, weren't we, Lieutenant?' William said, turning to Cazotte, who was still clutching his head.

The Italian glanced up and scowled. 'Only this time, British. Next time it will be different.' Cazotte's gait was groggy and a little unsteady, but he managed to get to the other side of the courtyard, and disappeared down one of the corridors.

Master Yu and the initiates followed quietly, leaving William alone with Kieran.

'So what have you been doing while I've been resting? Busy making enemies?' Kieran murmured.

William shrugged. 'No. Maybe just some competition. Cazotte has something against us. Especially me. He feels threatened.'

'I thought it was because you were an aristocrat in his eyes? A member of the gentry? You're saying he feels threatened by your authority? That's doubtful. He's a monk of the Order – you're not,' Kieran remarked.

William winced again, his nose throbbing harder.

'It would do us well to keep Cazotte on our side, Will. He killed our assassin. He might be competition but I would rather he was watching our back from now on than giving you a bloody nose.'

'You're right. I'll apologize the next time I see him, if he doesn't stab me first,' William said sardonically. He patted Kieran on the shoulder, glad that his friend had recovered.

△ IV △

The ride to Rome seemed longer than usual. The sky above was dark and cloudy and their driver spoke of a storm coming. It did nothing for William and Kieran's spirits in the wake of the urgent message they had received ordering them to report to the Secretariat immediately. Although the message had been carefully scrutinized to confirm its authenticity, they were jittery about travelling to Rome for the first time since the ambush a week before. Kieran was still recovering, though William felt fine apart from his bruised nose. Cazotte had kept out of his way since the sparring contest, and on those occasions when they had crossed paths, the Italian simply scowled and murmured something in his native tongue. At least it meant that William could train in peace and Kieran could recover without any trouble. Now, with the summons from the Secretariat, both men had an inkling that more trials were on the horizon.

When they pulled up outside the steps of the basilica, Engrin and Cardinal Devirus were waiting for them. Also present were a number of guards and the third cardinal they had met on their arrival at the Vatican. William and Kieran got out of the carriage and exchanged concerned glances with Engrin, who was somewhat subdued.

'Gentlemen, you remember Cardinal Grisome?' Devirus said.

William and Kieran nodded silently.

'Ah, the two British officers from the Army. I trust you find Rome satisfactory?' the cardinal said. Kieran and William nodded.

'I doubted that Pope Pius would approve of this,' Grisome remarked to Devirus. 'He doesn't wish to have outsiders meddling in Papal affairs.'

'The Pope would approve if only he understood what we want to achieve within the Secretariat,' Devirus said.

'Do not attempt to tell me what Pope Pius would agree to and what he would not. He has become weary from his time in captivity in France. Now is the time to rebuild our previously annexed states, not embroil ourselves in further turmoil. This is not a matter for the Secretariat but for the whole of the Papacy. We must talk.'

Both cardinals walked up the steps towards the doors of the basilica, leaving Engrin and the monks with William and Kieran.

'Engrin, what's happening?' Kieran whispered.

'One of the companies of the Order was massacred two days ago in the Carpathians. Word of this has returned to the Papacy. They are concerned.'

'Was it the traitor?' William asked.

'We believe Ordrane may have been forewarned, but we cannot be sure. Our informant was killed in the attack, as well as twenty other men. The Count sent us a message.'

'What message?' Kieran asked.

'The right forefinger of every man in the company – and the head of our informant,' Engrin replied grimly.

'What is Grisome's part in this?' William asked.

'The cardinal has been given special dispensations to relay information about our operations directly to Pope Pius. He might also be given extra powers to control those operations. That could jeopardize everything.'

'So why did you call us here? To tell us about the massacre in the Carpathians?' Kieran asked.

'Partly,' Engrin said. 'Partly other matters. You will learn of them presently. Come, we must go to the Chambers.'

William and Kieran followed Engrin up the steps and down the corridor they had first walked along on their arrival in Rome days ago. The monks followed behind, receiving derogatory glances from the Papal guards in their yellow and blue uniforms. None of them looked favourably at the monks, some muttering snide comments under their breath. William got the first real inkling of the gulf between the Order and the rest of the Vatican: the Order was despised. How deep this feeling went was unknown to William, but clandestine Papal organisations were probably only tolerated if they had a purpose, and judging by Engrin's revelations, the Secretariat was becoming increasingly redundant in the eyes of the Papacy.

Ahead of them, they could hear Grisome lecturing Devirus. It surprised William to hear Devirus being so vocal, though the voices were too distant and the Latin too complex for William to completely understand what was being said. Engrin appeared as humble as ever, trying not to listen.

'Is this about our conversation at the villa?' William asked, as they reach the main hall and made their way towards the Secretariat offices.

Engrin turned slightly but was non-committal. 'We spoke of

273

matters of theory. The facts will become clearer once we have met with Cardinal Issias.'

William grumbled at the ambiguous reply and picked up his pace. Kieran was lagging behind. He still felt weak and found it hard to breath after walking so quickly. The physician had told him to rest and take the next few days easily, but Kieran had to be active. He'd learnt from his time at Gembloux that if he stopped to rest his body would give up. He had seen too many good men turn into cripples because they had abandoned themselves to their wounds or maladies.

Outside the offices of the Secretariat, Engrin waited patiently, Cardinals Devirus and Grisome having already disappeared inside. Neither William nor Kieran knew what was happening. Looking up, William noticed some lines in Latin, which when translated read:

> *He who offers the truth, offers the burden of the truth,*
> *He who takes the truth, takes the burden,*
> *He who takes the burden, carries the torch*
> *across the Inferno.*

William swallowed hard and pictured himself holding the torch in both hands as Devirus appeared, beckoning them forward. They went inside, feeling apprehensive. This time Engrin stood to the right of Cardinal Issias, who was waiting for his guests with a troubled smile. In the centre sat Devirus, while Grisome sat rigidly on the left.

'Captain Saxon, Lieutenant Harte,' Issias beckoned and motioned for them to sit in the chairs opposite. 'You are not troubled by Cardinal Grisome's presence, I trust?'

William and Kieran both shook their heads.

'Cardinal Grisome is worried about the lack of security in the Secretariat,' Issias stated. 'And I must agree. So we have decided on new security measures. Firstly, the reception of messengers will be reviewed to avoid a repeat occurrence of that tragic ambush seven days ago. Secondly, the Secretariat will be under armed guard – though, at the request of Cardinal Grisome, the guards will no longer be brothers from Saint Laurence.'

Devirus shifted uneasily in his chair.

'Thirdly, we have decided that you shall be sent on your first mission. While you are away, we will endeavour to find the individual who has jeopardised our work. Engrin has assured me that you are fit enough to travel. Is that correct, Lieutenant Harte?'

Kieran nodded, a little surprised. 'I can travel if I need to.'

Issias beamed. 'Good, good. Then it is decided.'

'Where are we to be stationed?' William asked.

'We have decided to send you to the north, near a city called Aosta, close to the mountains,' Devirus began. 'We've had reports of a renegade French captain who is terrorising the borders there. We understand his force consists of a company of French infantry who escaped Waterloo.'

'This doesn't sound like something the Vatican would be involved in,' William remarked.

'The captain is a servant of Count Ordrane of Draak,' Devirus said, crossing and uncrossing his fingers.

'Of course, I understand. Who is this captain?' William asked.

'His name is Jacques Cuassard,' Issias said.

William fell silent.

'Cuassard?' Kieran said. '*The* Cuassard?'

Issias glanced furtively at Devirus and then up to Engrin who shrugged. 'You know this man?' Issias asked.

'The Butcher of Berlin,' William murmured. 'We know him only by reputation, and he is a murderer. I heard he was killed at Waterloo.'

'He clearly survived, Captain,' Issias said wearily, 'and now he is attacking the north of this country.'

'And you want us to find him and apprehend him?' William asked.

'Do whatever you deem necessary to stop this man, Captain,' Devirus said. 'If that means killing him, then do so.'

Grisome made a disagreeable sound under his breath and Devirus sighed. 'Cardinal Grisome, we have reason to believe this Cuassard has consorted with the Devil by spreading the pestilence that is the Scarimadaen across Europe. We have evidence to implicate him in witchery, Devil worship and conspiracy to invite daemons. All can be verified. This man must be apprehended or must perish.'

Grisome folded his hands. 'I must see this evidence. I would prefer to have the man arrested and brought here for trial. Would this not also fall under the provision set down by the Coalition for all surviving French officers of Waterloo?'

The cardinal stared at William, who nodded. 'He should be arrested, sir, yes,' said William. 'But Captain Cuassard's infamy precedes him. He will not surrender. He will die fighting.'

'Then die fighting he will,' Devirus said coolly. 'He is responsible for several confirmed deaths already. The man is a murderer.'

'Very well,' Issias conceded. 'Arrest Cuassard, and if he will not be taken alive, then bring his body to Rome.'

William nodded.

Devirus sat forward. 'To achieve this aim, you'll be leading a company of thirty monks to Aosta and the surrounding region. I know that thirty men seems slight, but it is a whole company of brothers and should easily match Cuassard's force. Understand that we don't want either of you riding off on any foolish exercises. Your duty is to the mission, the people of Aosta, and your men and the Papacy. Am I clear?'

Kieran nodded.

'Did you say *lead?*' William asked, nervously.

'You'll be the captain of the company,' Devirus replied. 'They will answer to you.'

'But I don't speak any Italian and my Latin is quite poor,' William said doubtfully. 'Surely another officer within the Order would be better suited ...'

'Lieutenant Cazotte will be accompanying you. He will act as translator and second in command, with no offence intended towards you, Lieutenant Harte.'

Kieran smiled, a little relieved to be spared the burden of such responsibility.

'Cazotte?' William murmured.

'If Lieutenant Cazotte is not the officer you had in mind, then I'm sure another from the Order could be appointed to you,' Cardinal Devirus suggested.

William shook his head. 'Not at all. Cazotte will do just fine,' he said, trying to look comfortable with the decision.

'Have you any other questions?' Devirus said.

'When do we leave?'

'Tomorrow morning,' Issias said. 'You must begin packing, gentlemen, and inspecting your men. The longer you wait in Rome, the greater the danger you're in.'

The cardinals rose from their seats and William and Kieran followed. Cardinal Devirus was the first to leave, not saying a word to Issias or Grisome. Issias stepped aside to talk to Grisome, and Engrin walked over to William and Kieran, trying to judge their reactions.

'Cuassard,' Kieran began. 'And it was he who was responsible for spreading the Scarimadaen across Europe?'

'The Secretariat suspects so,' Engrin replied.

'How did he become a servant of Count Ordrane yet still hold a rank in Napoleon's army?' Kieran asked.

'It has been said that Cuassard almost died during the long march home from Russia after Napoleon was defeated. He and his men were separated from the main army and were lost in a blizzard,' Engrin told them. 'He appeared in France months later, just after Napoleon fled Paris. We think the Count rescued Cuassard and his men, and turned them to his will. Few outside of the Vatican knew of this.'

Kieran seemed to tremble for a moment, his expression becoming angry. 'Was he responsible for the pyramid that appeared at Gembloux?'

Engrin didn't reply but held his gaze.

'Was he, Engrin?' Kieran pressed.

'Perhaps,' Engrin replied. 'No one knows. Somehow the Scarimadaen arrived in the town, and if William's description was correct, perhaps it was scavenged from the field of battle. Perhaps even from a fallen French soldier.'

Kieran closed his eyes, clenching and unclenching his fists. His face contorted as though he was fighting some sort of inner war deep within. He stumbled over to the wall and leant against it, his back towards them.

'Kieran,' William approached.

The Irishman held up his hand. 'I'm ... I'm fine. Honestly.'

William glanced at Engrin, worried at Kieran's swift turn to fury.

'Kieran, would you wait at the carriage for William and I?' the old man requested gently.

The Irishman looked up and then nodded, though his expression was stormy. William wanted to say something as his friend left them, but Engrin took him aside.

'Watch him, William,' Engrin urged. 'Kieran is looking for vengeance.'

'Wouldn't you?' William replied. 'That butcher may have been indirectly responsible for his lover's death. I'm sure under any code of honour that would entitle him to vengeance.'

'Not if it compromises the Secretariat,' Engrin replied sternly.

William stepped away from him. 'As you have pointed out, we were loaned from our regiment to help you return the pyramid to the Vatican. We fulfilled our side of the bargain. We are now under your protection, and we are thankful for it. But that hardly obligates us to undertake a mission for the Papacy. I'm no longer sure either Kieran or I wish to be part of your war, Engrin.'

Engrin took William's arm and they walked down the corridor slowly. 'This Frenchman is the residue of Napoleon's reign, and as such he is wanted by the Coalition as well as the Vatican. What you do will be done under both remits: you'll be serving king and country, and the Papacy.'

'And fighting daemons and vampyres,' William added, 'not to mention leading a band of monks.'

'There will be no daemons, nor will there be vampyres,' Engrin assured him. 'Issias has promised as much. All we want is to stop Cuassard spreading more Scarimadaen along our borders.

Can you imagine what would happen if daemons like the one at Gembloux ran amok in the Papal states?'

'There would be pandemonium.'

Engrin nodded. 'So he must be stopped. And Kieran must be reigned in. He appears calm most of the time, but there is immense anger inside that young man. If he allows himself to be governed by it, he will lead you and the entire mission into trouble. That is the nature of vengeance. It could mean his life; it could also mean the destruction of you and the company under your command.'

'I don't want this command,' William said. 'Let Cazotte have it.'

'Cazotte is a fine lieutenant, but he has little command experience,' Engrin replied.

'Nor have I,' William admitted. 'I was promoted only after Waterloo, when my own captain fell.'

'But you were a captain at Gembloux, yes?'

William sighed and nodded. 'Yes, I was.'

'Then you have already been tested, and survived. You also destroyed a daemon, which I must say is a significant test,' Engrin remarked.

'You didn't see the men who died that night under my leadership, Engrin,' William said caustically.

'All captains lose men under their command. It is the way of battle. I have no doubt that you will lose one or two more over the coming weeks, but as long as you apprehend or stop Cuassard and return home intact, the mission will be a success.'

'And if it isn't?'

Engrin stopped walking and folded his arms. 'If you fail, you won't come home at all, William. And you won't have to worry about the repercussions and the downfall of the Secretariat and the Order.'

'You're telling me the future of all of this hangs on our success?' William said.

'Yes. If this most simple of missions fails, then the Secretariat will be shut down by Cardinal Grisome. Your deaths would embarrass the Papacy. How would we explain it to your government and King? That is why it is important that both you and

Kieran come back alive. And that is why Cazotte was suggested to accompany you. He has saved your necks once already, he should be used to it by now.'

William shook his head and laughed, but with little humour.

'You must prepare yourself, William,' Engrin said as he led him back along the corridor. 'You haven't long before you leave. The brothers must be picked and Cazotte must be addressed.'

'That is the part I am looking forward to the least, old man,' William muttered. 'I'm sure our Italian friend will be overjoyed that I am his senior officer.' He touched his nose and felt the bump on the ridge, a reminder that the mission to Aosta might not be as simple as everyone hoped.

△ V △

As the carriage crossed the Ponte Sant'Angelo, William finally spoke, having been quiet since they had left Engrin on the steps of Saint Peter's.

'I have an uneasy feeling,' he said, and turned to face Kieran, who was busy looking along the streets at nothing in particular. The Irishman's expression was tormented.

'Sorry?' Kieran replied a little distantly. 'An uneasy feeling about what?'

'About Grisome,' William confessed. 'There is something about him that I don't trust.'

'Does it matter if you trust him or not?' Kieran said indifferently. 'We're headed for Aosta, and we're leaving this place.'

'We have to return eventually,' William said.

Kieran didn't reply, but after a short while of rocking along paving stones and driving past people on the street, he said. 'If I had my way, we would kill Cuassard and then march on the Carpathian Mountains. There I would bury my sword in the chest of the Count.'

William stared at his friend nervously.

'I want the Count dead as well,' he said. 'But we cannot

achieve such an aim with only two swords. We need the Secretariat's help, Kieran. Maybe, after we've completed this mission and apprehended Cuassard ...'

'*Killed* Cuassard,' Kieran countered, without glancing in William's direction. 'We're going to kill him, Will.'

William faltered, feeling even more uncomfortable in the face of Kieran's anger. His yearning for vengeance was indeed deep, and his merciless expression almost chilling. This wasn't the friend of old; something more callous and vengeful had taken Kieran's place, and William heeded Engrin's warnings. Had he been so foolish to believe that Kieran's mood had softened, that his heart was mending? The wound in his soul was festering, and Kieran's true murderous intentions were revealing themselves. For a moment it crossed William's mind to leave Kieran at Villeda.

'You're worried about me,' Kieran said.

William shook his head. 'Of course not. Cuassard deserves to die, and he will not surrender anyway.'

'And the Count? Would you follow me to the Carpathians?' Kieran asked.

William fell quiet and looked away.

They continued in silence for the next hour or so, riding through the countryside until they arrived at the arch of Saint Laurence, the sun casting shafts of light through the branches of the trees high above.

If their conversation had achieved anything it was to take William's mind off his imminent meeting with Cazotte. Thankfully, the lieutenant was in the main courtyard at Saint Laurence so William didn't have to go far to find him. William parted from Kieran, watching the forlorn figure trudge down the corridor away from the courtyard, his doubts making him seem hunched and wretched. William concentrated instead on Cazotte, who sat on the steps of courtyard eating the segments of an orange while watching the initiates spar with staffs, apparently oblivious to William's approach.

As he got within a couple of feet, Cazotte snorted. 'You'll have to do better than that to catch me unawares, British.'

William bit his tongue and tried to compose himself. He moved past Cazotte and sat down on the steps next to him.

William didn't turn to look at him, knowing that the Italian's mocking expression would only serve to anger him. Instead he addressed the lieutenant while watching the initiates spar. 'I want to bury the bad feelings between us, Cazotte,' William began.

Cazotte raised his eyebrows, clearly surprised. 'Bad feelings, you say? Bury them? And if there are these 'bad feelings' why would you wish to bury them? And why do you think *I* would?'

William tried to remain calm. 'Because we're on the same side, Cazotte. Like it or not, we are fighting a common enemy, yet right now we appear to be fighting each other.'

'I do not like you, British, and I doubt I ever will.'

'Maybe so, but we can cooperate, can we not?'

'That sounds like an order, British.'

'Engrin once told me there is no need to have officers barking orders here. The monks of the Order follow without discussion. Is that correct?'

Cazotte nodded.

'Does that apply to other officers of the Order?'

'Yes, British, *all*. Why do you ask?'

'Because I'm leading the company embarking for Aosta. I've been given the command.'

Cazotte was flabbergasted. '*You're what?*'

'Under direct instructions from the Secretariat, I will be assuming command of the company, and you will be my first officer and translator,' William said. He was trying to be civil, but secretly enjoyed watching the lieutenant squirm. Cazotte wanted to say something, the words trembling on his lips, but he was an officer of the Order and knew he couldn't speak out against the decision, no matter how unjust it appeared.

'I could find another lieutenant as my second,' William suggested.

'Then why don't you?' Cazotte hissed back.

'Because I would rather have you, Lieutenant.'

'Why? To gloat? To order me around?' Cazotte growled.

'Because you are a strong and capable fighter. And while I do not trust your feelings towards me, I trust your faith in the Order. You killed our assassin and saved our lives, I see no reason to mistrust you,' William replied calmly.

'Then you're a fool. I could have killed the assassin to stop his tongue. I could have killed him because he could have implicated me in the attempt.'

William regarded Cazotte a little suspiciously. 'So why *did* you kill him?'

The lieutenant's anger faded and he looked away, almost ashamed. 'Because he murdered two of the brothers I myself trained since they were boys. I had seen them grow into fine men, yet both were killed by cowards. Both were killed trying to protect you. It was so ... *unnecessary*.' He paused and looked pained. 'I could not stop myself. I beat the kafala to death with my own hands,' he said, staring down at his fingers.

'You care about the brothers,' William remarked.

'They are my family,' Cazotte replied gently, all menace in his voice vanished.

William stood up and put out his hand towards him. 'I need you as my first officer, Cazotte. I ask you not as a British officer, but as a colleague within the Order. Come with me to Aosta.'

The Italian looked up at William and gripped his hand tight, numbing his fingers. 'I care for my men. I will support you and will show you where you are going wrong; you can count on it. But believe me when I tell you that if the company is destroyed because of your incompetence, I will leave you in the mountains to die.'

William nodded bitterly. 'I can ask nothing more of you,' he said, and pulled his hand back, flexing it a little from Cazotte's strong grip. 'You know the men better than I. Will you select the company for me?'

Cazotte nodded.

'Thank you. If you need me I'll be in my room preparing.' William left the Italian on the steps of the courtyard, unsure if he'd made the right decision to retain him as his Second.

CHAPTER THIRTEEN

The Journey North

△ I △

William was rapidly learning the ways of the Order and was quick to inspect the contents of the crates stored on the cart. The closest crate contained ammunition while another long crate contained ten baker rifles, all pristine and shiny, their barrels well greased. He picked up one and looked down its length, regarding its weight, balance and alignment. The guns were of the highest quality and William admired their impeccable presentation. If they fired as true as they looked, then it would only bolster his confidence in the mission.

He was surprised to find that another crate housed a miniature gun-barrel. It was the smallest cannon he had seen, yet the spiral grooves inside were almost like a rifle's. The shot in another crate was something different: instead of a cannonball it was a flask of thick black glass.

'I wouldn't drop that,' someone said behind him.

William turned and found the disagreeable Wilcox looking up at him with his one good eye. He was loading another crate onto the cart, his big hands making light of the weight.

'Wilcox,' William said.

'Saxon,' Wilcox replied gruffly. William was tempted to correct him with 'Captain Saxon', but he quickly remembered that there was no recognised rank in the Order and fell quiet.

'What is this?' he asked, gesturing to the glass ball.

'Ammunition for the Calatan gun,' Wilcox replied.

'Calatan gun?' William asked.

'Invented by the Spanish. Very small, very manoeuvrable cannon. Can be moved in seconds rather than minutes. Has a long and accurate range due to the grooves inside it. It can fire conventional cannonballs but we prefer those glass ones there,' Wilcox said, grinning nastily.

'What do they do?' William asked, suspecting that the balls would be quite devastating.

'They are thick enough to stand the firin' of the cannon, but they soon 'eat up and melt, ignitin' slowly. When they 'it their target they explode, castin' a sheet of burning oil across a wide area. Like the catapults of ancient Rome, when they fired urns of burnin' oil at their enemies. But the Catalan gun is more accurate.'

William jumped off the wagon. Wilcox regarded him with contempt.

'Cazotte told me you were leadin' the company,' he said.

'And that worries you?' William asked.

'Yes,' Wilcox said bluntly. 'I admit you are good with a rifle, but still a little slow. I would have preferred trainin' you longer before you went on your first action.'

'This is not my first action,' William rebuked.

'It is, as far as the brothers of Saint Sallian are concerned,' Wilcox said sharply. 'I would have liked Cazotte to lead us, but it is not my decision.'

'Us?' William frowned.

'Of course. Cazotte picked me,' Wilcox said, satisfied to see that the news galled William.

'He picked *you?*'

'Someone needs to keep the brothers firin' quickly. Are you able to do that?' Wilcox asked.

William knew very well he couldn't. 'Then he's acted prudently, of course,' he said grudgingly.

Wilcox grunted back and turned away to load another crate. William watched the scarred man for a moment, weighing up the problems that could be caused by him joining the expedition. Cursing under his breath, William turned and stormed away from the courtyard and down towards the armoury, where Cazotte was busy talking to several of the brothers. William waited patiently, but was secretly seething.

Cazotte seemed to ignore William as he talked to the monks in Latin, looking over the extra equipment with care. He then made a joke and turned to address William, who tried his best to hide his anger.

'Why Wilcox?' William asked abruptly.

Cazotte smiled caustically. 'He is the finest rifleman in the Order. You are not. I need him, and so does the company.'

'Even though he might clash with Kieran?' William accused.

'He's been told not to come near Kieran,' Cazotte said. 'I told him that Harte was volatile after his tragic loss, and would not take any teasing.'

William frowned. 'How do you know about Kieran's loss?'

'He told us,' Cazotte shrugged.

'What?' William said, bewildered by the revelation.

'Is it so surprising?' Cazotte said.

'Quite frankly, yes. I thought Kieran considered it a private matter,' William admitted.

'You don't know your friend as well as you think,' Cazotte replied. 'Maybe you have not been listening to him.'

William fumed, his teeth grinding together.

'He told me and several of the brothers about Gembloux over a noonday meal during the training,' Cazotte said. 'I suspected that he had wanted to talk about it for a long time, that he had – how would you say it – "bottled it up"?'

William fell silent.

'If I was his friend, I would talk to him more,' Cazotte said, and smiled, knowing that this good advice would grate with William. 'We have a long ride ahead of us. Maybe you should try it then, eh, British?'

William ignored him. He tried busying himself by looking over the additional weaponry assembled across long wooden tables. He noticed the steel stars lying on a satin cloth.

'These are yours?' William ventured.

'My throwing-stars,' Cazotte replied, and picked one up between his fingers. 'Very deadly. They come from Japan, you know.'

William nodded. 'They're so small,' he remarked.

'But fast and accurate in my hands. They are easier to carry than throwing-knives,' Cazotte said, passing William the star. He took hold of it and winced, as one of the edges cut open his thumb. He dropped it and the forward point sank into the table with a dull thud.

'They are also quite heavy and sharp for something so small,' the Italian said, and pulled the star out of the wood.

William nodded whilst sucking his thumb. He was quite embarrassed and gestured to the rest of the weapons. 'Make sure you get them all loaded, Cazotte,' he said, trying to appear officious while blood seeped out of the small cut.

'Of course,' Cazotte replied coolly. 'It appears you have a visitor anyway.'

William turned about, his thumb in his mouth, and he found Engrin standing at the entrance to the armoury. Realizing that he looked like a big child, William took his thumb from his mouth and smiled weakly. 'Ah ... Engrin,' he said, and walked over, his cut hand behind his back.

'William,' Engrin replied warmly. 'Is there something wrong with your hand?'

William conceded and pulled it into view. 'I cut my thumb, that is all.'

'And the preparations?' the old man asked.

'We should be ready to leave very soon,' William said, and walked with Engrin out of the large hall.

As they strolled down the courtyard towards the training fields at the back of the monastery, William talked more openly of his concerns.

'Kieran is still angry. He does his best to keep his feelings within,' William said, patting his breast. 'I don't know what I can do, Engrin. He is my friend, but I think I'm losing him.'

287

'Talk to Kieran. Make use of the time you have,' Engrin suggested. 'Because the mission may rest on his actions.'

'Are we talking about prophecies again?' William asked.

'No. I am referring to something else. Cuassard,' Engrin said. 'He was seen near Aosta around the villages bordering the Swiss Alps. Two villages were completely destroyed a week ago, their occupants slaughtered. Almost 200 people.'

William nodded grimly. 'Cuassard did this. He's done it before.'

'But could he have achieved such a massacre with only a company of soldiers?' Engrin asked.

William pondered for a moment. 'It's possible. A night attack, perhaps.'

'But even from a night attack you would have thought that at least *some* of the villagers would have escaped,' Engrin remarked.

'You suspect that something more was behind the attack?' William said.

'It had crossed my mind,' Engrin admitted. 'Maybe Cuassard is more dangerous than Cardinal Issias believes. This Frenchman's infamy precedes him. With Count Ordrane as his master, his capacity for murder has increased ten-fold. Tread carefully, William.'

'You don't have to worry about Cuassard,' William grunted.

'It is not just the Frenchman that worries me, William. The region you will be entering is known as Piedmont. Aosta is an area the House of Savoy wishes to control. But at the moment a revolutionary group called the Valdostani governs the city. They are French sympathisers and do not wish a return to Savoy rule.'

'The French?' William said. 'That will make things difficult. Will they support Cuassard?'

'As long as they believe Cuassard is still a figurehead for Napoleon's dreams and not in the employ of Count Ordrane, then the French captain will indeed have the Valdostani's support.'

'Do the Valdostani know of our coming?' William asked.

'An anonymous letter was sent to us, warning of Cuassard's intentions. We know that it came from Aosta, but whether it was sent by the Valdostani or even someone from the House of Savoy, we do not know,' Engrin replied. 'Your success will be based on white lies and swiftness. Find Cuassard quickly, before the Valdostani know your true intentions. If there are complications, then perhaps you should tell them who Cuassard *really* is and what is *really* happening to people outside of the city. But only do this if you have no other choice. We try to keep our affairs confidential, as you know.'

William nodded, but he appeared concerned about something. 'This is not as simple an errand as the Secretariat believed,' he remarked. 'I would appreciate your candour, Engrin.'

The old man crossed his arms. 'You must be aware of the circumstances you lead the company into. This is no longer a mission to apprehend or assassinate an enemy of the Coalition and the Papacy. Italy is divided into separate regions, each with its own monarch. These monarchs bicker amongst themselves. Their subjects have little love for them, less still since Napoleon stamped his mark on this country. He may have been disliked here in Rome, but there are people in Italy who welcomed his tyranny. Aosta is one such place. The Valdostani do not like the Papacy, or the House of Savoy, their rightful rulers. The Valdostani lean more towards France than they do Rome. If Cuassard has been embraced by them this could mean they are helping the Frenchman. If that is true, then the logical conclusion is that you will be facing more than just a company of seasoned French infantry.'

'Indeed,' William mused. 'How much military might does the Valdostani command?'

'It is hard to say. Aosta has a large army for a city of its size. But they are not well trained, and may be still under the influence of the Savoys. And if not the House of Savoy, then the Liberals. If so, you should find the mission easier. But if it is the Conservatives who control the militia, they may see Cuassard as the thrust of a revolution. This would be disastrous. If Cuassard spearheaded a revolution in Aosta, the House of Savoy would be replaced by the conservatives and the Valdostani, and Count

Ordrane's sphere of influence would extend to our very doorstep.'

'It would indeed be a disaster. He would be within striking distance of Rome,' William murmured.

'Which is why Cardinal Devirus wants Cuassard dead,' Engrin said grimly. 'The French captain represents every danger to us.'

William sighed. 'Then why send us? I am not afraid of the danger, Engrin, just afraid of the politics. I am not a politician but a soldier. It will be awkward.'

'Actually you will find it awkward at *best*, especially when you pass from here through Tuscany to Piedmont. Perhaps it would be wise to wear our colours for the journey.'

'As a monk?' William said, already disliking the idea.

'You will be less conspicuous,' Engrin suggested.

'You said the Valdostani do not like the Papacy. Would it not be easier to dress as someone other than a Papal delegate?'

'The Order does not dress with any badge or insignia. No one knows who we are. We may even appear as militia to some.'

'But you are hoping they don't ask,' William said.

'Precisely. Do you have any other concerns?'

William laughed. 'Of course I do, old man. It sounds chaotic and dangerous. But who am I to argue against the prospect of another adventure. Especially if it is to rid the world of one more murderer. You have retained my services, Engrin.'

'Good,' Engrin said, and put out his hand, 'then I mustn't keep you. Good luck William.'

'Thank you, Engrin,' William replied, and shook his hand. He watched the old man walk away, feeling a little exasperated by this new information. It seemed that with Engrin nothing was ever straightforward.

William stretched and looked up into the morning sky. The sun was daring to come out of the clouds, just as the clouds themselves poured rain upon the land. It was a strange omen of the times ahead; an omen of uncertainty.

Kieran pulled the hem of his grey jacket down and puffed his chest out, taking an instant liking to his new attire. William was not so impressed.

'No rank, no insignia ...' he murmured.

Kieran ignored him.

'The only good thing about this blasted uniform is that it fits well,' William continued.

'The material is quite soft,' Kieran remarked.

'Italian silk,' William replied. 'Cazotte told me himself. The finest tailors in Villeda made these uniforms.'

'Then I will wear mine with pride,' Kieran announced.

William nodded. 'As will I,' he said, a little grudgingly.

Outside the monastery stood thirty mares, all different breeds, but powerful. William and Kieran were reunited with the horses from Naples and both animals recognised their riders instantly, stamping the ground with appreciation. The other monks were also ready, standing by as they waited for William and Cazotte. Behind them was the weapons-cart steered by two monks and pulled by two large mules.

Cazotte marched over to William, his hand on the hilt of his sabre. 'All the brothers are ready and accounted for. Each man is armed with a sabre; the rest of the weapons and provisions are stored on the cart.' He spoke without any of the malice or teasing of previous days. William was happy he'd urged him to ride with the company.

'Very good, Cazotte,' he said, and glanced at Kieran who appeared eager to ride. 'Gentlemen, I believe we have a long journey ahead of us. A column of two abreast, if you will' – he was tempted to say 'Lieutenant' but corrected himself before the word trembled over his lips – '*Cazotte.*'

'Very good, sir,' Cazotte replied, and turned away.

The company mounted their horses with precision and efficiency. William regarded Kieran and the brothers closest to him, before holding his arm aloft. 'Forward!' he ordered and kicked his horse into a trot, the rest of the company following.

As they trotted through Villeda, some of the children watched from the edge of the road or behind picket fences. Some stared, appearing a little scared of this column of horses marching through their village, while others cheered, their tiny voices drowned by the fall of hooves on stone.

William had not had the pleasure of leading a column of men like this before. Even after he was promoted as captain, there had been scant chance to lead the regimental company out of Brussels or even Deramere in England. Today was his first taste of true leadership, and he liked it.

Kieran watched as William kept glancing at the column trotting behind. 'Enjoying this, aren't you?' he remarked to William, above the noise of hooves.

'I don't know what you mean,' William said, grinning for a moment, before clasping his lips shut and staring down the road to Rome.

△ III △

'Where are we?' Kieran asked. Cazotte wiped the sweat from his brow and regarded the map he was holding up against the flank of his horse. Rome was now behind them, the journey so far having lasted several hours.

'We've just passed Rieti,' he said, pointing to the east. 'We should ride on through the hills until we get to Terni. Then we head west and down the valley towards a town that lies north of Viterbo. We can then make camp and water the horses at a lake called Bolsena. We must quicken our pace if we are to get there before sunset.'

'And after the lake, where then?' William asked.

Cazotte looked to the north of the map and pointed his finger there. 'There is an abbey in the hills near Siena. We use it occasionally to rest during the longest of rides. I know the friar there – he will be glad to see us.' Cazotte rolled up the map, slipping it back into his saddlebag. 'It will take us another day to reach the abbey.'

'Very well. I'll leave the details in your hands. This is your country, after all,' William said, and returned to his own horse. He took his canteen from the saddle and sipped. Despite the thinness of the uniform, he was perspiring badly under the afternoon sun. He closed his eyes against the glare and listened for a moment to the sounds of crickets in the long grass and the birdsong that seemed to come from all around. With his eyes closed he could almost imagine he was back at Lowchester again.

'Will,' Kieran said, and he opened his eyes.

'Yes? Something wrong?'

Kieran glanced down the column and then shook his head.

'Really?' William pressed.

'That man, Wilcox, he keeps staring at me,' he said.

William glanced over Kieran's shoulder and for a moment his eyes met the scarred gun instructor who quickly looked away.

'Are you sure? He's probably scowling at me. I was the one who threatened to hit him.'

Kieran nodded. 'I suppose so.'

'Just keep away from him,' William suggested, trying to sound like he was offering advice rather than giving an order. 'He's a bad seed, Kieran.'

'Then why was he chosen as part of the company?'

'That was Cazotte's doing. Wilcox is the best man for the job. No one can drill the monks with their rifles as well as he. He's a necessary evil, I'm afraid.'

Kieran shrugged again. 'Well then, I'll just keep out of his way, as you suggest.'

William brooded as he looked again down the column of monks. Wilcox was hiding now and it angered him. He would tell Cazotte his thoughts when they stopped at the lake, and if that meant a reckoning with Wilcox, then so be it.

'Mount up!' Cazotte shouted. William kicked his heels in and led the column trotting down the dusty track. The farmers labouring in the sun did not stop to acknowledge their presence, even when they were only a dozen yards away. In a country that had once been occupied, the people had learnt to mind their own business, especially when armed men approached.

William kept his eyes on the horizon and watched as the landscaped dropped into valleys and woodland. Eventually, as the sun began to fall, they sighted a golden shimmering lake on the horizon half-obscured by a row of trees that sat along the mountain-track. William guessed this was the lake Cazotte had spoken of. He turned about and pointed silently to the stretch of gold on the horizon.

'The sea?' Kieran queried.

Cazotte shook his head. 'Lago di Bolsena,' he replied. 'There are a few inns around it, and a few villagers living on the fishing here. The perfect place to rest for the night.'

'Indeed,' William said, 'and completely out in the open. And of course, no one could attack us while we are camped there?'

Cazotte couldn't hide his amusement at the Englishman's scorn. 'You think we'll be attacked, Captain?'

William kept Cazotte's gaze for a moment. 'We are probably being followed even now.'

'You are paranoid, British,' Cazotte grinned.

'No. I'm just careful. We were attacked outside Saint Laurence, as you well know. If there is a traitor in the Papacy, then our progress will be watched closely,' he said.

Cazotte stopped smiling and looked over his shoulder. 'Perhaps you are right. What can we do about it?'

'Nothing,' William admitted. 'Just be sure that, if it happens, we are prepared. Sentries will need to be posted.'

'I'll make sure it is done,' Cazotte said, and turned back down the column, leaving William feeling a little triumphant.

'I don't know how you dare to smile, Will,' Kieran said gravely. 'If you are right, then we are all in danger.' The Irishman rode ahead, leaving William chastened. He followed and caught up with him as the road descended into the immense bowl where the lake lay. Here and there were small islands near the shores, where little boats huddled. To the north William could see a settlement, probably one of the fishing villages Cazotte had mentioned.

As they trotted down the precipitous track to the lake there was sudden commotion behind them. William turned and saw the cart slowly tipping off the dusty road where the surface had fallen away, the brothers nearby leaping off their horses to assist. The cart's left wheels were trapped, and the cart itself was in danger of sliding over the edge.

'Damnation!' William cursed and got off his horse. He raced down to the rear of the cart, where eight of the monks were already holding on as best they could.

'Rope!' he shouted. 'Rope, now!'

Cazotte translated and a brother appeared at William's side with a length of rope. William looped it to the front right side of the cart, just under the driver's seat, and pulled both ends level, before passing them to the nearest two monks still on their horses. More brothers had dismounted and some were even standing beneath the cart to keep it upright. William could see a disaster in the making. At best they would lose the cart and the weapons, at worst it would take with it the four brave men now standing underneath it.

'Tie the ends to your saddles!' William shouted, turning sharply to Cazotte. 'Tell them!'

Again Cazotte translated and the monks obeyed quickly. 'Forward! Ride forward! And pull!' William shouted, grabbing hold of the rope. The horses stepped forward and more monks came to the side and the rope. They pulled as those beneath pushed, and slowly the cart tipped back onto the track.

The cart was safe and William leant against it, slightly breathless. His shirt was unbuttoned and his face streaked with dirt and sweat. Kieran looked down at him, amused by his dishevelled state, while the monks muttered to each other, obviously impressed by their leader's performance.

'Your friend is full of surprises,' Cazotte murmured to Kieran.

'That he is,' Kieran replied proudly.

With the drama behind them, the company trotted slowly down the lake's edge and the brothers dismounted, leading their horses to the water.

William glanced down at his grey uniform, dishevelled and covered with dust. His shirt was stuck to his back and his face felt grubby. 'I could do with a wash,' he murmured to Kieran, as they looked over to the glistening lake.

'You're the captain,' Kieran reminded him. 'I'm sure no one will object if you bathe before we eat.'

William dismounted, to lead his horse to the water.

Camp was set up quickly and two sentries were posted. William had washed while the others set up tents and started a fire in the camp. Instead of using up their valuable provisions, several of the monks rode to a nearby fishing settlement a mile up the bank and bartered for fish and bread. By the time William returned to the camp the meal was being cooked.

William sat down next to Kieran and gazed into the flames, the smell of cooking making his stomach rumble.

'How long until we get to Aosta?' Kieran asked.

'Days, I think,' William replied. 'Hopefully not weeks. I examined Cazotte's map and found we are riding the most direct route possible, but a route that will take us through hills and mountains. It will be a long and hard journey.'

'We've ridden worse,' Kieran remarked.

William nodded. 'Quite.'

Their conversation was interrupted by the passing of food, and William and Kieran sighed as the salted fish was dished out on a tin plate in front of them. A piece of coarse bread was added and although it looked a little unappetising, they devoured every last flake and crumb.

'Hungry work, Captain,' Cazotte said, grinning behind pipe-smoke. The Italian was laid back, smoking rings into the air contentedly. The rest of the company were quiet as they ate. Some seemed to be reflecting on the day, whilst others were checking their weapons. The remainder had disappeared from the campfire for silent prayer.

Wilcox kept glancing at William and Kieran with his one good eye; William scowled back, before getting up abruptly. 'I'm just going to have a quiet word with Wilcox,' he said.

Watching the captain go, Cazotte took the opportunity to talk to Kieran. 'Your friend is a strange one. He was quick to help out when the cart toppled. Most aristocrats would not have lifted a finger, even if it meant losing the ordnance.'

'William was brought up better than that.'

'Tell me more,' Cazotte said, interested in what this British officer was really like.

'William's father, the Lord of Fairway Hall, is a son of a great merchant. Like his father before him, his title and lands have come from fair business and a moral eye. They never hire slaves, and they pay their crews well. The Saxon family is one of the most respected merchant families in England – both by those they employ and their business partners. Lord Richard is also one of the most selfless men I have ever met. Did you know that he gave away a third of his hard-earned estate to the local people?'

Cazotte looked impressed. 'For what reason?'

'Lord Richard simply thought they would make better use of it.'

'He sounds like a good man,' Cazotte conceded.

'He is. And William is just like him,' Kieran remarked. 'He was given the captaincy of our regiment because he is a good soldier and a brave one. You won't find many like him.'

Cazotte puffed on his pipe and frowned thoughtfully. He had been surprised by William's tenacity, and maybe even his willingness to get 'dirty' with the men. But that didn't necessarily make him a good leader. For the moment, Cazotte decided to reserve judgement.

△ IV △

The following morning, they woke early and packed up the camp. It took more than an hour to move north around the lake, past the village on the edge of the waters. William could still taste the dust, which lingered regardless of what he drank or ate. It was something he was used to after the campaign in Spain, but he still disliked it.

William and Cazotte led the company on the second day, giving William time to tell the Italian what he had said to Wilcox.

'I simply warned him that I would not tolerate any antagonism towards either myself, or Kieran,' he said.

Cazotte didn't seem impressed. 'He knows his duty, Captain.'

'If he knows it, he is not always mindful of it,' William retorted. 'He is always staring at Kieran. I suspect he knows who Kieran is.'

'He may do,' Cazotte admitted.

William clenched the reins in his hands angrily. 'Was it you who told Wilcox?'

'Me?' Cazotte said innocently. 'No, it was Harte himself. He told the brothers he trained with. They must have told Wilcox.'

'We should send him back to Rome,' William growled.

'Nonsense. Wilcox is the best shot in the company. It would be foolish to send him back.'

William turned in the saddle and glowered at Cazotte. 'People like Wilcox killed Kieran's parents.'

'That was a long time ago,' Cazotte remarked.

'People do not change so much, Lieutenant,' William said. 'Wilcox hates me. But he despises Kieran. He is dangerous.'

Cazotte glanced back. 'He is a brother of the Order of Saint Sallian. He has taken vows to defend the Order and the Church at all cost. He has no political beliefs.'

William shook his head. 'I am not so convinced.'

'I will not let Wilcox harm you or Harte. If that means killing Wilcox, then I will do so, I promise you that. Even if he *is* my closest friend.'

CHAPTER FOURTEEN

Piedmont

△ I △

The farmer felt content with his lunch as he sat under the branches of the tree, resting his back against the trunk. The sun was particularly strong that day, and he was glad of the shade. From the hill he could see all the way down the field to the woods on the hill opposite, and even to his little home on the edge of the clearing, with its thin plume of dark grey smoke spiralling into the air. Roberta was probably making a good meal for him that evening, believing her husband to be toiling hard in the fields rather than relaxing in the sun. The farmer laughed to himself and stretched out.

His mood was only partly disturbed when he saw the train of horses and men in grey uniforms ride slowly by, forty yards from the hill, down one of the roads passing the Castle of Savino. In his time he had seen many merchants on this road, leaving or entering Piedmont. But these men were not merchants, and the swords at their hips warned him that perhaps it would be wiser to shuffle around the trunk and face the other way.

William saw the farmer hide, but wasn't surprised. In the ten days since leaving the abbey at San Galgano, they had spied plenty of people who either ignored the company or hid. People wanted nothing to do with them, which in a way was helpful: the less curious locals were, the better their chances of getting to Aosta unhindered. But at the same time, it was frustrating. On the fifth day of travelling from San Galgano (the ninth since leaving Villeda) the cart had broken a wheel and they had needed a carpenter. It took them the best part of a day to find one, losing precious time. Most people they spoke to wanted Italy to be reunited, while others even mourned the removal of Napoleon. That worried William. If Tuscany had people who supported Napoleon, then how strongly entrenched would that feeling be in Piedmont?

William kept his wits about him and made sure Kieran did too. Each night, they sparred; both were better swordsmen than they had been a month ago. Cazotte surprised William by asking to spar. William reluctantly agreed, but found that this time the combat was less competitive, and Cazotte often paused to offer useful advice. After a while, William was amazed to find that he liked Cazotte's company and they would often talk – usually of the mission, but sometimes about William's time in the British regiment, and Cazotte's as a mercenary.

William knew he would soon be called upon to prove himself. They were expecting a company of highly trained French veterans, and if the Valdostani were involved there would be another large army to contend with as well.

△ II △

Cazotte looked at his map again and held up his hand, halting the column in its tracks. William rode up to him and watched the lieutenant pull out his map.

'We're here,' he said. 'We're in Piedmont.'

'At last,' Kieran sighed, wiping the sweat from his brow.

'How many miles to Aosta?' William asked.

'Many,' Cazotte replied. 'Tonight we should rest near the Orba. It's a river that runs down from the north through Novi Ligure. I think it might be best to avoid the towns from this point forth. It may attract more attention than we would wish.'

'Will we make the Orba before nightfall?' William asked peering down at the map.

'We should do,' Cazotte replied, rolling the map in his hands.

'Send the order, Cazotte,' William said, and turned his horse to the head of the column of riders.

As they rode down into the valley, which was flanked by poplar trees and golden fields of grain, two riders from the rear galloped up to Cazotte. He pulled up his horse and spoke to the men.

'Is something wrong?' William asked, as the rest of company rode by.

Cazotte rubbed his chin. 'It appears your cautious approach was the correct one. We are being tracked,' he said.

William frowned. 'For how long?'

'Today is the second day,' Cazotte admitted a little sheepishly. 'Before you ask, I didn't bother you the first day as I thought they were most likely just peasants who were curious about us.'

William shook his head irritably. 'Did the men get a good look at them?'

'No. They're keeping their distance.'

'Uniformed?'

'No uniforms. Dressed in dark clothes,' Cazotte said. 'What do you think?'

'Well, they're not in uniform, so that rules out Cuassard's men, unless they are dressed as civilians,' William mused.

'The Valdostani?'

'Why would the Valdostani come out of Piedmont?' William asked.

'Unless they knew we were coming,' Cazotte suggested.

'It's possible. The House of Savoy may be riddled with Cuassard's spies.'

'What do you wish to do?'

'Maintain the riding formation, but post two riders on each flank. If our friends come within fifty yards, we'll give chase. Can our men fire from horseback?'

Cazotte nodded.

'Then issue the four riders with rifles. Tell them to shoot at the horses, I want the men captured alive,' William said.

Cazotte rode away to organize the four chosen riders while William galloped back to the head of the column.

'Problems?' Kieran asked.

'We'll see,' William replied.

As the company rode into view of the silver river winding through the fields, William signalled the company to slow, in order to select a good spot to pitch camp. There were very few hills around but finally William spotted a cluster of trees near some farmland a few minutes' walk from one of the bends in the Orba. The camp was erected with efficiency and very soon a fire was crackling away, spitting embers into the shadows as night fell. As usual, sentries were posted, but this time on horseback. William was insistent on capturing at least one of the spies alive.

That evening he dozed with his doubts, trying to quieten thoughts of traps, spies and Cuassard. But as before, he found something else to think about: *home*. And as he thought about riding into Dunabbey on a mid-summer's afternoon, his eyelids drooped and he slept.

△ III △

'Will!'

William stirred and put a hand to his face to bat away some unseen fly.

'Will?'

He opened his eyes and found Kieran staring back at him.

'What?' he said groggily.

'They caught a spy,' Kieran said, but didn't look pleased. William pushed himself up and pulled on his boots and followed Kieran out of the tent and into the ring of the camp, where last night's fire was still smoking.

It was barely sunrise and shadows still lay thick about them. As he followed Kieran, William noticed the grave looks on the monks' faces. For a moment or two, he entertained bad news; perhaps one of the brothers had been hurt, or worse.

Kieran took him to a tent guarded by two armed brothers. 'In here?' William asked, as Cazotte appeared from the tent, looking grave.

'Captain,' Cazotte Said.

'What has happened? Has someone been hurt?'

'We have one of our pursuers,' Cazotte said.

'Have you spoken to him?' William pressed.

'No,' Cazotte shook his head. 'The man is dead. The brothers fired from horseback and missed the horse. They struck the rider in the back and he fell. I think his neck was broken.'

William looked a little dismayed. 'I wanted him *alive*,' he groaned. 'What about the other rider?'

'Escaped,' Cazotte scowled, showing his displeasure.

'Let us hope he isn't from the Valdostani, otherwise we could have problems convincing them we are on their side.' William rubbed at his weary eyes.

'He's not,' Cazotte confirmed.

'Then he is one of Cuassard's soldiers?' William asked fearfully.

Cazotte shook his head. 'I wish he were.'

Cazotte looked uncharacteristically worried, and this rubbed off on William.

'What have you discovered?' William asked.

Cazotte pulled open the flap of the tent. 'See for yourself.'

William ducked inside the tent and found one of the monks kneeling by the body of a man wrapped in simple dark clothes. On his head he wore a scarf that had been partly unwrapped, allowing his jet-black hair to tumble out. The man's face was white apart from two streaks of blood running from his left nostril and the side of his mouth. His shirt had been torn open at the front and pulled down at the shoulder. William noticed the flecks of blood on the chest and the dirt around the shoulder where the man must have fallen to the ground. The monk moved the lamp closer to the shoulder. Under the dirt was a clear mark – a tattoo of a single wave.

'Oh God,' William murmured. He stepped back and held his

fingers to his mouth. Cazotte was behind him.

'A kafala,' Cazotte said.

'Yes,' William replied, his voice wavering. 'It appears so.'

William retreated outside and rubbed his cold hands together. Cazotte followed.

'I should not be so surprised,' William admitted and laughed bitterly. 'After all, Cuassard is serving the Count.'

'But now he knows who we are, and our intentions,' Cazotte replied.

William waved the worry away. 'Lieutenant, we were never going to creep into Aosta unannounced. I was prepared for some kind of "welcome", or a trap of some type,' he admitted. 'No. That is not my greatest concern.'

William continued to pace and Cazotte waited for him to express his worries further.

'If these are the only kafalas in Piedmont, then we can count ourselves fortunate,' William continued. 'But I doubt it. It seems likely that Cuassard has an army of kafalas at his disposal.'

Cazotte's expression grew ashen. 'We will not be able to fight an entire army,' he declared. 'We should return to Rome.'

William shook his head. 'Our mission is to apprehend Cuassard.'

'But not to start a war,' Cazotte argued.

'As Engrin has told me often, we are already in a war, Cazotte. Innocent people are at risk if we do nothing.'

'But what *can* we do?' Cazotte asked.

'We continue as planned. Once we have established the size of the enemy force, we will attempt to apprehend Cuassard or kill him. If it appears an impossible task, we will return to Rome. I will not risk the fate of the company and the Secretariat with another disastrous defeat, and I don't plan to ride into certain peril without hope of survival.'

'You're advising *more* caution?' Cazotte said, and smiled, agreeing with him.

William nodded, smiling also. 'The best tactic, I think.'

△ IV △

It took two days to circle the mountains around Aosta, the shadowy behemoth of Gran Paradiso – that momentous rock – towering over them. Only on the second day, when they reached the north-east corner of the mountains between the Alpi Grai and the Alpi Pennine, did they at last emerge from Gran Paradiso's shadow and descend into the valley to the city of Aosta.

They passed several castles and fortresses, and William realized how heavily fortified the Valle D'Aosta was. If the Count had control of this area, then the gateway to France and Switzerland would be closed. Piedmont could then fall. It was almost the perfect strategy to control the whole of Italy.

One of the brothers shouted from the rear and William and Cazotte pulled up their horses. The column of riders halted and stared down towards where the monk was pointing. On the far side of the valley, beyond the river, was a row of figures.

William galloped away towards the river across the valley plateau, Cazotte close behind him. They pulled up when they saw the figures more clearly and discovered they were merely villagers.

'Refugees?' William suggested.

Cazotte cupped his hand over his eyes against the glare of the sun. 'I have seen many people displaced and wandering. Those are indeed refugees, Captain.'

William sighed. 'So it has started. The war with Napoleon has ended, and now comes another, hot on its heels.'

'Perhaps it is our mission to stop another war before it starts,' Cazotte suggested. 'Perhaps these will be the last refugees.'

'Let us hope so,' William replied. 'Still, we will not learn about their plight on this side of the river. We need to speak with them.'

Cazotte cupped his hands again and noticed a ford less than a mile upstream. The Italian galloped back to the company and ordered them down the valley with Kieran in command. Meanwhile he took half a dozen monks and rode back to where

William was waiting. It was only a short gallop along the river to a ford.

On the other side they waited until the refugees appeared, a little cautious at first. Eventually an elder shuffled over and demanded to know their intentions. Cazotte's answer seemed to placate the refugees, who began gathering around, chattering nervously. William noticed the troubled looks and the poorly-bandaged wounds.

'Where do they come from?' William asked, above the cacophony of pleas and prayers.

'A village in the mountains,' Cazotte said grimly, passing his canteen to an old lady who looked as though she was dying of exhaustion. 'They are farmers. Their village was attacked two nights ago and destroyed. Most were killed.'

'Do they know who did this?' William asked.

Cazotte tried to find out, but the refugees, numbering over fifty, were clambering around them, crying for help and for shelter. William had seen this many times before, especially in Spain, but it was still a heart-rending sight.

Eventually the elder spoke to Cazotte.

'They were dressed in black, ' Cazotte said, rubbing the back of his neck in a perplexed fashion. 'They could not see their faces ... they did not see how many there were ... they know very little, only that they are hungry and tired.'

William nodded. 'What can we do?'

Cazotte shook his head. 'Nothing,' he said regretfully. 'They are heading for sanctuary in Aosta. If these raiders were kafalas, then we are running out of time.'

William licked his dry lips, feeling desperate. They could not help these people, yet it did not make it any easier to leave them behind. They gave them all the food they were carrying and William handed the weakest woman a blanket to wrap herself in against the chill of coming night. Then they remounted their horses and turned away to ride back to the company a mile or so ahead. William closed his eyes against the sound of weeping as they left them, and behind those eyelids was anger. Cuassard was responsible for this, as he had been for so many other atrocities.

The Butcher of Berlin would atone for his crimes, William vowed.

△ V △

The city of Aosta lay on a plain surrounded by a vast expanse of mountains. The city was nestled in the cradle of the sublime and even with the sun almost down, the snow-capped rocks glowed orange and red. Aosta was fortified by large walls, and a number of medieval turrets that looked out across the plain.

William saw another small column of people trudging towards the gates, more refugees. Cazotte had seen them also. 'It never ends,' he said.

'No, it seems not,' William replied. 'If the Valdostani condone this, we will have more trouble than we bargained for. We need to find out who they are supporting, how big an army the Valdostani command, and how many the kafalas really are ...'

The company of monks arrived at the city gates as the sun fell and the sky purpled. The militia at the gates regarded the armed men cautiously until Cazotte explained who they were and where they had come from. Still, the guards would not let the entire company inside the city walls.

'You and I must go in alone,' Cazotte said, dismounting.

William followed his example. 'I hope we'll be armed,' he murmured.

Cazotte grinned. 'Of course we will. Do you think I would let *these* bumpkins take our swords?'

William walked over to Kieran's horse. 'Make camp outside the walls, somewhere secure. And post sentries,' he said. His eyes caught those of Wilcox, who stared back, glancing ever so slightly at Kieran. William hated to leave his friend like this, but knew the Irishman could take care of himself.

William and Cazotte left the company at the gates and walked into the city on foot. The city was older than Rome but unremarkable in comparison. The Roman walls and arches were still standing, and even the medieval architecture had more than a little Roman influence. Churches appeared on almost every corner, towers of grey. It was only when they reached the main square, lit by golden torches and lamps in the windows of buildings, that Aosta seemed to shrug off its solemnity.

At the square they were approached by two militiamen who took them to a grand building of stone and oak, where they were delivered upstairs to a large but sparse room. In the room was a round wooden table where five men were seated, one in a velvet chair whose grandeur seemed out of place in the simple room.

The man in the velvet chair, a stern looking gentlemen with thinning grey hair and well-worn clothes, beckoned them both to sit, appearing to know who they were.

'Our fame proceeds us,' William whispered to Cazotte.

The Italian nodded gently as the thin-haired gent began speaking. William waited patiently for the translation, promising himself he would learn to speak the language soon. He didn't like receiving bad news second-hand.

'He welcomes us. And he knows who we are,' Cazotte confirmed.

'Does he appear pleased that we're here?' William asked Cazotte.

Cazotte shook his head.

'Is he Valdostani?' William asked and Cazotte translated.

After many words from the man opposite in the velvet chair, Cazotte replied. 'The short answer is 'perhaps'. I think we should assume they are *all* Valdostani.'

'And what do they know of us?' William asked and again Cazotte translated.

'They know we come from the Papacy, but for what end they are unsure,' Cazotte said. 'They are suspicious of our intentions.'

'Surely they know of the politics we are bound by. The Valdostani are subjects of the House of Savoy. Regardless of their feelings towards their monarch, we must observe etiquette in these matters,' William said. 'But also tell them we will not interfere in the affairs of Aosta and the Savoys.'

Cazotte translated and the man in the velvet chair seemed amused.

'Ask him about the French,' William suggested.

The man listened to Cazotte but showed no emotion as he replied.

'He says he knows of no French army in the Valle,' Cazotte replied.

'Then ask him about foreigners raiding his villages,' William said, and waited for a reply.

'He says he knows of no villages being raided,' Cazotte said, sounding a little frustrated.

'What about the refugees? Surely a man in his position would notice refugees entering their city?' William said.

This time the man with thinning hair paused and his stare faltered. He glanced at his colleagues who remained quiet.

Finally he replied to Cazotte. 'He says they are not refugees. They are simply coming into the city for their own protection.'

'Protection from whom?' William asked.

Cazotte repeated the question. The response required no translation: '*La Casa di Savoy.*'

△ VI △

William and Cazotte left the building, a little irritated by their lack of progress. If this was the best information the Valdostani could give them, then they had to be counted amongst the enemy. They denied everything, even what was happening in their own neighbourhoods. Worse still, it appeared to confirm William's suspicions that the Valdostani were condoning Cuassard's tactics.

'What do you suggest we do now?' Cazotte asked.

'We need to establish the whereabouts of Cuassard. If we find the man, we can stop this right now, without having to fight the Valdostani,' William replied.

Suddenly there was a sharp whistle behind them, and both

turned to find one of the Valdostani hiding in the shadows. William and Cazotte approached with their hands at their sides, their fingers on the handles of their swords.

'You speak English,' the man said.

William nodded.

'We must talk,' the man said. William recognised him as the youngest of the five heads of the Valdostani.

The man led them down an alley that smelt of urine and faeces, and stood talking to them in hushed whispers as rats scurried past them on the other side of the alley.

'My name is Veron, and I know some English. I was schooled at Cambridge, and confess it has been a while since I talk in this tongue. Please. Pardon my inaccuracies. I could not talk in that room. Angelo is a proud man, and old. He speaks for Valdostani, but not always for me. Please understand Angelo believes he is doing true ... sorry ... *right*, by all Valdostani. All we have wanted was our own rule, or the rule of the French. I am scared that we have embraced the wrong Frenchman.'

William looked surprised. 'Then you know of Cuassard?'

'I know of Captain Jacques Cuassard. We all do. A family have lent him their home while he is in the Valle, a castle in the Gran Paradiso, the Castle of Addrasio. It is well fortified. Cuassard has promised more will arrive in the coming months, an army to challenge the House of Savoy. Angelo believes Cuassard will pass control of Piedmont to the Valdostani.'

'But you don't believe him,' Cazotte guessed.

Veron turned to him. 'I have seen what has happened in the villages north and east of here.'

'Then it is true? There are attacks on the villages?' William said.

Veron nodded.

'Will you excuse us, just for a moment,' he said, and took Cazotte aside.

'He *could* be an ally,' Cazotte murmured out of Veron's earshot.

'I was thinking that as well,' William said. 'We may have to tell him things about Cuassard we have not told others on this venture.'

'What kind of things?' Cazotte frowned.

'Some truths. But also some of Engrin's "white lies".' He turned back to Veron, smiling.

'Is something of concern, sir?' Veron asked.

'Not at all. Before I tell you what I know, may I ask why you are talking to us?'

'Because it was *I* who sent the plea for help to the Vatican,' Veron replied.

'You?' William said.

'I could do nothing else. The others blind themselves to the horrors being perpetrated upon my people. I cannot. I wish for French rule, but not at this price. I have heard of the killings, and that foreigners are responsible, and I have heard that witchcraft is being used by this man Cuassard.' Veron leant even closer to them. 'He has made a pact with the Devil.'

'The Devil?' William said.

'Yes, the Devil,' Veron replied. 'He has let loose a monster in the mountains. They say the beast is rampant in the night, made of fire and ash. And it kills many. I could have involved the House of Savoy, as they have a large army. But if the Savoys marched into Aosta, there would be a rebellion! The only other help I could think of was Rome – this is, after all, an *infernal* enemy.'

William frowned and rubbed at his tired face. 'A monster?' he said to Cazotte.

'A daemon,' the Italian suggested grimly.

William groaned. This mission was getting worse.

'Saxon,' Cazotte said, 'this does not sit well. If the beast was mentioned to the Papacy then somewhere the message did not reach the Secretariat.'

'Or perhaps the information was suppressed,' William mused.

'The traitor?' Cazotte said, as though he had a bad taste in his mouth.

William nodded.

Veron was suddenly startled and bundled both men down the alley towards the next street. 'Leonardo!' he hissed.

As they ran into the next street, Veron panted and glanced wearily back.

'Who are we running from?' William asked.

'One of the Valdostani: Leonardo. He tried to stop my letter from reaching Rome,' Veron replied, his hand twitching nervously at his sword. 'He must not know that we have talked or it will be your downfall. He too knows of Cuassard and accepts what is happening.'

'I appreciate your candour,' William said. 'It feels dishonourable to ask for more.'

Veron shrugged. 'What else can I give you?'

'The whereabouts of Castle Addrasio,' William replied.

Veron nodded and looked again to the alley, listening for signs of Leonardo approaching. 'Very well. But then you must go. The castle can be reached through the Valle di Cogne.'

'And the villages that were attacked are near there?' William said.

'No. To the north and to the east. Cuassard has not attacked those in the Gran Paradiso.' Veron pursed his lips as he heard footsteps coming closer.

'Go now!' he hissed and William and Cazotte fled, without even thanking the man for his help. William was acutely aware that Veron may have sacrificed his own life for this information.

'I do hope that poor man is not executed for this,' he said quietly, as they walked quickly past a group of militia talking to a whore on a street corner.

'He would make a certain ally,' Cazotte replied. 'But that is not what most concerns me, Saxon. We are all quite mortal, and our lives mercifully short. If Veron is to die, then he will die knowing he may have saved many of his people.'

'Then what concerns you?' William asked.

'The daemon, obviously, but also the letter Veron sent to Rome.'

They came to the city gates and passed through them without being approached by the militia. William felt nervous, as though someone might pounce on them at any moment. Their pace slowed as they spied their camp half a mile down the road in a nearby field. With their pulses slowing, they continued their discussion.

'The letter must have reached Rome intact,' said William. 'But somehow, it failed to reach *us* ... Only Cardinals Issias and Devirus read the letter, correct? And it was they who devised the mission?' William then fell quiet, realizing what he was suggesting.

'The missions *always* come from Cardinals Issias and Devirus,' Cazotte confirmed. 'It has been this way since the Secretariat was formalised.'

'And no one else knows of the missions until the brothers are given their orders?' William asked.

Cazotte nodded.

'Then the traitor *must* be either Issias or Devirus,' William replied, though he took no pleasure in saying it.

'Impossible!' Cazotte hissed.

'Because they are cardinals, or because such a breach would be devastating?' William said.

Cazotte fell quiet.

'If you can think of any other explanation, now is the time to tell me,' William said.

'I cannot,' Cazotte conceded.

They walked on in silence as they considered the implications of such a revelation. William knew enough about the lieutenant to know that the hierarchy in the Secretariat was the one thing he had been able to trust, and now he was being asked to question it. It could only sour Cazotte's mood, and William feared it might dull his wits. If he began questioning his own integrity then the venture was surely in trouble.

'We should tell the Secretariat what has happened,' Cazotte suggested finally.

'No. We will send word to Engrin. He is the only one I completely trust. He had misgivings about this venture from the start. He will know what to do. We'll send a rider back to Rome. Perhaps then Engrin might discern who our traitor is.'

Cazotte seemed to agree, but was still unsettled.

'Cazotte,' William said as they stopped just outside the camp. 'You look distracted. And by rights you should be. You have soldiered under the Secretariat for a long while, and as you have pointed out so many times, I am but an outsider. I have no right to assume anything over what facts are presented to me. But I do have the right as the company's commanding officer to discern what cause of action should be taken on this and any other matter relating to our mission. I am of course bound to do what is best for the men under my command and the people we have come to save. I trust your judgement on both, but on the matter of the traitor you must trust *mine*.'

'You would have me believe that one or both of the cardinals are treacherous,' Cazotte seethed, seeming to return to the Cazotte of old.

'No,' William said defensively. 'I would simply have you believe that Engrin alone is impartial. He will know what to do and what is at stake. He is quite discreet, don't you think?'

Cazotte nodded reluctantly.

'Then you agree that the course of action I've suggested is the right one?'

'Maybe it is,' Cazotte grunted. 'But I respectfully abhor the decision.'

'It may be too late for any other course of action,' William said. 'We may already have stepped into the trap and only now is the net closing. I for one will run not around like a wet hen waiting to be caught. I believe we should let the Secretariat sort out their own problems while we continue with the mission. But I will proceed only with your agreement. Let me be frank,' William continued. 'Kieran and I are nothing more than puppets. This your country' – William cast his arms wide – 'and your people.'

Cazotte nodded, his confidence returning. He straightened his jacket, his dark ruminations fading as he considered their next course. 'We need to remove Cuassard, but attacking this castle with a small number of men would be futile.'

William agreed. 'The only way to succeed is to gather allies. We must have the Valdostani on our side, and to do that we must open their eyes. So I suggest that tomorrow we obtain evidence of the horror of Cuassard. Refugees may be too terrified to talk, but the bones of the dead will speak for them. If we dangle enough corpses in front of the Valdostani they may wake from their slumber and realize exactly who Cuassard is and what he represents.'

'And then we turn the Valdostani against him,' Cazotte said, appearing to like the plan.

They returned to the camp and joined the other brothers who were finishing up their food.

'Are there problems?' Kieran asked, as he handed his friend a bowl of broth.

'Aren't there always?' William replied.

'But you wish for us to stay on here?' Kieran pressed.

'Most certainly,' William said. 'Our mission is not over.'

'And Cuassard? What of him?' Kieran asked.

'He is in a castle two days away, in the mountains.'

'Are we to assault it?' Kieran was hopeful.

'Not with this small number of men,' William answered. 'We would be slaughtered. No, we wait for aid.'

'But from whom? We have no allies here,' Kieran remarked.

'Not true,' William smiled. 'I think we have at least one.'

CHAPTER FIFTEEN

Blood in the Mountains

△ I △

To the west of Aosta, nestled in the foothills, were a number of villages; some were lavish like Villeda, while others were simple settlements with simple homes. All – rich and poor alike – were abandoned.

'I haven't seen anything like this since Napoleon invaded,' Cazotte growled as he kicked over an empty barrel. 'The villagers have fled and anything of value has been stripped from this place.'

'This is the fourth village in two days,' William sighed, as he turned over the partially burned carcass of a goat with the toe of his boot. They had left Aosta the morning before at sunrise to scour the area for signs of Cuassard's men or the kafalas. Each village since then had borne the same marks of chaos and pillaging.

'There are no dead, nor are there graves. These people managed to escape with their lives,' Cazotte said as he knelt down to touch the muddy road beneath them. 'And these are not soldiers' tracks.'

William knelt down with him and examined the boot marks. 'Could be anyone,' he murmured.

Both men straightened up and William noticed several crows perched on a nearby thatched roof.

'They sense death,' Cazotte said to him. 'But today they missed out.'

'They shouldn't worry. There could be plenty of carrion on the other side of the ravine,' William said grimly and spat in the mud.

'We have been lucky,' Cazotte remarked. 'Four villages abandoned and only six dead.'

'Six fresh graves, you mean.'

'You think the kafalas would waste time dragging away corpses?' Cazotte said.

'At this moment in time, I'm not sure what to believe. We have refugees spilling from the valleys into the city, and a governing body who ignores the situation, thinking only of power.'

'Power corrupts,' Cazotte grunted.

'This is not corruption, Cazotte,' William said, marching away. 'It's murder.'

△ II △

On the third day they discovered a group of refugees heading south. There were more than forty men, women and children, and as before, William had to pass by without offering much comfort or aid. It was a desperate sight, and one that angered him.

Those who weren't afraid to speak told Cazotte a familiar story of raids and murder; the tactics of their attackers were all too clear: assault under cover of darkness. Yet this time Cazotte recounted a new detail to William as they rode on.

'They added something curious,' the Italian said. 'Something I've never heard of before.'

'About the attacks on their town?' William asked.

'No, no,' Cazotte replied. 'About something they saw two days ago, after they fled. They said they saw lightning hit the mountains, and when they arrived at the place it struck, they found many of their attackers dead.'

William pulled up his horse, the company halting suddenly.

'Where?' William said urgently.

'Miles from here, I think,' Cazotte replied as he reached down to pull out the map. Unrolling it, he peered across ravines and valleys until he found the place the refugees had spoken of. 'It is here, south of the border, near Tresta and Lenova. A few miles south of their town.'

'How long would it take to get there?' William asked.

'Less than a day,' Cazotte replied. 'What are you thinking?'

'I'm thinking a single kafala or French corpse would be better than all the dead in these mountains,' he said grimly.

Leaving a handful of monks to guard the cart, the rest of the company galloped down the pass, arriving before dark at the spot the refugees said was marked by lightning. It was a small field by a river, and looked slightly out of place against the looming rocks and gargantuan mountains. The company dismounted as they searched for bodies, but after half an hour they found none.

'Are you sure they meant *here?*' William asked, but Cazotte could only shrug, bewildered that they could not find any sign of the enemy.

Suddenly, one of the brothers yelled, and they gathered around a patch of grass stained with blood.

William knelt down. 'Someone bled badly here. And here,' he added, pointing to another patch nearby.

'Signs of battle,' Cazotte remarked.

'It looks that way,' William replied. 'Tell them to spread out and search the bushes. I'm suspect they took their dead away and buried them somewhere.'

'But who could have done this?' Cazotte asked.

William couldn't be sure until he found the bodies.

As the sun began to fall, several monks found discarded weapons hidden in nearby bushes. William assumed they belonged to the kafalas. Still, they didn't find a single body, much to William's displeasure. Suddenly Cazotte called over to William by the river. He jogged over and found the Italian looking down with disgust.

'I've found something,' he said, but clearly wasn't happy about his discovery.

William rounded his side and looked down, his nose

scrunching up at the smell of burnt flesh and sulphur. 'Oh God,' he murmured.

'Is that a man?' Cazotte said weakly.

'It was,' William replied. The corpse was black as charcoal and burnt to a crisp. It lay half in a bush with an arm and its head missing. William bent down, though not too close, for the smell was nauseating.

'What do you make of it?' Cazotte coughed.

'I think we have our evidence,' he said. 'Though I don't know if anyone would believe it.'

'You want to take *this* to Aosta?' Cazotte said, incredulously.

William straightened up. 'I've seen this before,' he said. 'Some time ago, in a town called Gembloux. This corpse has the mark of the Devil.'

Cazotte looked down at it. 'How can you tell?' he asked, seeing nothing but burnt flesh.

'It has no head,' William said matter-of-factly, and walked away.

Both men climbed the river bank again and stood a few yards away from their discovery to consider what had happened. 'Those are the remains of a daemon,' William continued. 'Only decapitation will kill them.'

'If it was a daemon, the kafalas must have been controlling it,' Cazotte said.

'I'm not so sure,' William replied. 'I've seen one of these things up close. I don't think it can be controlled. Perhaps what the refugees saw was the kafalas' own daemon destroying them. They somehow managed to cut off its head before it slaughtered them completely. Then they buried their dead and left.'

Cazotte thought about this. 'And the lightning?' he asked.

William shrugged. 'Embellishments. All stories have them. Strangely, I think the facts here are more terrifying than the fiction.'

Cazotte ordered the monks to throw the discarded weapons they had collected into the water.

'We need something harder to convince the Valdostani,' William said. 'We need evidence of the suffering of their people. Not bloodied weapons or burnt corpses.'

Cazotte nodded and returned to his horse and pulled out the map. He pinched his brow as he poured over the area, searching for another town or village. William mounted his horse and walked it over to the Italian. 'I think one more village will suffice,' he said.

'And if there is a daemon?' Cazotte asked, his eyes still on the map.

'It's more important than ever to conclude this sorry affair swiftly. If we cannot find enough evidence to show to this Angelo gentleman, then we will need to rely on Veron for support. We need the Valdostani on our side, if only to take that castle.'

△ III △

Since night was coming and there was still no sign of the next village, William decided to signal a halt to their travels. They were near a defensive position that looked out to almost every direction for several miles, and with a solid wall of stone at their rear they could not be surprised from behind. Thirty men with rifles would have had no problems staving off a modest assault.

Half an hour after camp had been made, however, they spotted a group of refugees huddled in the valley below.

'More refugees,' Cazotte pointed out.

'They're trying to hide from us,' William remarked.

'From this distance, we are all alike,' Cazotte said. 'We carry guns and swords.'

'Do you think it is safe to speak with them?'

'We will have to get down there first,' Cazotte replied. 'There isn't a path for another mile, and even then we couldn't take our horses.'

'It is growing dark. Too dark to waste time,' William observed, looking skyward. 'We need to get down there now. Do we have some rope?'

Cazotte rubbed his chin with a knuckle. 'Thinking of climbing down there yourself, are you?' he said.

'Unless you have a better idea,' William said.

'I do, as it happens,' Cazotte replied. 'I'll go.'

'You?'

Cazotte nodded. 'Unless you can suddenly speak my language.'
William backed down.

Cazotte approached the edge of the road with a long length of rope coiled around his shoulders. He bent over and assessed the drop, his boots dislodging a few stones that skittered down the cliff edge to echo in the valley below. He stepped back a bit, a little more cautiously, and rubbed his chin again. 'There should be enough rope,' he said. He pulled away his sword and passed it to William.

'Unarmed?' William asked.

Cazotte patted the narrow belt tied over one shoulder, on which the metal throwing-stars were strapped. 'I have these. And they are less threatening than a sword.'

The Italian wrapped the rope about his shoulders and waist and passed the remainder to William and the other monks who had come over from the camp. They held on tight as Cazotte clambered over the edge and began to descend. Kieran came to William's side and took over from him, letting William stand on the edge of the road to watch Cazotte's progress. The cliff face was jagged and William winced as the Italian clattered into one of the jutting rocks, grinding his side against it. To the Italian's credit he let out only a low groan, but continued descending until he reached the ground. Cazotte was obscured by bushes and shrubs and William couldn't help but fear the worst. The Italian was an experienced soldier, but a crowd of unarmed and panicked refugees could exact harm or even throw the lieutenant over the next cliff and down into the valley.

'Captain?' came Cazotte's voice. The gloom was thickening quickly with the coming dusk but William could see Cazotte at the bottom with several people at his side.

'What do you know, Cazotte?' William called down.

'They are refugees, and they are not afraid of us now. They want to come up!' Cazotte shouted back.

'Up here?'William said, and looked to Kieran and the monks. 'Can they climb?'

'No!' Cazotte shouted. 'But we can pull them up!'

William agreed to the request, but harboured concerns. It was growing darker by the minute and they were vulnerable to attack. In Cazotte's absence, the only translator he had was Wilcox, who was skulking back at the camp. William jogged over to the tents.

Wilcox glowered behind his scarred face, making no secret of his disdain for him.

'I need a dozen sentries,'William said to him abruptly. 'And I need a good soldier to lead them in case we are attacked here. It's only a precaution, and Cazotte assures me you are a good soldier.'

'I am,'Wilcox replied.

'Then organize the sentries. I need six men covering the north road, and six covering the south.'

Wilcox nodded and turned to say a few words in Italian to the brothers. At once, twelve men volunteered and Wilcox separated them into two parties, leaving William to return to the ledge and supervize the evacuation of the refugees.

'I am ready!' Cazotte called up, and William noticed that the rope was tied around a small figure wrapped in a shawl.

'Very well!' William said, and turned to the brothers. 'Haul away!'

The monks began to pull the rope, short lengths at a time, and William looked down into the shadows of the gully as the bundle hanging onto the rope swayed against the rock-face. It was hard work and already sweat was beginning to bead the crowns of the brothers as they pulled like machines, their arms working in unison. William marvelled at their speed, yet the refugee rose smoothly and soon reached the top.

William quickly untied the rope from the person in the shawl, and as he did so he caught a slight scent of flowers, perhaps perfume. The refugee was a woman, though under the shawl he could not tell how old she was.

They dropped the length of rope down the ledge again. Cazotte stood back to let it fall, before selecting another refugee from the crowd around him.

William led the woman away towards the cart and regretted his lack of Italian. He decided to try some Latin, and asked the woman if she was hungry. The woman looked up at him and William saw her big brown eyes staring back from under the hood. They locked on his for a moment and then she shook her head, turning away.

Back at the ledge, an elderly gent was having difficulty climbing over the edge of the road. William ran over and helped him up before the rope was lowered and the process began again and again.

△ IV △

It took them over an hour to haul fifteen refugees from the ledge below. With night upon them, the camp was reorganised quickly and spilled out across the road. Two fires were lit, and a mixture of refugees and monks sat around each, the brothers attending to the refugees' wounds and hunger. William and Kieran sat with Cazotte and the elderly man, along with the woman they had first pulled up the rock-face and a boy – perhaps her son or her brother.

'So it appears the nearest village is no more,' Cazotte said after he finished talking with the frail old man wrapped in one of the monks' blankets.

'He told you that?' William said. 'Is it completely gone?'

'Raised to the ground.' Cazotte spat and stoked the fire in front of them with a short stick. Little embers like fire-sprites sparked into the air and then melted into darkness.

'How many escaped?' William asked.

'They do not know,' Cazotte sighed. 'Some of the refugees fled deeper into the mountains. Others crossed over the border. He thinks most perished.'

'The kafalas did this?'

'Hooded men,' Cazotte said. 'That is how he described them.'

'Then this appears to be the work of the kafalas,' William said. 'And if we can persuade them to speak to the Valdostani, then maybe we have the evidence we need.'

'They are too frightened,' Cazotte scoffed. 'And too weak.'

William looked around the fire and studied each refugee's face. Cazotte was right, they were afraid and they were weak. All except the woman they had pulled up first. There was something else in her expression – a determination or pride. He wanted to talk to this woman, but he didn't want to use Cazotte as an intermediary. She barely kept the hood from her face, but he had noticed her red lips, her slender neck, her brown eyes and the way she held herself.

'Our situation is serious,' William announced suddenly, trying to take his mind off the woman. 'I think we need to call on our only ally here, if he is still alive.'

'Veron? Do you think he will help us further?' Cazotte asked.

'If he is genuine, then yes. We are blind pilgrims here. I realize we know little about Veron, but we have very little choice. He has conspired against his fellows, and against our enemy. He was also willing to place himself in danger just to talk to us. It will take time to get all these people to Aosta. If Veron can meet us near here with extra horses then it will assist our endeavours.'

'The passes will be patrolled,' Cazotte suggested. 'If not by Cuassard's men, then by the kafalas. A lone rider would be killed on his way to the city ...'

'Then send six,' William said. 'Our numbers here matter not if we are ambushed. Thirty men or twenty four ... if they attacked it would be bloody and disastrous. Only in the open would we have a chance. We can get there quicker with more horses.'

'Then it all depends on time. And we have little. I will send the men tonight.'

William held up his hand and shook his head. 'Not tonight. They'll go in the morning. They have travelled far and worked hard. They should rest.'

'You forget that these are monks of the Order, Saxon, not farmers,' Cazotte retorted. 'They can ride through the night if they must.'

'And you forget that these men have ridden far and are still tired. I am not questioning their ability, but their wits. If they are attacked at night with a day's ride dulling their instincts, they would be wiped out. And besides, one night will hardly make a difference to our circumstances.'

For the rest of the night William sat and looked into the flames, his thoughts on what lay ahead. Finally, when Kieran was asleep and Cazotte was snoring, William stood up and stretched, feeling the faint promise of sleep around the corner. He was about to leave the fire but noticed the woman with the brown eyes. She was still awake, her face blurred in the shimmering heat of the fire.

William reached down and picked up his blanket, before walking over to the other side of the fire. The woman was shivering slightly in her shawl and William sat down by her. He smiled and placed the blanket around her shoulders. As he did so, her hands touched his arm. Her fingers wrapped around his and she pulled herself close to him until she could lean her head on his shoulder. William put his arm around her and found himself hugging her close. She said nothing, uttering not a single sigh or noise as she held herself against him and began to sleep.

William drifted off soon after – not into the restless sleep that had dominated him since leaving Villeda, but an easy sleep with dreams of home.

△ V △

Cazotte's orders to the six riders were simple: 'Ride all day and night and stop for no one. Find the one they call Veron, but be discreet. Ask Veron for horses and a place for them to meet us, then ride back and rejoin the company.'

It took three days for the company to emerge from the mountains, and even then it wasn't without sacrifice. Two of the most desperate refugees, an old woman and a baby, died on the road. They had no time to bury them with decency, nor could they be burned on a pyre, as it would have alerted the enemy. Their bodies were bound and hurled down the mountainside, in the hope that they would fall into the river far below. It was the only thing they could do.

As they appeared on the incline towards the plain where Aosta sat, William and Cazotte consulted the map and recognised that it would take another five days to reach the city at their present rate. They were unable to move fast, even with the refugees on the horses and the monks marching alongside. The roads were rocky and made travelling slow; that and their frequent stops as they spied shadowy figures along the passes, impeded their progress.

Four days after finding the refugees, they came to a grassy plain that followed the river down gentler slopes. The mountains behind loomed with their grey walls and snow-capped summits, and the wind was cold at their backs. In front, it was more like summer, and the smell of flowers and grass was relaxing. The effect on the refugees was immediate when they stopped for water and rest by a hillock that was alive with rabbits. The brothers killed several with their rifles, both for target-practise and for much-needed food. William had not counted on having to feed refugees as well.

He watched the refugees dismount, the monks helping many of them from the horses. The woman with the brown eyes declined assistance and climbed down unaided. She had not yet uttered a single word, but each night she would huddle close to William and they both slept serenely.

Cazotte had been quick to comment, but had not come to any roguish conclusion, noting only that she was 'a strange and quiet woman'. Later, the Italian learned from another refugee that the woman was from a wealthy family, most of whom had been butchered before her eyes. Only she and the boy – her nephew – had survived. The child was being looked after by one of the older women, a nurse of some kind.

When eventually the brown-eyed woman pulled away her shawl on that fourth day, William found that she was indeed beautiful. She had long black hair that curled like night about her shoulders; across the ridge of her back, fine black hairs swirled like a whirlpool. Her skin was an olive colour and looked soft and smooth. She remained graceful and when she turned to look up at him, William's eyes faltered. She was stunning. Even beneath that cowl she had appeared pretty, but now he was bowled over. She was younger than William, no older than Elizabeth.

William tried to look away, his eyes alighting on anything but her: the cart, his horse, a monk helping an elderly woman to sit on a nearby rock, two children playing, even his own tired and worn hands. In the end he could not help himself and his eyes always returned to her: as she sat with her people, as she drank water from a canteen, as she ate the bread a brother persuaded her to have, as she stared up at the mountains behind them, and then looked over to William her eyes so beautiful, but so proud.

The sounds of horses approached and Cazotte was quick to organize a platoon of men to fan out as a screen around the clearing and the road. The grey uniforms of the Order blended into the landscape and they were hidden, their Baker rifles at their shoulders.

It was a relief to find that the approaching riders were neither kafalas nor French soldiers, but the six brothers they had sent to Aosta.

'They have ridden all night,' Cazotte said to William as they walked away from the others, 'and they bear good news.'

'Go on,' William implored.

'Veron has agreed to send us eight horses to an abbey at the foot of the main pass. It will take several hours to arrive there, but we should make it before dusk.'

'An abbey?' William said, as Cazotte unrolled the map and pointed to a small dot a few miles east of the mouth of the pass.

'I don't recall seeing this before,' William murmured as he assessed the distance between them and the abbey.

'Neither do I,' Cazotte agreed. 'But the map says it exists, and so does Veron. If it is hidden, then it can only aid us. The kafalas may not know of its whereabouts.'

'It could be up to nine miles away,' William said, and scratched the stubble on his chin.

'More like seven. Still, with these people it will take us until dusk to reach it,' Cazotte said.

'Then we should go now,' William said.

Cazotte gathered the brothers, and the refugees were led back to the horses. As William came to his mount, he stumbled into the woman; his flustered apology came out in a mixture of Latin and English. For the briefest of moments he thought he saw her smile, but when she turned again, that proud look had returned. She was a determined woman, but a mystery; William hoped he would have a chance to unlock that mystery, to find out who she was.

△ VI △

As the mouth to the pass widened, the sun caught the side of the hills and mountains and turned them gold. The lead riders had to cup their hands over their eyes to see ahead. William could make out the edge of the plain and the city of Aosta in the distance, only a day's journey once they had collected the horses.

William rode along the column of refugees and monks. Their food was running terribly low now, and he hoped Veron would be able to provide provisions at Aosta without the Valdostani finding out. If Veron was discovered, then their venture would be in dire trouble.

The column turned and they made an exit down a less trodden route. It was a narrow path, only just wide enough to accommodate the cart. After an hour's march, as the sun began to fall, they found a forest on the plain's edge. There, half hidden, was the abbey, a tall bell-tower looming behind the trees.

'The abbey,' Kieran announced.

William rode up to Cazotte, a little cautiously. Some of the refugees became excitable and began pointing to the building as it emerged from the trees.

'They are just happy they have found somewhere holy,' Cazotte explained to William. 'They think God can protect them.'

'I pray they're right,' William replied, his hand on his sword. The forest was growing quite dark and the sun had fled from this side of the mountains. As they neared the building, William grew even more cautious. There was no sign of Veron or the horses.

'They could have been delayed,' Cazotte said as the column came to a halt.

'And yet would they have been so far behind the brothers?' William said.

The air was quiet. Even the birds that had sung their songs in the deepest valleys barely an hour before had ceased to sing. Now there was nothing but the animated chatter of the refugees.

Something was wrong.

William dismounted, taking his rifle and walking away towards the tree-line. He stood at the nearest tree to look up into its branches.

'What are you thinking, Will?' Kieran asked as he came to his side.

'We need a lookout,' William said. 'I don't know why, but I feel uneasy here.'

Kieran regarded his friend for a moment but knew that it was unwise to question him. William had a keen sense of danger. For a moment, the refugees grew quiet, and William and Kieran heard twigs snapping.

William's hand went to his rifle just as a dozen flashes came from the shadows of the trees. The shots rang out a second later, as lead balls cut down one of the monks and two refugees.

'Down! Get down!' William roared. The brothers dived for cover as soon as the first shots rang out. The refugees reacted more slowly, and as another volley of fire sputtered across them, one more was cut down. She screamed, clutching her face, her dress turning red in waves, before she collapsed to the ground. The monks pulled the rest of the refugees to the floor as the woman fell, and even the brothers on the cart dived for cover, grabbing their rifles and using the wagon as a barricade.

William and Kieran were crouched in a ditch by the road, a mound of earth separating them from the firing in the tree-line.

'Trapped so easily, dammit!' William shouted, pulling the rifle from his shoulder. He loaded it as quickly as he could, still hunkered down as shots erupted on the bank just above his head.

Kieran had pulled his sword out and was grinning. 'Just like old times!' he declared, almost deliriously.

'Don't do anything careless!' William warned. 'They have guns. You do not!'

'It hasn't stopped us before!'

'We weren't outnumbered then. I fear now we are,' William retorted as he pulled back the lock into its firing position. He rolled to the side where the bank was lowest and crawled to a notch in the mound. There he rested the rifle and looked down the barrel. He could hardly see a thing, and although the monks were beginning to fire back, he was not sure if they were hitting anyone.

'Torches,' he murmured to himself and then turned over. 'Cazotte!'

The Italian appeared from behind the cart, his head ducking down as a piece of splintered timber flew past his nose.

'Torches!' William yelled. 'Throw some torches into the forest!'

Cazotte nodded and busied the two monks by his side as the shots flew closer. It would take time to assemble the torches and light them, so William turned back and narrowed his eyes to discern what was shadow and what was the enemy.

Eventually he spotted a figure creeping up between two trees. As he emerged from a third tree, William anticipated his next step and fired. The figure dropped and did not rise again. William was already lying on his back and loading again.

As he primed the pan, he looked up as one flaming torch after another sailed overhead, drawing a trail of fire behind them. Their arcs were high, and while some hit nearby trees, others went far into the thicket, destroying the shadows with their glare.

William rolled over again, found the notch in the mound and was greeted with a dozen men moving quickly towards them. He fired and dropped one, another three falling as the monks found their range. Reloading again, William raised his rifle and faltered as the enemy poured out of the forest before them.

William fired, loaded, and fired again before the first of the enemy reached the road. They came at them, cloaked in dark robes and their heads bound by black scarves so that only their eyes were visible.

'Kafalas!' William screamed as he launched himself at the nearest attacker with the butt of his rifle. He swung it wide, catching the man in the side before clubbing his head. Tossing the rifle aside, he drew his sabre and with Kieran fell upon the black tide as it engulfed them.

William cleaved and hewed his way through the massed ranks. At least a dozen fell to his sword before he reached the cart, where Cazotte was fighting hand-to-hand. On the ground, amongst the dead kafalas, William saw two dead monks – the drivers of the cart.

William skewered the kafala to Cazotte's right while Cazotte hacked down the one on his left. He glanced up with a grateful expression before he had to parry the sword of another assassin. Kieran had broken away from them, alone, as he cut his way through to the refugees. The monks had formed a tight circle around them, but already six monks were dead. Kieran yelled and startled some of the kafalas assaulting their position, before driving his sword down time and time again.

William pushed back a kafala assault as he and Cazotte tried to find a way out. The situation was growing more hopeless with every passing moment. They had lost a third of their men and the kafalas continued to attack in waves. There were at least 200 of them now.

'We have to get out of here!' William yelled.

'We need to get everyone to the horses!' Cazotte shouted back.

'Agreed! But we can't get to the refugees, look!'

William was right. The remains of the company were split almost in two, with William, Cazotte and eight brothers including Wilcox on one side of the road, while Kieran, the remaining dozen monks and the refugees were backed up against the walls of the ruined abbey. Between them and the Kieran and the brothers protecting the refugees there were dozens of kafalas.

'Cazotte!' William shouted as he parried another attack, cutting down his enemy before he could try again. 'Get Wilcox to form a firing line, four men front, four men on the second row. Help him organize it!'

'What are you going to do?' Cazotte yelled back.

'I'm going for the horses!' William shouted.

'Are you mad? Just you?' Cazotte screamed back.

'I can take care of myself!'

Cazotte shook his head, but didn't argue. He fought his way to where Wilcox and the others were driving off the kafalas, but he had already lost another man, and they were down to seven.

Without hesitating, William charged down the road, cutting down two kafalas who were in his way. Another came at him out of the shadows and it was only William's sharpened wits that stopped the attacker's knife from running into his throat. He dodged and the blade nicked his ear. William roared out angrily and his sword followed in a wild swing that cut through the attacker's back. Without stopping to see him drop, William charged on until he reached the horses. He gathered as many reins as he could and leapt onto his own horse as three more kafalas came at him. William turned the horses towards them and charged, only one of the kafalas managing to get out of the way. The other two were trampled to death.

Ahead of William there was smoke and chaos. Night had almost fallen. William charged on, through a line of kafalas that had formed to storm Cazotte's firing-line. Those who weren't trampled broke and ran; William wished he could free his hand and hack the bastards down with his sabre.

He pulled up the horses as he came to Cazotte, and put his hand out. The Italian took it and swung himself up behind William, who handed him the reins of the horses.

'Hang on!' he cried and drew his sabre to cut down a kafala who had the tenacity to charge at them.

Meanwhile, Wilcox was leading the small squad of men in two ranks, firing with discipline and accuracy. Already they had cut a small path through to the others, but had lost two more men, and were now fighting hand-to-hand.

'Retreat!' William yelled.

Cazotte had leapt from William's mount to another, still holding onto the reins as William did his best to keep the kafalas at bay.

Kieran turned to Wilcox, blood on his cheeks and forehead.

'Get out of 'ere, you fool!' Wilcox bellowed to him, staring at the Irishman with his one good eye. 'We're to retreat!'

'I'm not leaving these people!' Kieran yelled back.

'We'll provide a screen to cover them!' Wilcox snarled. 'Saxon has given the order!'

Kieran glanced over to where William was thrusting into the pack of kafalas. The Irishman nodded and began inching back as Wilcox barked to the brothers and the refugees.

A shot rang out and an elderly woman fell screaming, clutching her breast.

Kieran cursed and ran to the refugees, picking up the youngest boy and carrying him under his arm. Seeing the boy being taken away, the refugees followed blindly.

As Kieran looked back, he saw that Wilcox was holding their rear, but they were losing more men. The company was now down to half-strength and things were getting desperate: the line of monks was too sparse, and too weak.

Kieran handed the boy over to the old man and pointed to William. 'Go!' he yelled, hoping the old man understood. He did, and dragged the boy towards the horses as William trotted forward to provide protection.

'Retreat!' Kieran shouted, cutting his way back down the line of men to Wilcox, who was clubbing kafala after kafala with his spent rifle.

'Get out of 'ere!' Wilcox shouted again, as he swung the butt of the rifle at another attacker.

Kieran cleaved an assailant who swung an axe towards them both, and then sidestepped as another blade just missed his cheek. He swiped his own sword up and through the man's throat, more blood showering upon him. Behind, the monks were falling back to the horses now. Strangely, though, the kafalas were not following.

Then came the screams, and Kieran saw that the refugees had been surrounded. Kafalas were dashing their way from behind the abbey. It was hopeless.

'Goddam it!' Kieran cursed as he saw them being carried away by their attackers to an uncertain fate. He wanted to go after them, but knew it was too late. They were outnumbered and outgunned. The best they could hope for now was to survive.

'Fall back!' Wilcox urged and pulled Kieran away from the fighting. 'We have to retreat!'

'The refugees ...!' Kieran shouted hoarsely.

'They're lost!' Wilcox screamed, as the sounds of horses behind alerted him to William's rescue attempt. Wilcox clubbed another kafala and then discarded the rifle as he stumbled away with Kieran.

'Mount up! For the grace of God, mount up!' William implored, ducking as shots buzzed past him.

'They're firing at us!' Cazotte yelled. 'We must go!' He added something in Italian and the monks mounted without hesitation, turning the horses around to gallop away as quickly as possible, Cazotte leading them.

William would not leave until Kieran was on his horse. The Irishman put a foot in the stirrup just as a kafala charged with a pike. In the confusion he didn't see it coming.

Wilcox threw himself in the way and the pike ran through his stomach.

Kieran heard him cry out and turned, drawing his sabre and cutting down the kafala, before snapping the pike extending from Wilcox's stomach, and hoisting him over his shoulder. He put him on his horse and climbed on as another monk fell screaming, with a hole in his forehead.

'Kieran!' William shouted as the Irishman turned his horse and galloped away from the carnage, shots ringing out behind them.

△ VII △

'They've stopped following us,' Cazotte panted. 'My guess is that they couldn't keep up.'

They rested their horses under the hanging rocks of the pass. They had galloped through darkness for half an hour until the first horse collapsed through exhaustion. Its two riders had fallen, but thankfully were not injured apart from a few bruises.

But now William had realized they were lost.

'We should go no further until daylight comes,' he said as he dismounted. 'We can hide here for the night.'

'And if they find us?' Cazotte asked.

'If they find us, we fight again. And we will probably lose,' William replied starkly, knowing that only Kieran and Cazotte would understand his words. Wilcox was unconscious as they carried his skewered body from Kieran's mount.

The Irishman watched the remaining brothers take him under cover to work on his wound, the head of the pike still through his stomach. 'He saved my life,' Kieran murmured as William watched them work. William said nothing, but was moved: he had been wrong about Wilcox, as he had been wrong about many things.

Cazotte came by them and watched, his face betraying his sadness as his friend groaned and writhed while the monks did what they could.

'How many survived?' William asked bitterly.

'Excluding us, only eleven brothers live, and one of those might not make it through the night,' Cazotte said. William didn't need to look at him to know how upset the Italian was. But Kieran dared to, and saw the tears in his eyes.

'I'm sorry,' William said, and walked away.

They set up what shelter they could from the remaining blankets on the horses, and from branches cut from nearby trees, deciding not to build a fire in case it attracted their pursuers. All this was done in a mourning silence.

William thought sadly about the woman with the brown eyes and black curly hair. Only the old man and the woman's nephew had made it, and they sat away from the monks, the boy wrapped in the old man's arms.

Kieran stared out into the mountains, the moon casting a pale sheen over everything. His clothes were damp with sweat and gore, and he wanted so much to get rid of them. He felt grubby, soiled and ashamed. There had been so much killing that he had felt sick as they fled, and now there was the emptiness of defeat, with nothing to look back to except the memories of the fallen.

'Harte,' a voice said nearby. He turned and found Cazotte with William at his side.

'What is it?' Kieran asked quietly.

'Wilcox wants to speak with you,' Cazotte said.

William stepped in. 'You don't have to,' he assured his friend.

Kieran frowned. 'He saved my life,' the Irishman said, and brushed past William as he made his way to the makeshift bed where the wounded monk lay. The brothers had done their best to make the aging monk comfortable, but nothing could be done for his wound and the improvised bandages were sodden with blood.

Wilcox was dying.

Kieran stood over the man and looked down at his pale face, his one good eye only a slit and puffed up like the one buried beneath scar-tissue. The man was completely inert, no longer the energetic killing machine that had saved his life and helped them all to escape.

His eye opened a little wider and he murmured something no one nearby could hear. With his hands, he gestured for Kieran to come closer, and William was afraid. He put his hand to Kieran's shoulder as a warning, but Kieran shrugged him away. He knelt down close and took Wilcox's hand.

'So much to say ...' the man croaked. 'No time to say it ...'

'Save your breath,' Kieran urged.

'No ...' Wilcox said, and shook his head slightly. 'Must say these words ...'

William and Cazotte stood closer to hear the last testament of Wilcox, while Kieran held his hand throughout.

'I know you ...' Wilcox began. 'I know your family ...'

Kieran frowned. 'You know my family?'

'The 'Artes of Kerry ... a good family ... the kindest ...' Wilcox began, his voice weakening with every breath. 'I am also Irish ...'

Kieran patted his hand gently. 'A man of my country,' he murmured.

Wilcox coughed and a bubble of blood appearing on his lips. Despite his discomfort, he continued. 'I lived ... lived in the village near your home ... the rebels forced my family to help them ... help them fight against ... against ...'

Kieran, still holding Wilcox's hand, seemed to falter. 'Against my parents?' he whispered, his eyes narrowing.

Wilcox seemed to grip Kieran's hand stronger as his grip on life grew weaker. 'I'm ... so ... sorry,' he managed. 'I was not strong ... I believed their talk ... their speeches about the British ... believed that the 'Artes were no good ... the lies ... but I realized after ... *we were so wrong* ...' Wilcox groaned in agony and William saw blood running out from under him.

Kieran held his hand and put the other one to it, trying to hold the dying monk back in their world.

'I led them to the gates of the House of 'Arte ... I watched it burn ... Forgive me! Oh God, forgive my ignorance ...'

337

Kieran bent closer.

'I never dreamt I would find a chance to atone ...' Wilcox croaked and blood seeped from the corner of his mouth. Tears were running down the sides of his face and he pulled Kieran closer. 'Please forgive me ...'

William waited for Wilcox to continue but there were no more words from the poor monk. He stared out into the void and his hand went slack. Kieran stared back at him, his lips trembling. He released the man's hand and it fell to the floor.

'The British have been hunting him for most of his life. When he came to us, he was desperately sad,' Cazotte murmured. 'He confessed to atrocities he had participated in and witnessed. And he spoke of his disgust when innocents were murdered in anger. It has haunted him forever. He fought for us to repent his sins, hoping for the forgiveness he would never receive from those he and his cause murdered.'

'And this was his valediction,' William said.

'Wilcox wasn't his real name,' Cazotte sniffed. 'He changed it because he was a wanted man. His real name was Diarmuid O'Hearne.'

Kieran nodded and stood up from the body. 'Your sins are forgiven,' he whispered. 'Be at peace, my brother, Diarmuid O'Hearne.' He stayed staring down at him until the monks pulled the blanket over him, and even then he continued to look at the mound that had been alive not so long ago, fighting for the lives of his men, the refugees, and of course Kieran himself.

William glanced at Cazotte, who had closed his eyes tight, murmuring a prayer to send his friend on his way. He couldn't believe how wrong he had been about the man, and he was sorry.

'Kieran ...' he began.

Kieran smiled and put a hand on William's arm, smiling almost serenely. 'I am fine,' he admitted. 'Do not worry about me.'

William watched him go, followed by Cazotte. Finally he himself left, as the brothers wrapped Wilcox's body in the blankets. There would be a burial – they had the time now – but who would remember a grave so deep in the mountains?

CHAPTER SIXTEEN

Rallying the Rebels

△ I △

The following morning was colder than previous mornings, and William wrapped his blanket about him as he sat cross-legged on a bank of grass, one of the few places that wasn't rock. He sat away from the others, having scarcely slept. His head was buzzing with emotions and thoughts too great to allow him to simply shut down. With the sun rising, William got to his feet and walked through the hidden camp. Only a couple of monks were standing guard. They said nothing to William as he passed by.

Ammunition was very low, and William feared that an attack, however small, would overwhelm them. The loss of the cart was a particular disaster; it meant that most of their specialist weapons were now gone.

William paused to regard the nephew of the brown-eyed woman. He was about ten years old, and despite the horrors of the last few days, he still managed to smile up at William. His elderly guardian was not as oblivious to the events happening around them, and his face appeared haggard and haunted as he wrapped his fragile arms about the boy. William thought again about the refugees and couldn't take his mind off the woman with the brown eyes.

'William?'

He looked down to his left and found Kieran, propped up

against a tree not far from the boy and the old man, his blanket around him, rubbing his eyes wearily.

'Did I wake you?' William asked.

'Not at all,' Kieran groaned and pulled himself up from the floor, stretching. 'I should not have slept. I was on guard duty ...'

'I took your turn,' William murmured.

Kieran frowned. 'You shouldn't have done that. You're our captain ...'

'Some captain ...' William grunted.

Kieran stopped rubbing his eyes. 'This wasn't your fault.'

'Yet I must take responsibility for the defeat.'

'If you believe you must, then do so. But this isn't the end,' Kieran said. 'And we still live. Isn't that enough?'

William shook his head and walked away. As he came to the road, he kicked a stone across it, the pebble skittering amongst the rocks.

'You blame yourself,' said Cazotte behind him, making William start.

'Your friend is dead,' William replied. 'As the commanding officer, I *must* blame myself.'

'Indeed,' Cazotte agreed. 'But your men do not.'

William turned to him, expecting Cazotte to be angry or mocking. Instead he was overwhelmed with humility.

'We survive, and we have done so because of your actions,' Cazotte remarked.

'It was my actions that led us to the abbey,' William said, 'my failures that led us into that trap. If I had not decided to take the refugees with us, we would not be so defeated.'

Cazotte crossed his arms. 'I did not see this trap, either. How could anyone? It was foolish to trust someone we did not know well.'

William didn't want to return to Rome in defeat, yet how could they continue? He clenched his fists angrily. They had been tricked, and tricked easily; he needed to know if Veron was indeed behind the ambush.

William marched back into the camp and brought the horses

340

around. 'Saddle up,' he said, hoping Cazotte would translate.

'We're riding? To where?' Kieran asked as he went over to a horse. 'Back home?'

William shook his head. 'Back to Aosta.'

△ II △

The ride took almost a full day and most of the horses were exhausted by the time the brothers spotted the main gate to the city. The sun had risen and fallen with such speed that William could not remember a shorter day. The riders were battered, bloodied and tired, as their mounts lurched down the road towards the city. A mile from Aosta, the fields around them suddenly grew alive with militia. They advanced swiftly on the riders. William pulled his sword free, though his arm was leaden with lack of sleep and the struggle of the previous evening. Kieran also had his sword free.

Cazotte reared up his horse and galloped to William's side. 'Another ambush!' he growled.

'If so, we are too late,' William sighed. They were quickly surrounded by men with spears and pikes, dressed in a range of battle colours. They halted a few yards from the horses.

'What are they waiting for?' Kieran asked, as the militia parted and several figures moved out of the shadows, a man dressed in fine clothes with a sword at his hip, and an older man with silver hair and a short black beard.

The older man regarded them all keenly and his eyes alighted on the two refugees. 'Marco!' he cried and ran down the line of horses to where the boy was sitting. The boy, seeing the old man rush towards him, struggled free and leapt from the horse to run to the old man's arms.

William gave Cazotte a curious glance.

The boy Marco hugged the older man who carried him on his shoulders back to the head of the column. They talked and the boy cried a little, but one thing was unmistakable to William.

341

'They're speaking French,' he remarked.

'Of course,' Cazotte replied. 'Here they speak both Italian and French. The Valle was once a region of France.'

'I wish I'd known,' William sighed, thinking he could have communicated with the woman with brown eyes had he known this. 'I can speak some French.'

Cazotte nodded and gave an expression as if to say 'By all means, try your best.'

'Who are you?' William asked the older man, his French a little stilted. He wasn't sure whether or not the words were coming out correctly, but he was trying his best.

'My name is Leonardo,' the older man replied, and Cazotte and William suddenly realized who the man was.

'What do you want?' William demanded, fearing the worst.

'I know about the trap at the Abbey of Saint Michael,' Leonardo replied.

'Do you know who was responsible?' Cazotte asked, his French a little better than William's.

Leonardo nodded his head and said, 'Veron.'

'How can we trust what you say? It was you who tried to stop the message being delivered to Rome.'

Leonardo laughed. 'Veron told you this? No, my friends. It was not I who tried to stop the letter. It was I who *wrote* it.'

'You?'

'I have been working for the House of Savoy ever since Napoleon left the Valle. I have been their secret emissary here, employed to smooth over divisions and, if possible, stop a civil war. There are those who would seek a war with the Savoys, those who would make any allegiance if it were to their gain. Those like Veron. It was he who informed Cuassard about you, and those were Cuassard's men.'

'How do you know this?' Cazotte asked.

'We have spies in Veron's camp,' Leonardo shrugged. 'The heads of the Valdostani never trusted him. And they were right not to.'

'It seems we chose the wrong ally,' William whispered to Cazotte.

'Angelo Maldini and the other heads of the Valdostani were murdered last night by Veron and his supporters. Only I escaped. He is assuming control of this region.'

William bowed his head, confused, and exhausted from lack of sleep. 'But why? Why destroy the heads of the Valdostani?'

'Because Angelo discovered that Cuassard had attacked Tresta. And Tresta is the family village of the Maldinis,' Leonardo replied gravely. 'Once he learnt his family had been butchered, he vowed revenge. But Veron would not let Angelo spoil his plans. So, Veron's supporters arranged a meeting for the heads of the Valdostani, and then torched the building. Only I was late. They have yet to discover that I am alive.'

Cazotte looked up at Leonardo. 'But why keep it a secret? With you dead, Veron now has control of Aosta, does he not? Who will fight against Cuassard now?'

'If they knew I lived, they would hunt me down.'

'Then we are lost,' Cazotte whispered to William. 'If Veron controls the Valle D'Aosta, and he is with Cuassard, what hope do we have of usurping him?'

'Very little,' William conceded.

Noticing their dejection, Leonardo gestured to the militia around him. 'I still have many supporters in the city. If we can subdue Veron's people, we will regain control.'

'He may find you first,' William suggested.

'The Valdostani are not the only power in the Valle,' Leonardo said weakly. 'There are the Savoys. They can help us.'

'But will they not demand a price for that help?' Cazotte said.

'Yes,' Leonardo conceded. 'But what choice do we have? At least the Valle will be safe for the time being.'

William dismounted and walked over to the older man. 'We will need more than the Savoys.'

'The Aosta Militia are controlled by the Valdostani,' Leonardo said. 'In their eyes, the Valdostani is headed by Veron now.'

'We must deal with Veron first,' Cazotte warned William. 'But we are in no fit state for street-fighting.'

'Where is Veron now?' William asked.

'He is not in Aosta,' Leonardo replied. 'When he understood that the Valdostani heads were dead and that you had been all but destroyed at the Abbey, he rode to Castle Addrasio.'

William rubbed his chin and looked to Cazotte. 'For once, we are lucky,' he murmured.

'Can you deal with Veron's supporters while Veron is away?' Cazotte asked.

Leonardo looked unsure. 'It will be difficult and bloody.'

'Difficult and bloody? We have lost many men,' Cazotte told him. 'And the refugees from Tresta have been taken by Cuassard. Would you not do this for the memory of Angelo Maldini? Many more will be killed if this is not finished now ...'

Leonardo still appeared unmoved, to William's annoyance. 'What about this boy's aunt? She was also taken by Cuassard. Would you see her die because you did nothing?' he growled, even though he feared she was already dead.

'Marco's aunt? Mariana? Adriana? Which?' Leonardo interrupted.

'I don't know her name. She had ... brown eyes? Black hair?'

'Adriana ...' Leonardo replied cheerfully. 'Angelo's favourite niece. Quite beautiful.'

'Yes,' William replied in English. 'That she is.'

'The night has fallen, and the world is chaos,' Leonardo said. 'It will be difficult to destroy Veron's supporters, but destroy them we will. I will raise the militia to march on Castle Addrasio.'

'Meet us in two days' time, at the second turn in the valley towards the Gran Paradiso,' William suggested. 'Then we will go into the mountains to find Cuassard.'

'Together then,' Leonardo said, and put out his hand.

William shook it. 'Together.'

△ III △

Fresh horses were arranged for the monks as they slept in a farm a couple of miles away. Marco and the old man had returned with Leonardo to the city. William stared out across the night-covered plain to the glow of Aosta in the distance against the mountains. It was a clear night, and the stars glittered sadly in the darkness, the chill of the air numbing his skin.

Kieran stood by him, smoking a pipe that Cazotte had lent him.

'Are you enjoying that?' William asked.

Kieran nodded. 'Yes. It's quite agreeable. Your father used to let me smoke with him sometimes.'

William looked astonished and then smiled sadly. 'That sounds like my father.'

'He is a great man,' Kieran said between blowing out a weak smoke-ring.

'I wonder if we'll see them again, Kieran,' William sighed.

'You wonder about that every day,' Kieran remarked. 'Not that it is a weakness. Every man needs to be driven by something. I am driven by vengeance, as you know. You are driven by your love for home and family.'

'I had hoped that you too would be driven by that same love,' William admitted.

Kieran shook his head. 'I do love Family Saxon, Will, but they are not my family. They have taken care of me since I was a boy, and treated me like a son. But I am not their heir. You are, and it is a responsibility I gladly decline. My life belongs with others and along another path. Even if we were able to return home, I wouldn't. I belong here, in the Order.'

William nodded. 'I know. Somehow, I've known that for a while, although I denied it. We lost you in Gembloux, Kieran. I realize that now. I just hoped ...' He stopped and shook his head silently.

'Hoped for what?' Kieran pressed.

'That things would never change,' William said finally and then chuckled. 'Ridiculous, is it not?'

Kieran laughed with him. 'Not at all,' he said, and smiled, lowering the pipe. 'Things have not completely changed. You are my commanding officer, but you are also my friend.'

William nodded. 'Thank you,' he said. 'That means a lot to me.'

Kieran puffed on the pipe again and stared out into the stars. 'Do you know, I've been watching these stars every night,' he admitted.

'Every night?'

Kieran nodded. 'Every clear night. Ever since we were on the *Iberian*.'

'Why the stars?' William asked. 'What do you seek?'

'Him,' Kieran replied. 'The *Dar'uka*.'

'That creature?' William said, and paused. 'I doubt we'll ever see him again. He was only after one thing: the vampyre.'

'And the pyramid,' Kieran added. 'He'll come again if he knows a daemon is loose in the Valle.'

'That is quite optimistic, even for an Irishman,' William remarked. 'I admit, his assistance would be more than helpful. I wonder if we could call him.'

Kieran shook his head. 'You can't. Engrin told me no one can, but he may yet appear.'

'Why do *you* wish to see him again?' William asked.

'Because he is beautiful and terrifying all at once,' Kieran declared dreamily. 'Because he brings hope. And we are in desperate need of hope right now.'

William agreed, but didn't say so. He couldn't waste his time believing they would be saved by phantoms.

△ IV △

The next day they saw smoke coming from Aosta as they rode south into the mountains.

'The city is burning,' Cazotte observed.

William stared into the distance, feeling cold. 'It is,' he murmured, trepidation creeping up his spine. Perhaps Leonardo had failed and the city had fallen into civil war. The fire wasn't that large, but the thin trail of smoke meant that at least one or two buildings inside the city were burning.

'What now?' Kieran asked. 'If the city is fired and Leonardo lost, is it still wise to go to the mouth of the pass as arranged?'

'Harte has a point,' Cazotte said. 'If Leonardo is a prisoner, he may be forced to tell Veron's supporters of our plans.'

William couldn't give in to doubt.

'We ride on to the meeting place as we promised,' William decided. 'If Leonardo is dead and Cuassard comes for us, then so be it. At least we will have lured Cuassard out of his castle.'

Cazotte thought about this and nodded. 'That sounds reasonable. We ride to the pass, then.'

William kicked his heels in and began galloping across the plain on the fresh horse, Kieran close behind. Cazotte galloped behind with the ten remaining monks. They would gallop until their backsides were numb and their horses weary. If they arrived at the river that evening, it would give them two days to wait for a trap – and to set a trap of their own, just in case.

△ V △

Three days had passed since they saw the smoke over Aosta, and everyone was growing nervous. They sat in the shadows of the mountains, the occasional avalanche echoing in the valley. They spent their time on reconnaissance missions in the surrounding hills, or catching rabbits to eat.

After several false alarms, William was getting twitchy, and his anxiety increased when Leonardo and the militia failed to appear on the second day as planned.

'Maybe we should find out what happened in Aosta?' Cazotte suggested.

William picked absently at a clump of grass. 'If the city has fallen, then we are trapped. The only way out of this valley is back along the river, by Aosta,' he said, and pointed with the blade of grass to the mouth of the valley. 'Unless your map can show us another way out of here?'

Cazotte rubbed his chin. 'It cannot.'

The Italian looked up at the mountains, ominous blocks of

stone against the grey skies. 'This country conceals such dark deeds,' he said.

'You mean that village?' William prompted.

Cazotte nodded. The previous day, two monks had returned from their reconnaissance with grim news of a massacre high in the mountains. The village had not been large, but big enough to keep two dozen people, who had been slaughtered and left to rot near their burnt-out homes. A quick examination of Cazotte's map had told them the village's name: Cremona.

'How many more villages would this bastard burn?' Cazotte snarled.

'As many as it takes, Lieutenant,' William replied grimly.

'I thought this was the only way. But now ...' William said, and then paused as he searched the mountains. 'Perhaps we might have a chance. Remember when I said that Veron's supporters might alert Cuassard of our presence here? Well, perhaps if enough of us climb those mountains, we could creep into the castle while Cuassard is out looking for us. On his return we could surprise him, kill him and be back in Villeda ...'

'... Before you can say ten "Hail Mary"s?' Cazotte suggested and smiled.

William laughed. 'I suppose it does sound far-fetched,' he admitted.

'Well it is a better plan than waiting for Cuassard to butcher us,' Cazotte sighed.

'There is another option,' William suggested after a few minutes silence. 'One that might not send everyone to their doom.'

'Speak on,' Cazotte said, though the tone in his voice doubted this plan would be any more realistic.

'Your map shows some Roman ruins, just to the south of here. I noticed them the last time we looked because it seemed a perfect place for an ambush. An ambush of *our* choosing,' William said.

'Go on,' Cazotte urged.

'Our men are good shots. If we place a few sharpshooters in the ruins, we could assassinate Veron, maybe even Cuassard himself.'

While the two men were talking about the planned ambush, one of the younger monks climbed the slope to where they stood, his face covered in dirt from the past few days.

Cazotte stepped forward, annoyed by the interruption, but the monk spoke quickly and Cazotte's face changed. 'They've spotted a dozen men in the passes,' Cazotte said.

'Friend or foe?' William asked.

'They're not sure. They could be bandits, or militia, or Cuassard's men,' the Italian replied. 'But they are coming this way.'

'We can defeat a dozen men,' William remarked. 'I will take Kieran and some men to investigate.'

Cazotte shook his head. 'If you are killed ...'

'Then you will lead,' William said quickly. 'Under the circumstances, we are in a mortal position: out of supplies, out of men, and out of luck.'

'Riding to your doom will not help us, Saxon,' Cazotte growled.

'Nor will sitting here simply waiting for that doom to descend,' William retorted. 'I've been sitting around too long. I need to stretch my legs.' William walked back to the makeshift camp. He paused and put his hand out as rain came down. 'If we are not back soon, head for the ruins and hide there.'

Cazotte looked displeased. William didn't hear what the lieutenant said under his breath, but he knew it was far from charitable.

△ VI △

When the rain finally stopped and the sun came out, clouds of mist began forming, providing the perfect conditions for covert riding. William had taken two monks with him, as well as Kieran. They climbed into the hills along ancient paths and tracks. William imagined Roman centurions with golden armour marching these very paths, and for a minute or two it was a fine diversion from the humid climb.

Soon they came to a forest perched around the pass. William drew his sword and looked about carefully. The two monks and Kieran shifted uneasily in their saddles, and William turned around to them, silently gesturing to dismount. On foot, they followed William over to the tree-line.

'What did you see?' Kieran hissed.

'Nothing. But I heard people approaching,' he whispered back.

There was the sound of snapping twigs nearby, and William bundled the three men into a ditch. They rolled down a short embankment to land on their feet. He led on with his sword and moved swiftly, hunkered below the trees and bushes until they came to a natural gap and squeezed through.

William stopped suddenly and raised his sword. Before them was a group of armed men, who were now pointing their swords at them. They were militiamen, yet William had no way of telling if they were Leonardo's followers or Veron's.

The stand-off remained tense for several minutes as they pointed swords and spears, bayonets and knives towards each other. William licked his dry lips as his eyes danced over the dozen or so men that surrounded them.

'Leonardo?' he called out.

One of the militia broke through to the front, his short-sword before him. He spoke in French and only William understood.

'You know of Leonardo?'

Cautiously, William nodded.

'You are the men from Rome, are you not? I see your grey clothes,' the militiaman said, glancing down at their tattered jackets.

'What if we are?' William said.

'Then you are those we wish to meet,' the militiaman replied, and lowered his sword, signalling to the others to do the same. 'There is grave news.'

William sighed and lowered his weapon. 'Leonardo failed?'

'Leonardo is dead,' the man replied. 'Killed in a street battle with Veron's supporters.'

'The smoke we saw two days ago, that was the battle?' William asked.

The man nodded. 'My name is Castillio,' he said. 'I served Leonardo and his family for several years. When the battle was joined, we were forced to flee.'

William sheathed his sword and leant back against a nearby tree, wearily. 'Then Veron has the Valle,' he murmured.

'Will? What has happened?' Kieran asked. William told him and the Irishman looked down darkly.

'Veron's supporters are coming for you,' the man called Castillio said. 'They have sent an army from Aosta to attack you from the north, and word has been sent to Cuassard, who will most certainly attack you from the south.'

'A trap ...' William murmured in English.

'A trap?' Kieran exclaimed, though William wasn't listening.

'How did Veron's people pass us? We have stayed in this valley for three days? We would have seen them,' he explained.

'There are other routes through the mountains,' Castillio replied, 'secret routes known only to the people of Aosta.'

'Where is this army from Aosta?' William asked.

'Ten miles away. It is being led by a man called Paolo Gilledo, Veron's most trusted supporter. There are over a hundred men,' Castillio said.

'How do you know this?' William asked.

'We are from the army,' Castillio replied, gesturing to the others. 'But we are secretly loyal to Leonardo. We know what happened in Aosta.'

'And the others? Do they know of Veron's treachery?' William asked.

Castillio shook his head. 'They follow him blindly. Veron ordered the arrest of the Savoys' ambassadors and revealed Leonardo as an emissary of the Savoys. I fear that we will soon be at war.'

'You already are,' William said grimly. 'The moment the Valdostani joined with Cuassard.'

Kieran understood very little. 'Will?' he said, but William

waved his hand, not wanting to be disturbed.

Finally, he stopped pacing and regarded the man called Castillio. 'How many in this army are loyal to Veron?'

'Only a few; most are loyal to the Valdostani,' Castillio replied.

'Could you convince them that Veron is an enemy of your people?' William asked.

'That would be difficult ...' Castillio replied.

William turned to Kieran. 'Yesterday, one of the brothers spoke of a village that had been massacred not that far from here,' William said. 'Their bodies are still there, are they not?'

Kieran nodded. 'I would have thought so. No one has returned to bury them.'

'If these men can convince the militia army to head up to the village ...' William began.

'What army?' Kieran asked.

'An army has been sent to destroy us,' William told him. 'But we may yet stop them. Cuassard and Veron wish to ambush us somewhere around here. According to Cazotte's map, there are ancient ruins a day's march from here. If Cuassard and the Valdostani attack us there, we will be defeated. There will be nowhere to run ... except ...'

'Except for what?' Kieran asked.

'What if the Valdostani army was under *our* control? Cuassard would not know until it was too late,' William mused.

'Can it be done?' Kieran asked.

'If the Valdostani see what Cuassard and Veron have done to their people, they will surely turn against Veron and his supporters,' William said hopefully.

Kieran shrugged, wondering if it was too much of a gamble.

'It is all we can hope for,' William said. 'If this fails, then we are dead men.'

He turned back to Castillio and outlined his plan:

'Go back to this man Gilledo and tell him you have seen us making our way towards the ruins to the south. Tell him that an attack from the north would be folly as we are heavily armed and have a cannon. Tell him that if they march up the path towards that mountain' – William pointed up the slope towards the twisted summit and the plateau beyond – 'they can use another track to surprise us. They could even destroy us before Cuassard arrives. That would please Veron.'

Castillio frowned and William thought for a moment that he had failed to understand his French.

'Why would you wish the army to surprise you?' Castillio asked.

'We don't. We want you to take them to a village called Cremon, whose people were killed by Cuassard. If we can show the militia that Veron is responsible for the massacre, Gilledo will be driven away, and you can lead the army to the ruins. Cuassard will believe you are there to destroy us ...'

'... But we will actually be there to battle him,' Castillio grinned. 'A good plan.'

'It gets better,' William smiled. 'Only three of us will be at the ruins. The others will be hidden, ready to attack Cuassard at the rear. If we can confuse his men, we will destroy them. Cuassard has a company of French soldiers with guns. They are the most dangerous. They could kill us all if we are not careful. The others – the kafalas – are deadly, but only at close range. It will be a bloody battle.'

Castillio considered this. 'We fight for the Valdostani, and for Aosta!' he declared, punching the air with his fist.

William held his sword aloft. 'Then we fight. We will meet you at Cremona, and we will see if we cannot persuade your army to march on Cuassard!'

Castillio seemed cheered by this and, gathering his men together, retreated.

'We have two chances now,' William said as they returned to the horses. 'If this Castillio can convince Veron's supporters to head to Cremona, then we can help usurp them and drive the army to the ruins. We could yet defeat Cuassard.'

'But what if we cannot persuade the militia to help us?' Kieran asked.

William mounted his horse, but Kieran still pressed for an answer. 'Well?'

353

'If we are killed at Cremona, the pass to the plain will be clear. Cazotte can lead the company back to Rome,' William said. 'If we fail, the Valle will fall, and so will Piedmont. Rome must know of what has happened here.'

'And what if they don't come to Cremona?'

'That would not surprise me,' William admitted. 'But we have little choice, my friend. We are surrounded by enemies who know this country better than we. Our only chance is to turn the Valdostani army to our cause. If we don't, then we're dead. It's that simple.'

△ VII △

'This is not a wise plan, Saxon,' Cazotte said as William and Kieran departed for the village in the mountains.

'Wise or not, it is our only chance,' William had replied to Cazotte. 'If we do not make it, then make your own way home.'

Cazotte looked at the map to where William's finger was pointed, a small patch of green just off the main pass and several miles south of the ruins where William planned to launch his own ambush.

'Good luck, Captain Saxon. May God favour even the foolish.' The lieutenant shook William's hand.

The journey into the foothills took them until dark. They rode on through the thick mist that hung around the paths and dirt-tracks up to the village of Cremona. At this rate they would arrive some time in the morning. Then they would be able to view the carnage themselves. As the witching hour came and went, rain came down and a landslide of mud and rock impeded their progress. Eventually the sun began to rise again and the clouds burned away. William was aware that they should have arrived at the village by now, and feared they were lost. Just then Kieran dismounted and clambered over the rocks and mud, and stood on a newly-formed ridge. With the mud and water plastered over his face, he laughed and pointed. 'There it is!' he hailed and William clambered after him to see the outlines of huts and barns.

'Cremona,' William said, and wiped his face. 'Let us find some shelter.'

They led their horses over the mound of loose earth and rock, and down what was once the main road into Cremona. The huts were largely skeletal ruins, blackened and burnt out. Dead dogs and mules lay in stinking heaps, the rain doing its best to wash the filth away.

William was both pleased and revolted to find that evidence of the massacre remained. Two charred skeletons lay on top of each other, the vermin and the rain having stripped almost everything from their bones. The next hut they came to provided a more disturbing sight: three very small skeletons lying in the ashes.

'Children.' William spat and shook his head.

'If this doesn't turn the Valdostani against Veron and Cuassard, then they deserve to be damned,' Kieran murmured.

The third hut they came to held further horrors, as did the fourth; after a while they ceased looking, wishing only to find some shelter. It wasn't an easy task, and the kafalas had done a thorough job of annihilating the village.

Finally, they came to the only building that had not been successfully destroyed, a barn, charred but still upright. They led their horses inside and huddled in the gloom, water dripping through holes in the roof. It was cool but not cold and after stripping out of their jackets and shirts, both sat with blankets about them to dry off.

'Do you think the plan will work?' Kieran asked.

'I hope so,' William replied, not sounding terribly convinced.

'I miss home,' Kieran said out of the blue.

'You do?' William replied, a little surprised by the admission.

'I miss home,' Kieran repeated and sneezed.

William began laughing.

'You find that amusing?' Kieran said indignantly.

'Of course!' William replied. 'It's the first time you've said that.'

Kieran smiled. 'It's the first time since we came here that I have truly feared for my life, Will.'

William stopped smiling.

'How do you think it will end?' Kieran asked. 'Will we die like heroes, or just be forgotten?'

'I think we will die as heroes. Maybe we will even get our own plaques in the grottoes of the Secretariat.'

'If the Secretariat exists after all this,' Kieran replied.

'Are you tired?' William asked. 'If you are you should sleep. We are going to be facing at least a hundred militiamen in a couple of hours. We may have to fight our way out if we fail to convince them to join us.'

'I'm not sure a couple of hours sleep will help, but ...' Kieran sighed and then pulled up his knees and rested his head on them, closing his eyes.

William watched his friend fall into a shallow slumber. He would have tried to sleep himself, but he knew it was impossible. If they did survive the next couple of days, he promised himself he would sleep for a whole week.

△ VIII △

Paolo Gilledo, the overweight former bureaucrat, led the army of militia up the steep road into the mountains. As their scouts (led by Castillio) had suggested, it would be the perfect route to surprise the remaining enemies of Veron. The map, old as it was, showed a small unused road that ran through the mountains and would land them on top of the suspected base of the Papal monks in the Forest of Endilo. There also appeared to be a village along the way that would provide provisions. If the villagers stopped them, well, it was to be expected, and Gilledo had been told by Veron that sacrifices had to be made in the name of progress.

Gilledo turned in his saddle and surveyed the militia. They were tired and wet through but still they burned to be in battle

– just as Gilledo burned to please Veron. If he could destroy the monks before Cuassard appeared then he would surely be rewarded.

'On, you dogs!' Gilledo yelled. 'We should be at the top of this road by now! We have killing in the name of God to attend to!'

Castillio glanced around at the loyal men closest to him. They could not get close to Gilledo as he was flanked by two dozen of Veron's loyal mercenaries, hired from across Northern Italy.

As noon approached, the militia reached the level road and made their way down it until the edge of the village appeared.

'Cremona?' one of the guides said to Gilledo. The fat leader narrowed his piggy eyes and stared towards the burnt-out husks of huts before them. He had been warned that a few villages had been attacked, 'in the name of progress', so Gilledo was not too worried when he saw the first one. But he had to be sure how to explain it to the militia. He was tempted to blame the monks, but how could just ten men do so much damage? No, he had to concoct another explanation. A wide grin spread about his fat.

A civil war was coming with the Savoys, Veron had promised it, and maybe Gilledo could hasten its arrival.

The militia marched into the village, the expressions of the armed men darkening as they saw the dead animal and then the first corpses. Gilledo held up his hand and the militia stopped marching. He turned his horse about and addressed the men in French dialect.

'Men of the Valle. Look at the work of Savoy! They have destroyed this village. They and their corruptors, the Papacy. Their instruments have murdered man, woman and child!'

'Liar!' came a scream from one of the buildings. Gilledo froze and watched in disbelief as two riders in grey trotted out.

Castillio gave a start but stood firm.

Gilledo turned his horse back and drew his sword as William and Kieran stopped a few yards away.

'You are a liar! The one responsible for this is Veron!' William shouted. 'It was he and Cuassard who butchered Cremona, just as he butchered the villages to the north and the south!'

357

Castillio had his hand at his sword in anticipation. He glanced nervously around at those who had followed Aosta and not Veron or Leonardo.

'Do not listen to this man!' Gilledo cried back, his sword aloft. 'He is of the Papacy! He is in league with the Savoys! He will take your freedom and your land!'

'I will do no such thing!' William retorted, drawing his sword also. 'I will give you back your freedom and protect you from the likes of Veron, who murdered the heads of the Valdostani!'

Gilledo's small eyes burned with anger and he shouted down at the men below.

William faltered and glanced at Kieran. 'Oh damn,' he sighed.

'What is it?' Kieran asked as he pulled his sword free.

'He's told them to kill us,' William moaned, as the army charged towards them.

CHAPTER SEVENTEEN

The Battle for Aosta

△ I △

The first of the militia charged with pikes and William turned his horse to dodge the attack. One pike missed by a couple of feet, but the next ran through his mount's neck. The beast made a pitiful noise as it fell, and William was thrown. He hit the floor and his sword skittered over the ground. He would have been skewered by another pike had not Kieran struck down the militiaman, staving in the man's skull. He then galloped about and swung down to pick William up from the ground, crushing two of the militia under his hooves. The others rounded on them and charged, seeing three of their comrades fall. As William looked about to find Castillio, he found instead Gilledo's fat face, guffawing as he sensed victory. He wanted to cut the man's expression in two, but right now he had more pressing desires, like survival.

William held onto Kieran, the horse almost stumbling as they tried to escape back down the pass. But the militia had circled them, and as they drove down the road, past burnt-out huts, the men appeared at every exit. There was nowhere to run.

Panting in desperation, Kieran realized it was over. The militia began to close in. 'Do you think Cazotte will escape?' Kieran said.

'I hope so,' William slurred, dismayed by their bad luck. Ever since they had reached Rome, luck had turned against them. He had lost his horse and his sword, and could do nothing now but face death square in the eyes. He wondered how long it would take, and hoped he would not see his dear, dear friend die before him.

'Farewell, Will!' Kieran cried, his sword swinging wildly in front of him. William gasped hopelessly, still holding on to his friend's waist, his head reeling.

Had time been against them, they would have surely died. Perhaps fate, or whatever controlled their destinies, was trying to teach them a lesson; whatever the explanation, neither man could have predicted the events that followed – nor the lightning bolt that fell among them.

The light was blinding, the thunder deafening. A storm engulfed them and a gale hurtled through their hair, whipping up dust in a blinding swirl of darkness and light. Kieran shielded his eyes and looked into the storm around them, a bubble of light expanding, and throwing pieces of matter across the road. Inside the light was a swimming shadow, a figure like a ghost, which seemed to be frozen in time. The light expanded with a shuddering bang and exploded with a rapturous roll of thunder that shook the very air.

Gilledo and the militia stared on in utter terror as the ball of light exploded, the storm abating suddenly. As the chaos faded, it revealed a man dressed in black robes, his arms tucked out of view. His hair was golden and hung down to his shoulders; his skin was white as ivory. He stood motionless between the militia and their prey.

'Who are you?' Gilledo demanded.

The man said nothing.

'In the name of Veron, rightful leader of the Valdostani, move out of the way!' Gilledo demanded.

Again he did nothing.

William and Kieran, still a little blinded by the entry of the stranger, were struck dumb with surprise and did not even think to flee as Gilledo ordered some of his men towards the figure. Slowly they came at him, their pikes swinging this way and that, but the man was immovable. As the first pikes came towards him, he raised his head. His eyes were completely black, without an iris or sclera. The militia panicked. The closest man thrust his pike forward and it entered the stranger's shoulder – but instead of falling, he simply stepped backwards, before pulling himself from the tip of the blade. The militiaman screamed in terror and fled, dropping his pike as his colleagues lunged in with theirs.

This time the golden-haired warrior was not so motionless. He pulled his arms free from the cloak, and in his hand was a short silver sword. In a blur and within a heartbeat, six of the militia were felled.

Kieran gasped.

Gilledo looked down at the dead men and blanched. 'I ...' he stammered weakly, 'I demand you remove yourself! These are enemies of the people!'

The warrior raised his sword and looked threateningly to the militia.

'Attack him,' Gilledo murmured, and then turned his horse around. 'Attack him, you fools!' he screamed, having found his voice again.

But the militia were hesitant, and only Veron's guard came forward. The warrior jumped into the air, appearing to climb invisible steps as he appeared above them and struck down with his sword, cleaving the skulls of three on his right and three on his left. As he landed, he turned and rushed forward with his short-sword and ploughed through the rest, hewing them down with great sweeps of silver metal.

William and Kieran did not move a muscle as the last of Veron's guard slumped to his knees, the gaping wound in his stomach causing some of the militia to vomit, while others fled.

Gilledo, holding onto his distressed horse, cried to the other militia, but they would not listen. 'Kill them! Kill them, I say!' he yelled. He then turned about and charged at the warrior. The warrior slipped to the side and under Gilledo's sword as he passed by, and William saw a sudden flash of metal.

Gilledo's horse stopped a few feet from theirs and Gilledo stared dumbstruck at Kieran and William, before the top of his head slid off and his body tumbled from the saddle.

Silence fell, and all seemed to be regarding the warrior before them. It was Kieran who said the first words. 'Hail *Dar'uka*, warrior of light!'

The greeting was the only thing he could think of. The golden-haired warrior turned, sheathing his sword as he walked towards Kieran. He regarded him with his jet black eyes, blood dripping from his brow.

'Hail, Kieran Harte,' the warrior replied, his words hollow and echoing as though there were many voices within his one voice.

Kieran gasped again. 'You ... You know me?'

'We know *everything*,' he said, and turned away.

The militia were retreating, a good third having fled the village. Castillio remained but looked terrified and needed only the slightest nudge to flee also.

William climbed off Kieran's horse and limped towards the warrior of light. 'You were there on the *Iberian*,' he said. 'Why are you here now?'

'I have come for the Scarimadaen,' the warrior replied. 'The Scarimadaen that you found in the village of Gembloux is now here in Piedmont.'

'Impossible!' William scowled. But as he thought about it further, he realized it wasn't impossible at all.

Kieran had dismounted now and took his place by William. 'That pyramid is *here?*'

'It has been used in this place,' the warrior continued. 'You failed to destroy it.'

'It was stolen from us by a traitor,' William protested.

'Cuassard has the Scarimadaen of Gembloux!' Kieran gasped and his expression was suddenly furious. 'Goddam it! We must stop him, Will. More than ever, Cuassard must die.'

'Agreed,' William replied. 'As must Veron.'

At the mention of his name, some of the remaining militia gave an angry start and the *Dar'uka* turned to meet them.

'No!' William shouted, coming to his senses. 'Stop!' He pushed his way past the warrior to the head of the militia. He raised his unarmed hands and spoke in French.

'Sons of the Valle, this man is not your enemy, and nor am I. It is Gilledo and Veron who are you enemies. Veron has deceived you all! He has been poisoned by the Devil! Hear me, sons of the Valle, your land is besieged and a new tyrant is coming! You will all die if you do not fight! You will all perish, your families will be murdered, and your lands will be burnt if you have not the courage to join us!'

Some of the militia looked doubtful, others hostile. Suddenly, one man yelled out defiantly and ran at William with an axe, but Castillio was there and knocked him to the floor, kicking the weapon out of his reach.

'Listen to him!' Castillio shouted. 'What he tells you is the truth! It was Veron who burnt the guesthouse, killing Angelo, Leonardo and the other heads of the Valdostani! It was Veron who persuaded the Valdostani to accept whatever wrongs this Cuassard has brought upon us! We have been weak in the face of adversity! We have allowed our people to be slaughtered! But no more! Today we must fight! We must fight for salvation and the Valle!'

'Who is with us?' William cried, holding his hands in the air.

There were some murmurs from the crowd, and some who had begun to flee returned.

'I say again, who is with us? Who will fight for the Valle?' William cried, his voice hoarse with the effort.

Instantly the militia raised their weapons into the air, and shouted defiantly, 'We will!'

Δ II Δ

William showed the militia the easiest route over the landslide and back down the valley to where Cazotte and the brothers would be waiting. The army was now less than seventy strong but William was glad they were on their side against an enemy four times larger.

Kieran was talking to the plainsman, who remained to watch the militia move out.

'Please, I must know ...' Kieran began. 'Have you the name of a hero?'

The golden haired warrior looked across to the Irishman. 'I am Anitekos.'

'I expected the name of an angel,' Kieran laughed. The plainsman appeared to be devoid of humour and simply stared at Kieran curiously.

William walked over. 'Your intervention has been most helpful,' he began. 'We have a mutual interest: Cuassard. We could do with your help now, just as you helped us on the *Iberian*.'

'I am here for the Scarimadaen,' Anitekos stated coldly.

'Cuassard knows where it is, I'm sure.'

'What is your plan?' Anitekos demanded.

'We will ambush Cuassard and his men at the ruins a couple miles north of the Castle Addrasio. I have men who can attack them from the rear while the militia will attack at the front. When the battle is joined, come to us as you have today. Fall amongst them and destroy them. This will force Cuassard's hand.'

'You believe Cuassard will try to conjure the daemon?' Anitekos asked.

William nodded.

'Then I will come when the battle is joined, William Saxon.'

'Do I have your word?' William asked. The warrior ignored him and turned away.

'I hope that is a *yes*,' Kieran whispered.

The plainsman bowed as if to pray and light suddenly erupted from his hands and fanned out like incandescent wings. With a rumbling sound and flashes of light, he seemed to dissolve into bright blue flames, which shot upwards, flashing to the sky with a crack of thunder, until nothing of him remained.

Kieran stared after him and wiped his blurry eyes with the back of his hand. 'Beautiful terror,' he murmured. 'If he comes, Cuassard will surely be defeated. But I have just one doubt. How do we get Cuassard to come to the ruins in the first place? How will we lure him into our trap?'

William smiled grimly. 'I was hoping you would not ask,' he

admitted. 'For the plan to work, we will need a bait. And that bait will be you and me.'

△ III △

The skies darkened grey. A column of infantry and men dressed in pitched robes marched out of the Castle of Addrasio and down the mountain pass. At their head was Veron, the young noble of Aosta, his eyes alight with ambition. To his right was Captain Jacques Cuassard, the charismatic leader of the Cavalry Guards of Lyon, the Butcher of Berlin, and now the servant of Count Ordrane of Draak. The French captain, his dark hair slicked back across his skull, his thin moustache waxed and his blue eyes gleaming, sat high on his charger. He received nothing but admiration from his troops, the men he had saved from the winters of Russia and promised a life of unparalleled success and pleasure under Count Ordrane.

They would follow Cuassard into Hell itself if necessary. It was that simple.

As for Cuassard himself, he had other plans, which he was very near to realizing. Already his shoulder burned with the three waves with which it had been branded. Soon he would have the final blessing and a taste of immortality.

Soon he would be a vampyre.

The column of 250 men continued to march down the pass towards the ruins a few miles away. This was where their scouts had last seen the enemy, and this was where the militia of Aosta was also converging. The enemy from Rome would be trapped between two armies, with nowhere escape.

The very thought made Cuassard chuckle with anticipation.

△ IV △

William sat on the ruins of a Roman temple. There were words engraved along the wall, but time had all but obliterated them.

365

William looked north and then south, noting the dust rising from the south.

'Cuassard,' he muttered and looked down at Kieran who had also seen it. 'Make yourself visible, gentlemen.'

The two monks who had elected to stay with William walked over to their horses and mounted, checking that their Baker rifles were loaded. Kieran walked over to another part of the ruins, an old bathing complex now overgrown with weeds. William stayed on the wall and closed his eyes, feeling the mountain breeze on his cheeks. It was growing cooler, and the black clouds above threatened rain.

Slowly, Cuassard's army appeared, and then, to the north, the militia. At the head of the militia rode Castillio. He was wearing the late Gilledo's jacket and had padded it out with grass until he looked twice the size he was. From afar he would pass for Gilledo.

William licked his lips eagerly and looked to the hills where Cazotte and his sharpshooters were hiding. Finally, William looked back at the enemy approaching from the south. At the rear was a tail of darkness: 200-or-so kafalas, dressed in hooded cloaks and armed with an assortment of weapons. Leading them were the blue uniforms of the French, carrying their muskets. At the head were Veron and the French captain, who was already ordering his men to spread out along the width of the ruins. In response, the militia did likewise, cutting off William's escape.

'Nowhere to hide,' Kieran said.

'And nowhere to run,' William added as he jumped from the roof and landed, knees bent, on the grassy verge. He pulled his sword free and remembered what he had said to the plainsman: 'Only intervene when the battle is joined.'

The company of French soldiers formed into two ranks and began marching towards them with their bayonets pointing forward. William examined his sword. It was a little crooked from the fighting at Cremona.

'Kieran? Good luck!' William called over to his friend.

'And you,' the Irishman replied, and walked over to stand in view of the approaching French …

Very soon it would be obvious to Veron that the man leading the militia was not Gilledo. It was all a question of timing, William knew. He had to make sure that Veron did not suspect anything until it was time for the Valdostani to reveal their true loyalty. He walked past a ruined wall and climbed to the top of a pillar, hunkering down to evade a volley if one happened to come his way. He stared down at Veron, who was trotting with Cuassard behind the two ranks of approaching French infantry.

Behind William the militia were beginning to reach the outskirts of the ruins. William glanced to the hills where Cazotte was waiting. Very soon, he needed them to attack; but not yet. Too soon and the element of surprise would be lost. Too soon and Cuassard would escape.

The French were close enough for Kieran to hear their shouting, and the mounted monks turned as planned, riding away through the ruins towards the militia. Veron began shouting to the Valdostani, pointing his sword to the runaway brothers.

William gritted his teeth as he noticed Veron halting his horse. He seemed to stare towards Castillio and then shake his head, muttering something to Cuassard, who suddenly held his hand up.

They had discovered the masquerade.

William turned to the mountains and swung his sword in the air; as he did so, there was a shout from the militia behind him and the Valdostani army charged through the ruins to where William stood. When they got within thirty yards of the French, Cuassard ordered his men to load their rifles. As that order was passed down, Cazotte and the seven remaining monks began firing down from the rocks. Their positions were perfect, as was their aim, and instantly eight French soldiers fell to the floor, Cuassard's surprise evident as he turned to glare at William, his eyes narrowing with anger.

Withdrawing the initial command, Cuassard ordered his men to charge, and French soldier and kafala alike ran towards the ruins and the charging the militia. As the militia passed by, Castillio discarded Gilledo's jacket, and Kieran joined them. William saw his friend swept up in the charge and signalled the two monks on horses to come around. As they galloped near, William leapt from the pillar and motioned for the brothers to dismount. The two monks ran to the top of a nearby ruin, where they began to shoot at the ranks of French and kafalas.

Half a mile away, Cazotte's rear guard fired another volley, and several kafalas fell. They reloaded and fired again, cutting down several French soldiers who had tried to fire back at the hills. A third volley signalled the end of their ammunition, and Cazotte discarded his rifle, pulling his sword free, and opening his jacket to reveal the throwing-stars on his shoulder-strap. He yelled 'Attack! Show no mercy!' and the brothers clambered down the slopes towards the ruins, where the militia were trading blows with the French and the kafalas.

Kieran was in amongst the worst of it, but he seemed to lead the way without any fear, as he cut down the enemy troops. In minutes, eight had fallen under his sword and he was thirsty for more.

William had taken one of the horses and charged forward into the deepest flanks of the kafalas. Veron looked desperate as he searched around blindly for someone to protect him. Cuassard had forsaken his side and was now deep in the battle, cleaving a number of militiamen. Cazotte dashed forward, his right hand at his chest, his left holding the sword. As he approached the kafalas, he took a throwing-star and hurled it at the nearest. The flashing star of metal struck the neck of the kafala who fell instantly, followed by another who clutched the strange metal object now buried in his chest.

'Onto them!' Cazotte cried, showing the brothers the way. They plunged into the kafala ranks at the rear, showing the surprised mob no mercy.

Cazotte, pulling his sword free from one of the dead kafalas, found Cuassard and threw his final star towards him, but the Frenchman struck it away and marched forward. Their swords clashed and clashed again, the two soldiers locked in combat. Cazotte had not traded blows with a Frenchman since the days of the Coalition, and as he struck time and time again, he used his hatred of all that Napoleon's men had wrought on his people to push him forward. For a brief moment, the Italian seemed to have the better of the exchange, but Cuassard had not been riding for many days, and had not fought a hard battle in weeks. His strength was supreme and slowly his blows grew stronger and stronger, driving Cazotte to his knees.

As the Italian parried another blow, the French captain swatted the blade aside and ran Cazotte through. Cazotte had no sensation from the waist down, but he pulled himself up the blade towards Cuassard who marvelled at the Italian's determination. When he got to the hilt, Cazotte used his last strength to strike Cuassard defiantly twice in the face, before the Frenchman drew back his sword and Cazotte fell face-forwards to the ground.

William had seen none of this. He was busy trying to get to the traitor Veron, but the kafalas swelled around him, bringing down his horse. William fell and rolled, almost losing his sword. But he regained his feet and struck out at the nearest fighter, a French soldier who was spitting insults at him. William kicked aside the soldier's bayonet and cut out his throat with a single sweep of his blade. He then turned and regarded the battle as best he could. It was a mess and with the militia wearing no uniform, it was difficult distinguish friend from foe, or to tell who was winning.

Parrying a kafala blade, William chopped through the melee until he could see Veron. At the same time, he saw Kieran making his way towards Cuassard. Of the brothers, William saw only three in the thick of battle, surmising that the sharpshooters who had climbed onto the ruined roof were still there, patiently picking off the enemy troops.

There was still no sign of the plainsman.

'The battle is joined!' William cursed, fighting forward despite being attacked by three French soldiers in quick succession. They lunged with their bayonets; if this had been Waterloo, William's poor training would have cost him dear. But his lessons at Saint Laurence had taught him some tricks, and he jumped back, kicking down one rifle before using the other to shove away the third. With all three bayonets momentarily awry, William swung down with his sabre, slicing one soldier's arm, another's chest, and a third's neck. With their blood spurting down his jacket, William wiped his face and noticed for the first time that it had begun to rain. It came down gradually harder and harder, until a mist rose from the battlefield. William gritted his teeth and hurtled forward again, sliding on the wet and muddy grass, as he launched himself wildly at another kafala.

△ V △

Kieran had found Cuassard. The French captain strode across the field towards the next soldier in grey. Cuassard did not know who this man was, only that Count Ordrane's orders were that all men from the Papacy should die. Kieran surprised him, leaping forward, his hair matted to his scalp, shouting 'Bastard!'

His sword connected with Cuassard's, driving the Frenchman back. The sheer force broke Cuassard's composure, but he struck back, and Kieran slipped on the sodden ground, recovering his balance as Cuassard swung his blade low to try and cut him in half. Kieran's sword was there to block it, and he pushed Cuassard away with a strenuous grunt, turning the block into a swing that took a lock of Cuassard's sodden hair. The French captain put his hand to his neck to feel for blood, angered that Kieran should come so close to cutting him. He swore at him in French; Kieran just smiled and said, 'Go to Hell!'

Of the monks, only the two firing from the ruins were alive, and they had now run out of ammunition. They looked at each other with trepidation. From what they could see, they were losing the battle.

An old injury had opened up in William's shoulder, staining his jacket. Still he fought on, felling one enemy and then another, before going to the aid of Castillio, whom he found almost disappearing under a crowd of kafalas. He managed to drag the Valdostani free and both men fought back to back against the overwhelming tide of kafalas. There were no militia around them now, and William, too, realized that they were losing.

As Kieran swatted away another of Cuassard's blows, a number of fighting men fell between them like a curtain. At that very moment, there was a heavy roar and a crashing roll of thunder that shook the ground. Kieran was faintly aware of the flash of bright light nearby.

William had seen Anitekos fall to earth as a streak of light. It struck the ground somewhere in the battlefield. The plainsman turned on the nearest kafalas like a storm. In moments, the kafalas around him broke and ran as their brethren were slaughtered. It took only a few minutes for the confidence of the kafala force to be broken by this terrible onslaught.

The remains of the militia, who had retreated into the heart of the ruins, watched with joyous horror as the warrior destroyed half as many of their enemy in a few minutes as it had taken the Valdostani to kill in the entire battle so far.

William was transfixed by Anitekos' brutality as the enemy struck at him, seemingly unable to inflict any damage. At one point several Frenchmen fired a volley from their muskets; Anitekos barely flinched. This warrior was invincible.

Cuassard had seen the plainsman, too, and Veron looked ready to wet himself. Cuassard leapt on his horse and gestured for Veron to flee. The traitor did not need a second prompting and kicked in his heels. Before leaving, Cuassard regarded the battlefield for a moment, noting how easily this invincible warrior of light was massacring his men. He could not believe how quickly the battle had been lost. Spitting, he turned his horse and galloped away.

Kieran, having freed himself from the melee, stumbled after Cuassard, finding a stray horse that had since lost its rider. He leapt onto the saddle and rode hard after the two fleeing figures.

'You'll never escape me!' the Irishman yelled through the downpour, as he galloped swiftly down the pass to the Castle of Addrasio.

CHAPTER EIGHTEEN

The Beast

△ I △

Mesmerised and blinded by the plainsman's arrival, William had not seen Kieran charge after Cuassard. The rain too had conspired to hide everything within about twenty yards, and the mist was so thick now that very few knew that the battle was all but over. The militia who remained could be counted on two hands. Castillio stood amongst the carnage, his face red and wet, his clothes in tatters. William had no idea of the fate of the monks as the sound of swordplay clanged weakly in the distance. He had also lost sight of the plainsman.

'What now?' Castillio said.

William shook his head sadly. 'Are there no more survivors than this?' he asked.

Castillio looked about them, over the carpet of bodies. Some of the survivors were calling names William did not recognise.

'Have we won?' one of the militia asked, his right eye clotted with blood.

William bent double for a moment, his hands on his knees. He felt desperately tired and sick to the stomach.

Out of the mist came two figures, carrying a body between them. As they emerged, William saw it was the brothers who had been firing at the kafalas from the ruins. Both men seemed to have aged several years in a matter of minutes, and their faces were caked in blood and mud. William wondered how old he himself looked at that moment in time. As his thoughts wandered, he recognised the body in the brothers' arms. His heart sank.

'Cazotte,' he murmured and stumbled towards them. The monks slipped to their knees in the mud, despairing at their fallen lieutenant. William knelt by them in the filth and turned the Italian's pale cheek towards him. He looked calm now, as though he was sleeping comfortably. William put his fingers to his neck and found no pulse.

'I'm sorry, Cazotte,' he whispered. 'I hope you find some peace, my friend.'

He straightened up and sighed. There was no sign of Kieran and the only sounds he could hear now were of the dying. He sheathed his sword and stumbled across the field of battle, stepping over the mounds of dead.

Finally, he found a figure in the mist and approached it cautiously. It was Anitekos, standing amongst the carnage he had wrought. His golden hair was dripping with rainwater as he regarded William closely.

'Where is Cuassard?' the warrior demanded.

William shook his head. 'I don't know. Did he escape?'

'I saw him flee,' said a voice nearby, and William turned to discover a militiaman standing beside Castillio, his hand at a wound in his side. 'Him and Veron.'

'To the castle,' William remarked. 'It would be his last refuge.'

Anitekos flinched for a second and then a strange frown crossed his expression. 'Kieran Harte has followed him,' he said, in that curiously echoing voice.

'How do you know?' William demanded.

'Because his light is not here,' he said, his eyes searching the mists.

'His light?' William asked.

'Every soul has a unique light,' Anitekos explained. 'It is how we track our prey. Kieran Harte fights Cuassard alone.'

'But Veron is with him, and who knows how many others!' William exclaimed. 'We must go to his aid!'

'I am here for the Scarimadaen, not to save your friend,' Anitekos said coldly.

'Damn you! Kieran is after Cuassard, and Cuassard has the pyramid!' William shouted and threw up his hands in disgust. He pushed past the plainsman in search of a horse. With so much lost already that day, William was not about to lose his best friend as well, even if it meant riding into certain death himself.

△ II △

Kieran had galloped for two miles when the star-shaped castle of Addrasio appeared, the Gran Paradiso looming over it, its summit hidden by cloud. Ahead, Veron and Cuassard were about to make the gates of the castle. Kieran hoped he too could reach the gates before they closed.

Most of the troops stationed inside the castle had been involved in the battle, and the handful that remained needed to be roused to close the entrance. None had the slightest inkling that Cuassard had been defeated. When they saw Kieran driving his horse hard and fast towards them through the mist, few realized what was happening until Veron screeched out a warning and Cuassard ordered the gate to be closed.

Kieran saw the large double doors swinging to and he kicked his horse faster and faster, feeling the beast weakening. He had never beaten a horse so hard as he did now, and yet he felt no sympathy for the beast. He was furious. How many men had been left on the battlefield because of Cuassard? How many people had that bastard butchered?

Kieran growled under his breath as he neared, and gunshots echoed from the battlements. The shots didn't even came close. Kieran drove his horse towards the bridge of the castle, drawing his sword as the horse slipped through into the courtyard, where the animal collapsed to the floor, throwing Kieran off its back. Kieran rolled, landing with a thud against a pile grain-sacks near an old well.

Above him, along the parapets, feet scampered and muskets turned to fire again. Kieran scrambled to his feet and ran over to the old well. He dodged another short volley, throwing himself through a door into a stone building in which was a kitchen. He jogged between the fireplace and the preparation tables as two kafalas burst in and fired their muskets. Kieran squatted down at the last second and the shots missed. Jumping up, he seized a sharp carving knife which he hurled with deadly accuracy at one of the kafalas, before throwing another that struck the second man in the shoulder.

Kieran ran on through the next door and into a hallway decorated with tall tapestries. He crossed the floor, looking for any sign of Cuassard or Veron. Both men had disappeared inside the castle somewhere, leaving only the few kafalas and French soldiers behind.

There was a crash of breaking glass, and footfalls from the kitchen. The Irishman dashed to a large oak door. He pulled on the great iron handle and it swung open with a groan before he slipped through and down the passageway beyond, lit by torches and quite gloomy. He pulled one of the torches from its fastening and began running again, glancing behind him as shouting echoed down the tunnel.

△ III △

Cuassard marched into the main hall with Veron close behind, his lips gibbering slightly, his eyes full of fear.

'Who was that?' he kept demanding.

Cuassard was feeling nothing but contempt for the former head of the Valdostani. With the people of Aosta rebelling against him, he had outlived his usefulness – in his current form, at least.

'He came out of nowhere! He was ... like a Devil!' Veron continued, mopping his brow with a handkerchief.

'Are you afraid?' Cuassard snarled, as he unlocked the box on the table.

'You are not?' Veron said, baffled by Cuassard's indifference. 'He killed your men as well as mine.'

'*All* those men were my mine,' Cuassard said, turning to Veron angrily. 'You have no men, Veron of the Valle. Your men turned against you, do you not remember?'

Veron looked weak and wretched, his floppy fringe matted to his forehead, his face smeared with mud, his clothes smelling of urine.

'They betrayed me,' he said weakly. 'And Gilledo, what happened to dear Gilledo?'

'All your allies are dead,' Cuassard said, his eyes shining as something within the box began to glow, 'as are most of mine. The battle is lost, and it is *your* fault.'

'Mine ...?' Veron uttered weakly. 'No!'

Cuassard turned around. 'Oh yes. Completely *your* fault. If you had warned me earlier, we could have destroyed the Papal men at the abbey. If you had been able to control your troops we would have never been ambushed. If you had been stronger, and not a coward, the Valle would have been yours to control. So many *ifs*, Veron. You have failed me.'

Veron dropped to his knees and sobbed. 'What am I to do? They will execute me for treason!'

Cuassard smiled humourlessly. 'There is an alternative. A way for you to take your revenge, and salvage some dignity.'

Veron looked up, his eyes red. 'Yes! Yes! Please tell me! What must I do?'

Cuassard glanced back at the box. 'Salvation lies here.' He pointed to the glowing box. 'But first I'll need a drop of your blood.'

△ IV △

Coming upon a series of steps leading down, Kieran cursed under his breath. Knowing that he wouldn't be able to double back without meeting his pursuers, he charged down the steps and stumbled around the corner at the end, crashing into a wall. He winced but ran on, gasping a little as his heart pounded away.

Beyond was a light. Kieran dashed towards it and came to a circular room, surprising two French guards. They looked blankly at Kieran, who took only moments to register the danger before he ran through the first, and cleaved the second through the shoulder. Both men fell on their faces and Kieran kicked away their rifles and swords.

Catching his breath, he looked around. He was in a prison. The circular room was surrounded by cells. As he looked about, he saw fingers appearing at the bars to each door. Voices came soon after and Kieran realized there were people alive down here. Knowing that time was against him, Kieran went to the bodies of the guards and fumbled around for the keys to the cells. All the while, the voices from the tunnel were growing louder.

As footsteps rang down the steps behind him, Kieran triumphantly found the keys and began trying them in the locks. Miraculously, the first key fit and he pulled the cell open to reveal three refugees, the same refugees that had been captured at the abbey – including the girl with the brown eyes.

He went to the next cell and tried the next key, but it would not fit. He tried another, but again it would not turn.

'Blast it!' he cursed – just as the kafalas appeared at the entrance to the prison. Kieran didn't even see them coming. But instead of cutting the Irishman down, the first kafala groped at his stomach, a sword imbedded in it. The hooded man looked down and saw a woman with brown eyes staring back, her hands on the handle of the weapon, before he keeled backwards. Kieran dropped the keys and attacked the other kafalas, killing two in as many strokes. The woman screamed as another grabbed her by the hair. Kieran severed his arm and then his head, and the woman fell to the floor.

Kieran went to help her up but she swatted away his hand angrily and picked up the keys he had dropped. Bewildered though he was by her apparent ingratitude, he was relieved to be able to leave her to free the remaining refugees.

Before he left, he pulled the French sword from the kafala's stomach and handed it to her. She returned the gesture with a faint smile and pointed to an exit at the far side of the wall. '*Aller!*' she shouted and then went back to unlocking the cells.

Kieran stayed to watch her at least open the second cell, before she turned angrily and shouted '*Aller!*' again. Kieran hurried to the door. As he pulled the wrought iron ring-handle, he heard more prisoners being set free and it gave him hope that perhaps this would be their day after all.

Beyond the door was another passage, this one leading to steps that ran up and up towards a single light. Kieran grinned and gathered his strength as he climbed the stone steps. He didn't doubt there would be enemies waiting for him, but that mattered not. He would not be stopped now.

Even the sudden shudder through the stone steps – like a minor earthquake – followed by a distant roar, like a caged beast had been let loose nearby, failed to shake his nerve as he continued upwards, his bloodied sword before him.

△ V △

William was riding hard to the south, unaware of his friend's fate. Kieran had wanted vengeance for so long that it had blinded him to reason, just as Engrin had warned. William had failed in his responsibility to restrain him; he could only hope that when he arrived at the castle he would not find his friend's corpse hanging on the battlements.

Back in the ruins, Castillio was rounding up the remaining militia and trying to find survivors amongst the dead. It was no easy task, hampered by the mist and rain, yet they sensed a grim victory.

The two surviving monks likewise tried to locate their fallen brothers, and began arranging them under cover of the ruins, Cazotte's body already lay in state upon the tomb of some unknown Roman. The victory had been bitter for them. Having seen their company almost completely destroyed over the past week, and now Cazotte as well, it was difficult to drive despair from their minds.

Strangely, since the battle had ended, the warrior of light had simply stood amongst the bodies of the fallen. Waiting ...

'The daemon is loose,' he said finally, startling the militia nearby.

Castillio watched as the plainsman put his hands together as if to pray, and light began fanning out from his hands and across his body. He started to dissolve into light, with a shuddering sound that caused a little panic in the militiamen. Then there was a cracking roar that sent Anitekos flaming into the sky. He rose dozens of feet, before shooting south and away from the ruins.

The brothers, seeing him pass overhead, squinted, and wondered about his destination, and what havoc he would wreak there.

△ VI △

Anitekos flew down the main road and the valley towards the castle. It took him mere moments to arrive within sight of it, whereas it had taken William a good thirty minutes to gallop – something that barely crossed his mind as he looked up at the searing blue light exploding across the sky towards the castle walls.

On the battlements, the few kafalas who were not trying to find Kieran saw the light coming and were transfixed by its beauty. It roared over the fortifications and landed with a shuddering crash in the courtyard. The flash of light blinded many around it, and as the ball of energy expanded few saw the dark shape rising from within, until the sphere cracked open and Anitekos stood with his short-sword sheathed, his black eyes darting about for signs of the Beast.

△ VII △

Kieran kept close to the barrels and sacks as he crept along the walls of the castle. He had heard the sudden commotion in the centre of the courtyard. He suspected it was the plainsman, yet he couldn't be sure, and did not want to risk exposing himself. He had to find Cuassard, wherever he was.

The inner building, a large keep cornered by four stone towers, had several storeys, each with an array of narrow glass windows. At the top a coat of arms fluttered from the flag pole, but it appeared burnt and rotten as though infected by some plague. Above, the sky was still black with storm and the rain was coming down harder.

Kieran rushed towards the large wooden doors of the entrance and stumbled into a long room, which was empty apart from a table that was smoking and several tapestries that were smouldering. A fire had erupted there recently, but all trace of what had started it had now gone.

Kieran stayed near the doors, looking around for a moment. He found a small door under a wooden balcony, which led to a room filled with an array of crudely-made weapons.

As he looked over them, he heard footsteps ringing above. Kieran held his breath and backed up against the weapons, fearing he would be discovered. As he waited in the gloom, his sword pointing to the door, he heard a French voice shouting urgently, and then came something else, something neither French nor Italian, nor English. It was bestial and guttural, like an animal in pain.

It was a sound he recognised. It was the monster from Gembloux.

Suddenly, overcome with emotion, Kieran struggled to keep himself from flinging open the door, realizing that against the daemon alone his chances were distant, but against kafalas as well, there would be no chance for revenge.

The daemon roared with a sound that shook the very walls. 'Oh Mary, full of grace ...' he muttered. 'Our Father, who in art heaven ...'

Above, the voices stopped. Kieran closed his eyes and clutched his sword. There would be no salvation; there would be no running away. He had come here to slay Cuassard, and now he had to slay the daemon beyond that door as well. His hand trembled on the handle as he gritted his teeth and began to pull. As he pulled, something blew the small door back and he was thrown across the guardroom into the weapons. As his world wheeled about in a flash of white pain, something struck his head and he fell unconscious.

△ VIII △

William made it to the castle walls only to find them deserted. The gate was ajar, and there were very few sounds from within. It was all too eerie. William brought the horse to a halt and shook his drenched hair. Coughing harshly, he trotted the horse to the gates where he dismounted and unsheathed his sword.

The courtyard was in a state of devastation: barrels were cracked and broken; grain was spilt across the flagstones; here and there were bodies of men, mostly kafalas. He began counting, stopping as he reached fifteen dead. There were yet more near the building in the centre of the courtyard, and probably others elsewhere.

William had his sword ready just in case, but almost doubted he needed it. The plainsman had done his work well. A few crows had already begun feasting on the dead. At any other time he would have scared the birds away, but not this time. Today the dead and the scavengers deserved each other.

William examined the bodies in case Kieran was among them, but he didn't find the grey jacket of the Order amongst the dead.

As he walked past the kitchens, he heard movement and flattened himself against the wall. The door opened cautiously and then someone stepped out.

William swung his sword but it was parried strongly away. He stepped back, raising his blade and then stopped as he met the brown eyes of the woman from Tresta. She stood glowering at him, her sword raised to his, her hand out towards the other refugees huddled behind her. For several breaths they could do nothing but stare at each other.

William smiled, and then laughed as he lowered his sword. 'Adriana?' he said.

She frowned, her brow creasing with the effort, then rushed forward. William feared she might stab him. Instead, she dropped her sword and flung her arms around him, sobbing quietly. William felt almost weak with joy. Seeing her again made him feel such happiness. She pulled away to wipe her tears, and then kissed him. William returned the kiss fully and passionately, barely remembering that they were still in danger.

She smiled through her tears and looked him in the eyes. But the sudden explosion from the keep made them realize that the nightmare was far from over.

△ IX △

It was Anitekos who had crashed through the two large doors to the keep, knocking them open in a flash of light and terrible thunder that lit the main hall like a magazine explosion. The force of his entrance had thrown Kieran back across the adjoining guardroom. The plainsman stood in the centre of the room now, regarding the scene. The daemon was hunkered down on the flagstones, a brute of a creature almost eight feet tall, built like a rock and armoured with charred bone that smoked and groaned as the monster moved. Its left hand retained a claw with long black talons, while its right hand had been fashioned into a blade of bone. Its back was ribbed and its small head was pushed so far into the shoulder plates that it was barely visible, save for two incandescent eyes, burning and steaming within.

Anitekos stepped forward and raised his sword.

The creature grunted and raised itself upon its fat legs. It clicked its swollen neck and smoke rose out of its mouth and nose, forming a small cloud about it. It stepped forward, just the once, the floor resounding under the creature's weight. It lifted its bone-blade to full height, roared to the ceiling high above and lurched forward. Anitekos did not move his feet, but swung his sword up to the giant charred weapon, the parry sounding like metal on metal, but ten times louder.

It was that noise, of sword and bone-blade, which roused Kieran. He opened his eyes groggily, feeling a bruise blossoming on his temple where some armour had fallen upon him. He kicked aside spears and a couple of muskets that lay across him, and struggled to his feet as the sound of a titanic fight rang from the next room. Still feeling the effects of being knocked unconscious, Kieran stumbled to the doorway and peered into the main hall.

He was struck dumb by the sight of the two immortals locked together in combat.

Anitekos was matching the beast easily. Each time the monster struck down with its weapon, Anitekos held his ground and parried it away. If anyone else had tried such a tactic, they would have surely been driven into the ground or cut in two where they stood. No normal sword would have coped with such a beating, yet the warrior's short-sword flashed with each parry and the creature's bone-blade looked worse for wear with each strike. The daemon seemed weaker as it tried to grapple with the plainsman, who toyed with it, matching its movements with ease.

Finally, the daemon lunged forward and Anitekos sidestepped swiftly, bringing his sword down on the creature's wrist. The blade cut through the creature's armour without effort, and at once blue flame spewed forth from the severed limb and the creature screamed to the heavens, its severed claw twitching with light. The beast stumbled back, guarding its wound with the bone-blade, its eyes burning furiously.

Kieran wanted to cheer but could not find his voice. Anitekos turned the sword around in his hand and stepped forward, cutting down towards the beast's legs. The blade struck the fat calf and more light belched out, followed by a spray of grey motes, like moths, that melted into the air under the burgeoning blue fire. Again the daemon cried out, its pain shaking the foundations. Kieran, his sword in his hand, stumbled out of the doorway and leant against the wall, grinning hysterically.

And then he heard movements above. Over the edge of the balcony, Kieran saw a dozen musket barrels appear, levelling on Anitekos. He wanted to warn the warrior, but again he could not find his voice.

The muskets fired with a roar. Kieran ducked, wrapping his arms about his ears as the air was torn apart. The muskets all found their mark and riddled the back of Anitekos, tearing up his great black cloak and tunic. As they struck, blue flares erupted and the plainsman staggered for a moment as though hit by a strong gust of wind.

Kieran looked on desperately, expecting the warrior of light to fall. But Anitekos stood still, and then turned, almost nonchalantly, to view the cause of the irritation. He hadn't even been marked.

Anitekos appeared to look straight at Kieran with his deep black eyes. And that was when they both realized their error. With a blur – from behind the nearest tapestry – came Cuassard.

The muskets were not intended to kill Anitekos, but to distract him.

Cuassard swung his sword towards the plainsman. Had Kieran been on the receiving end he would have been killed for sure, but Anitekos was unnaturally quick, and his sword swung about to meet Cuassard's within a fraction of a heartbeat. It was all so sudden, Kieran doubted what he had seen. Cuassard and the plainsman stood staring at each other, their swords held fast together.

And then the daemon lurched forward, having suddenly recovered from the wounds Anitekos had inflicted. Anitekos tried to recover his sword, but Cuassard parried it down, just as the bone-blade swung low, cutting through Anitekos' arm. The plainsman was eclipsed by his own radiance. Through the bright glare, Kieran could still see the outline of the warrior as he stumbled back, his severed arm trailing fire and lightning. The golden-haired warrior faltered, stared at his hand and then back at the daemon, as it thrust its blade through his abdomen. More light erupted, and now Anitekos stood pinned by the giant blade, unable to move.

Bewildered, Kieran could not understand exactly how the warrior of light had failed. Now the orchestrator of his downfall, Cuassard himself, stood by Anitekos, his laugh almost drowned out by the roar of fire, as he raised his sword and decapitated the plainsman.

Anitekos did not cry out when he perished, his expression was passive. But on his destruction, the blinding light that poured forth offered its own death cry; a song of light that even those beyond the Living could hear.

Kieran peered between his fingers, his heart pounding, his credulity stretched. The plainsman was gone, nothing more than a heap of clothes and dust on the stones. He couldn't believe it – that seemingly invincible warrior had been felled by a mere mortal.

But instead of driving Kieran from the keep, it angered him.

How dare he? His hurt growing, Kieran scrambled through the shards of wood for his sword. His fingers wrapped around the sword-hilt, but his eyes remained on Cuassard who was laughing triumphantly as he kicked at the smoking mound of clothes. Remembering Katherine, Kieran stood up and pushed himself away from the shadows under the balcony to the centre of the room.

Cuassard didn't notice the Irishman approach as he bent down to lift the plainsman's sword. The beast, however, saw him coming, and took a step forward, its claw knitting itself back to its wrist, and roared, causing Cuassard to shudder fearfully. 'How much control do I *really* have over you, I wonder? he murmered.

Cuassard's thoughts halted suddenly, invaded by the terrible pain in his back and stomach. It seemed to twist for a moment and then there was no pain at all. He looked down at his belly to find the tip of a sword jutting out through his guts, blood spilling down his shirt to his groin. It twisted again, and he began to choke on his own blood. He looked into the daemon's eyes, hearing not the expected roar of anger from the monster's jaws, but instead several words of English, whispered by his ear, 'And now you die, you bastard!'

Kieran withdrew his sword with a little satisfaction, forcing himself to watch as the Frenchman fell to his knees. Cuassard bowed slightly as a pool of blood formed about him, before falling on his side, his eyes staring out into nothing.

Kieran felt triumphant, having revenged both Katherine and the plainsman. But it did not last. The daemon roared and charged towards him. Kieran found his legs and scrambled away as the creature lurched forward with its bone-blade, crashing it against the floor with such force that the very flagstones were shattered. It swung again, but Kieran slid on his side, just under the blade. The Irishman rolled onto his front, pushed himself up and ran full pelt towards the tables, just as the kafalas came to their senses.

Having seen their leader slain, they turned their guns on Kieran and fired a volley. The urgency caused them all to miss, but several went close, one hitting the heel of Kieran's boot and knocking him off balance. The daemon lurched towards him but his accuracy was poor and the bone-blade crashed into the wall, pulling masonry down upon them both. A piece of rubble struck Kieran's shoulder and buried his sword, another piece driving him to the floor.

Coughing through the dust, and kicking away the rubble, Kieran limped away, just as the kafalas raised their muskets again. But they delayed too long, and as they fired, they caught the daemon, their shots ringing off its hide. It was enough to distract the beast, and Kieran fled to one of the half-burnt tables at the top of the hall. He glanced back in case the creature followed, but heard the daemon roar out as it charged angrily towards the balcony. Those kafalas who realized what would happen next, tried to flee into the adjacent room, but most were caught as the beast tore down the balcony.

As Kieran crawled under the table, he heard the cries of the kafalas as they were torn apart by the crazed beast. There was an arch to Kieran's right; if he ran quickly, he could make it. As the daemon pursued the last kafala and stamped on his head, Kieran realized that he no longer had a sword. The Irishman could see only one replacement, but that meant facing the beast again.

'To Hell with caution,' he murmured, as he crawled out from the table.

The daemon lifted the corpse of the last kafala and tossed it across the room. The beast bellowed angrily, and its eyes burned more strongly. It no longer appeared wounded from its encounter with Anitekos, and turned its attention to Kieran as he scrambled for the late plainsman's sword. Bowing, its blade and claws brushing the floor, the creature clucked in its throat and stampeded towards him.

Kieran looked up, his hand on the hilt of the short-sword still lying in the dust that was once Anitekos. He pulled the sword away and rushed towards the arch, leaping over a few struts from the ruined balcony. Behind him, the stampeding daemon followed, his lumbering footfalls echoing in the hall, shaking the ground. The daemon lurched into the walls, tearing portraits from their frames and ripping up the crimson rugs running along the floor. The heady smell of sulphur hung unpleasantly in the air, and Kieran tried desperately not to look back as he reached the three doors at the end of the hall, kicking open the first door as the beast pounced towards him. Kieran heaved the door back and locked it from the inside. He knew it was a hopeless gesture – too big to get through the door, the creature would probably just tear down the wall – but at least it gave him some time to look for an exit.

Kieran glanced about and found that he was in a small chapel. It was a simple room, with only a couple of stained-glass windows, and two flanks of pews arranged in six rows. There was a small, unimpressive pulpit to the left, and at the top of the aisle was an altar.

But where a cross or a figure of Christ might have been, there was the Scarimadaen, its bronze sides shining.

Kieran stared at the object with absolute hatred. He suddenly forgot the daemon, which was now pounding at the door so hard that the hinges were coming loose. All that mattered to the Irishman in those few moments was the pyramid and the need to destroy it. Purposefully, he marched down the aisle, Anitekos' sword in his hand, and approached the altar. Looking down at it, he wanted to strike the blasted object with the sword, but was not sure how it would react. Engrin had told him the pyramid needed to be 'exorcised'. Kieran angrily swatted the defiling pyramid off the altar and let it land clumsily on the floor. He spat at it, and was about to kick the Scarimadaen, when the wall to the chapel collapsed in a cloud of dust and masonry.

Kieran leapt away from the altar and raised his sword as the monster tore up the pews on the left and right. Kieran was struck on the shoulder by a chunk of timber. He yelled out, and fell to his knees, feeling his left arm was broken.

The daemon swung for him, but Kieran brought up Anitekos' sword. The blow swept Kieran off his knees and sent him crashing into the debris of the broken pews. He screamed out and rolled as pain flashed up his arm and into his head. His arm seemed to twist at an awkward angle, making him feel sick. Still he clambered to his feet and held the sword out before him.

The daemon, completely enraged, flung aside the pews and stepped forward as Kieran retreated. He didn't want to leave the Scarimadaen, but had no choice. There was no obvious way of getting past the daemon, whose angled bulk and tall body seemed to rise above him. Its claws twitched and its bone-blade hovered a few inches above the floor as it regarded Kieran tentatively.

'What are you waiting for?' Kieran hissed. 'I have beaten you before ...'

The eyes peeking from its sunken neck glowed like embers and then seemed to erupt, spewing smoke as the beast rushed forward, swinging its blade close to Kieran, and hitting the floor a foot from him – before the claw swooped and knocked the Irishman to the ground.

Dazed and bloodied, Kieran stared up from the wreckage of wood about him, the pain in his arm making him nauseous. His right hand still gripped the sword, but he doubted he would have much strength to parry a blow. It was over, but at least he would die fighting.

But as he looked up, he noticed the short-sword flicker with blue light. And then the windows of the chapel shattered and blue flames fell from the shards of glass. From the light sprang two warriors in black cloaks. They assaulted the daemon instantly, their swords clattering at once against the beast's back. The first, a giant albino, with long white hair, clattered an enormous broadsword against the beast, piercing the daemon's hide. The beast turned and tried to grapple with the second warrior who was smaller than the first but equally lithe. The shorter warrior slid aside swiftly and cut down with his sword, severing the beast's arm again.

Bellowing with rage and pain, the daemon swung the bone-blade to defend itself, parrying the albino warrior's blade, before the shorter warrior sank his sword into the belly of the beast. Kieran got to his feet and rammed Anitekos' sword into the creature's back, adding to its pain. He then climbed its hide with his one good arm before pulling the sword free. With his last efforts he shoved the blade between the shoulder-plates, where the neck was buried, and heaved, ripping the monster's atrophied skull completely away from its shoulders with a terrible groan and flash of light.

Kieran fell, hard, onto the floor, tears of pain falling down his face. He didn't even bother to watch the daemon burning up, its body purifying itself of the daemonic spirit. He could hear it well enough, a voice of defiance in a tongue he had never heard before, yelling angrily to anyone who would listen. Beneath the voice was another, pitiable and contemptible – Kieran supposed it was the soul of the host. The chapel shook and the body of the beast fell in a smoking pile amongst the smouldering pews.

A hand went under Kieran's shoulder and he was pulled up to his feet. He looked to the one who had helped him up and found it was the albino warrior, who stared at him with black eyes, a faint look of admiration in his expression. To his side was the shorter warrior; his eyes, too, were black, and Kieran realized that these were also plainsmen.

'I don't believe it,' he gasped. 'There are more of you?'

The albino nodded and gestured to what remained of the

doorway to the chapel. There, standing in the rubble, were two others: one was a giant like the albino, but covered in tattoos; the other appeared to be Chinese.

Kieran was ready to fall to his knees again, and would have if it wasn't for the albino who kept him upright. '*Four* plainsmen,' he murmured and then chuckled gently.

'Not just four,' said the shorter warrior.

'Always are the five *Dar'uka*,' the albino said.

'Five?' Kieran murmured.

'I am Chow-Yuen,' said the Chinese.

'I am Tzicothe,' said the tattooed warrior.

'David,' said the shorter warrior.

The albino stared down at Kieran. 'And I am Gregor.'

'Names of heroes. And I expected names of angels.' Kieran looked down at the charred remains of the daemon host. 'It is done?'

'The body is destroyed. The daemon returns through its gate,' Tzicothe said, gesturing to the Scarimadaen lying by the altar.

Kieran smiled softly, glancing down at the short-sword. He then held it up to David. 'This was his,' he said faintly. 'Your fallen comrade's.'

David sheathed his own sword and took the weapon from Kieran's hand. He looked at it coldly, without any sadness.

The one called Tzicothe plucked the Scarimadaen from the ground and brought it over, the object flickering with light. 'You must destroy this, Kieran Harte, before it is used again,' he said.

Kieran nodded and gingerly took off his soiled grey jacket, wrapping the object in it. 'I will see it destroyed personally, I promise you. Never again will it be allowed to ruin the lives of the innocent.'

'And there is another matter,' Chow-Yuen said.

'A matter that does not require an answer quite yet,' Gregor added.

'An answer?' Kieran asked.

'There have always been five,' David said, still holding Anitekos' sword.

'Always are the five *Dar'uka*. No few, no more, to face this war,' Tzicothe said, almost as though it had been said many times before.

'But now there are four,' Kieran said.

'No,' Chow-Yuen said. 'There will be another.'

'Who?' Kieran asked.

'You, Kieran Harte,' David replied.

Kieran's legs buckled, but again Gregor's hands held him up. 'Me?' he said weakly.

'Twice you have destroyed the daemon,' David continued. 'You have shown you are worthy to join us.'

'To become a plainsman?' Kieran said, almost too shocked to say much more.

'There must always be five *Dar'uka*, and we wish you to become one with us,' Gregor said. 'An immortal to fight an immortal war.'

Kieran shook his head. 'I don't know ...'

'Then do not make your decision now,' David said. 'Your choice must be made by the next full moon.'

'In nineteen days, we will find you, Kieran Harte,' Tzicothe said as he placed the wrapped Scarimadaen on one of the few pews that was still partially intact. Gregor lowered Kieran to the seat and stepped away, a slight smile on his lips.

All four plainsmen looked down at Kieran, a pitiful state with his bloodied temple and broken arm, and covered in dust. Yet Kieran was a victor. He had avenged Katherine's death.

'Until then, Kieran Harte,' the plainsmen said in unison. Only when the plainsmen had left the chapel did Kieran realize that he was crying. He wasn't entirely sure why, but when he glanced down at his jacket with the pyramid bundled within he felt a great surge of relief.

When William and Adriana entered the room they found Kieran within the wreckage of the aisle, with the charred body of the daemon lying prostrate across it and Veron's head lying near the altar.

CHAPTER NINETEEN

The End of the Beginning

△ I △

The sound of feet ringing down the catacombs caused the two monks at the entrance to the vaults to stare at each other with unease. Their disquiet was justified when Cardinal Devirus appeared with two guards of the Vatican, both armed with muskets. Devirus looked wrathful – a terrible expression of anger on his already pointed features.

'Stay here until I call for you,' he hissed to the armed guards and then turned to the monks. 'Stand aside, and be sure to follow on my call.'

The monks nodded and stepped out of the way, their spears tight to their sides. Devirus stormed into the room beyond, clutching a document. He marched down the tight corridor and then into the gallery, mounting the steps to the balcony above the Map Room. There was nobody about and it was quiet apart from the gentle sound of scribbling coming from one of the lecterns on the far side of the gallery.

Devirus screwed up his face and marched over to the lectern to the hunched figure sitting behind it. The man continued to scrawl in the shadows, but stopped as he noticed Devirus approaching.

'Scribbling new orders, are we?' Devirus mocked.

The hunched man turned fearfully and narrowed his eyes on the cardinal. 'What are you doing here, Devirus?' he asked and stepped down from the lectern.

'I might ask you the same question, Cardinal Issias,' he replied. Issias flinched and stepped back into the shadows.

'Where are the other secretarial staff?' Devirus asked and looked about the abandoned room.

'Sent back to their chambers,' Issias said.

'By you?'

'They can't be trusted!' Issias spluttered. 'None of them can!'

'Can *I* be trusted?' Devirus asked.

Issias nodded slowly. 'Of course you can.'

'So you can trust me,' Devirus said, and walked about the gallery, glancing down at the shimmering regions of the map below, 'but can I trust *you?*'

Issias flinched again. 'What do you mean?'

'There is a daemon loose in the Valle of Aosta,' Devirus said angrily.

Issias frowned. 'Are you sure?'

Devirus nodded, circling the cardinal. 'A message was sent by Captain Saxon to Engrin, of all people. In the letter he stated that he could not take the risk of delivering the news to the Secretariat as he suspected we had been compromised at the highest level.'

Issias looked shocked. 'Surely he's mistaken.'

'I wish he was,' Devirus said solemnly, 'but there is certain evidence to suggest he is correct. Captain Saxon met with our contact in Aosta and he told him of their suspicions that a monster was loose in the Valle. According to the contact, his letter to Rome explained this.'

Issias put a shaking hand to his lips. 'I see. I see. But that is a lie ...' he explained. 'I saw the letter from Aosta, and it never mentioned a daemon ...'

'Are you sure?' Devirus asked.

Issias frowned at Devirus. 'What are you implying?'

Devirus shrugged. 'I am only saying that I myself never had sight of the letter. I relied on you to present all the facts.'

'And I did present all the facts!' Issias hissed at him. 'Are you accusing me, Devirus?'

Devirus held up his hands disarmingly. 'Accuse my fellow cardinal? I would never do such a thing,' he said, and then glanced at the paper clenched in his hand ' And yet, I *did* discover something.'

'Tell me!' Issias demanded.

Devirus unfolded the letter. 'I discovered the letter from Aosta.'

Issias looked down at it. 'Where did you get that?'

'Is there a problem?' Devirus asked.

'You know that such correspondence can only be found in my office! How dare you go through it!' Issias seethed.

'You should have nothing to hide,' Devirus complained.

Issias stepped forward to take the letter. 'I *have* nothing to hide!'

Devirus stepped back, lifting the letter out of Issias' reach. 'Are you sure?' He looked down at the letter and read: 'As for the matter of your presence, I would not normally presume to request your assistance in such earthly matters; but assistance is needed, for something infernal is responsible for recent happenings in Aosta.'

Issias turned pale. 'Lies,' he murmured.

Devirus looked up from the letter. 'Excuse me?'

Issias grew angry. 'Filthy lies! That was not in the letter!'

Devirus glanced down at it. 'This is signed by the contact, a certain Leonardo of the Valle!' he exclaimed, holding it up in front of Issias. 'This was found in your chambers!'

'You're accusing *me!*' Issias shouted.

'I'm simply telling you the facts,' Devirus explained.

'I did not know of a daemon in the Valle!'

'Did you not read this?'

'I read it all!'

'Then why was I not informed? Why did we send those men to Aosta? They could all be dead by now!' Devirus growled. Issias stepped away until his back was against the wall of the gallery.

'I am not the traitor!' Issias cried.

Devirus stopped still and smiled thinly. 'I never said you were.

And I never really thought you were ... But now I have my doubts.'

'Don't come near me, Devirus!' Issias warned.

'What are you talking about?' he said, and raised his hands, still clutching the paper.

'I'm not the traitor and you cannot prove I am,' Issias said, and pulled a knife from his robes.

Devirus halted and looked stunned. 'What is that?'

Issias looked down at the weapon, somewhat ashamed. 'It is only for self-defence. These are precarious times!'

'Indeed they are, Cardinal. Indeed they are. But you are carrying a weapon with you, and that is unlawful. Only the monks of the Order and the Papal guards are allowed weapons in the Vatican.'

The cardinal waggled the knife about in front of him. 'It is for my protection! And that is all!'

'From the traitor? I think we both know who the traitor is, don't we, Cardinal Issias?' Devirus stepped forward.

'Keep back! I'm warning you!' Issias whimpered, retreating.

Devirus followed at a respectful distance. 'Issias, this is not the way,' he said calmly.

'I am not a traitor, damn you! This was not my fault! None of it was! I didn't know there was a daemon in Aosta!' he shouted. 'I never knew of this, until now. It is ... it is a different letter, I tell you!'

'If that is true, then you have nothing to fear,' Devirus said, approaching him slowly. 'You might not be the traitor, but with that knife in your hand you appear guilty of this and more.'

Issias looked down at the blade and lowered it slightly. 'You do not understand what it has been like. People have been spying on me. I have seen shadows in the corridors, and I've received threats,' he moaned.

'From whom?'

'I do not know, but I fear for my life, Devirus,' Issias replied.

'You must tell me who, Issias. It will be the only thing that saves you,' the cardinal said as they stepped near the rail at the gallery. Issias looked doubtful and raised the weapon again.

'Saves me? How could you?' Issias sobbed. 'How could you think this of me? I am not responsible ...'

'You are a fool, Cardinal Issias,' Devirus growled. 'If you are not a traitor, you are certainly not fit to command here. Either way, Cardinal Grisome must know of what has happened and what you have done.'

Issias shook his head. 'No! Please, Devirus! He'll remove me from the Secretariat!'

'Yes, he will. Maybe even send you to the outermost monastery in Europe, but that is the price you must pay for your foolishness. And do not think to lie about what has happened. This document is your folly, and will be given to Grisome shortly enough.'

Issias snapped and rushed at Devirus. He went to take the paper, but the cardinal dodged out of the way. Issias swung his knife about and cut across Devirus' arm. He yelped and dropped the document, Issias taking it quickly before retreating back to the rail of the gallery. He turned and dropped it onto the golden map below.

'There will be no evidence, Cardinal Devirus,' he said desperately as the letter landed on one of the markers and burst into flame. 'We will continue as we always have, and you and I will find the *real* traitor in the Papacy.'

Devirus squinted with pain and looked down at his bloodied hand where he clutched the wound. 'You are mad, Issias!' he groaned and stumbled forwards. 'Drop your weapon before you do something you regret.'

'Only if you agree to *drop* this ridiculous slur upon my name!' Issias cried.

'Disarm yourself now, Issias!' he said, and turned about. 'Guards! Guards!'

'No, Devirus! No!' Issias shouted and rushed forward. He put his hand over Devirus' mouth and they struggled. Again Issias tried to cut Devirus, but this time the cardinal backed off. He shouted again and Issias grabbed him at the balcony, smacking him across the face.

'Shut up! Shut up!' he cried hysterically.

'Damn you!' Devirus shouted back, blood dripping from his lip. 'Traitor!'

Issias snarled and held the blade near his throat. 'No!' he cried.

There was a sound of movement by the steps from the room below and Issias turned around to see two Papal guards aiming their muskets at him. Everything seemed to halt and time froze as they pointed their weapons. Devirus struggled and moved back, stumbling over with a yell.

The monks fired their muskets and smoke filled the air. Issias felt the lead-shot tear through his shoulder and chest. The small of his back hit the top of the rail and he felt himself rock backwards. Pain flashed in his skull and he saw the world turn upside-down, before he was surrounded by air.

Devirus saw Issias plummet, and heard the cardinal hit the Map Room floor with a sickening crunch. Devirus clambered to his feet, still clutching his wound, and stepped to the edge of the gallery to peer through the smoke. The handrail was sticky with blood, and below it, spread out across the map, was Issias' body, a small trail of blood running across the Mediterranean Sea.

Devirus slumped against the rail as the guards came to his aid. 'Send for a surgeon immediately,' he ordered. 'And find Engrin. I need to see him, *now!*' The guards complied and rushed away quickly, leaving Devirus to stare again at the cardinal, lying dead on Europe, his hand, still holding the knife, resting on the Carpathian mountains.

△ II △

William and Kieran left the city of Aosta just a day after returning from the castle with the surviving brothers. Those who had fallen were buried in the ruins, but Cazotte was not among them. William was determined that he should be laid to rest in a tomb in the Vatican. Cazotte's death had been particularly bitter for William, despite all that had passed between them.

The bitter taste was tempered only by their travelling companions who journeyed with them to Rome: Adriana and her nephew, Marco. Having lost their family during the attack on Tresta, and with Angelo killed in Aosta, they elected to go with William.

The boy did nothing but chatter over the two weeks' ride from Aosta to Rome, and while at first it irritated William, he soon became accustomed to the boy's gaiety.

As for Adriana, William was smitten with her. Each night they slept hardly a foot apart, and often he would wake to find her staring and smiling at him. She told William, in her mix of French and Italian, that she simply enjoyed watching him sleep. Sometimes, when the brothers were collecting wood for the fire, William stole kisses from her, and occasionally those kisses became something more passionate. He was falling in love, for the first time, and as he did so, William began to understand why Kieran had been so hurt by Katherine's death.

The Irishman was a changed man. His arm was not broken but seriously dislocated. The brothers took care of it, as well as his other wounds. But beyond the physical scars of the last weeks, there were deeper ones that had hardly healed. Kieran seemed more aloof than before. William knew his friend was hiding something, for his description of the battle with Cuassard and the daemon was vague at best. There was something missing. William had the feeling that the end of the story was yet to be told. He hoped that Kieran would come to him eventually. In the meantime, he wallowed in Adriana's affections.

On returning to Rome, William and Kieran consulted Engrin immediately. He told them the news of Issias' conspiracy and eventual death. It had sent shock-waves through the Church, and Pope Pius had been close to disbanding the Secretariat completely. Yet he was stilled by an entourage from the House of Savoy, thanking the Pope personally for assisting in the Valle d'Aosta.

Reform would visit the Secretariat, Engrin had told them, with Cardinal Grisome as supervisor and Cardinal Devirus as the sole commander of the Order of Saint Sallian. It didn't surprise William to hear it, but he was surprised how quickly change had come.

William left with Engrin to be debriefed, while Kieran left for the Chambers of Deconstruction, a workshop within Vatican City. It was built half underground, with two large chimneys from which grey smoke came, as something burned within; something unholy. The workshops were manned by monks of the Order, brothers who had been trained for a single task: the deconstruction of the Scarimadaen. Here were giant stone presses, intense furnaces, and all manner of hammers and cutting instruments. It was here that Kieran observed his promise to the plainsmen, by bringing the bronze pyramid to its end. He personally watched the brothers taking the Scarimadaen of Gembloux with a pair of clamps before submerging it slowly into the molten fire of the furnace. At once the pyramid seemed to flare with bright blue light, struggling against the heat, before it began to dissolve away, hissing – and seemingly screaming – into oblivion.

The brothers left Kieran to watch as the topmost point of the pyramid sank and sizzled into the fire. While their backs were turned, Kieran fumbled in his breast pocket and pulled out the handkerchief with the pressed tulip within. He knew what he had to do, and now he was ready to do it. He would never forget Katherine.

Smiling, a single tear spilling down his cheek, Kieran tossed the handkerchief into the flames. 'Goodbye, my love,' he whispered, and turned his back on the fire.

△ III △

Cazotte was laid to rest in the catacombs following a muted service. In attendance were several brothers, Engrin, Cardinal Devirus and Cardinal Grisome, as well as Kieran and William. It was William who led the service, as Cazotte's commanding officer, and he did so soberly, reflecting on what had been lost.

Kieran approached his friend after Cazotte's tomb was sealed, presenting him with a pipe. 'It was Cazotte's,' the Irishman said. 'I never returned it to him. I think he would have wanted you to have it.'

William smiled sadly. 'I do not smoke,' he said, but took it gratefully.

After the service, William was taken to one side by Cardinal Devirus and agreed to stay with the Order for the time being. After the defeat of Cuassard, both agreed that Count Ordrane would be watching Rome quite closely, and William and Kieran in particular.

Kieran walked with Engrin down the catacombs.

'Remember during the ride from Naples, I asked you about the plainsman?' Kieran said. 'Even though you never said it, I suspected you had met one before. When I pressed you, you avoided the subject, and since then you've done your best to avoid telling me what happened.'

Engrin nodded and sighed. 'Yes, I remember. And you are right. Sometimes it is difficult to look back at your own life and see missed opportunities. I was not much younger than you are now when I first saw him,' Engrin said. 'The plainsman appeared after the daemon I was pursuing was despatched, and he praised my strength and swiftness of sword. I, in turn, wanted to become one of them. To be a plainsman. That might sound strange to you ...'

Kieran shook his head. 'Indeed it does not.'

Engrin sighed. 'But it did not matter, since he would not have me.'

'Why not?' Kieran asked. 'You defeated one daemon ...'

'And by then I had also defeated two vampyres,' Engrin added. 'But that wasn't enough for him. He would not take me, but said only that "Always are the five *Dar'uka* ..."'

'... No few, no more, to face this war,' Kieran finished.

Engrin looked surprised. 'How did you know that?'

'Because I have heard the saying before,' Kieran admitted.

Engrin held his arms. 'You met him again, didn't you?'

Kieran nodded. 'It will be in my report, when I write it. Though I believe William will not be so quick to detail their hand in what happened in Aosta.'

'*Their* hand?' Engrin frowned further.

Kieran nodded and beamed. 'All five *Dar'uka* came to us.'

Engrin rubbed his beard and clapped his hands. 'All five! So it is true. There are more of them!'

Kieran nodded again.

'I confess, that I am bewildered by this,' Engrin said. 'I'm sure it was a miraculous sight!'

'It was,' Kieran agreed.

'And who was among them? Was there an albino warrior?' Engrin asked eagerly.

'Gregor,' Kieran smiled back, knowing that he was fulfilling some part of Engrin's dream.

'Yes ... Yes ...' the old man murmured distantly. 'Gregor. The giant. And he is still alive after all these years? It was he who came to me and it was he who told me about the five *Dar'uka*. Why would he tell you such a motto, my friend?'

'A plainsman was destroyed by Cuassard,' Kieran said.

'He killed a plainsman?' Engrin whispered, his eyes narrowing. 'But they are immortal.'

'I know, but fall Anitekos did,' Kieran replied.

Engrin laughed. 'You know all their names! What else did they tell you?'

Kieran paused. 'They told me they had to recruit another plainsman, to replace Anitekos.'

Engrin's expression changed to shock. 'They asked you to become one of them, didn't they?'

Kieran nodded.

'And did you agree?'

'They told me I had nineteen days to decide. Those nineteen days conclude tomorrow night,' Kieran replied.

'And your decision?'

'I suppose I decided in Aosta.'

'What does William say?' Engrin asked.

'I haven't told him.'

The old man shook his head. 'You must! If you value your friendship, you must tell him, or he will never forgive you.'

'I'm not sure he'll forgive me anyway,' Kieran replied, 'but you are right. And I will tell him in time.'

△ IV △

Villeda had decided to celebrate the return of the Heroes of Aosta. It was a subdued celebration; joy at William and Kieran's return was tempered by the loss of so many.

William sought the opportunity to simply relax, to drink and chat with Engrin and Kieran – but most of all he wanted to show Adriana the hospitality of the village. He knew they would welcome her and Marco, and was pleased that she had decided to live there.

During the weeks since the battle in the mountains, they had bonded quickly. He longed to make love to her, but bided his time – this would not be something he would rush into. Adriana was the most determined woman he had ever known. A truly fiery woman with a strong arm, yet she was also tender and affectionate. William found her stunningly beautiful, and he felt proud as he led her by the hand to the village square near the tavern.

Villagers young and old raised their tankards to him as he walked passed. Children played around his legs before running off into the tavern, and Marco seemed to get dragged along with them, much to Adriana's delight.

'Marco will enjoy it here,' she said.

William smiled and kissed her gently on the lips. 'As I hope you will.'

Inside the tavern, he met up with Kieran, who was talking with Engrin.

'Apologies for my tardy entrance,' he said proudly, though

Kieran could tell he wasn't sorry at all. In fact if he had been three hours late because of Adriana he wouldn't have been sorry.

'I'll get you some drinks,' the Irishman said, and wandered over to the bar. The tavern was thick with pipe-smoke, and around them curled clouds like mist hanging over mountains.

Some locals at the table made room for Adriana and she sat down as they began talking to her in Italian. She found it a little awkward at first, French being her native tongue, but after a while William was amazed she could talk back quite clearly.

'You'll need to teach me this language some day,' he whispered. Adriana smiled and took the wine from him.

Kieran looked a little distant; only Engrin knew why. William, attempting to start some kind of conversation between the three of them, began with his report to Devirus. 'Cardinal Devirus was pleased with our progress in Aosta. He was surprised we escaped with our lives,' he said.

'Indeed, William,' Engrin remarked. 'You have had a busy few weeks.'

'And it will not stop there,' William admitted. 'I have decided to stay a while longer.'

Kieran smiled. 'You have?'

'I know ... It is a surprise, but ...' he glanced down at Adriana, 'I have realized there is much to do here in Rome. I hope this pleases you.'

Kieran nodded. 'Yes. It does,' he said, and patted William's shoulder. He drained his tankard and walked outside for some fresh air.

'Something is wrong with Kieran,' William remarked and shook his head. 'He is still brooding.'

'I see,' Engrin said, trying not to give anything away.

In the distance came a roll of thunder and some locals began to walk inside, mentioning something about a summer storm.

'Cuassard is dead, so you would think Kieran's need for vengeance would be satisfied,' William continued. 'He even killed Cuassard himself! As for the daemon, he oversaw its destruction. Never again can that beast be used to kill innocent people. Yet still Kieran is not satisfied. Is this the "nature of vengeance" you spoke of before we left for Aosta, Engrin?'

Engrin lowered his tankard and pursed his lips. 'Always to me you ask such questions. Would it not be better to ask Kieran? You have been friends longer than I have known you. What do you fear, William?'

'I fear nothing except maybe losing my friend. I have pushed him hard over the last few weeks. I've asked questions that have cut deep, and sought answers he has been reluctant to give.'

Engrin nodded. 'Then perhaps it is time you talk straight to one and other. Time is not forgiving to those who do not.'

William thought about this for a while. 'Then I will,' he announced eventually, bending down to kiss Adriana on the cheek. He left the table and made his way outside.

The air was fresh, but there was no sign that a storm was coming, and the sky was quite clear. Puzzled, he walked out to where Kieran was standing by a tree, looking out towards some fields in the distance.

'It is too stuffy and hot in there,' Kieran said, glancing over to William as he approached.

'Indeed,' William replied, though he knew something else was wrong. He looked down at something propped against the tree and frowned as he studied it in the light of the full moon.

'A sword?' he said. 'A broadsword?'

Kieran nodded. 'I didn't think anyone would notice if I took it. Cazotte once said that it was too big for me to wield. I believe he was right then, but now things have changed.'

William picked up the sword. It was incredibly heavy and he doubted he would be able to swing it with any great power. 'Lords, Kieran, it's immense! It is a sword for burly men with tree-trunks for arms. You are not that strong, surely!'

'Not today, no,' Kieran admitted.

'Then why take it?' William asked.

'Because I will be, and quite soon,' Kieran said.

William shook his head. 'You are riddling as badly as Engrin. What are you talking about?'

'I've made a decision, Will. And I think it is a decision you may not like,' Kieran replied.

William's expression darkened. 'Tell me,' he started, but halted as something caught his attention. From the shadows appeared four men, emerging into the light like ghosts.

William stepped forward, his hand reaching for his sword.

William sighed. 'A storm was not coming after all,' he murmured, his hand moving away from the sword handle. 'Are these the plainsmen you mentioned?'

'They've come for *me*,' Kieran replied. 'And I must go with them.'

'With them?' William said, and then he began to realize what his friend was saying. He shook his head strongly. 'No, Kieran, no. You can't go with them ...'

'William, please,' Kieran said. 'Do not worry. Do not fear.'

'Kieran, they're not even men!' William exclaimed.

'No, they're much, much more!' Kieran said, placing his hands on his friend's shoulders. 'And I have decided to join them.'

William shook his head again, his eyes pleading.

'They asked for me at Aosta, and I have decided to go,' Kieran explained. 'It is such a great honour, Will. Thousands like me must have asked for this honour throughout history, and yet it is I who has his wish granted.'

'Is it *truly* your wish, Kieran?'

Kieran looked up at the four plainsmen standing calmly by. He smiled and looked back into his friend's eyes. 'Yes. It is.'

William breathed out hard, and backed away. 'I see,' he said softly.

'Do you understand, Will? My search for vengeance is over. Cuassard is dead, yet I know now that there are others in this world who will suffer the same fate as Katherine unless the forces of Hell are stopped.' Kieran walked over to pick up the broadsword from the base of the tree. 'What would you give to go home, Will?'

William stared at his friend and smiled, tears in his eyes. 'Everything in the entire world.'

'I can never go home,' Kieran admitted. 'It was taken from me when I was very young. Now I have chance at a new home that will last for all eternity, and a cause. *Our* cause.'

William looked away as a tear slid down his cheek. 'Our cause,' he repeated.

'And once it is won, you can go home,' Kieran insisted. 'Back to Fairway Hall. Back to Lizzy. Back to Father. Back to Mother.'

William laughed gently. 'Back to riding through the fields in summer. Back to teasing Skinny at the stables ...'

'Back to sitting on the hill and looking across Dunabbey,' Kieran added, his eyes glazing over. 'Isn't that worth fighting for?'

'Of course it is,' William whispered. 'But you will never be able to return there.'

Kieran lowered the sword to the ground. 'Yes I will. In you,' he said, tapping William's shoulder with an outstretched hand.

'It is time, Kieran Harte,' Chow-Yuen said, his voice echoing in the night.

William closed his eyes. 'Then this is goodbye? The end?'

Kieran shook his head. 'No. Only the end of the beginning.' He reached forward with his hand for William to shake, but his old friend could only look at it. He paused, looked up through his tears and stepped forward, wrapping his arms around his friend. Kieran hugged him back, and they parted.

'You are my commanding officer. You are my friend,' the Irishman said. 'And you are also my brother.'

William nodded, grinding his teeth against the sorrow welling up from his chest. He glanced at the plainsmen, who began to melt back into the darkness. Kieran picked up the broadsword and followed them. The Irishman paused as he came to the shadows, looking back at his friend with a smile. And then he was gone.

Only Chow-Yuen remained.

'Will I meet him again?' William asked.

'You fight now, in the war against the Infernal,' Chow-Yuen replied. 'As long as you continue that fight, the *Dar'uka* will be there, William Saxon.' And then he was gone also.

William closed his eyes and felt his sorrow lifting. Had this been such a surprise? Perhaps not. Perhaps Engrin and the prophecy had been right all along.

A fresh evening breeze came out of the darkness and stroked his cheek. It was followed by a warm, soft touch and he opened his eyes to find Adriana standing by him.

'Come back, William,' she said, her fingers gently pulling on his. 'The celebrations are no fun without you.'

William nodded, his head bowed as she pulled him back to the tavern.

'Are you alright?' she asked as they walked. 'You look sad.'

'I've just said goodbye to a friend,' William replied.

Adriana frowned. 'Is he coming back?' she asked.

In the distance came the sound of thunder, like a distant storm approaching. William glanced over Adriana's shoulder and saw four lights shooting to the heavens.

A few moments later, a fifth light erupted from the ground and sped towards the clouds. William laughed, another tear falling from his cheek. 'Yes,' he replied, 'I think one day he will.'